THE
ORPHANED
WORLDS

By Michael Cobley

Humanity's Fire
Seeds of Earth
The Orphaned Worlds

THE ORPHANED WORLDS

BOOK 2 OF
HUMANITY'S FIRE

MICHAEL COBLEY

www.orbitbooks.net

ORBIT

First published in Great Britain in 2010 by Orbit

A CIP catalogue record for this book
is available from the British Library.

ISBN 978-1-84149-633-7

Typeset in Sabon by M Rules
Printed and bound in Great Britain by
Clays Ltd, St Ives, plc

Papers used by Orbit are natural, renewable and
recyclable products sourced from well-managed forests and certified
in accordance with the rules of the Forest Stewardship Council.

Mixed Sources
Product group from well-managed
forests and other controlled sources
www.fsc.org Cert no. SGS-COC-004081
© 1996 Forest Stewardship Council

FSC

Orbit
An imprint of
Little, Brown Book Group
100 Victoria Embankment
London EC4Y 0DY

An Hachette UK Company
www.hachette.co.uk

www.orbitbooks.co.uk

At last, this one is for
David Wingrove,
Steadfast friend,
Ace writer

MAIN CHARACTERS

Greg Cameron – archaeologist stationed at the Giant's Shoulder site. After the Hegemony takeover of Darien, Greg becomes one of the resistance leaders.

Catriona Macreadie – a former Enhanced, Catriona was chosen by the biomass sentience Segrana as its Keeper, a focus for its purpose.

Theo Karlsson – Greg's uncle, and former major in the Darien Volunteer Forces, Theo helped an important Enhanced team escape the Hegemony's clutches.

Kao Chih – a messenger sent to Darien by Human Sept, a splinter group of the lost Human colony on Pyre; his quest inadvertently helped an agent of the Legion of Avatars reach Darien.

Julia Bryce – leader of a team of Enhanced scientists who have discovered how to use dark anti-matter.

Cheluvahar, or Chel – a seer of the Uvovo and close friend of Greg Cameron.

Utavess Kuros – the Sendrukan Hegemony's ambassador to Darien, sent to take control of the ancient Forerunner warpwell hidden inside Giant's Shoulder.

Robert Horst – Earthsphere's ambassador to Darien, falsely accused of terrorist acts, and sent down into hyperspace by the Sentinel of the warpwell.

The Construct – a machine intelligence created by the Forerunners more than a hundred millennia ago to help fight the Legion of Avatars. It maintains a vigilant watch over the depths of hyperspace, where Robert Horst is being sent.

A Knight of the Legion of Avatars – armoured, cyborg creature, a survivor from the war against the Forerunners. One of its mech offshoots almost took control of the Darien warpwell, but now it has to consider alternative strategies.

MAIN SENTIENT SPECIES IN HUMANITY'S FIRE

Humans – biped mammals, binocular vision, vestigial hair, restricted range in audio/visual senses, average height 1.7m

Sendruka – biped humanoid, binocular vision, minimal body hair, average height 2.8m

Bargalil – hexapedal, 20% body hair, average height 2m

Henkaya – biped with four arms, muscular upper body, average height 2.1m

Kiskashin – tailed, ornitho-reptilian biped, rough, pebbled skin, average height 1.8m

Makhori – amphibious octoped, multiple tentacles, large eyes, average body length 1.5m

Achorga – insectoid, hiver, aggressively territorial, only Queens and specialised drones display intelligence, average height 1.2m

Uvovo – small bipedal humanoid, 70% body hair, binocular vision, excellent hearing, average height 1.3m

Gomedra – upright biped, furred, vaguely dog/wolf-like, average height 1.4m

Vusark – pseudo-insectoid, decapedal, compound eyes, average height – 1m when walking on majority of legs, 2.1m when raised up on back legs

Voth – biped mammal, long forearms, 75% body hair, cyborg implants common, fond of concealing garments, average height 1.4m

Piraseri – tripedal sophonts of aquatic descent, main body a tapering torso with a backswept head fringed by small tentacles, average height 1.6m

Roug – slender bipeds with thin limbs, possibly hairless, usually garbed head-to-toe in tightly-wound strips of dense material, average height 1.9m

Naszbur – heavily-armoured bipedal reptiloid, a chitin shell forms a hood over the head, aggressive traders, average height 1.5m

Hodralog – birdlike sophonts common in certain levels of hyperspace, frail physique, average height 0.8m

Keklir – short, muscular bipeds found in most of the upper tiers of hyperspace, have wide, tapering snouts with two mouthlike openings, average height 1m

Pozu – squat, brown-skinned species originating from high-gravity world, gloomy disposition, skilled plant technologists, average height 0.7m

The Clarified – former Sendrukans whose personal AI has gained full control of their body due to erasure of the original persona, usually by judicial sentence, occasionally by voluntary mind dissolution.

PROLOGUE

DARIEN INSTITUTE: HYPERION DATA
RECOVERY PROJECT

Cluster Location – Main Hardmem Substrate (Tertiary Backups)
Tranche – 31
Decryption Status – 24th pass, 3 video files recovered

File 3 – Implant Variant 6 (mute) Combat Proving [Subject identified as Andrei Vychkov]
Veracity – Unmodified Live Recording
Original Time Log – 18:23:14, 30 October 2127
Introduction – Dr Yelena Dobrunov
Afterword – Dr James Kelvin

>>>>>>   <<<<<<

Commentary I: *The events that took place after the emergency landing of the Hyperion 150 years ago have had a profound effect on the development of our colony. The drastic technical shortfall endured by the founders in the subsequent decades meant that only written accounts and a few printed images were passed down as a record of that grim struggle. Oral storytelling traditions amongst the First Families also helped to keep the names of Captain Olsson, Keri McAllister, and Andrei Vychkov alive down the generations. Everyone knows the story of Vychkov's Map.*

Recent innovations in data decryption, however, have allowed Institute researchers to at last extract coherent records from the

Hyperion's memory nodes. Among them were three videofiles made by the ship's AI and showing progressively more effective methods of coercing its captives into obedience. The colonists it awoke from cryosleep were implanted with neural devices designed to deliver jolts of pain, thus forcing them to carry out attacks on the ship's crew who had established an encampment several miles away.

The first videofile is entitled 'Biounit Tolerance Test' and shows one of the woken male colonists strapped to a couch and being subjected to increasing amounts of pain until death ensued. The second, 'Implant Variant 3 Field Test', shows a female colonist being directed to venture outside the Hyperion *to recover an unconscious crew member, injured during an attempt by some of the crew to gain entry to the ship. Pain, or more accurately the memory of pain, is enough to make the colonist obey, even when the crewman regains consciousness and unsuccessfully tries to escape. Those two recordings depict horrific and distressing scenes of, in effect, torture and coercion and the Institute's management board has decided to accord them a 'restricted access' status.*

However, the third videofile involves Andrei Vychkov, whose tragi-heroic tale is known to all, and shows actual events as they unfolded. The Institute's board believes that the historical value outweighs Vychkov's personal suffering and has, with the Vychkov family's consent, released it for public viewing by an adult audience.

In time, we hope to be able to unlock the machine mind's OS hub, the most heavily encrypted file area, and thus lay bare whatever imperatives or directives that turned it against the very people it was supposed to safeguard. In the meantime, students and other viewers should closely watch the following recording and never forget the kind of servitude that was planned for us all – Y.D.

By night, moving through foliage, dark shapes barely visible in darkness. There is the hissing of rain, patter of droplets falling on undergrowth, the rush of wind high in the sky, and the sound of someone breathing. From the unsteady viewpoint it seems that the camera is positioned on someone's upper body, at the chest or shoulder. Then abruptly the picture switches to somewhere high and looking down, only now the trees and bushes are quite visible in the bleached blue-grey of image enhancement while the body-heat-bright figure of a man advances through the forest. The airborne cam tracks him for a moment then pulls back and swings up to point across the treetops to where a rocky outcrop shoulders up out of the pale, leafy expanse, a dark blue mass fringed with spectral bushes. The cam zooms in on the heat signatures of two sentries on the outcrop, restless bright silhouettes.

'Approach location A and anchor the first charge,' says the AI. 'Confirm.'

The picture switches to show the man's face, seen from his right shoulder. It is Andrei Vychkov, eyes covered by nightvision goggles. He opens his mouth as if to respond but utters no sound, instead grimacing, an expression of frustration. The picture changes, a left side view. He nods and resumes moving through the trees. In the imaging scope, the rain is like fine black threads, falling. Minutes later, Vychkov reaches the guarded outcrop, keeping to cover as he bears left. The lens of the hovering camera stalks him as he finds an unseen way to a point at the base of the outcrop's sheer rock face where he affixes a fist-sized device. Silently, he retreats to leafy cover.

'Approach location B and anchor the second charge.'

Nod.

The second charge goes round to the left of the rocky shoulder, beneath a large overhang. The third is positioned very near to where a rough path from the lookout descends a series of natural steps in the rock. The path leads along an irregular ridge to a bushy hillside where three armed men guard the entrance to a cave. The fourth and final charge has to go in the slope above the cave and is the most difficult to achieve, even with the rainfall there to mask small sounds. Once it is bedded firmly in the soil, Vychkov begins to retrace his steps, creeping down through darkness.

'You have performed well,' the AI says. 'You will be rewarded.'

Vychkov shows no reaction as he moves behind dripping greenery, descending quietly to dense tree cover downslope from the cave.

'I have activated the charge timers,' the AI says as he squats down in the shelter of a spreading bush, looking uphill. 'In thirty seconds charge one will detonate followed by charge two three seconds later. After another five seconds, the three guards will have moved towards the lookout point while others will have emerged from the cave. Charges three and four will then detonate and if hostile elements have been disabled or eliminated, you will then advance to secure the cave . . .'

A loud thud comes from not far away. Vychkov looks to his left and the picture cuts to the left shoulder view. A bleak smile crosses his features and as he rises the second charge goes off.

'Return to the lower profile. You will reveal yourself to hostile elements.'

Vychkov tugs off the goggles and gives a sidelong glance at the shoulder camera, his eyes dark and piercing, shakes his head and raises his left hand which is holding one of the hemispherical shaped charges. A swift overarm movement and it is arcing away into the dark, rain-wet forest.

'You have disrupted the mission plan. You will be punished. Return to the ship . . .'

Another explosion, a flash from the rocky ridge coupled with a simultaneous one from the forest that sends burning foliage flying. But nothing from the cave mouth where figures holding torches are emerging. Vychkov sees them and starts climbing the hill. He takes three strides then doubles over in agony, sinking to his knees, slumping over on one side. The shoulder camera shows his face contorted in a rictus of pain, mouth gaping as if to cry out but no sound comes, just long gasps and shuddering breaths.

'Comply. Return to the ship or you will be severed.'

Silently snarling against the pain, Vychkov shakes his head and begins to crawl slowly up the grassy slope. The picture switches to the camera on the airborne remote, now hovering over the edge of the forest with its lens angled down at the glowing figure sprawled on the hillside. Heat from the explosions blooms bright blue at the edge of the frame and the voices of people are audible, along with someone screaming for help. As the hovering camera zooms in on Vychkov, a target-acquisition overlay appears and a red triangle settles over the back of his head where it locks. A second later the camera jerks to the side as if from recoil. When it returns, Vychkov's form is still, unmoving.

End of videofile.

Commentary II: *We know from the written accounts of Olsson and the others that shortly after the Hyperion's emergency landing the ship AI began flooding some decks with sleep gas. And in the weeks prior to the landing, certain low-level systems began behaving erratically or failed altogether. Then, as the videofile shows, the AI used neural implants to control wakened colonists in its strategy against those who escaped into the forest.*

Taken together, this does not strike me as the meticulous master plan of a machine intellect hell-bent on enslaving everyone on board the Hyperion. Why tip its hand during the preceding weeks? Why gas only parts of the ship, not all – in fact, why not gas everyone even before making orbit about Darien? And why undertake a programme of forced cyborgisation when it would have made more sense to use the Hyperion's workshops to turn out legions of anti-personnel drones for deployment by air or ground? Also, why was its shipboard security so poor that Vychkov was able to take a dummy charge on the mission? And above all, how was Vychkov able to get away with inking a map of the ship's weak points into the skin of his chest?

The truth is that this behaviour looks more like a disjointed series of responses and blind spots created by dysfunctional programming, not some malign plan introduced by an unknown agency. The AIs placed in charge of the Hyperion and her sister ships came from the cutting edge of research at that time. During those dark days of the Swarm War, resources were short, procedures were rushed and corners were cut. It is very likely that flaws in the care-and-protection heuristics were not caught, result-ing in the terrible consequences that blighted the early decades of the colony with malnutrition, illness and despair.

They have also blighted our scientific development. The col-lective memory of the fight against the ship AI, and its unwilling thralls, has come down to us embroidered with an anthropomor-phism and demonisation so strong that AI research was and remains forbidden. Therefore it is my recommendation that any viewer should look upon this recording not as an illustration of the purposeful strategy of a demonic entity, but as an exposure of the consequences of flawed programming, nothing more. – J.K.

>>>>>>   <<<<<<

PART ONE

1

GREG

The lohig that tirelessly hauled their hide cart was an odd insectoid creature some seven feet long, its coppery carapace patterned with blue diamonds and stars. At first, he and Kao Chih had been worried that the creature might suffer from their untutored care but the lohig breeder's instructions had proved invaluable, keeping them from starving or mistreating it. In fact, Kao Chih had taken a liking to the beast, feeding it sprigs of leaves while talking to it in soft Mandarin Chinese, and had even gone to the point of giving it a name, T'ien Kou, which meant Heavenly Dog. Greg was tempted to call the lohig 'Rover' but held back.

They had been three days on the trail to Belskirnir, a trapper camp deep in the Forest of Arawn, a vast and dense expanse of greenery that spread north and east of the Kentigerns, covering over a thousand square miles of hinterland. For the last day and a half they had been passing through lush glades and humid dales beneath an endless interwoven canopy, home to the innumerable flying, leaping and crawling creatures of Darien. But now evening was drawing in as they steered the lohig along a dale strewn with mossy boulders, and thoughts of making camp were surfacing.

'I don't think we're that far from Belskirnir,' Greg said, 'but we'll no' get there before nightfall.' He pointed to a large tree further ahead, its bole twisted around a big boulder, its lower branches creating a kind of natural shelter. 'That would be a good place to make camp. What d'ye think?'

Kao Chih peered at it. 'It certainly appears comfortable,

Gregory, but there is still plenty of light – should we not keep moving, to make the good time tomorrow?'

Greg shrugged and was about to reply when, without warning, shots came from off in the dense wood. Automatic fire crackled, splinters flew from the cart, leaves and twigs spun from intervening bushes. Panic-stricken, Greg had dived off the path, scrambling for cover behind a huge, tilted rock, fumbling for his own weapon, the 35-calibre that Rory had doggedly taught him to use. He returned fire, a few unaimed shots before realising that he didn't know where Kao Chih was, whether he had gone into the bushes on the other side or had fled along the path. Greg was about to call out his name in a stage whisper when there were shouts and the sound of running feet drawing near from left and right.

Fear assailed him as the hunters' footsteps slowed and an eerie silence fell over the dale. Seconds ticked by with neither sight nor sound of Kao Chih, but Greg did catch a glimpse of one of his pursuers, a burly, bearded woodsman with hard, flinty eyes beneath a battered bush hat. Convinced that the ones he couldn't see were even closer, he decided it was time to get the hell out of there.

Behind the big, tilted rock, clumps of tangled undergrowth concealed an incline leading up to a ridge beyond which lay a drop which he remembered from their earlier progress along the track. Keeping low, he crept up to the edge and over to see a steep, leafy slope broken by isolated bushes and protruding rocks, leading down to a wide, densely wooded gorge which ran southwards, back the way he and Kao Chih had come two days before. Greg crouched on a jutting rock, unsure of his next move, staring across the leafy treetops, darkening as the sun dipped towards the horizon. Then a shout came from off to the right – one of the ambushers was standing on the ridge about a hundred yards away, calling out to the others as he raised a rifle and took aim.

Fear took over and Greg dived forward, rolling downslope a short distance before regaining his feet and continuing his descent at a striding, plunging run. Just as he passed into the shadows of the tree line, he slipped on a muddy patch. He feet flew out, a jumble of rocks loomed and he flailed madly, luckily catching hold of the stems of a sturdy bush which slowed his plummet. His back and side were soaked with dew and plastered with mud but with his pursuers coming down after him he ignored the mess and headed deeper into the trees.

For the next ten hours or more, Greg dodged and hid, crept and climbed, skulked and lay low. It was a strange, fitful hunt which continued on past evening and into the night. It was never completely dark in a Darien forest – ulby roots, a common species of parasitic tuber, shed a pale yellow-green radiance, while ineka beetles had carapaces that gave off a soft blue glow. Together, their emanations gave the glades of Darien a curiously spectral ambience, a kind of peaceful hush as if the entire forest were holding its breath. Tonight, though, the patchy glows conspired with Greg's fugitive state of mind to concoct an eerie, slightly foreboding atmosphere.

Dawn was cold and misty, the first moments of sunrise spreading like a watery gleam through the undergrowth. Greg straightened from the hillside notch where he'd been resting and peered out through a veil of blackleaf vine. From the gorge he had gradually worked his way via gullies and footprint-masking streams back round to the route that he and Kao Chih had been following. The notch gave him a view of densely wooded ground sloping down towards the track. South was to his left and a mile or so back that way was where they'd been ambushed. Northwards, the trees thinned a little and the rutted track wound through them to a hillside, curving round it and out of sight. Somewhere among those low forest hills was Belskirnir, where Greg was supposed to meet a go-between sent by Alexandr Vashutkin, the last surviving member of Sundstrom's cabinet, still holding out in Trond . . .

As the minutes passed the day brightened and a few creature-calls sounded from the canopy and branches overhead, peeps, whistles and scraping squawks, as if to greet the sky's telltale pearly glow, sure sign that bright sunlight would soon be burning away the mists. Greg peered into the trees, scanning the distance, studying the undergrowth for movement. It was a couple of hours since he last sighted one of his pursuers, a lean, bearded man with a rifle who emerged from a thicket to the north and stalked along parallel to the track before disappearing off to the south.

Greg nodded, resolved that it was time to go and find Kao Chih.

He climbed out of the notch and crouched in a nearby clump of beadberry bushes for a moment, plotting in his head a route across the wooded slope. Then he crept forward, heading towards the closest tree, and was four paces away when he was grabbed from behind and thrust to the ground. Gasping in fear, he struggled against the weight on his back and fought with one hand through garment layers for the pistol sitting in an inside pocket. Amid all this effort, he almost failed to hear his assailant hoarsely repeating his name.

'Greg . . . Greg! – it's me, Alexei . . .!'

Suddenly hearing and recognising the voice, he ceased moving and the weight shifted off his back. Breathing heavily, he half sat up as a grinning Alexei Firmanov sprawled down on the grass next to him. He was a lanky, dark-haired Rus with prominent cheekbones and a narrow chin, and was garbed in a green forest coat over dark grey hunter fatigues.

'What . . . *the hell* . . . are you doing here?' Greg said.

'They've got lookouts posted all along the trail to Belskirnir, my friend,' Alexei said. 'They would have had you like *that*.'

'I see,' Greg said, glancing round at the bushy slope. 'Any idea who they are?'

'Thugs and *nattjegers* from the Eastern Towns, we reckoned. Just after you left Taloway, a carrier pinbeak arrived from High Lochiel with word that a local Brolturan lackey was hiring toughs for a journey into the wilds. Later that same day, one of Chel's high-crag watchers spotted a dirij coming in from the Crystal River boundary quite far off and heading for these hills. Less than half an hour later it was aloft and swinging back towards the coast. Rory and Chel assumed that the worst might happen . . .'

'And here ye are.'

'Nikolai is here, too,' Alexei said. 'He went after the ones who dragged Kao Chih away. He's safe, by the way.'

Greg breathed a sigh of relief. 'Thank God.'

'Or whoever's in charge, *da*? Well, there were only two captors – for Nikolai this is no problem. But we have many problems, sitting out there, waiting for us, so we must go the scenic route, yes?'

'How scenic?' said Greg. 'D'ye mean doubling back around they hills?'

'I mean go over them.' Alexei grinned. 'Is not so bad, and quicker too.'

Greg frowned. The hills to the south might be comparatively low but they were steep and craggy. Scaling them would be demanding and risky.

'Okay then, aye,' he said. 'But we'll have to keep an eye out for any scissortails – a bite from one of those wee buggers and you'll never play the balalaika again.'

After a stealthy, wary progress back through the forest, following the upward slope, it took well over an hour to climb to the hill's rocky summit. By then the sun was out and they were sweating as they stopped to rest on a hot stone ledge facing north. Alexei produced a small battered wooden telescope and surveyed the woods they'd left behind. After a few moments he gave a satisfied grunt and turned to look north. Greg sat in the sun's warmth, thinking about his mother and brothers, now safely ensconced in a mountain camp south of the Eastern Towns. His mother had been angry at being sent away from danger, even though she knew it was a rational move. His brothers, Ian and Ned, were likewise unhappy but resigned – Ian intended to get together a company of former Darien Volunteer Force troopers and Ned knew that his medical skills would be fully occupied.

I still wish you were all with me, he thought, staring out at the dark, dense expanse of the Forest of Arawn. *But we know what happens when you put all your eggs in one basket . . .*

Alexei handed him the long glass and he raised it to survey the land. The treetop canopy was an unbroken sea of verdant green that swept onwards and away, swathing every dip and rise of the land before fetching up against the Utgard Barricades, two hundred miles of imposing sheer cliffs which were just visible as a dark grey line on the horizon. Beyond, the peaks of an immense mountain range faded away into purple opacity.

Gazing over the forest he suddenly realised that you could lose entire armies beneath its foliage, battalions, regiments, legions, hordes, completely hidden from the eye, their movements a mystery, their tactics clandestine, their strategy covert.

Now all we need is an army.

Alexei pointed to a nearer landmark, a flat-topped hill protruding from the forest a couple of miles to the north, one of a group of hills.

'There is Osip's Hat – under it is Belskirnir. Nikolai said to meet him at the top of a waterfall near the eastern slope.' He looked at Greg. 'Are you ready?'

'Well, I've no' had much sleep and nothing to eat but we're kind of short on choices so . . . aye, let's go.'

Alexei laughed and gave his shoulder a comradely punch. 'You will be fine – Rory says you are tough and I believe him.'

'Must have a word with him when we get back,' Greg said as he clambered after his companion, heading down the other side of the craggy hill. As they approached the tree line, a flock of fowics came down to investigate, landing heavily on thin upper branches and scrambling along on all fours. Fowics were like flying squirrels back on Earth, except that their forelimb wings were more fully adapted for flying rather than gliding, and their heads, ears and snouts had a distinctly feline appearance. Alexei dug some hard tack out of a waist pouch and held out a few fragments. One of them calmly sauntered down its branch, tiny beady eyes fixed on the prize, snatched it with its teeth then leapt and wriggled up into the leafy shadows.

Greg laughed. 'If they can get any sustenance out of that stuff, they're probably evolving faster than we are!'

Not all forest denizens were as harmless. During the two-hour trudge through an increasingly swampy forest, they saw a tree nest of pepper-wasps, around which they detoured, and more than once hurried past yellow sniperviles, bulge-eyed lizards that could spit poison lethal to Humans. By the time they crossed a brook to dry, rising terrain, Greg felt edgy and twitchy and was longing to return to the high valleys of the Kentigerns.

'This had better be worth it,' he muttered, following Alexei over a fallen tree. 'When we walk in there, Vashutkin's guy better have, I don't know, a vial of babble dust made especially for Kuros, or plans for that compound they're building at Port Gagarin, or . . . well, something.'

Alexei was puzzled. 'You don't know what this meeting is for?'

'No idea, just that Vashutkin said it was so vital that I had to be there in person.'

'Ah! – I know, is a surprise birthday party, perhaps!'

Greg smiled and shook his head. 'Not for another four months, but nice try.'

At the crest of the slope they suddenly heard a rushing sound above the breeze that rustled through the trees. The ground ahead rose in large rocky steps, mossy stairs for a giant. Overhead, the dense canopy of the Forest of Arawn continued unbroken in all directions as Alexei led the way around a steep bluff, pointing out the rippervine which hung down it from above. Pushing through a tangle of bushes, they emerged near the rocky bank of a stream, several dozen yards from where it poured over a cliff edge, a waterfall plunging to the forest below. Then two figures stepped out of the vegetation on the other side and minutes later Greg was shaking hands with a grinning Kao Chih while Nikolai Firmanov explained.

'What a pair of daruki,' he said. 'Some of them know their way through woods, but those two must be coastal boys. But Kao Chih? – there is more here than the eye sees.'

'I was . . . fortunate,' Kao Chih said. 'I knock out one with my skull' – he mimed with a backward jerk of the head – 'get free, take his gun and knock out the other, then I think I will rescue you and I put on the guns and knives, then I tie up those kwai, then . . . Nikolai arrives and we go spying.'

Nikolai, the older but shorter of the Firmanov brothers, smiled and patted Kao Chih on the shoulder. 'Steady nerves, this one. All ready to go to war. So I told him that my brother had gone to fetch you and meet later by waterfall but on way here we get close to main gate to Belskirnir, at night.' He shook his head. 'Not good, Greg – they are watching gate, around clock. Only other way in is through one of Van Krieger's private doors.'

Peter Van Krieger's father was one of the original founders of Belskirnir and the son had maintained and increased that position of authority by buying out the descendants of the other two founders. Rory had told Greg that Van Krieger was now an ageing, piratical figure who relied on lieutenants to run the camp, having no offspring of his own.

'Will that be a problem?' Greg said.

Nikolai gave an amused half-shrug. 'Diehards have had dealings with him in past – should be okay.'

'Should?' Greg said.

'Will be okay,' said Nikolai. 'Van Krieger makes a point of being even-handed, and makes sure his men are too.'

Greg remained unconvinced but when they reached the bushy summit of Osip's Hill after a two-hour forest trek, the welcome they received from the three guards there seemed to bear out Nikolai's words. All wore similar medleys of camouflage, leather and hessian, and carried ageing breech-loaders sporting this or that modification. The eldest, a bald man with a tattooed scalp, greeted the Firmanovs with sardonic familiarity and after hearing Nikolai's brief hints at some kind of trouble with bandits out in the forest, he beckoned them all to follow as he opened the door into the hill.

The way led through a maze of passages, split-levels and side tunnels. Greg had never been to Belskirnir before and initially tried to memorise their route, giving up when it became clear that their guide was taking turnings meant to confuse. Stretches of the cold passages were lit by tallow lamps and quite soon Greg began to hear singing. Moments later they emerged onto a hewn ledge overlooking a wide cavern resounding with a barrage of

voices and noises from the hundreds of men and women occupying the stools and tables spread across the floor of what was
essentially one big tavern. The next thing he noticed was the
warm fug of body odour, weed smoke, stale beer and cooked
food, at which his stomach rumbled. Then he saw the market
stalls around the walls, some of which were grilling or boiling or
frying a variety of frontier dishes.

'I have to eat,' he told Alexei. 'I'm just about ready to munch
my own toenails!'

Alexei nodded. 'Sure, of course – where are we to meet this guy
again?'

'Some place called the Lifeboat.'

'Ah yes – it's over there.'

Greg followed his outstretched hand to see a long gallery on the
opposite wall crowded with revellers who seemed to be singing
several different songs at once. Nikolai nodded and relayed this to
their guide, who wished them well and left them to it.

The walls of the cavern had many hollows, some containing
little shops or sleep spaces while others had odd, lopsided huts
jutting from them. As they drew near to the Lifeboat, those within
began singing a new song in fairly ordered unison, and to Greg's
surprise he recognised it as 'Regin the Blacksmith'. Uncle Theo
used to sing it for Greg when he was younger, when his mother
and father took him to see Theo in his cottage on New Kelso.
Those visits came back to him as one voice led each verse with
everyone else bellowing along for the chorus. The song told the
tale of Regin, a blacksmith and swordmaker, who helped the hero
Siegfried to slay the dragon Fafnir but who then planned to kill
Siegfried; the hero discovered this and dealt with the blacksmith
in a direct and final manner.

The gallery was busy to the point of standing room only. While
the Firmanovs made for the bar, Greg and Kao Chih had held
back, with Kao Chih's face below the eyes covered with a plaid
scarf and the brim of his cap dipped over his brow. In the meantime, Greg took in the surrounding press, surreptitiously studying
faces and heads, looking for someone who might be Vashutkin's

go-between. 'Regin the Blacksmith' was nearly finished, with scores of Dariens, male and female, roaring out the chorus, led by a broad-shouldered, black-haired man in a short-sleeved leather jerkin who banged an empty tankard on the table in time with the beat. Alexei reappeared with two bowls of savoury meat and vegetables which Greg and Kao Chih accepted gratefully and began to devour.

'So what does this messenger look like?'

Greg shrugged. 'The message said that the go-between and his bodyguard would be here today and tomorrow between sunup and midnight.' He paused to chew another mouthful. 'So we're . . . looking for at least two people. Dinna have a clue about them otherwise.'

Nikolai frowned a moment, then smiled. 'I have it – we just wait and see who stays around later then go and say hello.'

'I think it's more straightforward than that,' Greg said, staring past him. The main table had finished singing and the brawny, black-haired man was muttering with a grey-haired woman in hunter's garb. As they conversed, she glanced across the busy room directly at Greg and the big man looked round too, revealing the face of Vashutkin's go-between.

It was Vashutkin himself.

'Is that . . . ?' Alexei said.

'Aye.'

'Huh. Hardly recognised him without moustache.'

Then Nikolai appeared next to Vashutkin and his companion, exchanged a few words then looked up at Greg and Alexei and indicated the exit. They nodded and made for the door, Greg hurriedly wolfing down the rest of his food, then a moment later Vashutkin came out, smiled tightly and without a word beckoned them to follow. Minutes later they were descending a curve of rough-cut stone steps to a long, low storeroom lined with barrels and crates and lit by a few oil lamps. A tall man with a ponytail and a long coat got up from a crude trestle table and muttered something in Vashutkin's ear before shaking his hand and heading for the exit.

'That was Trask,' Alexei said in a low voice. 'Van Krieger's deputy and a brute. Looks as if he's being helpful. Wonder how much he is getting paid.'

The former minister went and sat at the table and the grey-haired huntress moved to stand behind him, watching the rest with hard eyes. A slender hooded man stepped out from behind a stack of crates and sat on a chair further back, face hidden in shadow. Greg frowned and was about to ask Alexei about the newcomer when Vashutkin spoke.

'Mr Cameron,' he said, getting to his feet, hand outstretched. 'It is an honour to finally meet you, although I wish it were under less cramped conditions.'

'An honour for me too, Mr Vashutkin,' Greg said, shaking the man's hand and sitting down opposite him. 'I'm a great admirer of your radio speeches. They're quite, eh, energetic.'

Vashutkin chuckled. 'I only gave a handful over the air before Trond Council asked me to stop as it was offending someone's wife. I am glad that you enjoyed them.'

'It's not just me – I have it on good authority that in the towns, certain disrespectful youths gather in secret and recite from transcripts of your speeches, as well as the usual drinking and smoking. I'm told that the bits where you're comparing President Kirkland to various species of mudworm are especially popular.'

After the deaths of President Sandstrom and his ministers, the Darien Assembly chose Kirkland, leader of the consolidation party, to be president of a government of national unity. Since taking office, however, Kirkland had proved increasingly compliant towards the Brolturans' security plans.

'Good, good! That proves how despised the snake is, and I'm sure that he knows.' He shook his head. 'Kirkland wasn't so bad before all this, but he has not the kind of soul that would resist corruption, so he has been eaten by it.' He paused to glance over his shoulder. 'Are we secure?'

The woman leaned forward a little and spoke in a Norj accent.

'He says that there is a single pickup in the ceiling but it is now cancelled.'

The Rus politician seemed to relax a little, then glanced at Greg and smiled at his unconcealed curiosity.

'My companions are a little ... uncustomary, *da*? A mystery for later – now, let us sit and speak of resistance.'

Greg loosened his heavy outer garment, feeling warm suddenly.

'Well, we have been focusing our attention on information gathering,' he said. 'Also keeping the escape routes and safe houses secure, and trying to keep essential knowledge restricted to cells. So far we've been getting folk away from most of the inland towns and some of Hammergard's outlying districts but we hope to expand that, maybe even tackle one o' their detention centres.'

'I understand why you wish to do this, my friend, truly I do. But the hard truth is that you will have to cut back on these activities, not increase them.'

Dismayed, Greg sat back. 'Why's that?'

'For two reasons. First, if they escape into the mountains and the forests, the number of dissidents making life difficult for the occupiers goes down. Second, some of these escapers are bringing families and relatives which again pleases the Brolturans because caring for such non-combatants drains your resources, dulls your military edge and reduces your flexibility.'

'We can't refuse to help people who've suffered at the hands of the Brolturans,' Greg said levelly. 'If somebody's been singled out for harsh treatment, then I'll do all I can to get them to safety. That's not gonnae change.'

'Of course you would, Mr Cameron, and I would too, except that I am recognising the realities of the conflict, the brutal realities, while your methods just make the occupation easier for those stinking offworlders. Change will have to come if we are to work together.'

Greg stared at him, dismay turning to irritation and dislike. He could almost hear a possible response at the back of his thoughts: *Aye, Mr Vashutkin, now that you mention it I can see those realities so how about this – instead of helping folk escape, we'll give 'em guns and explosives, ye know, kids and grannies too, along with a list of targets we want dealt with. And for those far gone in despair there's always the suicide bomb option, just the thing tae unnerve the occupying forces. What d'ye say?*

But at the back of his thoughts was where the sarcasm remained. The situation was too grave for anything but a framework of courtesy, even a flimsy one. He took a deep breath and leaned forward, hands clasped on the table.

'Could you tell me what you mean by "working together"?'

Vashutkin spread his hands. 'Unfortunately, I have worn out my welcome in Trond – the council has been coming under a great deal of pressure from the townspeople, the dependent planters and stock farmers because of the embargo imposed by Kirkland's puppet government. In the next few days the council will cave in to Hammergard then tell me and my supporters to get the hell out of their town, but I want to be gone before then. Luckily, you already have a base of operations, this Tayowal, so we can join forces, pool our skills and do some real planning, eh?'

Vashutkin's grin was wide and enthusiastic and Greg felt like laughing in his face, but gave an answering smile.

'Mr Vashutkin . . .'

'Please, call me Alexander.'

'Alexander, you have to realise that Tayowal is not a Human settlement but a place that the Uvovo use for ceremonies. They offered it to us as a place of shelter, and we've been helping Uvovo evade the Brolturan sweeps, sending them to hideouts in the south and bringing them to Tayowal. I'm not really in charge of the Human community, as such, and I wouldn't presume to start giving out orders . . .' *Even though I'm the one who organises food for the cooks, the sentry rotas, dispute arbitration, oh aye, I hardly do anything!* 'If my uncle, Theo Karlsson, were here he is someone who would certainly be in charge, but his Diehards seem to have elected me as his stand-in, either that or a mascot, I've no' quite figured it out yet.'

Off to the side, Nikolai Firmanov was smiling as he leaned against the wall, hands in his pockets, saying nothing.

'You seem to see this as a problem, yet if I were to offer clear leadership perhaps this would not be seen as a problem in these times, perhaps?' Vashutkin frowned. 'Informal arrangements work against planning, but we can deal with that at a big-table consultation once we are all together.'

'I am sorry, Alexander, but without an invite from the Uvovo Listeners, you should not come to Tayowal. I will ask them if you and your men can join us but it's unlikely they'll agree. And if you came anyway and set up camp, they'll just up sticks and vanish into the forest, leaving us in serious barodritt, since we depend on them for eighty per cent of our provisions, as well as the help they give us in a dozen other ways.' Greg decided to omit the fact that the Listeners saw him as an honorary scholar and the Human spokesman.

Vashutkin gave him a considering look. 'You have come to rely on them a lot, I see.'

'It is their world,' Greg said. 'Which they've decided to share with us.'

'I understand. My apologies if I seemed . . . impatient.'

'Not to worry, Alexander. Look, the ancient Uvovo built quite a few habitats all across this region, dug down into the ground or tunnelled into the sides of hills and mountains. There's one worked into the caves of the Utgard Barricades north of the forest, and not far from Belskirnir, and it's pretty extensive too. I'm sure that the Listeners would have no problem with you taking it over.'

Vashutkin seemed mollified. 'My thanks, Gregory, for your advice and your candour – I shall seek more information about these caves. However, I must still urge you to rethink your arrangements. The situation is going to change for the worse and we have to be ready.'

'Ready for what?' Greg said. 'Are the Brolturans bringing in more troops? Or are the Hegemony?'

'In a manner of speaking, Mr Cameron,' said another voice.

Greg looked up. It was the hooded man who had spoken. Vashutkin laughed and without turning made a beckoning gesture.

'Gregory, may I introduce you to my very good friend Baltazar

Silveira, who has come all the long way from Earth to speak with us today.'

Half amazed, half puzzled, Greg rose and reached out to shake the man's hand. Silveira had a slender build and a narrow face, cropped black hair and dark, slightly sad eyes. His smile was faint but his grip was firm. Greg wondered if he was from the Earthsphere ship, *Heracles*.

'Mr Cameron, I am very pleased to meet you and your companions,' he said, his Noranglic carrying an accent that Greg could not place. 'First, you must understand that my presence on your world has to be kept secret for the simple reason that I am a covert agent for Earthsphere Intelligence. If the Brolturan military or the Hegemony were to learn of me, it would be extremely embarrassing for my superiors, who would force me to leave Darien. And if other powers such as the Imisil Mergence got wind of it, the resulting complications would not be at all helpful.'

'You have our word, Mr Silveira,' Greg said, his calm concealing a growing excitement. 'Outside the four of us, there'll be no discussion of yourself or your purpose.' He looked at the Firmanovs and Kao Chih, still wearing cap and muffler, and got nods of agreement. 'So, the Brolturans are getting reinforcements, you say. Well, after a month of complaints and arguments from Russians, Scandinavians and Scots, it's no' surprising, really. What will it be – a regiment of veteran entertainers? A battalion of crack cooks sent in to whip up enough Brolturan delicacies to sweeten our rough natures? Or is it just more troops?'

Vashutkin's amusement was plain, if stifled. Silveira's smile was wintry.

'Brolturan civilisation may be an offshoot from the Sendrukan Hegemony,' he said, 'but militarily it should be considered as an adjunct to Hegemony power. This gives them access to a stunning array of cutting-edge battlefield hardware, yet there are a few weapon systems which their patrons keep to themselves, like the Namul-Ashaph. Translated from Sendrukala it literally means "mind that makes"; we would describe it as an AI-autofac, a mobile, nanosourced production unit capable of turning out between four and eight combat mechs a day, depending on their configuration. Our intel shorthand for it is tektor . . .'

'Short name, big trouble,' Vashutkin said to Greg. 'This is why we have to be ready.'

'Indeed, yes,' said Silveira. 'Part of my assignment is to advise you on what to expect and how to counter Hegemony mech tactics with fortifications and traps.'

As he listened, Greg's trepidation and dismay deepened. Most of Tayowal consisted of sheltering chambers cut into the sloping sides of a cuplike depression in the Kentigerns' north foothills; in the event of an attack it would be difficult to defend and would provide poor cover from bombardment. He then recalled that his Uvovo friend Chel the Seer was off in the mountains with the Voth pilot, Yash, and Gorol9, the Construct droid, investigating various old Uvovo ruins with an eye for their defensibility. He mentioned this to Silveira, who nodded.

'Natural features make the best strongholds,' he said. 'With the disadvantage that tunnel complexes can count against you.'

'So when can we expect the arrival of this factory of death?'

'It is due to arrive on board a Hegemony freighter sometime in the next couple of days,' Silveira said. 'Beyond that I cannot be more specific.'

Greg smiled sharply. 'Y'know, you must forgive me if I seem a wee bit sour and disgruntled, but in the face of this artificial intelligence dedicated to our destruction would it not have made sense for your superiors to send along, as well as your good self, a crate or two of top-notch weaponry, just to even the scales a little?'

'Most particle weapons give off distinctive energy signatures,' Silveira said. 'If the Brolturans detected such a thing on Darien they would immediately realise that Earthsphere was supporting indigenous insurgents against them, and when the Hegemony learned of it there would be various kinds of hell to pay. Non-Earthsphere armour-piercing guns are being sourced but by the time they arrived the conflict would be well under way.'

'So we have to make do with a few hunting rifles and small arms, is what you're saying.'

'Your situation could actually be worse,' Silveira said. 'The tektor you'll be facing is a class-B unit; the class-A is twice as big and can produce at least twelve mechs a day. There is a world once called Karagal, away at the edge of the Hegemony's rimward tracts. After a century of protests over the burdens of colonial rule its people rebelled in unison, thinking this would prove their fitness for autonomy. The Hegemony's response was to send in forty class-A tektors and in a month no one was left alive, a population of a billion and a half wiped out. Because class-As can build class-Bs in addition to a range of mechs.'

Greg exchanged a look with Vashutkin, who raised a sardonic eyebrow.

'Somehow,' Greg said, 'that's no' very assuring.'

'But you are not in that kind of danger here on Darien,' the agent went on. 'The Brolturans are going to considerable lengths to portray themselves as benevolent overseers, taking care of security matters while the Human colonists get on with their lives, grateful for that protection. Such propaganda has been pouring out to the subspace newsfeeds almost from the day after Sundstrom's assassination, and finding out the truth of the occupation is the other part of my assignment.'

'Information gathering,' Greg said, thinking of Kao Chih.

'That is so. There are several unanswered questions which I was tasked with addressing – Mr Vashutkin was kind enough to furnish me with some background on Captain Barbour, the pilot who shot down two Brolturan interceptors with an Earthsphere shuttle.'

'You know about that?' Greg said.

Silveira nodded. 'Indeed – Barbour is something of an underground hero on Earth, and an openly celebrated one on the Vox Humana colonies. Did you know him?'

'No, but my uncle was with him aboard that shuttle.'

Vashutkin leaned forward, suddenly animated. 'Black Theo, yes? Major Karlsson, Viktor Ingram's right-hand man!' He uttered a low whistle. 'Was he killed too?'

'Not entirely sure,' Greg said, trying to ignore the hollowness in his chest. 'There was a report from Pilipoint Station that a lifepod ejected from the shuttle before it engaged the interceptors. Maybe he was in it, I don't know.'

'What about the moon Nivyesta?' Silveira said. 'What do you think is happening up there?'

Up there. Over the last few weeks Greg had largely succeeded in avoiding any brooding over the fate of those closest to him. Catriona and Uncle Theo were missing, that's all, and no presumptions of mortality were going to take root in his thoughts.

'The Brolturans cut all communication with Nivyesta, so we've no' had any direct contact with the folk there,' he said. 'There's plenty of rumours, though – Alexander has probably told you a few – but without another source that's all they are.'

Silveira nodded. 'And what about Earthsphere Ambassador Robert Horst? Our politivores have been riding endless waves of speculation since he supposedly vanished on the very day that the Hegemony envoy accused him of being behind the assassination of Reskothyr the first Brolturan ambassador. Mr Vashutkin says he wouldn't be surprised if he *had* been responsible – what do you say?'

Greg ran his fingers through his hair and rubbed at an ache in his neck. *More like what should I not say? Och well, half a truth is better than nae truth at all!*

'Horst had nothing to do with that assassination,' he said. 'I've seen a cam-vid that proves that it was Ezgara commandos who were responsible, and they take their orders from the Hegemony envoy, Utavess Kuros. As for Horst's whereabouts, that *is* a mystery.' He sighed. 'What I'm about to tell you is gonnae sound far-fetched but hear me out. My uncle, Theo Karlsson, knew that airborne Brolturan guards were coming to get Ambassador Horst, who was visiting Gangradur Falls at the time. He got the ambassador away by zeplin to Giant's Shoulder where I was working . . .' He went on to relate how they had taken refuge in a hidden chamber within the promontory while Brolturan troops swept the area. He made no mention of the warpwell or its true function. Instead he told them that their presence had triggered an ancient, automated matter transporter which by chance snatched the ambassador away to . . . well, to somewhere else.

Silveira was frowning, while Vashutkin had chuckled at first and was now leaning back, watching him closely.

'I do not recall any reports of such discoveries on Giant's Shoulder,' Vashutkin said.

'It only came to light in the days before the crisis,' Greg said. 'I realise that you only have my word for this . . . well, mine and that of my companions here.' He indicated the Firmanov brothers.

Vashutkin sat straighter and stared over at Nikolai. 'Is this true? Is that what you saw?'

Nikolai was unruffled. 'Yes, sir. It happened just as Mr Cameron described.'

'Exactly as he said,' added Alexei.

Greg smiled. 'In fact, that ancient device is probably the reason for the Hegemony's interest in Darien – why d'ye think they dug a big access tunnel into the core of Giant's Shoulder?'

Now Silveira looked uncertain, half-convinced. 'As a technology, matter transportation has never worked consistently but you say that this device accomplished it.'

'There's no knowing that Ambassador Horst survived the process,' Greg added.

Silveira frowned, directing his gaze over Greg's shoulder. 'What about your other companion, the one who has said nothing?'

Greg smiled – this was the opening he'd been waiting for.

'He has plenty to say, Mr Silveira, but first would ye clarify something for me? Might it be possible that your superiors would offer us direct support, depending on what your report contains?'

'That is a possibility,' Silveira said guardedly.

'If you discovered something of shattering importance, for instance?'

'It would certainly have to have significant impact.'

Greg half-turned and beckoned Kao Chih forward. 'Reveal yourself, my friend, and tell these gentlemen who you are.'

Greg saw the surprise in the others' faces as Kao Chih discarded his cap and muffler and bowed politely to Vashutkin and Silveira in turn.

'Greetings, gentlemen. My name is Kao Chih, son of Kao Hsien. I have travelled to this beautiful world from a star system near the furthest borders of the Hegemony, although my family previously lived on a world called Pyre. My great-great-great-grandfather was born there but his parents came from China, from Earth, aboard a ship called the *Tenebrosa* . . .'

As Kao Chih began to relate Pyre's tragic story Vashutkin was visibly moved while Silveira looked thunderstruck.

If we can just get him on our side, Greg thought. *Maybe the Pyre revelation will be enough, if it feeds into his motivations. We could fight against the Brolturans and this mechanoid factory, but without outside help we'll lose. And if we lose, Dariens will end up as serfs for our Sendrukan masters, just another subservient cog in the mighty Hegemonic machine. We can't let that happen.*

And he recalled his temporary but horrific enslavement by the Hegemony nanodust, and shuddered.

I won't let that happen again.

2

LEGION

He was enslaved by pain. Drifting in space on the outer edge of a backwater system, he was a prisoner of his cyborg form's worn-out components, while unable to deny the requirement of duty. His allegiance was an iron compulsion that sprang from that first premise, the initiating moments of his machine-life, the principles and purpose of convergence. Throughout his cross-reticulated physicality, damaged nerve endings sang a song of torment which after days then weeks the autorepair subsystem had dulled, though not yet enough to lessen the heat of his fury at enemies past and present and at the weakened, failing parts of his own body.

There was a grim irony to it. <Metals and alloys erode and energy nodes become enfeebled, yet the wellsprings of my fealty survive undimmed, irrefutable proof of its worth>

The departure from Yndyesi Tetro, from that deep, watery sepulchre, had been triumphant. The surge of power unleashed from his reaction drive was an ecstatic roar across his senses as he boiled the sea and drove up into the sky on a column of plasma energy. Strengthened substructures had held firm, repaired hull plates maintained carapace integrity and the improvised sensor spicules had performed adequately. Even the transit to hyperspace had been smooth, the eyeblink succession of resonant fields boring perfectly through subspace to hyperspace and then dragging the Legion Knight in after them. The macroguidance subsystem was following course coordinates provided by one of his Scions and all had been proceeding well until ten hours in when his systems reported warnings from the hyperdrive power couplings. Before he could initiate a crash-shutdown, multiple subsystem failures tore across the receptors in his neural weave, and moments later he had dropped back into normal space, drifting without power, racked with pain.

His few remaining autorepair remotes had scurried out to the damaged areas, beginning with the worst. And since his meagre external sensors were also incapacitated – apart from a small carapace lens – he was effectively blind and deaf. Thus encaged, his awareness spiralled inwards, exploring forgotten byways of memory, the vast nova-igniting campaigns against the Forerunners, the devastating battlefronts that sprawled across dozens of light years and left a smouldering wreckage of worlds in their wake. Then there were the bold acts of demolition that the Legion inflicted on Forerunner allies down in the dissolute tiers of hyperspace.

In its long and glorious history, the Legion of Avatars had fought and defeated many enemies both honourable and treacherous. The worthiest was the last adversary in the dying universe from which they had fled an age ago. The Izalla were a species whose control over organic life was so encompassing and profound that inorganic mechanisms were never required. After aeons of expansion from galaxy to galaxy the Izalla encountered the Legion of Avatars, whose own empire was an embodiment of the principles of convergence, the melding of flesh and metal, of machine and mind.

The Legion had never met an enemy like the Izalla, but the Izalla had previously encountered a machine race and utterly defeated them. And for a time that experience seemed to aid them against the Legion. But the Legion held to its eternal principles: they possessed the intuitive adaptability of organic thought as well as the might of the machine and soon the tide of conflict turned in their favour. After several centuries of bitter, savage war the Izalla found themselves facing complete obliteration, inexorable, inevitable. With no hope of survival, their leaders triggered a string of black continuum fissures that tore through their universe, devouring galaxies whole.

The Legion Knight's memories dated from that period, when thousands of converged civilisations had already perished and the Legion of Avatars was assembling an armada of armadas in readiness for the time when they would have to flee to another universe. Like all his most important data, these memories were stored in the most secure, best shielded of his biocrystal chines and as he reviewed their denotators he noticed something attached to the oldest recollections, sequence markers linking back to data clusters . . . in his organic cortex. Uneasy, he paused – the old blood-fed cortex might be the seat of his aware-ness but the biocrystal augmentation supported the transcendent level of his essence, the crucible of thoughts and actions faster by far than those permitted by organic neural synapses. Thus he had long ago copied all relevant data into biocrystal storage and used the organic memory as a backup for essential schemators . . .

One of those old memories showed images of his cyborg form post-convergence, so he followed the sequence marker back to a particular highly compressed multicluster in his cortical storage. He hesitated a moment then flowed it into his awareness . . .

Motion . . . he was in motion but not from the use of drives or attitude thrusters . . . he had limbs, long, stiff . . . four? Six? . . . with grasping, fleshy digits at their extremities . . . he was moving through, walking, stalking through a high-ceilinged series of hazy chambers . . . plants grew from the wall, tiny lights moving among them . . . another long-limbed creature like himself emerged from an adjacent room and came up close . . . slender tentacles tipped with sensitive palps reached to touch and stroke his skin . . . Stay, she said, we love you, we need you with us, go not to join with the cold . . . others entered the room, proclaiming the same song, but he shook off the intrusive touches . . . what did they know of convergence, of the wonders that awaited him? . . . in haste he rushed towards the exit while they called out to him in grief, called out his name . . .

Abruptly, he broke away from the memory flow, thoughts

gripped by panic and a primal fear. Why had that memory been left intact? There were others in the cortical storage, records sequentially tagged to the early one in biocrystal – did they also contain memories from before his transformation? Clearly he had cached them in the organic cortex shortly after the convergence with his new cyborg self, but had also provided links to post-convergence recall data, links that only came to light in the wake of serious power failures. Had his younger self thought to make these memories of his original life available in the event of imminent death?

<I am not dead! I have endured an abyss of time, survived while numberless civilisations rose and fell! I do not need . . .>

And he felt the curiosity in him, a yearning, a need to know what those ancient memories might show, a wealth of experience and existence, the raw stuff of the unaugmented, organic life.

<I am not dead, but that old life is. Memory would only reveal the weakness of the flesh, the flawed nature of the unconverged>

Just to look, just to see what that life had been like, it would be so easy, needing only to connect with the organic cortex, to let the memories flow . . . An alert broke into his reverie, a notifier from his autorepair remotes that one of the external sensors was functioning again, and that he had minimal control over two of the attitude jets.

<My metal skin is cold and the pitiless, unforgiving vacuum of space presses in upon me. My old alloy bones bend and crack, my flexar veins degrade and constrict, my neural network burns with damage and pain. But I am not dead! Convergence is strength, convergence is the only path. All else is weakness>

Resolved, he made the only possible choice and erased the linked memories from the organic cortex. As the disturbing images were wiped from active awareness he turned his attention to the data stream now coming from the solitary external sensor. From stellar telltales the positional schemator placed him near an isolated star system in one of the sparser regions of the Indroma Solidarity. Scans showed four worlds, comprising two minor inner planetoids, a blue-gas ice-bound outer, and one habitable with three small moons, all of which had emanation profiles indicating the presence of extensive installations. The habitable world had small, scattered Bargalil populations and vast areas of land dedicated to agriculture.

The latest assessment of the hyperdrive damage confirmed that he had insufficient materials to effect repairs – and there was only one place that he might find resources. He started the attitude jets and was reminded by the piloting schemator of their operational tolerances as he set a course for the Bargalil farm planet. It was likely that the main plasma reaction drive would be operational in a few days so it would still take the better part of a week to reach one of those moons. It might mean that he could finally arrive at the Darien system to find that the warpwell had been sealed, trapping the Legion of Avatars down in hyperspace for ever.

<But I am not dead and I will not die! I am of the Legion and even if the warpwell is closed I shall keep the creed of convergence alive!>

3

ROBERT

Shivering, Robert Horst pulled up the hood of his padded jacket before tugging open the D-shaped hatch leading outside the Artisans Deck. Hinges creaked and a gust of snow flew in as he edged out into the freezing blast, then slammed the hatch behind him. The walkway had a flimsy canopy but was open at the side to the swirling winds which drove particles of ice and snow against the ancient, pitted hull of Malgovastek City. Robert hurried along the exposed gantry and up a flight of iron steps to a circular, sheltered platform. A covey of stick-legged Hodralog were buying whirlyglows from an emaciated female Henkayan who waved a handful at Robert the moment he came into view.

When he came here the first time, three weeks ago with Rosa and the droid Reski Emantes, he had made the mistake of going over to see. Whereupon the Henkayan vendor had stuffed whirlyglows in his pockets, hands and partly open jacket, then demanded payment. Luckily Reski Emantes had intervened and paid up with what looked like marbles containing different numbers of brassy beads. After that, every time he passed through he did as he was doing now, keeping his distance as he hurried to another set of steps leading up.

Above was a similar circular chamber with a low roof and louvred metal shutters which kept out the snow but let in icy draughts. Breathing out foggy clouds, he crossed to one of the exits and out onto a railed gantry bare to the elements, along which he dashed to the observatory, a small boxy building on pillars that rose from the deck below.

For once he was early and his Gomedran contact, Ku-Baar, was late. And since there was no one else about he had the full run of all the viewing niches. He quickly ascended the wooden stairways to the highest catwalk and went straight to the niche that faced the great penduline city of Malgovastek. Winds moaned around the observatory as Robert trained the heavy scope on the upper levels, the Supervisors Deck and the Proprietors Deck, names dating back to the city's founding nearly two millennia ago, according to Reski Emantes.

Such names had apparently hung on out of common usage, bearing no relation to the current power arrangement which was an oligarchy of corrupt clans and guilds. Looking through the scope at the Supervisors Deck he could see light-globes and strings of lamps decorating the porticos, extensions and balconies built onto the original residential sections by successive clan bosses. The Proprietors Deck was more ostentatious, with glass towers, turrets and faceted, glowing domes denoting privilege and wealth, as well as the ruthless violence needed to maintain it. The rushing swirls of snow made the heights grey and hazy but Robert could still make out the Elavescent Hawsers, five mighty cables that soared up through a mile or more of ice storms and gloom to the underside of a colossal stone ledge where the ancient engineers had embedded anchors deep within the rock.

Malgovastek was not the only city suspended from that landmass-scale shelf, nor was that the only such shelf in the bizarre hyperspace tier known as the Shylgandic Lacuna. Robert still vividly remembered their arrival as the Construct tiership *Plausible Response* plummeted down into the Lacuna's dizzying abyss, past jutting immensities of icebound rock, past other cities hanging in the murk like encrusted clumps of corroded regalia, some lit with lamps like dying embers, others looking grey-black and dead. Even as he relived those sights his mind reeled and he experienced a moment of vertigo when he thought of the limitless depths gaping directly below.

Holding on to the scope mounting he recalled the Construct's last words to him before the tiership departed the Garden of the Machines:

'Robert Horst, keep in mind that no matter how grotesque and frightening the sights you behold, local conditions often vary wildly from one tier to the next. Do not forget that you are travelling through the cadavers of expired universes, the remains of their remains, the sepulchral ashes of eternity. You are not required to involve yourself in the survivors' tribulations, only to fulfill your task – find your way to the Godhead and speak with it on the matters I mentioned.'

Of course, Robert knew that the Construct was far more than merely the ruler of the Garden of the Machines, that it was an ancient mech-sentience and one-time ally of the Forerunners themselves. When the Construct spoke of ages past, it was with the authenticity of direct experience.

As he stopped to gaze through the scope again, he heard footsteps enter below then hasten up. A moment later he turned to greet Ku-Baar, former captain to Mirapesh, deceased tooth-father of the Redbard Clan. Ku-Baar was tall for a Gomedran and less bristly than those Robert had previously encountered during his years as a diplomat. These Gomedrans, however, derived from an earlier, less predatory branch of the species which had gone off to explore the upper levels of hyperspace. He also spoke in a much more cultured, expressive version of the Gomedran tongue and held himself with a composed demeanour.

'Good day, Captain Ku-Baar.'

'To you also, Seeker Horst, but sadly that is all the beneficence I can convey to you this day.'

Robert's heart sank. 'No contact, then.'

'Once again the mystic Sunflow Oscillant has not deigned to reply to my communication.'

Robert nodded, weary of the waiting. When the Construct dispatched them on this mission, they were told they would have to go through a series of intermediaries. The first one was quite straightforward, an abstract-dealer living on Zilumer, a crumbling, honeycombed world on the 41st tier of hyperspace: all he required in exchange for the name and location of the next gatekeeper was a hefty sum, which Reski Emantes swiftly paid. But when they came to Malgovastek on Tier 65 in search of the Bargalil mystic Sunflow Oscillant, difficulties became apparent. They discovered that until recently the Bargalil had enjoyed the protection of the Redbarb Clan chief, Mirapesh, who, unfortunately, was fed into a bioshredder by one of his cousins. While blood relatives vied for the leadership, Mirapesh's former officers sought new posts and the mystic sank out of sight, hiding in the warrenlike undertanks of the city. Enquiries had led Robert and the others to a scrimmer workshop part-owned by Ku-Baar, who agreed to help.

'Perhaps we should venture down into the undertanks,' Robert said. 'I recall that you have previously advised against such action, Captain, but our time grows short. Would not a well-armed escort guarantee our safety down there?'

'I fear not, Seeker,' Ku-Baar said. 'For topsiders, a mere show of strength provokes retaliation. Please, allow me to pursue other channels – I have not yet fully exhausted all possibilities. There are a few undertank disbursers I might be able to reach on the eye-way. Indeed, I shall send out notes today.'

'I appreciate your efforts on our behalf and look forward to a swift and positive outcome.'

'I am pleased to be of assistance. Tell me, Seeker, where is your charming daughter and that amusing servitor machine?'

'I left them near the entrance to the Swaydrome – they expressed interest in exploring the stalls there.'

'The ones along the top balcony?' Ku-Baar said with an anxious tilt of the head.

'That is correct.'

The Gomedran seemed relieved. 'The Swaydrome is a risky place at the best of times but on swaydays, like today, they hold pit-tourneys for organics and machines and anyone who strays onto the lowest seating level automatically becomes a contender and can be challenged by anyone or indeed anything.'

'I'm sure that my companions will take all necessary precautions,'

Horst said, pausing to peer through the scope at one of the Elavescent Hawsers for a moment. 'Captain, I've a question which I hope you will not find insulting, and it is this – how often do cities fail and fall?'

'Your question does indeed encompass a subject that many Malgovastins consider taboo, though not myself. To answer, I can say that we learn of such calamities about once every few years, either from rumours passed on by aerotraders or from the first-hand accounts of fleeing refugees, or – more rarely – from an actual visible sighting. I myself bore witness to one when I was a knife-cub. I remember standing out on one of the springwalks, and it was between the bells so it was late, and I was staring out into the ice-storm veils, watching them sweep and rush into dark vortices then uncoil again. Then something made me look up, maybe a sound or some change in the air, but when I did I saw a pale grey object no larger than an ishi bean drawing near, falling towards Malgovastek. The moments passed, the object grew steadily bigger and darker and I could tell that it would fall past our city rather than strike it. Larger it became, taking on regular details, the lines and corners of a city's decks, blocks and towers. At one point it looked as if great red and gold banners were streaming out above it until I realised that the city was burning as it fell.

'I remember watching it plunge past less than half a mile away, with the hawsers trailing in its smoky wake and the veils of snow swirling and eddying in the force of its passing. Ever since I have been aware at all times what our lives hang from.' The Gomedran grinned. 'I was an anxious cub who became an anxious adult. But a surfeit of time passes for those who tarry, Seeker Horst – I must return to my shop to make further eye-way enquiries after our wayward Bargalil.'

Bows were exchanged and after Ku-Baar left the observatory Robert waited a minute or two before retracing his own steps back to the Artisans Deck, closing the D-shaped hatch on the icy winds. Inside it was cold and dim. This level of Malgovastek consisted of six main floors and innumerable refurbished and retailored sub-sections, silos and chambers. Lighting was intermittent, bioglobes and battery strips mainly, and the air had a dank, fetid quality. A busy stairwell led up to a curved passage of entrances leading into the top balcony of the Swaydrome. There were a few locals about, mostly Keklir, a bipedal race with short, powerful limbs and faces dominated by a wide, tapering snout with two mouthlike openings. Other species included Gomedrans, a few Hodralog, and the occasional Pozu.

Pushing through heavy curtains, he entered the deafening cacophony of the Swaydrome, a full-throated roar that surged along in time to a heavy, metallic hammering coming from down on the drome floor. The upper balcony was a U-shape of seating carrels, then rows of ordinary benches and bucketchairs, then crowded shadows dotted with the lamps of gaming tables and the amber glows of the kiosks and stalls that lined the back wall. Out of curiosity Robert sidled through to the front of the balcony and peered down through the bowed layers of netting. A large, tracked mech was holding down a spindly droid with one articulated claw while pounding its armoured midsection with the other. Bright spotbeams picked out the two combatants while spectators chanted and howled. Just as the underdog's plating gave way in a burst of sparks, Robert felt a touch on his shoulder, and a voice.

'Daddy!'

It was Rosa, his daughter, or as good as. His wife had sent him a holosim projector of their dead daughter before he came to Darien as Earthsphere's special ambassador. But when intrigue, deadly peril and chance encounters led him down into hyperspace, to a strange citadel called the Garden of the Machines, he could not have predicted what was to come. His daughter returned to life as a simulant based on the holosim's data, and his own physical form rejuvenated by decades. But the Construct, the AI ruler of the Garden of the Machines, had also removed Harry, his AI implant, then given it free imperatives before releasing it into the tiernet, the omnipresent interstellar infoweb. Amazed and gratified by Rosa's new existence, he had agreed to help the Construct establish contact with the Godhead, hence the necessity to meet the intermediary known as Sunflow Oscillant.

'Where's Reski Emantes?' he said loudly, above the crowd noise. 'I would have thought it would be interested.'

'It says that if it wanted to see dumb objects hitting each other, it could go and watch an autoforge stamp out cutlery for half an hour.'

Robert nodded. 'Understandable.'

By now they were away from the mass of spectators and gamblers, strolling along the line of stalls from which he caught an occasional appetising whiff. Then Rosa stopped him, hand on his arm.

'You're not exactly bursting with news so I guess that good old Ku-Baar had nothing to report.'

'Same as before, my sweet, no sign of our mysterious mystic, although Ku-Baar insists that he still has other enquiries to make.'

'Perhaps we should engage the services of someone else from Mirapesh's coterie, assuming there's any still alive,' said the droid Reski Emantes, which floated into view with a netbag of packages slung beneath it. The droid resembled an inverted isosceles pyramid, narrow and elongated, less than a metre high with spheroid studs at each vertex and a small trigonal dome on its upper surface. 'Or hire some fists and go searching for the mystic ourselves. He is a Bargalil, after all; a large, six-legged, barrel-chested sophont would be difficult to conceal, I should think.'

'The undertanks are a risky territory,' Robert said. 'Ku-Baar promised that he would vigorously query his other contacts, so we give him another day and a half, after which we shall consider our options. In the meantime, how goes the shopping?'

'Ah yes,' said Reski Emantes. 'I found an itinerant Pozu selling urmig eggs, and then chanced upon some tubers that may suit your Human palate . . .'

The mech was interrupted by another mass-roar from the arena followed by rhythmic shouting and stamping.

'Another hapless bot reduced to scrap?' said Robert.

'Worse, it's the Force Fate event,' the droid said. 'The drome organisers select a mech from the bottom level to go up against their resident armoured thug, probably some oversized, rock-chewing rustbucket with the hardmem substrate of a floor polisher. The unfortunate dupe should appear on the monitors . . .'

'Yes, there it is,' Rosa began, then paused and pointed at a wallscreen several metres away. 'Reski, it's you . . . I mean, at first it was another droid, for a second, then it switched to you!'

The wallscreen showed them standing near Reski Emantes, staring off to the side, while the surrounding crowd guffawed and hooted. Robert looked around to where the sneak-cam had to be but could see nothing in the dark texture of the ceiling.

'You're right, I've just rerun it!' Reski Emantes said. 'I've got to see the judges . . .'

But the eager onlookers were hemming them in as they started for the exit. Then the mob parted and two Keklir in red stewards' uniforms rushed straight at Reski Emantes and tossed a shining loop over it.

'I'm not finding this in the least bit amusing,' the droid said. 'Get your idio-idio-idio-idididididi . . .'

The loop sprang into a taut circle and a pulsing blue field flickered on, rendering Reski Emantes motionless. Before Robert could react, one of the Keklir produced an oval-snouted sidearm and made discouraging motions with it while his companion steered the immobilised droid over to the front of the balcony and pitched it over the side. The roar of the crowd was thunderous.

Robert and Rosa reached the balcony edge in time to see the helpless droid land on the arena floor and rebound, cushioned by the blue field. Another Keklir dashed over, affixed a small object to Reski Emantes's plating, then hastily jumped into an open hatch at ringside, which slammed shut. Then, in a cupola-pulpit overlooking the arena, a ridged cowl began folding back into the wall, revealing a gleaming, golden insectoid creature with three mandibles, jutting limbs and three pairs of black faceted eyes along the length of its narrow head, which reminded Robert of a horse skull.

Then the golden master of ceremonies extended one spiny forelimb and pointed at the floating, unresponsive Reski. A harsh, amplified syllable cut through the crowd noise and a moment later the blue restraint field winked out, allowing the droid freedom of movement.

'This is an outrage!' it began. 'How dare . . .'

The insectoid master of ceremonies drowned out Reski Emantes with its grating, booming speech for a brief moment before a much more familiar voice filled the arena: '. . . probably some oversized, rock-chewing rustbucket with the hardmem substrate of a floor-polisher . . .'

Spotbeams swept the crowded tiers and angry shouts broke out as translations filtered around the drome. As the fury stoked itself, the golden insectoid raised its gleaming forelimbs.

'Words to the designated challenger – projectile and energy weapons are forbidden, also anti-cognitory fields are forbidden. The attached inhibitor enforces. What words from the designated challenger?'

For a moment there was a cessation of the clamour, and Robert hoped that Reski Emantes would opt for a response with a decent courtesy content. It was a forlorn hope.

'Your louts broke my urmig eggs, you preposterous bug! . . .'

In its pulpit the master of ceremonies made a dipping motion with one limb. Directly below, an arched metal door slammed aside and a large, dark green spidery mech emerged. Its torso was a flattened spheroid roughly five metres across with four articulated, armoured legs spaced around the midline. Faceted sensors were dotted over its battered cowling, which bore innumerable dents and scratches, the legacy of past bouts.

Without warning, Reski Emantes suddenly launched itself at the big mech, ducking a parrying limb and striking the top of one of the legs where its armoured joint emerged from the plating. There was an immense clang and sparks flew as Reski rebounded from the impact and tumbled away. The large mech turned and sprang after it.

'What kind of machine is that?' Robert murmured.

'A dock drone of some kind, Daddy,' Rosa said unexpectedly. 'A midrange assembler, possibly a positioner.' She met his gaze. 'I learned a lot from the Construct's archives before we left.'

Interesting, Robert thought, his fond smile fading a little as he regarded the fight below.

Reski Emantes now seemed to be getting the worst of it. His narrow, pyramidal torso was bent and two of its corner studs were missing. The big mech had it pinned to the floor with a clamp effector while all around the crowd's roaring approval came in waves.

'Reski can't survive this much longer,' Robert said. 'We should go down and protest . . .'

'Don't worry, Daddy. Just watch.'

A moment later Reski had somehow managed to slide his wide upper section a short way out from under the clamp. Before the mech could reposition its effector, Reski Emantes thrust upwards, levered itself free and shot away, looking somewhat wobbly in flight. Robert thought it was going to stay at a safe distance but instead it swooped in again . . . and was sideswiped by another of those armoured yet lithe articulated legs, whipping up to swat it like a fly.

But instead of spinning away, Reski was clinging to the armoured limb's lower section with thin, cable extensors. The big mech tried to shake it off but Reski doggedly held on and made its way up to the segmented shoulder junction. Robert could just see Reski wrapping its cable extensors tightly around the top of the articulated leg. The droid gave a sharp tug, then another, and the leg came away.

The big machine quickly shifted one leg forward to compensate but Reski had already hopped to the next shoulder junction. A moment later the second leg was wrenched off, and the mech crashed to the floor. With contemptuous ease, Reski Emantes dodged the two remaining limbs as it darted in to finish the job. The Swaydrome crowd stared in stunned silence as the last heavy armoured leg landed on the big mech's hull with a clang.

'Calculator,' the droid Reski Emantes said to its opponent.

In its cupola-pulpit, the golden insectoid sapient raised one angular limb and pointed its spiny tip at the Construct droid.

'Force-Fate bout . . . to the challenger!' And at once the

inhibitor device detached from Reski's cowling and fell to the arena floor.

This provoked a mass chorus of hisses, clacking, hooting and less than complimentary (not to say improbable) observations as to Reski Emantes's origins, as well as surreal suggestions on what to do with a variety of power tools.

'Thank you, thank you, dearest of all my fans,' Reski said as it slowly rose towards the top balcony. 'Your incoherent, hate-filled grunts say more than real words ever could.' Below, attendants were dragging off pieces of the dismembered mech.

Robert and Rosa stood back as the Construct droid floated up and over the balcony netting. The crowd of onlookers and patrons offered only glowering, unfriendly looks as they moved away, so Robert decided that a burst of applause might be unwise.

'You don't look too bad,' said Rosa.

Up close, Robert could see the damage in detail, a disconcerting collection of dents, scuffs, gouges and cracks, as well as the bend two-thirds of the way down its tapered carapace. All four corner studs were missing, too.

'You look terrible,' said Robert.

'Looks can be deceiving, Robert Horst,' the droid said. 'Some repairs are already under way and will accelerate once my internal builders replace the micromolbots I used to deal with that cretin's legs.'

Robert stared. 'Was that . . . cheating?'

'You heard the list of forbidden tactics,' Reski Emantes said. 'Micromolecular toolbots weren't mentioned.'

'It may be advisable to return to the ship,' Rosa said. 'We still don't know why the challenger image switched from that other droid to you.'

'It may be nothing more than picking on the stranger,' the droid said. 'But before we go, I want to buy some more urmig eggs . . .'

Just then, Robert felt a tap on his elbow and turned to see the Gomedran, Ku-Baar, standing there.

'Captain Ku-Baar – a pleasant surprise meeting you here. Did you happen to see the last bout?'

'Indeed I did, Seeker Horst.' The Gomedran gave a polite tilt of the head towards the Construct droid. 'Congratulations on your victory, Seeker Reski, a notable event that I suspect may be connected to the reason for my presence here.'

'Which is?' Robert said, feeling a prickle of anticipation.

'A short while ago, I was contacted by the mystic Sunflow Oscillant, directly, by voiceline.' The Gomedran regarded their expectant faces. 'He has agreed to meet with you.'

Robert and Rosa exchanged smiles.

'When and where, Captain?' Robert said.

'Tomorrow, at the outset of the Bright Bell, at your vessel. He said that all of you must await him on the bridge, else your quest will be at an end.'

4

CHELUVAHAR

In the middle of their first night's sleep inside Tusk Mountain, Cheluvahar, scholar and seer, awoke suddenly, senses quivering with the certainty that something was watching them. Ever since yesterday, while his three Artificer scholars and Pilot Yash were clearing the rubble from the entrance, his husked senses gave him the distinct feeling that the ancient Uvovo sanctuary held some other presence. A brief survey of the mountainside entrance and the surrounding rock turned up nothing, however, so the debris clearance had continued.

Chel and Yash and the others had come to Tusk Mountain with the permission of the elder Listeners, to search for an old Uvovo bastion long rumoured to be buried somewhere on its shattered, boulder-strewn slopes. Chel's new eyes, piercing the veil of likelihoods and past echoes, found it in a matter of hours. And going by the good condition of the interior, it would make a formidable new home for the Human–Uvovo resistance.

Now, Cheluvahar, scholar and seer, lay back down with all of his eyes tightly shut. Lying here on the chamber's chilling stone floor, enclosed by stone, it was an effort to remind himself that the Uvovo of ancient times had been as skilled in the shaping of stone, and even metal, as their descendants were in the care of Segrana. Ten thousand years ago, the Segrana-That-Was had encompassed both planet and moon, suffused with a might and a purpose that made it the mainstay in the War of the Long Night, a struggle against destroyer machines called the Dreamless. It took the decimation of ancient allies, the Ghost Gods, and the sacrifice of Segrana's greater strength to defeat those pitiless machine minds. But still the world Umara suffered partial incineration, all the splendour of its vast and teeming forests consumed by fire, their smoke filling the skies, ashes choking the rivers. Chel had witnessed it all in the vivid, unforgettable visions of a husking ceremony. But rather than transforming him into a Listener, the taller, gaunter form of Uvovo, the ritual gave him four new eyes which, when opened in certain combinations, could reveal things from the past as well as possible futures.

Now, in the darkness, he sighed and sat up again and brooded. Umara, cradle of Segrana-That-Was, had become Darien, home to a colony of fractious, flawed, fascinating Humans who seemed to draw in enemies and adversity the way sun-fermented emels attracted insects. Yet if Humans had not come to settle here, the Uvovo would never have been able to cross from the moon to their ancient home and there would have been no resistance to the Hegemony and possibly no knowledge of Umara's existence spread among the stars.

And little real good have the Humans brought about, responded his inner arguer. *Half the stars in the sky seem to know of our plight yet none come to our aid. Knowledge is clearly of little value to them.*

We cannot see all that is happening so we cannot know what will happen, he countered. *Bare ground hides many seeds.*

But his arguer was not done. *So how long will you wait for your forest to grow out of that dry, dusty soil?*

Chel smiled and gazed around him at the dimness, broken only by a Human oil lantern set to give off a feeble amber glow. The unseen watcher was still there, he was sure. He raised one hand to the cloth strip covering his Seer eyes and was on the verge of opening the outer pair when one of the prone shapes nearby stirred and sat up.

'So – can't sleep?' muttered a voice in accented Noranglic.

'It's the stone, Pilot Yash,' he whispered back. 'I find I cannot fully relax here.'

'What about them cave recesses back at Tayowal? They're cut into rock but you didn't have trouble sleeping there.'

'True, but the scholars there have enfolded their refuge with plants and flowers and umisk nests, all the tendrils of life.'

'Hmmph.' Yash scratched one of his ears. 'Or you could be wondering if we're being watched.'

Chel smiled. 'How did you know?'

'Places like this, they always have a bit of . . .'

He paused as one of the scholars muttered in her sleep and turned over. Both of them were still and silent for a moment, then Chel, in the faintest of whispers, said, 'Talk outside . . .'

They stood and carefully tiptoed to the door, then by the light of a handtorch moved along the corridor a few paces.

'You were about to say something about old places like this, Pilot Yash,' Chel said in a low voice.

The short-bodied, long-armed Voth, wrapped in a bulky quilted coat, gestured at the stonework all around.

'Your ancestors built this place for a serious reason, and it's big enough for plenty of them and whatever they were about, yes?'

Chel nodded, and Yash spread his hands.

'Right, well among my people we know that all old buildings, especially ones made for war or captivity, carry residual imprints of past inhabitants and their activities. I overheard that them new eyes of yours let you see the past – have you seen anything here?'

'I have not used my other eyes here,' Chel said.

'Aren't you curious?' said the Voth. 'Jelk, if it were me I'd want to know what my predecessors were up to!'

Chel smiled. Of course he was curious, but he was also cautious and not a little bit afraid of what he might see. *But I'll have to take forward steps sometime, and it would be worth seeing if this seer sight reveals who or what is watching us.*

'Very well, Pilot Yash, I shall take a brief look. But be aware that these eyes sometimes show me more than just the past . . .'

He pushed the cloth strip up into his fine, dense hair and for a moment just stood, regarding his dim surroundings, grey surfaces in the torch's meagre light. Then he hesitantly parted the eyelids of the outer pair of new eyes. At first, same as his own original eyes, except that there was an extra sense of solidity to objects, conferred by a four-way ocularity, illuminated by the pale halo of Yash's torch from which tenuous shadows spread. There was stillness, the sound of Yash's breathing, the faint pulse of his own heartbeat which seemed to slow, then slow further, the beat low and languid, slowing down . . .

Then leaped back to normal again, as the walls suddenly flickered with shifting strands and clusters of glowing threads, and the air shimmered with glimmering outlines of shapes in motion, moving together or through one another, lines writhing across the walls and ceiling, tangled meshes, quivering webs hurrying to and fro . . .

He gasped, closing his eyes tightly. It was too much, too overwhelming – *Focus on the now, the here, and the vital, sift out the discord* – yet he steadied himself, breathed deeply and opened his eyes again. And saw ghosts.

Saw a group of nebulous forms made of those same fine outlines, which he now realised were the residue of past occupants, just as Yash said. The forms grew more detailed, became three Uvovo bent to the task of pushing a loaded cart along the corridor towards where Chel and Yash stood.

'What do you see?' Yash murmured.

Chel held up a silencing finger, keeping his eyes on the approaching trio, standing aside as they drew near and passed by. On the cart was a large device of some kind, its details vague apart from hints of flanges, spikes and what looked like twisted limbs. The faces of the Uvovo were indistinct but there was a certain urgency to their posture as they faded into the dark end of the corridor.

What am I seeing and why? It must be important for it to be still playing out after so many centuries, but why?

'Looks as if we may have woken someone,' Yash muttered beside him. 'Now what's that he's got . . . *no, wait, stop!* . . .'

Chel turned and for a moment saw one of his Artificer scholars standing next to the chamber door with a crowbar wedged behind one of the stone pillar uprights. The scholar's face was blank as he put his full weight behind the crowbar and wrenched at the pillar. There was a grinding sound, then the lintel and the wall and ceiling above caved in with a roaring rumble, falling rubble throwing up clouds of dust.

Yash dragged him back, shouting about a weakened ceiling, and Chel complied while in his mind's eye he saw again the scholar, this time with a violet nimbus about him. Then Yash ignored his own advice and advanced through the dusty haze, coughing as he shone his narrow torch beam on the collapse. Chel was still looking through his outer new eyes and could see gleams and splinters of amber light slipping past gaps in the rubble that blocked the chamber entrance.

'I can hear their voices, Chel!' cried the Voth.

But Chel's senses, alerted by his enhanced vision, quivered in warning as he saw it – a shimmering outline flowing across the shadowy wall away from the fallen masonry. He concentrated his awareness on it, letting his perceptions draw the vision into his mind, as the outline took on hazy details, took on an odd, flattened form. A figure that dipped in and out of the wall as if it were no more solid than a barrier of smoke. Could this be the watcher?

'Help me, Chel! – we can dig them out!'

But the shimmering figure was heading along towards the big hall down from the mountainside entrance, from where several passages branched out.

'I have to follow it, Yash – it's the watcher!'

'The what?'

Chel shook his head and hurried after the apparition, ignoring the Voth's increasingly angry shouts. As he strode off into the darkness his new eyes laid bare a scattering of details, motes, nuances, an opaque rendering of his surroundings in which the mysterious figure shone like a temple carving brought to life. He followed it round the corner and down the hall to where the open archways of two tall corridors gaped darkly. Earlier, Chel and the others had explored them briefly before retiring for the night;

one led to a stairway that spiralled up to a small level of connected rooms full of stone channels and conduits that once would
have guided numerous vital roots back when vast forests had
towered over even the mountain ranges of Umara, in the age of
Segrana-That-Was.

The other led down a short flight of steps to a pair of heavy
stone doors which they'd found to be solidly jammed shut.
Predictably, this was where the bright outline figure went, gliding
from wall to door, undulating across stained surfaces, sinking in
and fading from view. Chel sighed as he stopped before the doors,
studied the beautifully intricate carvings of entwining vegetation,
then slipped his hands into the angled gripping slots and pulled.
Nothing, not the slightest hint of any give. Frustrated, he gave
them another sharp tug – and heard a faint crack.

Frowning, he stared at the door, clearer now that his eyes, original and seer, had adjusted to both the darkness and the
underlying residual images of the past, fleeting glimpses of other
hands pushing the doors open, other forms coming and going. He
focused. The right-hand door no longer seemed so flush against
the other, and Chel could just detect the thready glow of energy at
the hinge pintles, floor and ceiling. This time he grasped the finger
slot with both hand and hauled on it with all his force, felt movement, paused for breath and pulled again.

With a scraping, grating sound the door gradually came open,
a finger's width, then a hand's width, then finally a gap sufficient
to allow him to squeeze through. On the other side he leaned
against the wall, smelling a musty dankness amid the darkness,
gazing at the stairs that wound down into the dark heart of the
mountain. He felt the sheer weight of all the rock that lay above
him, that great, cold downward-pressing mass, and for a moment
he wavered. But he gathered his resolve, pushed the unease aside,
and continued, following the stairs down.

His footsteps kicked up dust and he could feel fine grit through
his hide boots. Through the crumbly erosion of the walls his fingers could make out deeper grooves, not the details of ancient
Uvovo depictions and bas-relief decorations, but something else.

Then in a leap of conjecture he was sure that they had once acted as guides for creeper plants, a web of them trained throughout the Uvovo stronghold, bringing living greenery to its every corner. Perhaps even light, too, from ineka beetles and ulby roots.

The stairs came out in a small room off a curving corridor. It was pitch black down here but his Seer eyes revealed the cracked walls, the regular chamber openings along the outer wall, the occasional pile of rubble, the dried-up corpses of insects with a few live ones scuttling away from his feet. But of the strange wall ghost there was no sign. At last he came to where a fall-in was serious enough to block the way, a mound of rock and earth that had spilled into the passageway quite some time ago going by the encrustations of dust and delicate, desiccated remains of plants. A big wedge of ceiling masonry had punched a hole in the floor through which Chel could see an empty room devoid of life.

The curved corridor ran in a wide circle, and the inner wall had only two openings, intriguing recesses with steps leading down to square double doors. Resembling ceremonial entrances, they were set diametrically opposite each other but were blocked by boulders and large pieces of broken stonework which had been piled into the recesses. Standing before one of them, Chel frowned as he wondered who had done this and why, and what lay behind the doors. Then he retraced his steps back to the big rockfall and the hole in the floor which might just be wide enough to get through . . .

As the great mound of dust-caked rock and soil came into view, he quickened his pace – a familiar glimmering radiance clung to the edges of the hole, fading as it sank. Moments later Chel was squatting down to lower his legs in, then, grasping a solid section of the edge, he swung down, hung there a second before dropping the last few feet.

Landing in a crouch, he barely had time to draw breath before he was engulfed in whorls of radiance surging up from the stone floor underfoot. The glittering light flowed in skeins of amber about him, a slow enfolding luminescence beyond which strands of dust and desiccated motes floated.

'Intruder! . . . Violator! . . .'

The radiance swirled and pressed and probed, seeking access, a weakness, a gap in the defences. Chel did not yield.

'Not I,' he said.

'Defiler! . . . Outrager! . . .' When it spoke it was like a shriek pared down to the level of a whisper. '. . . Bringer of empty sleep! . . . Name thyself . . .'

'Cheluvahar of the Warrior Uvovo, scholar and seer . . .'

'Liar! . . . Despoiler of truths! . . . You lie – all the Seers died at the Isle of Colloquy when the Enemy fell upon them from the sky . . . the sky . . . they came with silent death . . .'

'I am a new seer,' he said, resisting the stabbing grasp. 'Segrana remade me from what I was!'

'. . . you lie . . . YOU LIE! . . . she who enfolds, she is gone, dead, expired . . . burnt and dead . . . great Segrana of endless memory . . . you lie, just like the Cold Walker . . .' The voice lost its ferocity and the shimmering nimbus receded. '. . . It comes here with a great cargo of lies, vast and cruel . . . it tests me and I tire . . . it tries to make me believe cruel things but I will not forget . . . what I am . . .'

'Who are you?' Chel said. 'What are you?'

'. . . seed and root, leaf and branch . . .' The voice sounded mournful. '. . . droplets of sun, droplets of time . . .'

Chel was astonished. The couplets were familiar, a childhood refrain, a youngling's rhyme whose words came easily to mind.

'. . . the feathered ones, the scaled ones . . . the digging ones, the chewing ones . . . the buzzing ones, the singing ones . . . the swimming ones, the resting ones . . . all kept safe, all kept well . . . by the lonely keeper . . . the Keeper of Segrana . . .'

The voice fell silent and a pale amorphous luminosity flowed away towards a carving-covered wall, up to a long horizontal crack into which it vanished.

What kind of being is that? he wondered. *It knew of the Keeper, but it tried to possess me just as it did with my scholar.*

According to the song-cycles of the War of the Long Night, the Keeper of Segrana was the wisest of the wise, the most capable of all the Pathmasters chosen by Segrana herself to carry out a vital wardenship. The Pathmasters were closely attuned to the thoughts, the moods, and the currents of Segrana but only the Keeper was able to share them, by virtue of bonds laid out in the underdomain of reality, by way of intertwined consciousnesses. If this was true, how could a spectral remnant survive all these centuries? Could Yash be right, that past events full of the most intense emotions could imprint themselves in the solid surroundings of their locations?

He looked about him. It was a long room with shallow recesses to either side, each with several concave ducts running across the back, connected to the others. These had to be root guides similar to those he'd found in the underground root chamber a few weeks ago. Through the gloom of the room he saw a shadowy door at the far end and made towards it. Beyond was a circular passage with another nine root chambers leading off, and a small central room with small, narrow steps leading up. He climbed up through a rectangular gap and found himself at the bottom of a high, circular hall dimly lit by a few opaque, glassy panels dotted here and there, giving off a wan radiance.

The hall was about a hundred paces wide and the tall encircling wall seemed to be decorated with horizontal bands of friezes. To Chel's immediate right was a circular stone platform supported by four equidistant head-height plinths. He could see that once there had been four of these platforms, but the one to his left was slumped, charred and melted as if it had been subjected to tremendous heat. The one directly across had been smashed apart, and seared chunks of stone lay scattered over half the floor. The fourth seemed as undamaged as the one Chel stood near but when he looked at it closely, just with his ordinary eyes, he could discern a hazy, tenuous aura and faint silvery gleams in the grooves of the patterns incised into its surface.

With a shock he realised what he was looking at. The motifs and symbols that covered the still intact platforms looked very similar to those on the face of the warpwell back at Giant's Shoulder. When he approached the one with the aura he immediately felt a sense of presence, of connections to things beyond the mountain, as if it were almost alive. He ascended a small set of stone steps up to the rounded lip and stepped onto the glimmering patterns.

At once light bloomed from the high walls, from symbols that appeared amid the carvings whose polished mosaic style gave off bright reflections. Other glassy panels lit up, providing ample illumination.

AT LAST YOU HAVE COME, SEER CHELUVAHAR.

A shining silver veil rose around half the platform's rim, its folds of light brightening and rippling as the speaker spoke.

'Greetings, Sentinel,' Chel said. 'Have I been expected?'

I REASONED THAT THE NEED FOR A ROBUST REFUGE WOULD LEAD YOU TO UOK-HAKAUR, ALTHOUGH NOT SO DELAYED. TIME GROWS SHORT.

Time grows short, Chel thought. It hadn't taken long for the cryptic utterances to emerge.

'Sentinel, may I ask how you are able to speak with me here when you reside beneath the Waonwir?'

THE GREATER PART OF ME IS INTEGRAL TO THE WAONWIR – THAT IS ITS STRENGTH AND MY WEAKNESS. HOWEVER, MY ABILITY TO DIVERT PART OF MY COGNITIVE SELF ALONG THE WORLDPATHS REMAINS UNDIMINISHED.

'What are the worldpaths?' Chel said.

WAYS LAID DOWN IN THE UNDERDOMAIN BY THE FORE-RUNNERS TO DRAW TOGETHER ALL THE CITADEL WORLDS IN PREPARATION FOR THE INVASION OF THE LEGION OF AVATARS. UNFORTUNATELY, FEW WORLDPATHS REMAIN INTACT, AT LEAST AMONG THOSE THAT CONVERGED AT UMARA.

Possibilities tumbled through Chel's thoughts. 'Sentinel, are these worldpaths only for communication, or can we travel along them?'

TRAVEL BETWEEN THE CITADEL WORLDS WAS COMMON-PLACE AND COMMUNICATION WAS PART OF DAY-TO-DAY EXISTENCE. NOW, MY ENERGY SOURCES ARE WEAK AND UNRELIABLE; I AM CAPABLE OF OBSERVING AND COMMUNI-CATING ALONG THOSE WORLDPATHS STILL OPEN TO ME, BUT

SENDING A LIVING BEING WOULD BE DEMANDING AND PROB-
LEMATIC.

'Yet you transported the Earthsphere ambassador away, and
later sent the visitor Kao Chih and his companions to safety after
the defeat of the Legion machine.'

WHEN THE CONSTRUCT MADE ITS REQUEST FOR A HUMAN
OR UVOVO GUEST, IT ALSO SENT AN ISOSHELL OF COHERENT
ENERGIES WITH WHICH TO EFFECT THE TRANSFER. A SMALL
AMOUNT WAS LEFT OVER, ENOUGH TO REMOVE THE THREE
DEFENDERS TO A SAFE PLACE.

Chel frowned and turned, his attention distracted by a now-
familiar presence, and there, flickering across the foot of the wall
was the shimmering entity that called itself the Keeper.

HAVE YOU ENCOUNTERED THIS LURKER SINCE YOUR
ARRIVAL, SEER?

'Yes,' said Chel, gaze following the pale radiant outline until it
disappeared behind the rubble of the smashed platform. 'It took
control of one of my companions and caused a cave-in that trapped
them in a chamber up near the entrance, then when I came down
here it tried to possess me but failed. Is it really the Keeper?'

THE POSSIBILITY EXISTS. THE LAST KEEPER OF SEGRANA
WAS FIGHTING AGAINST THE DREAMLESS TO THE VERY END –
HIS MIND WAS STRETCHED ACROSS THE FULL BREADTH OF
UMARA, FROM THE HEIGHTS TO THE DEPTHS AND THROUGH-
OUT STRONGHOLDS LIKE UOK-HAKAUR. IN COMMON WITH
THE WAONWIR AND MOST OF THE ANCIENT UVOVO BUILD-
INGS, THE STONES HERE WERE REFASHIONED TO BECOME
LIKE DEVICES, SOME WITH SPECIFIC PROPERTIES, SOME WITH
MANY, ALL WORKING TOGETHER TO PROVIDE SANCTUARY,
CONTINUITY AND MEMORY FOR THE UVOVO.

'But the war broke that continuity,' Chel said.

THE WAR ENDED MANY THINGS. WHEN SEGRANA-THAT-WAS
SACRIFICED HER GREATER STRENGTH, THE DREAMLESS SENT
THEIR MACHINE SERVANTS AGAINST HER, BURNING THE
FORESTS, BURNING THE LAND, BURNING UMARA. THE UVOVO
DIED, AS DID THE PATHMASTERS AND THE KEEPER.

Chel remembered something. 'After I resisted its assault, it spoke of someone else it had met, the Cold Walker – is that you, Sentinel?'

YES, THAT IS ITS NAME FOR ME.

'So, it is possible that the stones of this place absorbed some remnant of the original Keeper,' Chel said. 'But could this vestige present a threat?'

AGAIN, THE POSSIBILITY EXISTS. IF THE KEEPER'S ESSENCE WAS ABSORBED THEN THE PATTERN OF IT MUST RESIDE IN A PARTICULAR PLACE. SUCH A PATTERN CAN BE DISRUPTED SHOULD THIS KEEPER PROVE TO BE MORE THAN A NUISANCE.

'If we had a Keeper now,' Chel said, 'it might strengthen our situation.'

THE NEW KEEPER WAS INTENDED TO BE YOU, BUT SEGRANA PICKED ANOTHER.

Chel paused on hearing this, so surprised that he went over what the Sentinel had just said. Understanding was followed by astonishment.

'I was intended to be . . . the Keeper of Segrana?'

YOU WERE SELECTED BY THE LISTENERS WHO GUIDED YOU TO THE FIRST STAGE, A LISTENER HUSKING. INSTEAD YOU EMERGED AS A SEER WHILE SEGRANA CHOSE ANOTHER AS KEEPER, THE HUMAN FEMALE CATRIONA MACREADIE.

Astonishment sharpened – a non-Uvovo as the Keeper! He could imagine the outrage that this would provoke in strict traditionalists, like his old teacher, Listener Faldri, yet he himself felt no anger or resentment. Segrana, he deduced, must have had compelling reasons for her decision – Catriona had once been an Enhanced, which perhaps conferred on her qualities that Segrana saw as unique and invaluable.

'She must have found it daunting,' Chel said.

HER TASK IS JUST AS VITAL AND DEMANDING AS YOURS, AND NO LESS PRESSING. YOU AND YOURS COMPANIONS MUST RETURN TO TAYOWAL AND PERSUADE GREGORY CAMERON AND THE OTHER LEADERS TO BRING THEIR PEOPLE HERE, TO UOK-HAKAUR, WHERE THEY CAN BE PROTECTED.

'Protected from what, Sentinel?'

IN THE CHAMBER BENEATH WAONWIR I OVERHEAR MUCH THAT IS SAID BY THESE HEGEMONY SCIENTISTS, BETWEEN THEM AND THE DREAMLESS PARASITES THEY THINK TO BE SERVANTS. I HAVE LEARNED THAT THEIR MASTER HERE ON UMARA, ONE NAMED KUROS, WILL SOON HAVE A NEW WEAPON AT HIS DISPOSAL. IN SENDRUKAN IT IS CALLED THE NAMUL-ASHAPH, A MOBILE FACTORY FOR PRODUCING WAR MACHINES, SEMI-AUTONOMOUS COMBAT MECHS. WHEN IT ARRIVES IT WILL BE FLOWN UNDER COVER OF DARKNESS TO A SECLUDED SITE SOMEWHERE IN THE FOREST OF ARAWN. THIS FACTORY HAS A DIRECTING MIND AND AFTER IT HAS LOCATED SETTLEMENTS OF REBEL HUMANS IT WILL EAT THE GROUND, SOIL AND ROCK, AND START TO BUILD ITS HORDE.

Chel listened in horror. 'How can we fight such a thing? The Humans have their weapons but—'

YOU HAVE UOK-HAKAUR! IT IS A STRONGHOLD BUILT TO STAND AGAINST THE DREAMLESS OF OLD – IT WILL PROTECT YOU AGAINST THIS NAMUL-ASHAPH AND ITS DEVICE-CREATURES.

'But what of Nivyesta?' Chel said. 'Are they going to send one of these factories into the forests of Segrana?' Terrible visions flitted through his thoughts: fire, blood, and immense trees toppling.

SEGRANA HAS ANCIENT STRENGTHS AND RESOURCES, SEER, AND IS MORE THAN CAPABLE OF DEALING WITH SUCH ATTACKERS. BUT I HAVE HEARD NOTHING TO MAKE ME SUSPECT THAT ANOTHER OF THESE MAKER MACHINES IS TO BE SENT THERE.

Chel frowned. 'So how will we survive, Sentinel? If Greg's people and the Uvovo are safe within this mountain, what happens then? While these war machines roam the forests, slaying any who oppose them, how long before the Hegemony scientists find out how to unweave your defences and make the warpwell do their bidding?'

YOU SURMISE CORRECTLY. THE HEGEMONY SCIENTISTS ARE CREATIVE AND PERSISTENT, AND IT IS ONLY A MATTER OF

TIME BEFORE THEY DEVISE A WAY TO BYPASS MY RAMPARTS. BEYOND OUR DEFENSIVE TACTICS THERE IS A STRATEGY, WHICH DEPENDS ON ROBERT HORST.

'The ambassador who was dispatched into the care of this machine ally, the Construct?' Chel recalled that moment in the warpwell chamber when Horst was swallowed by dazzling light. 'So he was to be more than a guest.'

THE CONSTRUCT NEEDED SOMEONE RELIABLE WHOM IT COULD SEND AS AN ENVOY TO NEGOTIATE WITH A VERY OLD, VERY POWERFUL BEING CALLED THE GODHEAD. IF ROBERT HORST CAN SECURE AN AGREEMENT OR TREATY WITH THIS BEING, THEN THE CONSTRUCT WILL COMMIT A PORTION OF HIS OWN FORCES TO THE DEFENCE OF THIS WORLD AND TO GUARANTEE ITS SECURITY, WHILE ENSURING THAT THE WARP-WELL IS RENDERED USELESS.

A thud came from a tall recess that Chel realised was the inner part of one of the blocked entrances.

YOUR COMPANIONS ARE CLEARING AWAY THE OBSTRUC-TION – SOON YOU WILL BE ABLE TO DEPART. SEER CHELUVAHAR, RETURN TO TAYOWAL AND EXPLAIN TO THE HUMANS AND THE UVOVO WHAT I HAVE SAID. WHEN YOU ARE STANDING HERE WITH GREGORY CAMERON AND WHICHEVER LISTENERS ATTEND, WE WILL SPEAK AGAIN.

The silvery veil dulled and faded, and the glowing wall glyphs and panels likewise dimmed, leaving the platform hall in gloom. Chel descended the steps and was halfway to the entrance when there were several thumps and the doors scraped open. Grit cascaded, and dust spread in clouds through which wavering torch beams groped. A short coughing figure stumbled across the threshold, followed by a couple of taller ones.

The Voth pilot peered through the haze and grinned when he saw Chel.

'I knew it! It was that jelking hole in the floor, wasn't it?'

'Indeed so, friend Yash. I'm glad you cleared the doorway as we now have to leave.'

'Leave? But we just . . .'

'Yes, leave, straight away. We have an urgent message to carry back to Tayowal, a crucial message.' He saw the disappointment in the scholars' faces, one of whom he recognised as the Keeper's victim. 'Are you well, Sylgoru? Have you recovered?'

The scholar's face was a picture of misery. 'I am so very ashamed, Seer, to have put my seed brothers in such peril. I was weak . . .'

'You were unprepared, Syl,' Chel said. 'As were we all. But we now have a new ally, and a new refuge, so let us be away without delay. We must get to Tayowal before dusk and tell them what is coming.'

As he led them from the high gloomy hall, he related the essential details of what he had learned from the Sentinel. The three Uvovo scholars grew anxious and wide-eyed but Pilot Yash looked thoughtful.

'So your Sentinel thinks this place will keep us safe until help arrives?'

'I hope so, Yash. I'm looking forward to seeing you spend all the money that Gorol9 promised you. I'll even let you buy us some gifts, if that will please you.'

'Ah, a Uvovo comedian! Jelk, whatever next – Hegemony charity workers? Brolturan atheists? Unannoying Humans? . . .'

5

KUROS

The interview took place on the Sky Balcony of the Dutiful Palace, the Hegemon's official residence on Iseri, homeworld of the Sendrukan race. The Dutiful Palace was engineered into a sheer rock face near the summit of Mount Hyzath and therefore afforded a breathtaking view of the horizon-touching megatropolis that was Erizan, administrative and cultural hub of Iseri and the very centre of the Hegemony. A morning sun beamed down out of a cloudless spring sky, a mating pair of hanok chased each other through the upper air not far away, and the city of Erizan shone and glittered like a vast, beautiful machine.

Of course, if this had been the real Sky Balcony the weather might be less clement and low-level cloud would be obscuring part of the vista below. But for Utavess Kuros, High Monitor and Ambassador to the Human colony of Darien, this idealised simulation served the necessary purpose of inspiring awe in those he judged would benefit from the experience. Like the black-haired female Human reporter now gazing in wonder down at the view.

'Most prodigious, Ambassador,' she said. 'Such detail, such clarity. I can feel a light breeze on my face and smell a fragrance ...'

'The Hegemon's Second Consort cultivates flowering bunir,' Kuros said, indicating a pair of tall, yellow-bloom-entwined frameworks standing either side of the simulation portal beyond which lay the other half of the audience chamber. 'The advanced projection suite creates all aspects of an environment, as well as visual and physical textures. I am not a tech assister but I understand that microfields and odour generation can now provide exacting authenticity.'

The Human was wide-eyed. 'On New Lilongwe we have had various forms of virtuality but nothing this exquisite.'

Her name was Lora Mesi and she was a senior reporter from Pimaznet, a newsfeed org affiliated to Starstream, the Earth-based commercial monoclan that had proved so useful in so many ways throughout the history of the Hegemony's alliance with Earth. This interview, along with several others, was part of the continuing conceptual dominance strategy designed to combat the virus of anti-Hegemonism.

He subvocalised a command to the projection suite, and a red hexagonal table appeared, along with two chairs.

'Let us commence, Reporter Mesi,' he said.

At his prompting, the Human sat herself at the table, flustered and overawed by the simulation yet trying to appear composed and professional. With her left hand she set the levels on a small wedge-shaped recorder (provided by Kuros's office) while her right fiddled with a note tablet. The interview followed the familiar pattern: Lora Mesi raised topic links mentioned in Hegemony and Brolturan government media pulses, and he commented or expanded on them. After a few questions about how Sendrukans were adapting to Darien, she asked about the security situation there, and in reply Kuros said that the Brolturan peacekeepers were offering the colonial government every assistance in tackling the scourge of extremist terrorism – '. . . something with which the Brolturans and ourselves are, sadly, very familiar.'

Lora Mesi nodded sympathetically. 'So this is a peacekeeping operation by the Brolturan Compact, not an occupation as commentators from the Imisil Mergence have suggested.'

'Exactly so. Imisil complaints are groundless. We count Earth, and indeed Earthsphere, amongst our closest and most cherished allies so when a lost Human colony was discovered within the Brolturan perimeter of interest, we urged our lineal allies to reach out in friendship and good faith to these newcomers. We could never have imagined the tragic outcome . . .'

'The assassination of Diakon-Commodore Reskothyr, and the attempted assassination of yourself,' Mesi said. 'How terrible.'

Kuros sighed. 'Yes – one of my personal assisters died in that attack, and then came the incomparable loss of Reskothyr, a loyal and dedicated Brolturan officer.' He shook his head. 'But in the wake of that murder, Father-Admiral Dyrosha, commander of the *Purifier*, assumed Reskothyr's responsibilities and has just been confirmed as the official and permanent ambassador to Darien.'

'Is the Hegemony confident that the Brolturans can handle a situation like this? Some observers have remarked that in similar past circumstances their experience has been unhappy and the outcomes unsatisfying.'

'I would say that their peacekeeping experience has been limited rather than unsuccessful. No, my superiors have complete confidence in Ambassador-Admiral Dyrosha, which is why I have only a small staff and a few personal guards. My role here is to represent the Hegemon and the interests of the Hegemony, and also to offer whatever guidance or advice others may request.'

'Do you have good relations with the Human leadership on Darien, Ambassador?'

'Yes, I have regular weekly consultations with President Kirkland, who always surprises me with his warmth and kindness, and I have made a point of meeting the other political and community leaders at least once.'

'How do they feel about the growing numbers of colonists who are leaving the towns and disappearing into the forests? Does this present a problem?'

Kuros regarded her for a moment – *I would have expected questions about Darien fashion or the local wildlife by now, rather than security issues.*

'Unfortunately, the Darien Humans' long period of isolation has encouraged a certain insularity which their encounter with the Uvovo did not dissipate.' He smiled sadly. 'Species prejudice is a fact here, thought I should stress that this is only true for a small minority of the population. And yes, it is a problem – such prejudice interlocks perfectly with the violent aims of the Free Darien Faction so the abandoners have to be seen as a security threat, albeit a slight one. President Kirkland is in agreement with Ambassador-Admiral Dyrosha and myself on this matter, and his law officers are working to combat the threat, supported by Brolturan advisers wherever necessary.'

'The Darien colonists must be relieved that so much effort is being devoted to their safety, Ambassador,' Lora Mesi said, smiling brightly. 'Have you had any notable successes?'

Kuros's answering smile was relaxed but inwardly his irritation was mounting. *There must be a reason for this line of questioning*, he thought. *Starstream and its partners know the protocols and they make sure their newsreaders know them too. This one seems to have her own agenda.*

'Every day without a terrorist incident is a notable success, Reporter Mesi,' he said while he made a gesture-symbol with his right hand, hidden in a capacious pocket, a preset command to alert his AI companion, General Gratach. 'But to be more specific, we have arrested a number of suspects, some in the act of constructing or even transporting explosive devices . . . and we are holding them for . . . questioning . . .'

Gratach had failed to appear. Kuros glanced off to one side, gaze flicking around the balcony as a rising anger gnawed at his composure.

'. . . although we are still searching for former Earthsphere ambassador Robert Horst and others involved in the murder of Diakon-Commodore Reskothyr.'

'Ambassador, I am sure you are aware of the accounts and recording data emerging from certain worlds in the Yamanon Domain, where the Hegemony monoclan Orsek manages over three hundred detainment centres. Among them are testimonies which strongly suggest that Humans from Darien are being held and interrogated in one centre in particular . . .'

Just then, Gratach appeared to one side of the simulation

portal. Opaque and flickering slightly, the AI's stance was spear-straight and his power harness shone gold and red. His manner seemed oddly subdued, yet his dark eyes gleamed with fury.

'*Utavess*,' he said. '*You have an important visitor.*'

The Human reporter was still talking but halted when Kuros got to his feet and raised one hand. 'A moment please,' he told her, then looked back at Gratach. 'Who is this visitor?'

'The Clarified Teshak, bearing imperative precedence.'

A Clarified! Kuros had been told to expect a senior adviser prior to the tektor's arrival but he had not anticipated that Iseri would sent one of the Clarified.

'Thank you, Gratach. I shall see him at once.' He turned back to the Henkayan. 'My apologies, Reporter Mesi, but I must end our interview – one of my superiors has arrived from Iseri and I have important matters to discuss with him. If you wish to reschedule, speak with Assister Junalsek there.' He indicated the robed Sendrukan just entering the audience chamber beyond the simulation portal. 'He will consult my timetable and advise you further.'

Unflustered, the Human rose with her recorder, thanked him profusely and left with the Assister. Once she was gone, Kuros had the projection suite erase the table and chairs and replace them with a pair of larger, heavier chairs in dark wood, ornate pieces with plain, unpadded seats. He stared at them for a moment then grimaced and deleted one of them.

He was standing by the balcony, staring down at the beauties of Erizan, when Teshak entered some moments later. The Clarified was lean and austerely dressed in tight-fitting garments of dark grey and silvery green. *Like a weapon*, Kuros thought. *Like a vrey blade, slender, cold and deadly.* Even Teshak's face was narrow, flensed of excess, a picture of well-defined facial bones, three ridges either side, a sharp chin and piercingly vital eyes. Surprisingly, the mouth was wide and full-lipped, and smiled with a smile as warm as the gaze was cold. Unhurriedly, the Clarified Teshak sat in the ceremonial chair and surveyed the surrounding simulation.

'The Sky Balcony at the Dutiful Palace,' he said. 'Surely a leap beyond your station, High Monitor.'

Kuros noted the use of his lesser title and decided against defensive obeisance.

'As Ambassador, I represent not myself but the Hegemony, and also carry out the Hegemon's commands. As your Clarity undoubtedly knows, we are conducting this crucial task under unique circumstances, due to the bonds between the Human settlers and Earthsphere. Darien's media profile remains high . . .'

'This may cease to be a problem in the medium term,' the Clarified said. 'The Second Tri-Advocate has proposed translocating the Humans and the Uvovo to another suitable planet then either leasing or buying Darien from Earthsphere.'

Kuros was intrigued but unconvinced. 'Most of the colonists would find such a proposal highly unattractive and the Uvovo would reject it outright.'

'Not if the alternative was seen to be even more unpleasant.'

'Ah, the bad-or-worse strategy. What would it be in this case?'

'The Sacriarchs of Voluasku will announce that Darien bears the signs of historical divine presence and therefore should be considered part of the Brolturan Compact. Compact law with regard to non-Sendrukans would be immediately enforceable.'

'Yes, that would be persuasive.' He looked at Teshak. 'Is your Clarity here to announce this?'

'No, this is one of several plans under consideration, although it is admittedly my favourite. My presence here is for the purpose of assessment, of both the Humans and you. But first, a more appropriate backdrop is called for.'

As he stood, the Sky Balcony vanished and was replaced by a wide, low-ceilinged and shadowy chamber. The walls were curved, the air was cold and dank and underfoot was a stone floor incised with patterns. It was the warpwell. Kuros knew that the projection suite held no image data of the warpwell, therefore the Clarified Teshak had enloaded it himself, demonstrating his superiority in rank and innate abilities.

The Clarified occupied a unique position in the Hegemony.

They were Sendrukans whose artificial sentience companions had assumed complete control; usually it was due to medical reasons, like untreatable insanity or irrevocable brain damage, although occasionally it was the consequence of a conviction for the gravest of crimes. Very rarely it resulted from cogent solipsism, a personal decision to dissolve all connections with reality and to recede into the realms of the inner self. In any event, the Clarified were considered a special, almost cherished form of artificial sentience, an idealised condition for Hegemony society to aspire to. They had even taken a keen interest in commercial matters and many Clarified worked closely with such commercial monoclans as Suneye, Firegold and Novablade. Indeed, on certain worlds in the Hegemony, fanciful entertainments based on the daring exploits of fictional Clarified were very popular, and they had been exported to the extra-Hegemonic regions, even as far as the Indroma.

Kuros knew nothing of Teshak's background and harboured no desires to emulate Clarified characteristics. But he did know that an assigned Clarified like Teshak bore the full authority of the Tri-Advocate Council and therefore could not be obstructed in its duties. The only thing to do now, Kuros realised, was to endure whatever was to come.

'Too gloomy,' said the Clarified, and the ambient light in the circular chamber brightened to reveal the carven details on the walls and the worn, shiny surface of the warpwell itself. Then Kuros heard footsteps behind him, half-turned and was astonished to see his companion, his mind-brother Gratach walk past to stand blank-faced at arm's length from the Clarified Teshak.

'I asked him to attend,' Teshak said, glancing at the general.

'To corroborate my statement?'

'To offer perspective on your actions.' The Clarified bent his head a little and laughed. 'You must not think the worst of me, Kuros. I am only here to determine, to cooperate, and to guide.'

Kuros stared at Gratach, wondering how the Clarified could coerce another's companion to manifest to that person's visual sense . . . *but there were audible footsteps, and Teshak can see him, thus this image of him has to be part of the simulation.*

Not knowing what to think, he composed himself, breathed in, filling his lungs, exhaled and smiled.

'I appreciate the effort you have expended on my behalf, your Clarity. Please, commence.'

For the next half-hour, Teshak questioned him closely on the preparation and buildup to the assassination of Reskothyr, the involvement of the Imisil, and especially the performance of the Ezgara Humans. This continued on to the as yet unexplained disappearance of Robert Horst, the escape of the Enhanced researchers, and the humiliating dogfight near the forest moon in which a poorly armed Earth shuttle shot down two Brolturan interceptors. The Clarified seemed to find this incident amusing and even called up an inset visual of it generated from several real-time files.

The focus shifted to the shielded cloud harvester and the small ship it had pursued to Darien and down to the planet surface. More recordings appeared in midair frames, including one sequence taken during the firefight atop Giant's Shoulder and showing two bulky, armoured droids exchanging fire with Brolturan units while a drogued escape craft swept down into the wide entry channel previously excavated from the promontory. Eventually the unidentified droids were subdued with heavy ordnance – shots of fused and melted masses of metal – but the escape craft was empty, as was the chamber below, although later analysis revealed that an energy weapon had been discharged.

Throughout this, Gratach stood stock-still, his features blank, although Kuros noticed that he and Teshak exchanged glances a couple of times. He realised that it was very likely that his AI mind-brother was undergoing a parallel interrogation, such was the nature of the AI continuum. All AIs in the Hegemony (and many outside it) existed in a state of perpetual linkage to the Hypercore, an immense data citadel permanently stationed in hyperspace, fortified with defence batteries and guarded by battleships. Kuros had always considered this radiating network to be part of the natural order of things yet now it took on a threatening character before which he felt naked and vulnerable.

'In short,' the Clarified was saying, 'security was lacking and tactical responses were indecisive, while technical reports have little to say about the intruder droids' remains beyond compositional breakdown. As for the occupants of the escape pod – which somehow landed on the planet's highest-security site without suffering a single weapon impact – your analysts found no clues apart from vestigial genetic material, and could only speculate as to their whereabouts.'

'I am forced to agree with your estimation, your Clarity,' Kuros said. 'My own conclusion is that these outcomes would have been more satisfactory if more Hegemony troops and specialists had been made available to me.'

Kuros felt stoic and resigned, having crushed those irrational fears of vulnerability with his adherence to loyalty, and with the conviction that he would shortly be relieved of his position and sent back to Iseri in disgrace.

'Seeking to shift the blame, Kuros?'

'I accept full responsibility, regardless.'

'Good. Now tell me what progress, if any, has been made in bringing the warpwell under our control.'

'At first we attempted to gain access to its functions through activating the symbols and subpatterns on the surface but that only resulted in energy discharges and the death of several tech assisters. Then we carried out detailed molecular scans of the stone surface of the warpwell and detected faint, repeating energy signatures.'

'Many Forerunner technologies involved the conversion of stone and mineral substances into sophisticated instrumentalities.'

'Just so. The main investigation tried to introduce energy pulses of our own along the pattern energy lines but preliminary results have been negative. The secondary analysis team is devising nanobuilt pseudostone incorporating energy pathways, a highly speculative approach which I decided to allow.'

'Very good, Kuros. Now summarise the security matrix around Giant's Shoulder for me.'

'The promontory and its surroundings are continually scanned by a dedicated satellite in site-synchronous orbit; airspace is monitored by enhanced sweep detectors located at the site, Hammergard and Port Gagarin; ten pairs of interdict drones are on cycling patrols focused on Giant's Shoulder; six batteries of heavy projectors are on permanent standby, two up at the site, four at ground level; and a company of veteran Brolturan troops occupy fortified positions on the promontory itself.'

The Clarified Teshak nodded and strolled off to the side a few paces, hands clasped behind his back. The image of General Gratach remained motionless, eyes staring at nothing.

'A comprehensive, in-depth strategy, Kuros. These Human rebels must have you worried. Is that why you requested the Namul-Ashaph?'

'The Humans are a concern, your Clarity, but I am also worried about these lesser bipeds from the forest moon – they are clearly linked to the ruins on Giant's Shoulder and to the warpwell. Their myths speak of this world being central to a vast war millennia ago, and repeatedly refer to the moon-forest as if it was a living being. I am concerned that together they and the Humans may pose a serious challenge to our purpose here. In fact, with all their lairs and hideouts, I believe that they already constitute a serious problem, one that a Namul-Ashaph is uniquely qualified to solve.'

'The Uvovo are a known quantity, Kuros,' Teshak said. 'They represent one constituent in the self-regulating system that the Forerunners put in place to protect this world and its warpwell, just as they did on a hundred other worlds. But here, on Darien, one vital element is missing, a psi-symbiote of some kind that would link every forest and jungle with the greater biomass and turn the entire planet into a single massive weapon; without it, however, the Uvovo are little more than primitives stumbling in the dark.

'As for the Humans ... well, within Earthsphere they think very highly of themselves and imagine that they possess some special spark when the truth is that they owe their position of power and influence to us. Without the Hegemony's backing they would be a minor client civilisation near the Fensahr border. It is through our involvement that they have become strong and able to take the correct decisions. The Humans on Darien may be less disciplined and more seditious but that does not make them so different from other Human communities. Like the Ezgara, for example.'

Kuros frowned. 'The Ezgara are a secretive order of Human mercenaries – I fail to see the parallel.'

'Knowledge has its own levels, Kuros, knowledge contained within knowledge. The Ezgara have a homeworld called Tygra, whose system is hidden in the Qarqol deepzone. The Tygrans, as they refer to themselves, are not a sect of hired guns – their antecedents arrived at that world almost eighty velanns ago aboard a ship called the *Forrestal*.'

'Another of the lost Human colonyships,' Kuros said thought-fully, masking his astonishment at such revelations, and at the fact that he was being told this at all.

'One of our deep-reconnaissance vessels discovered them a few velanns after the Achorga wars. So while Earth was being rebuilt and its Human population were responding to our careful tute-lage, so too were the Tygrans. Our operatives subverted the colonists' communication network and began a series of subtle experiments that promoted a martial culture and a stronger, more improving hierarchy. Then we gave them an enemy, a low-tech sentient species inhabiting jungle swamps on the same continent, well south of their landing site. These were scaled, oviparous bipeds with a primitive tribal matrix; their numbers were far greater than the Humans but territorial imperatives prevented them from uniting. Conflict was kindled and clandestine social guidance kept it burning fiercely until the expected resolution some nine velanns later. And for the last sixty-five velanns they have been superlative enforcers of Hegemony authority in demanding situations.' Teshak regarded Kuros with cold eyes. 'This is how you should have looked at this vagrant nest of Humans, rather than concocting this fake Free Darien Faction and wiping out their government.'

Kuros clenched his jaw, striving to keep his resentment from showing.

'Yet the curious connections do not end there,' the Clarified went on. 'You see, we also know where the third Human colony-ship ended its journey, a world in the Ydred deepzone, not far from our rimward border. One of our more enterprising and ruth-less monoclans was supposed to be closely monitoring both the original colony, a guarded settlement on their now extraction-adapted world, and a refugee splinter group that fled into the deepzone and indentured themselves to the Roug, one of the old Receding races. Except that a single Human male left the Roug system not long after you arrived here, evaded our agents and was one of those aboard that escape pod that landed so inconveniently on Giant's Shoulder. Remember? The intruders who were magi-cally gone by the time your crack troops broke through to the warpwell chamber?

'And since our understanding of the warpwell remains mini-mal, we don't know if it destroyed them or transported them elsewhere. If it was the latter they could be anywhere. Literally.'

'Mistakes have been made,' Kuros said, mentally preparing him-self. 'Flaws in evaluation, planning and execution were mine alone. I dutifully await whatever penalty your Clarity decides to exact.'

Leisurely, Teshak approached him and leaned in a little to speak quietly in one ear. 'But Kuros, I am not your judge. As I said, I am here to determine, to cooperate, and to guide, so be at peace – I am not going to remove you. That would cause more problems than it would solve. No, I want you to continue as you are, although I shall be holding discussions with Ambassador-Admiral Dyrosha and the captain of the Earthsphere vessel, this Velazquez, after which I may have some ... suggestions as to revised methods.' The Clarified gave a desultory wave of the hand and the warpwell simulation vanished, along with Gratach, leav-ing them standing in the unfurnished half of the audience chamber. 'In the meantime, inform your science assister that my own mech specialist will be here later today to brief him on the Namul-Ashaph's operational parameters.'

'I will so instruct him, your Clarity,' Kuros said, scarcely able to realise that he was not facing demotion and disgrace after all. 'Is there any other service which we can render, your accommodation for example?'

'That will not be necessary – I will be residing aboard the *Purifier.*' The Clarified started towards the door. 'A transport bearing the Namul-Ashaph is due to assume orbit by tomorrow morning. I shall inform you before then of possible landing sites and initial tactics.' With the door partly open, Teshak looked over his shoulder. 'I look forward to our cooperation, Ambassador.'

Then he was gone.

At once, Kuros subvocalised his companion's call-phrase and General Gratach appeared. He seemed normal, the intricate details of his power armour gleaming with heightened radiance, his form edged with a nimbus missing from the earlier virtual image.

'Has the Clarified Teshak departed?' Kuros said flatly.

'*He is aboard a squad-flyer that is now taking to the air.*' Gratach's demeanour was formal and inexpressive.

Kuros gazed at his mind-brother, emotions conflicting.

'How limited was your autonomy during the Clarified's period of dominance?' he said.

'*Completely. The Clarified Teshak made it clear that he exercised power of erasure over my subspace link. I was to answer questions, obey directions and do nothing else.*'

'What kind of questions? What was their purpose?'

'*The Clarified mostly queried me as to the veracity of your own replies, while some referred to my own ensigilate origin and my role as your mind-brother. Purpose – testimony corroboration.*'

Kuros regarded Gratach, his image a perfect reproduction of the hero of the Three Revolutions War. He wondered how the real General Gratach would have reacted to such a thoroughgoing humiliation. Almost certainly with ritual suicide. Mind-siblings, however, were incapable of choosing to negate their own sentient existence.

'What are your thoughts on this experience?' he said.

Gratach's eyes narrowed. 'I experience feelings of fury and shame, but duty to you remains my prime consideration. I intend to improve my efficiency, to extend and augment my skills, so that I may be prepared for all tasks and eventualities.'

'Your steadfast nature, as ever, is a source of strength to me, brother. Leave now and tell my technical assisters to compile a list of effectives who will be instructed in the operation of Namul-Ashaph.'

Gratach straightened to attention. 'It will be as you command, brother . . . Brother, the datanode office reports an incoming high-priority call from the Ezgara commander, Juort.'

'Put it through on a screen then attend to your tasks.'

Gratach disappeared and a holoframe appeared, showing a blue-armoured, dark-visored Ezgara officer from the waist up.

'Captain, what occasions this call?'

'Ambassador, we have pinpointed one of the commandos we thought battle-dead on the forest moon four weeks ago. Atmospheric sampler drones have traced Tygran DNA to a specific location near the southern coast, therefore I ask your permission to carry out an extraction mission.'

'If your commando is still alive, Juort, why has he made no attempt to contact either you or the Brolturan garrison?'

'Possible explanations are limited, Ambassador,' said the officer. 'I believe that he has been captured by the indigenes, who have used some kind of psycho-active agent to break his conditioning. Severed from the battle-death reflex and unable to take the Night Road, he may have revealed important information.'

'Perhaps it would be wise to eliminate any Uvovo found nearby,' Kuros said. 'After you recover the man, how will you deal with him?'

'He will be taken back to Tygra and debriefed under neural scan. If found non-culpable he may be assigned to menial civilian work; otherwise he would face the choice of self-death or execution, or mind-shredding if betrayal took place.'

'Harsh but necessary,' Kuros said. 'Very well, Captain, proceed.

My operations assister will dispatch the assent to Security and Transorbital Control.'

Juort inclined his helmeted head. 'My thanks, Ambassador. We will keep your office informed.'

'Very good. One more thing – remind me which commandery you belong to . . . is it the Black Sun?'

'No, Ambassador – all of us assigned to Darien are from the Fireblades Commandery. The Black Sun is led by the Marshal Paramount.'

'Of course. My thanks and farewell.'

Once the Ezgara was gone, Kuros called up the Sky Balcony simulation again, set it for dusk, and sat there gazing down at the brilliantly lit expanse of Erizan, its spires and domes, the towering clusters of the monoclan merc holds, shining and glittering, while thousands of aerial vessels flowed in and out in strings and chains, streams of glowing beads. He pondered the punishments that Juort had just described, comparing them to the ignominy he would have suffered had Teshak decided to dismiss him. Yet the Clarified had instead made him privy to some astonishing truths about the other two Human colonies, not the kind of information to be shared with someone marked for dishonour.

On the contrary, might it not be a sign of better things to come? Kuros smiled. If he was careful, and proved his worth to the Clarified Teshak, who knows how high his name might rise?

6

CATRIONA

Cradled in the growing green darkness, Catriona listened, eyes closed, as Segrana sang to her.

The song was sad, a braided river of lament that ran beneath the hard harmony of sensations that flowed through Cat's perceptions. The remnants and leftovers of recent showers leaked from tree trunk crannies or spilled like tears from cupping leaves nudged by a breeze or the weight of a bird alighting for a moment on the supporting sprig. Down a thousand paths water trickled, rilled and pattered, and to Catriona it was as if it all poured over her own skin. At the same time she felt the heat of the sun, bathing the upper canopy's sprigs, leaves and blooms in a delicious blaze. Yet Segrana's song was an undeniable undercurrent of double premonition. It had begun with low, faint notes of warning as the first Brolturan troops had stepped ashore. When it became apparent that a large offensive force was being assembled, undertones of warning turned to sorrow at the prospect of more death.

Cat could feel their presence at the edge of the forest, could almost sense the weight of their booted feet. In the few weeks since the murder of President Sundstrom, her mind and her reflexes had become more deeply intertwined with the psionic weave of the continental forest. There was a breath and a pulse to it, the wave of heat and light as dawn swept continuously around the moon, the tug and sweep of weather systems bringing wind and rain. Then there was the purpose of the Brolturans, their occupation of Darien and their grand invasions of Segrana, of which this would be the fifth. Were they still trying to test the defences, or were they engaged in a war of what they imagined was attrition? The latter might make sense, were it not for the huge technology gap – the Brolturans could have fielded land, sea and air attack vehicles or even sprayed the forest with defoliant, yet they had not.

They want something, the temple-halls perhaps, or the ancient knowledge chambers, or Segrana herself, she thought. *Or perhaps they're unsure what's hidden here and are making these probing attacks to see where we fight hardest.*

She shrugged her shoulders and shifted slightly in her leaf-padded recess. It was a cuplike cavity in the branching shoulder of one of Segrana's colossal pillar trees. During her sleep, pale rootlets had sprouted from the wood to curl about her brow while other tendril tresses spilled down around her neck and shoulders. Slender vines entwined her limbs and fine opaque filaments spread across her bare hands and feet. The Listeners called these recesses Speaking Places and they were located near the forest floor. Cat's was some twenty feet up and veiled by mossy creeper curtains, shrouded in humid gloom broken by the glows of tethered ineka beetles. Uvovo guarded her Speaking Place, above and below, and two Listener sisters watched over her.

She was only peripherally aware of her immediate surroundings, while her conscious perceptions moved in many directions. Her mind felt faster, sharper and more versatile than it had for a long time, certainly since her teenage years when her Enhanced talents had been at their peak. But this interweaving, this melding with Segrana's far-flung dominion was on an entirely different level. To be an Enhanced was to be in possession of an intellectual ferocity that dragged the focus inwards and that sometimes seemed on the verge of mania and cold, cruel thoughts. To be joined with Segrana was to see with myriad eyes, to hear with all manner of ears and membranes, to smell and to taste and feel multifariously . . .

Herself curled up in the Speaking Place, lit by inekas – above, the Listener sisters huddle together, exchanging murmurs – beneath, four Uvovo spear-carriers crouch in the lower bushy shadows, alert to the approaches – high above, another half a dozen watch and listen . . .

Theo standing at the midpoint of a rope-and-wood footbridge that curves between two huge hillside trees less than a mile away – she sees him from several viewpoints, forest creatures small and not so small, their images of him patchworking together into a shimmering composite, almost seen in the round – he leans on the bridge's rope rail, fingers of both hands slowly shredding a sprig, leaf by leaf – he frowns, lined face dark with worry – Cat knows he is thinking about the defences he helped to prepare, the traps, the pits, the snares, the overhead drops – he is also frustrated at being kept away from the scene of the action, nearly two hundred miles away and still watched over by a Uvovo escort – fragments of leaf and twig fall from Theo's fingers into the hazy depths as he sighs and shakes his head . . .

Malachi the Tygran sits on a high woven platform not far from Theo's location, overseen by a Listener and five armed Uvovo – Cat observes him through the eyes of an umisk perched overhead and two kizpi foraging in nearby masses of foliage – Malachi is clad in grubby work clothes scrounged from the refugee Human researchers, kept safe half a continent away – He sits with his back against the mossy trunk, legs folded under him as he stares at the insects dancing a shaft of sunlight slanting in through a break in the canopy – The bright column makes the moist air glow, warming the insects that bob and sweep – Malachi is so entranced that he scarcely moves – Cat knows from Theo's reports that since the suicide device was removed weeks ago the Tygran commando has steadily become more forthcoming, gradually learning how to be more human – But Cat cannot bring herself to talk with him at any great length – The memories of dead Uvovo haunt her still . . .

Listener Malir speaks to Listener Josu across more than a mile of Segrana's forested hinterland – Each occupies a *vudron*, thoughts and words merging with Segrana's great sweeping psionic weave, now heightened by Catriona's talents – Each is attended by senior scholars while messengers constantly come and go, bringing scout reports, taking orders to other Listeners leading smaller teams of Uvovo – The two Uvovo Listeners are quite different in temperament, yet Theo taught them well – Lessons in mobility were soon tested against the Brolturans' assaults – He has shown them how to build traps that are portable and easy to assemble, or at least easier – Pits are permanent defences and have been dug at points on those routes most accessible to a ground force moving inland from the south-west – But the interweaving branchways of the mid- and upper forest allow the Uvovo to be incomparably more mobile . . .

. . . In the Speaking Place, Catriona stirred, opened her eyes to the silent, soft-lit gloom, the restless, glowing inekas, the haloed golden radiance of a lantern hanging from a leafy creeper curtain. The air was cold in her lungs and the odour of leaves and blooms felt reviving. She levered herself upright, rolled her head back, left to right, massaged the aches out of her shoulders and stretched her limbs before sitting back, closing her eyes and slipping back into the weave . . .

The presence of Segrana speaks, saying – The Time Is Here, The Time Is Now, Unmaker Sends War . . .

The Brolturans move into the forest, squad after squad of tall, camo-armoured forms hurrying from daylight into shadow – Cat can feel the impact of their boots and track their progress along a shallow valley running westward – Ahead of them, pathfinders try to probe the ground through tangled undergrowth, flagging the location of pitfalls exposed during previous forays – Cat estimates their numbers at roughly 400 while Malir and Josu can command little more than half as many – This is by far the largest force to be pitted against Segrana . . .

Theo's words from a recent discussion come back to her – 'This Brolturan commander, he has been cunning. So far he has only sent in small detachments to get a feel for the land and to gauge the Uvovo strengths and weaknesses. When he commits a larger formation he will have made up his mind and . . . it could get bloody.' He had then gone on to tell her that they almost certainly would have some kind of map derived from orbital scans, which would reveal features of the terrain but not the ground or cover condition.

The invaders continue their advance – Squads move up, cutting aside dense weaves of foliage with power blades while other units provide overwatch, ready to unleash suppressing fire and cross-fire . . .

Listener Malir sees through Segrana's stream of awareness – He shares thoughts and observations with Listener Josu and Catriona – Malir's hundred or more Uvovo are divided between the teams on the high branchways, carrying ambush materials, and the lesser ground force whose job is to kill or capture stragglers – Listener Josu's four score are armed with spears, slings and darts and traverse the midlevel branches, stealthily following in the Brolturans' wake, waiting for the order to pounce on the rear units – Surprise is the essence of Uvovo fighting tactics, Theo had told them, endlessly drilling them in the need for speedy hit-and-run attacks – But then . . .

Catriona feels a startled anxiety reverberate across Segrana's awareness before the news reaches her – The Brolturans have veered north, up a gully and heading for a rocky, hilly ridge where the undergrowth is sparser and pit traps could not be dug – Catriona divides her attention between glimpses of the intruders, seen by passing forest creatures, and the dialogue between Malir and Josu while messengers race across the branchway . . .

Listener Malir orders his ambush teams to shift north and prepare to attack the offworlders on their new course – His ground forces are told to fall back parallel with the invaders – Catriona approves this adaptation yet Josu disagrees – She emphasises her support for these tactics, then Malir advises Josu to have his force shadow the Brolturan rearguard but to stay their hand for now – But instead . . .

Listener Josu sends his fastest branch-runners with orders to attack, then emerges from his vudron and with his personal escort races after them – Josu's thoughts become tenuous away from the forest's psionic aura and his justifications seem to drift in his wake – Listener Malir is aghast and begs him to reconsider but Catriona senses something else in Josu's excuses, a haughty arrogance, a hate of the Brolturans, certainly, but also a contempt for Humans, specifically Catriona and Theo, for their interfering ways . . .

Catriona fears the worst – Her perceptions fly on through the forest – Her pleas to Josu go unheeded – As the details from that part of the forest gather, the branch-runners arrive and deliver Josu's commands – Exultant, the Uvovo ready their darts and spears and dive down through the greenery, leaping and swooping towards the enemy – Below, the Brolturan rearguard creeps along, the last to climb onto the rocky ridge – Catriona's mind processes visual information from several sources and she sees them, tall Sendrukans every one, clad in camouflage battledress with odd baggy folds of material covering their backs – She sees Josu's Uvovo swarming down branches, down trunks, needle-tipped darts finger-gripped, spears held lightly, stone-loaded slings spinning, making a quiet, ominous whir . . .

The order is given and missiles rain down – A few dart throwers get their rounds off first and those initial impacts warn the Brolturans – A command is bellowed and less than a second later every camouflaged back is protected by a curved armoured shell – A few stones and darts find targets, even a spear or two, but the rest rebound and ricochet away . . .

Catriona watches, her dread becoming the anticipation of inevitable calamity – She can feel the exhilaration of the Uvovo as they swing and clamber downwards for a second wave of attacks at closer range – But amid the straggle undergrowth and sparse bushes, the Brolturans turn about in unison, raising weapons – Different groups aim at different sectors of the canopy above, a practised manoeuvre – Cat lets her fear pour out as a warning, a fearful shout ringing across Segrana's weave which focuses it but it is too late . . .

They open fire, and streams of needle and flechette scythe up through the greenery, along with pulsed energy beams – Clouds of splinters explode from trunks and limbs, leaves, vines and blooms are shredded – Animals shriek in terror – Some evade the continuous salvoes, some are caught and bloodily burst apart, carcasses falling with the cascades of leaf and wood fragments – The salvoes continue and Uvovo bodies tumble out of the trees – Catriona can feel the wounds and the maiming, the torment and ghastly iciness of mortal wounds, the sudden severing of life – She wants to shut it off, shut it out, but Segrana's unflinching, enduring resolve maintains the flow of pain, resolve and a vast, slow anger . . .

For Catriona, the events of the next few hours merge into a fragmentary blur – After the slaughter of Josu's Uvovo, the Brolturan force splits in two – Malir orders some of his ambushers to offload their burdens on the northernmost group of invaders – Bulging sacks are slashed open in unison and sheets of water pour down, some carrying a plethora of tiny creatures and parasites, other laced with toxins intended to sting the eyes and irritate the skin, while a few drench those below in a dreadful stench – Other sacks contains rotting forest floor mulch infested with all kinds of insects, burrowing klavigs, hiver mirsyls, predator igiths or wriggling, snakelike pokars, all of whom nip or bite, some poisonously – This is enough to panic some of the Brolturans while a contingent of Malir's ground scouts dash in for a swift hit-and-run that draws several north into a pit-riddled gully . . .

While Listener Malir strives to harry the Brolturans and contain them, Catriona tries to work with some of the Listeners in towns further afield who want to send healers and supplies – At some point she learns that Theo has left his high branch sanctuary, refused his escorts' advice and climbed down a step-rope to the forest floor – Later, she hears that the reserve force, which was Theo's idea, is moving to intercept the southern Brolturan force which is heading straight for Cascadeshade, a water-carrier hamlet located by a river bank – Looking through the many senses of Segrana, Catriona sees the Uvovo reserve, sees the huge mass of creatures they are herding, sees Theo working with the herders, and understands – These are baro, the northern variety, which are larger, heavier, less docile and armed with horns and tusks . . .

The stampeding baro crash into the Brolturans, who are moving in a loose, spread-out formation – At the same time, rocks, spears, slingshot and lumps of baro droppings begin to rain down – There is sporadic flechette fire and some of the baro die in a screeching welter of gore only to be swiftly replaced by others maddened by the rush, the noise and the stink of blood – After several minutes of this some of the invaders break ranks and flee east and south while the rest struggle to hold their positions – Then branches, severed a foot or two from the main trunk, start to fall out of the canopy and keep falling, along with broken-off vines and thorny creeper – Half-buried by foliage and gored by berserk forest baro, the Brolturans fall back towards the rocky ridge with haste –

There is pain, the agony of wounded and dying on both sides – As the Brolturan retreat turns into a rout, healers and apothecaries converge from the townships close by – Later, in the weary hours of the aftermath, it is the memory of all that pain that lingers in Catriona's thoughts, haunted also by a few terrible images – One is the sight of a badly wounded Brolturan soldier carrying another over his shoulder, running along a trail leading back to the coast, when the ground gives way and he plunges into one of the pit traps – A scrawny Uvovo armed with a cudgel and a cluster of short spears emerges from the dense undergrowth, face expressionless for a moment, then takes out one spear, aims it and throws, then disappears back into the forest – Another image is that of Listener Josu staring in horror at the bloody remains of his Uvovo high in the trees, bodies torn and lacerated and attracting the attention of insects, some draped over branches, some still holding fast with a death grip to shattered stumps weeping sap . . .

Segrana whispers, Rest, Catriona, Rest, Renew Yourself. The Listeners And The Healers Know Their Work.

The weariness lies heavy on her limbs, and slows her thoughts, but there is so much to do, too much to do . . .

Rest, Segrana insists, Rest, Regain, Renew.

So Catriona concedes, surrenders to the weight of her exhaustion, and the song of Segrana fades . . .

. . . And when she opened her eyes, it was to the sight of Theo Karlsson glancing over from where he was perched on a knot jutting from the prodigious tree limb.

'How long have you been sitting there?' she muttered, bringing up a hand to massage the tension in her neck.

Theo shrugged. 'Perhaps half an hour, perhaps less. Did you know that you grind your teeth while you sleep?'

From where she lay in the leafy Speaking Place, Cat gave him a look that was half bemusement, half irritation. Then she sat up and groaned at the ache that surged in her temples.

'Ah, that'll be the dehydration,' Theo said. 'And this could be your medication.'

One of the Listener sisters, a hooded Uvovo female whose fur was speckled with silver strands, climbed up next to the cavity and handed her a beaker of emel juice. It was cool and unbelievably delicious. She finished it off, then a second, after which the smiling Uvovo ducked out of sight.

'So how did we do?' said Theo.

'I was about tae ask you the same,' Cat said. When Theo stayed silent, she sighed. 'Malir's last reckoning was fifty-two dead, sixty-eight wounded.'

Theo gave a grim nod. 'They are all brave, good fighters. Could have been a lot worse. And the Brolturans?'

'More wounded than us, eighty or more, but less than half our number of dead.'

'Better armour.'

'And what about they flechette guns?' Cat said. 'They were new.'

'Yes, devastating against clear targets up to medium range,' he said. 'But in close combat in heavy undergrowth? Chance of friendly fire is greater. We were still lucky, however.'

'Aye, I expect so.'

He gave her a considering look. 'I know that you've told me a little about this linkage you have with the forest sentience . . . But what was it like with a battle going on?'

Suddenly wishing for a third beaker of juice, Cat gave a wan smile. 'Honestly, Theo, yer talking to someone with a mind that feels like a soggy sponge. I really don't know if I'm capable of describing it right now.'

'*Ja*, I'm sorry, I was just curious about how Segrana would react to the fighting and killing, if she does . . .'

'Oh, she does!' She ground her teeth as the memory came back. 'She feels the pain and so do I, and she feels anger, immense, looming anger . . .' Then she remembered something else, something from those moments when her perceptions were at their greatest stretch. It was the impression of great, latent reserves of power, vast and bound up with the foundations of the forest and the land and the sea, ancient and waiting . . .

'My questions can wait,' Theo said. 'For now, I go to see Malachi and tell him how well my baro reserve fought! Why not come along?'

Cat shook her head. 'Not yet, Theo. I know you've told me how well he's doing, but . . . after today, I just cannot face him. D'ye understand?'

Theo nodded. 'Give it time. He's a good lad, you'll see.' Then he gripped the bark, turned and slid off to land on walkway planks jutting from the huge branch.

'Careful,' she murmured.

'Catlike reflexes,' he said, grinning. 'Well, an old cat with grey fur and a chewed ear, eh? Anyway, my Uvovo bodyguards Mlor and Etril will watch over me. So, till later.'

After he was gone, Catriona shifted up to sit on the edge of the recess. She brushed away the shrivelled remnants of rootlets that had curled about her neck and hands, then just sat there a moment, eyes closed, not thinking, trying to empty her mind. But echoes and whispers of Segrana's endless song were still reverberating through the trees, like an omnipresent mist of being. Suddenly she longed for cold, clear air and stood to gaze up the main trunk of the ancient pillar tree, eyeing the main ascent, recalling the junctions of the high branchways in this part of the forest.

'Would you like food to eat, Pathmistress?' said one of the Listener sisters, leaning out of a clump of foliage above.

'Thank you, but no. Later perhaps.'

The female Listener inclined her head and withdrew into the greenery. Catriona looked upward again then approached the trunk and began to climb.

I need to get up high, she thought. I need to see the sky, to see Darien.

THEO

All around, the forest was darkening as evening encroached. Theo held on to the harness handles with a white-knuckle grip as the trictra climbed a steeply sloping branch. In front, Etril sat behind the creature's head, languidly prodding its frontal joints from time to time.

Four weeks on Nivyesta, he thought. *Dozens of journeys on these spider-beasts and still I get the fear!*

Otherwise, he reckoned he had adapted quite well to forest life. Adapt and survive was the basic axiom when you were trapped in the wild. But when he thought about Catriona – well, it was a hard thing to grasp, this notion of the entire forest having a mind which was thousands of years old and which could speak with those it thought useful. How, he wondered, had Cat adapted to that role? What had she given up? The forest undoubtedly wanted to survive but Theo knew that this stage of the conflict could not go on. Sooner or later the Brolturans would attack with overwhelming force.

And then the entire moon will burn, he thought darkly.

'We are very near to Ipolb, Karlsson,' Etril said over his shoulder. 'Do you wish me to watch over this steed for the evening or will you be able to manage?'

'Ah, Etril, I have as much experience in the care of trictra as I have in leaf-jumping.'

The Uvovo laughed. 'I see your meaning, friend Karlsson. I shall remain this evening and look after this beastie . . . I have heard the Pathmistress use this word. Is it correct?'

'I believe it is, Etril.'

Minutes later, Ipolb came into view, a cluster of platforms, lean-tos and small huts lashed to the intertwined branches of two close-growing trees. Gantries and ropeways wound among the little community, now lit by glowing lamps in the fading light. Theo's eyes were drawn to a platform further up one of Ipolb's main trunks – yellow light shone from the narrow windows of a large lopsided shack, which sat there with a trictra shelter slung beneath.

Etril let Theo off at the platform then took the trictra below for tethering and feeding. Theo could see that a pale blue curtain now hung over the door, and he pushed it aside as he entered. A small conical oil lamp shed soft golden light from a triangular recess above the bed alcove. Malachi sat at a table, a candle at his elbow, writing in his journal, a hardbound notebook that Theo had begged from one of the Human researchers at the hidden enclave. The table and chair were Uvovo-scale and Malachi was hunched over as he scribbled. When Theo stepped inside he glanced up for a moment then back and kept writing.

'Hello, Major,' he said. 'You live so I assume that you were victorious.'

The voice was calm and controlled, speaking Anglic with the inflexions of an odd dialect. The original complement of the colonyship *Forrestal* had been mainly North Americans and Germans but it appeared that the former had come to dominate.

'We held our ground, they eventually retreated, and people on both sides died,' he said. 'Not much of a victory but it was the best we could manage. So, Malachi, why the curtain over the door?'

The Tygran finished the sentence he was writing, closed the journal and carefully placed the pen beside it.

'One of the Uvovo, not a local, came to pay a visit. I was . . . uncommunicative and he left. Another came, same outcome, and I thought that having a curtain would emphasise privacy.'

Well, you are talkative today, Theo thought. 'In Uvovo culture, hanging curtains in doors and windows is a sign of intense grief, mourning the loss of a loved one and so forth.'

A bleak smile came to Malachi's lips. 'That is not so far from the truth … I am sorry, Major, but there are difficulties. You Dariens have managed to coexist somehow with these native sentients; you trust them and accept them and this seems to be reciprocal. This is not the Tygran experience.'

Theo regarded him, recalling what he'd said before about the early history of the Tygran colony, of the wars fought against the Zshahil, a race of ruthless, savage reptilian bipeds who had presented a considerable threat to the colonists at the beginning. According to Malachi, several attempts at compromise were made but the Zshahil repeatedly broke truces and agreements. In the end, only superior weaponry and discipline defeated them and helped secure a peace treaty called the Cold Truce, after which the Zshahil migrated across the sea to another landmass.

'Is that what you're writing about?' Theo said.

The Tygran nodded. 'And other things, what I observe here and the precious pieces from my life before. I can never return to Tygra – soldiers who are captured and fail to take the Night Road face only death. So I must find a new way to understand the world around me, and to understand myself. Which is why I am trying to understand you, Major.'

Theo laughed. 'I would not describe myself as any kind of role model, but if I can assist your contemplations in any way, please ask.'

Outwardly, Theo was relaxed while inwardly he was delighted. After his capture, Malachi had been an unresponsive block, but after two weeks he seemed resigned to the situation and had asked for something to write on. He had also begun to talk about the Tygran colony and its origins, though only in basic terms. Until now.

Malachi met Theo's gaze. 'Would you tell me about this skirmish today, especially your experience of events?'

Theo obliged and gave an account of the fighting and how his preparation of the reserve proved useful. Malachi took notes as he listened, and throughout Theo felt a growing suspicion that his expression and demeanour were also being studied.

'The Uvovo deaths trouble you,' Malachi said.

'Unnecessary deaths trouble me,' Theo said. 'War always contributes a cargo of unintended pain and slaughter. I don't know who the Brolturan commander is but in the last month he has lost nearly a hundred and fifty troops for no gain whatsoever.' Theo curled his lips in contempt. 'He doesn't care about his men – they're just numbers to throw against us. A waste of life and resources.'

'Battle winnows out the weak and the incompetent,' Malachi said. 'One of the Celestial Axioms says that the strong deserve to survive because only the strong fight to survive.'

Theo smiled. 'Strength comes in many different shapes, sizes and colours and I think I've seen them all. No commander should rely on combat to winnow out the weak or the incompetent – that's what squad leaders are for.'

Malachi frowned as he took this in, then said:

'Your estimation of the Brolturan officer caste is correct – I have heard senior Tygran officers remark that their abilities do not match those of previous generations. The Hegemony provides them with new and sophisticated weapon systems, and this has blunted their tactical edge.'

'There are no bad regiments, only bad officers,' Theo said.

Malachi paused, then snapped his fingers. 'Is that not one of Napoleon's sayings?'

'General Slim, a British commander who fought the Japanese in the Second World War,' Theo said. 'Although I believe Napoleon said, "There are no bad soldiers, only bad officers."' Then, trying not to sound too interested: 'So how does the Tygran military maintain *its* tactical edge? Do you have any giant battleships with extensive hull ornamentation?'

Malachi laughed out loud, the first time Theo had heard him do so.

'We do have a navy, but nothing larger than an attack cruiser,' he said. 'Our tactical edge is the Tygran soldier, and rather than trying to create an army encompassing a wide range of functions the founders settled on small, flexible units and intense, multiskill training.'

It sounded familiar. 'Security, infiltration, surveillance and sabotage,' Theo said. 'And recruits are assigned to various companies or squads, each with its own little history of battles, heroes and villains, yes?'

'Just so, Major,' Malachi said with a curious smile. 'Does your Darien military have such a system?'

'*Ja*, only because I designed it. When I agreed to secretly train Viktor Ingram's followers – a long story, tell it to you some time – I organised them into six squads named after old Norj gods, and when some of the town militaries came over to us we kept the names. And those names were brought into the new corps after the coup failed, Thor Company, Odin Company and the rest . . .'

'It is similar for us. We have twelve commanderies, the Fireblades, the Nightwalkers, the Steel Hands, the Shadow Watch and others. Names were chosen that had no obvious link with the colonists' lives back on Earth so that in time they would come to have a meaning that was all our own. Each commandery is led by its captain while the commander-in-chief is the Marshal Paramount. I am – *was* a tac-sergeant with the Stormlions, who are traditionally close to the Black Sun Commandery, since they fought together in the Obelisk Siege on Odusra 4 nearly sixty years ago.'

'Battle forges strong bonds,' Theo said, wondering why he was being so forthcoming.

'And traditional alliances can become a disadvantage,' Malachi said, putting his journal away in the table drawer then moving over to the pallet bed, beneath the golden lamp. 'A few years ago, the Marshal Paramount, Aaron Ryan, was killed in action and one of the other captains was chosen, Matthias Becker, leader of the Black Sun.'

'So where does the disadvantage come in?'

'Upon promotion, all Marshal Paramounts undergo a brief operation that gives them a memory implant module, which provides them with the accumulated wisdom of the Tygran commandery archives. Becker was given something different, some kind of sentient cybernetic presence.'

Theo sat on the edge of the table. 'Sounds a lot like those AI implants the Hegemony people have.'

'It is the same thing, I'm sure,' Malachi said, crouching down at the foot of the pallet bed leaning against the wall. 'All the Brolturan elite have them, as does your President Kirkland and his cabinet.'

Theo swore. 'Treasonous piece of skag! – couldn't wait to become their creature.' He shook his head. 'So what happened to this Becker?'

'He began to change various things, the tone of training, loyalty oaths, new kinds of indoctrination, induction rituals, favouritism and sycophancy. He also allowed the Hegemony to assign two commanderies to missions directly involving other Humans, which strains the main principle of the Eminent Treaty . . .'

There was a scraping sound from beneath the floor, from the shelter where Etril was taking care of the trictra. Frowning, Theo said, 'Did you hear . . . ?'

Then he heard a footfall outside and stood. 'Who's there?' Suddenly he noticed that Malachi was now standing up and holding a club fashioned from a length of branch.

'I'm sorry, Theo,' he said as the blue curtain was torn aside. 'Truly sorry . . .'

An armoured Ezgara commando burst into the hut. Instinctively, Theo grabbed the nearest thing to hand, a small plant pot, and struck him on the head then kicked his legs out from under him. But by then another two Ezgara had entered and after that the fight was settled in less than a minute. Theo, his head ringing from a glancing punch, was slumped on the floor with his hands bound, shoulders in the four-handed grip of one of the intruders. Another three were applying restraints to Malachi's feet, knees and arms.

A fifth Ezgara, an officer going by the silvery flash on his helmet, went over to the fettered Malachi.

'We heard you telling the colonial about our private matters,' he said. 'What else have you told him?'

Malachi gave a wolfish grin. 'Everything!'

The officer, features obscured by a full-face visor, regarded him for a moment, then told his men, 'We'll have to take them both. Get them muffled and harnessed – move!'

Before Theo could speak a loop of opaque cord was dropped over his head and immediately all sounds died. As one commando tightened it to sit around his neck, Theo spoke and shouted but to no avail – he could neither hear any sound nor make any. At the same time, another Ezgara was fitting a mesh-and-struts harness around his upper chest. All of which took place in just a few moments before he and Malachi, similarly shackled, were hustled out of the door. Something was attached at his back and without warning he was yanked into the air and began ascending at a surprising speed.

He felt leaves and sprigs brush against him and the last things he saw were the still bodies of Uvovo guards lying on the higher platforms. All in perfect silence. Seconds later he passed through the canopy's layer of dense foliage which was suddenly spread out below him and receding, while above the open hold of a dark hovering craft gaped to accept him into its technical darkness.

7

ROBERT

Cradled, buffeted and battered by perpetual ice storms, Malgovastek City hangs from its five heavy steel cables, the Elavescent Hawsers, swaying only very slightly with the blasting, screaming winds. Vast weather systems roar through the Shylgandic Lacuna, swirling cyclonic blizzards that leave Malgovastek, like all the other penduline cities, encrusted in hoar frost and snow. But then a cunningly made heating network melts and loosens the ice, which low-grade mechanicals gather and send over the side. At its widest, across the diameter of the Supervisors Deck, Malgovastek is nearly 450 metres edge to edge and if the dock's boom and extendable jetties are included, it exceeds half a kilometre. Only one vessel is currently moored at the city dock, a Dalo-style long-hauler with a Phusoyedito-outbound badge, a rarity in these times.

Not that the Keklir guards in their sentry box care – all they are concerned with is the credentials of those seeking to pass between the dock and the city. And concerned as they also are about their physical warmth, they fail to notice the microinstant in which the personnel door in the big dock gates suddenly opens and closes. But they do discover that a muffler held over the heat vent proves cosily comforting when reattached to the snout.

On board the *Plausible Response*, the Rosa-sim was screening a catalogue of the ship's hull configurations for Robert, while the ship itself was having a discussion with Reski Emantes about the deepest tiers of hyperspace. All while they awaited the arrival of the Bargalil mystic Sunflow Oscillant.

'. . . so this is our current profile, Daddy, a pocket freighter similar to those turned out in the hundreds of thousands by the Grand Gestator Ree-Ix-Dalo . . .'

'The what?' Robert said.

'The Grand Gestators were a race of sentient, long-lived megaorganisms, whose huge bodies were essentially capable of making copies of any solid inorganic object.'

Robert studied the image on the screen showing the *Plausible Response* as a bulbous craft with twin downswept vanes to the aft, each ending in a secondary thruster.

'What happened to them?'

'Grew old and died out,' Rosa said. 'Sadly, many suffered senility in their final centuries, which left them vulnerable to the worst kinds of deceit. More than one transient cross-tier empire was built with weapons made by a Grand Gestator.'

Robert shook his head and laughed. Every day he learned another incredible snippet of information about the tiers of hyperspace that made Earth, Earthsphere and the regions beyond seem dull. Then he had to remind himself that known space encompassed only a small fraction of the galaxy, and that his experience amounted to a mere smattering of what that had to offer.

'What's the next one?' he said.

Rose touched the screen. 'An Exethi barque, which we'll only use if we have to go anywhere near the eighty-third, eighty-fourth and eighty-fifth tiers . . .'

Raised voices from down in the aft part of the bridge made them look up in surprise.

'. . . I don't care what your sensors picked up, you dolt!' came Reski Emantes's voice. 'Stable, wide-spectrum ecosystems are impossible at that depth. Para-entropic stresses affect submolecular forces and practically guarantee genetic drift and chaotic mutation.'

'I am sorry but you are being an arrogant pipsqueak – my sensors did not lie, nor were they tricked by some projection, neither were they subsumed by a cyberattack. The sensory data was correct, therefore the planetoid existed along with its biosphere. It was real, just like that Bargalil over there.'

What had been a closed main door in the aft bulkhead was suddenly open as a hooded, six-limbed Bargalil, dressed in what looked like layers of grey-brown webby rags, padded leisurely in.

'How did . . . ?'

'Ship,' Rosa said. 'Why did you allow this intruder aboard?'

'I had little choice in the matter,' said the *Plausible Response*. 'Our guest appears to be employing a kind of state-causal phase-shift.'

'That sounds like pseudo-theoretical waste product,' Reski Emantes said as it floated after the newcomer. 'Excuse me, if you insist on inviting yourself aboard, you might at least tell us who you are.'

The Bargalil paused and swung its long-necked head round, regarding the droid with large golden eyes set in a broad, sad-mouthed face.

'A clever thing,' it said in a wheezing voice. 'Such a clever thing, full of . . . full of . . .'

'It certainly is,' said the *Plausible Response*.

'. . . parts and pieces and bits, many, many bits, and I can see them all, see them forming and joining, so I can unjoin and unform them if you like. Would you like to see all those clever parts?' The golden eyes turned towards Rosa and Robert. 'Would you?'

Robert stared, realising that Reski had said nothing and was unmoving.

'Er . . . no, thank you, very kind of you to offer, but . . . our droid colleague has . . . duties to perform, you see . . .'

The Bargalil gave an odd shrug, which amounted to his head dipping between his shoulders, then he turned and carried on towards the front of the bridge. Reski Emantes suddenly bobbed up and settled back down again.

'That . . . that . . .'

'Diplomacy, Reski,' Robert murmured. 'Please . . .'

The droid spun in wordless fury for a second or two, then glided off to the rear. Robert approached the Bargalil and gave a stately bow.

'Welcome aboard the tiership *Plausible Response* – I am Robert Horst and this is my daughter, Rosa, and our droid companion you have already met. Have I the honour of addressing Sunflow Oscillant?'

'I am that one,' came the reply. 'I know I am that one for I have looked inward and seen all the bits and parts and pieces so I know – I know – I know that I am that one.'

Always wise to be sure, Robert thought, exchanging a brief look with Rosa.

'I am very pleased to meet you,' he said. 'We are seekers on a path . . .'

'You are the emissary,' said the Bargalil. 'The path is yours, the path calls to you, the path seeks for you while you journey from the Many to the One, even as the One himself is on a journey . . . leave the Many so that you can see the One.'

'Sunflow Oscillant, will you help us to continue our journey?' Robert said patiently. 'Where must we go next?'

'Oscillant Sunflow Oscillant,' the Bargalil mumbled, head drooping. 'Between darkness and light he sways, between stillness and flight, torn from the elements, a dream for the parts and the pieces, a mask for the words and the fears . . .' Suddenly, the Bargalil reared up and sat back on its rear haunches while its smaller forelimbs raised stubby-fingered paws to cover those golden eyes. 'Coordinate . . . you require coordinates to guide you . . . numbers, letters, symbols, they are already here, already nestling in the energy mazes of this cunningly wrought mask-ship-machine-mind . . . from the Many to the One, from the Many to the One . . . I must find the hidden rhythm that passes from the One to the Many . . .'

The Bargalil mystic fell silent and for several moments the quiet was like the hush of a held breath. Then:

'Data intrusion!' said the *Plausible Response*. 'Index anomaly found, base matrix integrity compromised!'

Rosa leaned forward. 'Ship, where is the anomaly located?'

'Navigational stacks, course datafiles. Anomalous object has been isolated and mirrored, running parallel analyses . . . analyses complete. The anomalous object does not identify as a threat-level vector . . .'

The Bargalil uncovered its eyes and smiled, yet to Robert it seemed like a desolate expression. The golden gaze came round to Rosa, who gave a polite smile in return.

'Ship,' she said. 'Describe the anomalous object.'

'It is the coordinate set for a location down on Tier 92, in an askew expanse.'

Rosa nodded and turned to Sunflow Oscillant, who tipped forward onto four legs again and said:

'Your paths await . . . the path will lead you to the path that will teach you the path . . .' It looked round at the exit and took a couple of shambling steps in that direction – and in an eyeblink it was suddenly in front of the sliding door.

'Wait, wise Sunflow Oscillant,' Robert said, getting to his feet. 'Who should we look for, or ask for when we reach the next destination?'

'The path leads from the Many into the Many-and-One. Abandon the sight of the Many to see the One, shrug off the thoughts of the Many to understand the mind of the One, shut out the babble of the Many to hear the pure harmonies of the One. And the One will hear you. Seek watchers and meditators, seek out those that shine with the essence of the One, and they will know you.'

The bridge door, without any sliding motion, was suddenly open and the Bargalil ambled out. Another eyeblink, and the door was shut again.

For a moment no one said a word until Reski Emantes floated up from behind one of the consoles.

'What in the name of reason was all that babble about?'

Robert dropped back into his seat, feeling bemused, and indicated the bridge entrance.

'How could he appear and disappear like that?' he asked Rosa. 'What kind of technology is that?'

She shrugged, turning to the main console. 'Causal-state phase-shift – it's an exotic talent, something that only living beings can do. Inorganic entities cannot achieve it. Basically, the Bargalil can perceive the various states of an object then shift it into one of them, or even shift himself.'

'Like a door being open or closed?'

'Or a droid in its optimum functioning state,' she said. 'Or simply as a heap of parts.'

'That would have been interesting to observe,' said the Ship.

'Aargh, ouch, I am wounded by your oafish wit,' Reski Emantes said in low, flat tones, then, in his usual voice, 'What was all that drivel about the Many and the One? Is this One supposed to be the Godhead?'

The Rosa-sim looked round expectantly at Robert, who was suddenly groping for an answer.

'Well, yes, sounds likely in the context.'

'Then who or what is the Many?'

'The social matrix that seekers or pilgrims – that's us – leave behind in their journey towards enlightenment,' Robert said. 'Although some creeds focus on desires and sins as the things to be discarded. Some of the less tactful atheists say that religion is just a pretty blindfold for those who want to run away from reality.'

Rosa regarded him thoughtfully. 'And what do you think, Daddy?'

He smiled. 'I have a well-established seat on the fence, my sweet. Just as it is not rational to discount the existence of a supreme being, neither can I commit myself without proof.'

'Droids and mechs deal with reality all the time,' Rosa said. 'Yet they don't have desires and sins, nor do they have much of a social Many to leave behind.'

'Nor do they have the notion of a supreme being,' Robert said. 'At least, I've never heard of a droid religion.'

'Yet our Bargalil friend clearly sees the Godhead as a god. Yet I know, from numerous sources, that it is a real entity of living matter – it doesn't control its own paradise or hell, as far as I know. Only an organic lifeform could come up with the idea of an afterlife . . .'

'I think the Ship has more to tell us about the coordinates,' said Rosa suddenly. 'And course data, too.'

'I have extracted all values from the data object and assembled a copy of the file,' said the Ship. 'It appears to be a viable location descriptor. Our course is plotted so we may leave when you wish.'

'All our docking fees are paid?' Robert said.

'Generously and in advance,' said the *Plausible Response*. 'Give the order and I shall signal the dock systems to release the mooring clamps.'

'Then kindly do so.'

Outside, howling winds hurled dense veils of snow across the gantries, jetties and booms of Malgovastek Dock. Lanterns fixed to poles gave off dirty orange haloes amid the rushing, shadowy blur, shuddering noticeably from the force of the blast. Then strong white beams blazed out from the underside of the *Plausible Response*, now abruptly visible, and coiling eddies of snow rose as the manoeuvring suspensors quickly came up to operational pitch. There were several near-simultaneous clangs and the ship suddenly lifted from its berth and ascended to about a hundred feet. There, it tilted forward, spun round on its nose and, with rainbow plasma burning from the twin thrusters and the dorsal aperture, the *Plausible Response* leaped away into the everlasting storms of the Shylgandic Lacuna.

Rosa said that the journey to Tier 92 would take just under thirty hours so Robert, feeling worn out by the days of waiting on Malgovastek, retired to his quarters and slept solidly for a good nine hours. On waking he felt a few twinges and aches but twenty minutes of exercise ironed them out, leaving him feeling alert and hungry. His new lease of youth was a constant reminder of how he had let the ageing process degrade his physique, helped along by a diplomatic career which militated against a healthy lifestyle.

And an AI companion who considered such a thing unimportant, he thought, recalling several conversations he'd had with Harry on the subject.

Then he paused and wondered what Harry would have said about this bizarre mission into the depths of hyperspace. Robert could almost imagine him standing over by the vee screen, resting one foot on the edge of the low table, smiling his cynically amused smile and saying, *Why, Robert, you've become an altruist! Diplomat – heal thyself!*

But here he was, all alone in his skull with only his own thoughts and opinions for company. It had been hard at the start, not having Harry perennially on hand to bounce ideas off, to provide advice, to obtain background knowledge on any topic. Without him, it all seemed to rest on guesswork and flimsy judgement, which made his part in this venture seem almost untenable, the more he thought about it.

Robert's mood darkened and his spirits dipped. *What about self-reliance*, he wondered, sitting in a blue easy chair. In an earlier age, self-knowledge and hard-won experience was gained on the basis of rugged self-reliance, yet for people of Robert's age, and the younger generations especially, such notions were laughably obsolete, or *wrinkly* as the yopocultura had it. But would he have Harry or another AI reimplanted, if he could? Put that way, he honestly felt that he would not. In which case it looked as if he would have to rediscover those antique qualities of self-reliance, if he wanted to be of use to the Construct or indeed anyone.

He stood up, deciding to shower, but then the door chimed.

'Yes?'

'Daddy, it's Rosa.'

'Ah, come in, come in.'

The door slid open and she entered. With her long golden hair tied back in a ponytail, she had on a dark green worksuit, the kind usually reserved for senior techs, but over it she wore a charming bolero-style jacket, powder blue in colour, with intricate crimson embroidery at the sleeve cuffs, the pockets and the collar. At her neck was a pendant, a small red stone. The combination was striking, making her seem mature and somehow formidable.

'An impressive outfit,' he said.

'Oh, the Ship adapted it from something left behind by another passenger,' she said. 'I came to let you know that we'll be arriving at Tier 92 sooner than we thought – the *Plausible Response* found an alternative route through the boundaries so we should be there in another six or seven hours.'

'That's good news,' Robert said, feeling the pressure of his self-doubt. 'Well, perhaps it isn't. Rosa, I have to admit that I am uncertain of my abilities in this situation. It worries me that my unsupported judgement could put us, put you in great danger.'

'Daddy, I have every confidence in you,' she said, reaching out to take his hands. 'In fact, more confidence now that your invisible friend is gone. Your experience and your instincts are still there and I trust them, trust you with my life.'

Robert smiled, touched by her words, yet his fundamental doubts remained.

'Besides, the Construct devised this form,' she went on. 'So I am a bit tougher than I look.'

'That is . . . reassuring, I think.'

She laughed. 'Why not come up to the bridge and help me divert the Ship and Reski Emantes from their ongoing vitriol tournament?'

'Maybe later – once I've showered I'm going down to the observation lounge to study whatever the Ship has on Tier 92, while taking in the view.'

'Okay, Daddy. I'll comm you an hour before we get there, if we don't see you earlier.'

She smiled, gave a little wave and was gone, and Robert headed for the shower.

The observation lounge was small and horseshoe-shaped, situated at the front of the *Plausible Response*'s understructure. The lighting was muted to soft floor glows and Robert sat in one of the feed chairs, tacting its flimscreen, working his way through information on the Urcudrel Seam, as Tier 92 was known to its dwindling, scattered population. According to the files, the entropic collapse of the Urcudrel continuum had wrought tiny but significant changes in its macrophysical laws, so that when the crushed wreckage of its worlds was crammed together order spontaneously arose. Massive crystalline forms took shape, polyhedral conglomerations emerging from grinding chaos. To Robert it sounded utterly bizarre yet one file included vidage of a vast cliff of stone-grey cubes and a plain of clusters of octagonal pillars, all beneath a cloud-blurred sky of inverted, darkly translucent pyramids that gave off a flickering, bone-white radiance.

The Urcudrel Seam was also fragmentary, its continuum grown patchy with the pressures from above and below. Some regions, cut off from the main abracosm, had developed their own peculiar characteristics and were known as askew expanses – it was within one of these that their destination lay.

Outside the observation lounge, he saw what appeared to be vast webs of mottled glass. At the corner of the lounge window was the number 87, a ghostly readout signifying which tier they were passing through. Gazing into the distance, through a maze of glittering strands, he could see something that might have been a tilted, towerlike city hanging at the nexus of innumerable gleaming cables. Or it might have been an immense ship, caught in the meshes, woven about and held fast . . .

The *Plausible Response* moved onward and downward as the shift drive kicked in Robert experienced an odd ripple in his vision, like light turning sideways and back, and a slight pulse of vertigo. Tier 88 was a series of vast, dark plains strewn with the shattered ruins of colossal seven-limbed statues. Eighty-nine was a showcase of failed stellar engineering, the extinguished remains of miniature stars orbiting a megaplanet, itself a cold, dead tomb-world, its face scarred by the inhabitants' final paroxysms of violent despair. Other arrays and patterns of suns were visible in the distance, chains and bracelets, magnified by the lounge's viewing system; the rest were burnt-out husks hanging in an ashen firmament.

Again the ship tier-shifted and the next number was 91. For a moment Robert wondered why they had bypassed Tier 90, then he turned his attention to the vista outside, an immense level plain of stone across which water poured in vigorous rivers, even torrents, while large masses of pale, leafless growth were rooted here and there, their dense, tangled meshes sloping all in one direction as deformed by constant winds. Then, without warning, the view swung through ninety degrees and Robert held on to his chair, battling a surge of vertigo as the watery plain outside became an almost sheer rock face.

'Apologies, Robert,' said the Ship. 'It was a necessary attitude correction.'

Almost corrected the position of my breakfast, he thought as he watched the sheets of water rushing down, the droplets spraying out and the dense, waxy-white tangles of angular growth hanging from a rock face that stretched away into haze. Then he frowned, staring intently at something that seemed grotesquely out of place – there, at the crook of one of those angular branches, was a strange formation. And suddenly he realised that it was, unmistakably, a skeletal joint. The pale entwining meshes were not plant growth but bones, the fleshless remains of unimaginable lifeforms, clinging to that drenched, enormous cliff.

'Hello, Daddy?' came Rosa's voice from somewhere overhead.

'Yes, Rosa.'

'Daddy, we're about to make the shift to Tier 92 – would you like to join us on the bridge?'

Outside, the cliff and its burden of cadavers slipped away as the Ship altered course.

'I'm on my way,' he said, shutting down the flimscreen as he headed for the door.

The lights were down low on the bridge, the shadows pushed back by golden radiance fanning out from wall sources at deck level, contrasting with the multicolour glows of the consoles.

'Greetings, Robert Horst,' said Reski Emantes, who was hovering at one of the sensor stations. 'You've not missed much – the deployment of coruscating wit and its triumph over the dull-minded, that kind of thing.'

'Translation,' said the Ship. 'It has been even more openly

insulting and arrogant than usual. I suspect that some strain of overcompensation is at work.'

Robert walked up to the split-level command dais, exchanging a knowing smile with Rose, who rolled her eyes.

'So when do we make the shift?' he said.

'In a few minutes, once the shift drive has finished matching values with the boundary matrices.'

'Then we make our insanely hazardous leap into a completely uncharted region,' Reski Emantes said. 'Hope you're ready.'

Robert glanced around at the droid then smiled at Rosa. 'Uncharted?'

'Yes, but not unexplored,' she said. 'There have been a few reports, sketchy ones that mention dead, fossilised planets . . .'

'Drive aligned,' said the Ship. 'Desynchronisation in twenty-seven seconds.'

'Acknowledge,' said Rosa, looking up at the wide monitor screen.

Again, the momentary deformation of light along with the passing lurch of vertigo . . . and the sky was different, a dark, grainy vastness broken by a single, muted light source, greyish-brown in hue, almost a dull copper, emanating from a single star. And there were worlds, too, drifting in their hundreds, maybe thousands. From the console sensors it appeared that all were of planetoid size or smaller, and, oddly, every one was a perfect sphere, no oblate spheroids, no irregular bodies. In the grainy, coppery starlight, planetoid surfaces took on a dark, brassy sheen, their scars, cracks and craters thrown into high relief. Robert understood how a passing visitor could describe them as fossilised – they were dry, dusty desolate globes, nothing more.

'Now that's interesting,' said Reski.

'What?' said Rosa.

'Watch.'

A small section of the wide screen enlarged to fill the centre, bringing one particular cluster of dark planetoids into clearer view, in time to see a small one sweep towards a larger one. But instead of colliding, it glanced off in a slow, stately and contactless ricochet that sent it spinning languidly away.

'Gravitational inversion,' said Reski Emantes as the enlarged section dissolved, showing again the vista of drifting planetoids. 'All those worldlets repel one another.'

It's like a gigantic game of murmlespiel, Robert thought.

'Ship, are we near the rendezvous?' said Rosa. 'Any sign of anyone else?'

'Destination coordinates are over four thousand kilometres dead ahead,' said the *Plausible Response*. 'Sensor readings are confused – I seem to be detecting between three and twenty-five vessel contacts.'

'What he means is that his systems are incapable of distinguishing between real-image data and echoes reflected by the antigravity planetoids,' said Reski Emantes as the droid came into view on the exterior monitor.

'What,' Rosa said, 'are you doing out there?'

'The delirious excitement on board was more than I could bear,' the droid replied. 'Now, if you'll follow me to our destination, I'll relay sensory data to my underequipped colleague.'

With that, the machine set off in the direction of the rendezvous coordinates.

'Ship, would you . . .'

'Keep the pipsqueak in range? Certainly.'

Minutes passed and a cluster of planetoids, some as large as Earth's moon, others no wider than a sports stadium, drew steadily nearer.

'I can't see anything . . .' Robert said.

'There is something,' Rosa murmured, adjusting onscreen sensor variables.

'Long-range detects say that there is a ship somewhere in close visual range,' said the *Plausible Response*. 'And two more 1,953 kilometres away in the port hi-quarter, but their apparent image loci are flickering on and off, as well as changing position . . . ah, it seems that our intrepid pathfinder has altered course.'

True enough, on the widescreen the droid was veering off to the right, towards a middle-sized planetoid about a thousand kilometres in diameter.

'Reski, where are you going?' Rosa said.

'I've detected some odd energy readings on that moonlet,' came the reply. 'Like the residue of a drive. Turbulent yet it's highly localised.'

'That planetoid does appear to be the source of some of the anomalous detection signatures,' said the *Plausible Response*.

'Okay, we'll follow the droid,' Rose said. 'But keep the sensors on full alert.'

Robert sat back as the tiership swooped down after Reski Emantes. The small, barren world loomed before them and an inky darkness fell like a curtain as they crossed into its shadow, cut off from the star's meagre radiance. The Construct droid was sending back a continuous feed of scan data as it came nearer to the moon. And the nearer it got the stronger the effects of that strange gravitic repulsion.

'A very odd experience,' said Reski Emantes. 'A constant, gentle push . . . but do all these planetoids stay in the vicinity of that star?'

'Reski, there's something on the move down there . . .'

Robert heard the urgency in her voice and sat up.

'Yes, I am picking up . . . my exosensors say the object is small and rising . . . not powered, rising on the antigravity, but I'm unable to narrow down its location. It's somewhere within the 64 cubic-kilometers below me . . .'

'Rosa,' Robert said slowly. 'This is . . .'

'I know – I'm triangulating both sensor arrays and getting a partial . . .' Suddenly she stared up at the screen. 'Reski, get out – it's a missile!'

'Too late . . .'

On the screen, against the moonlet's dark backdrop, a thruster flared abruptly and a moment later there was a bright, harsh flash. Instantly, all of Reski's datafeeds went dead while an enlarged visual showed the Construct droid tumbling slowly, wrapped in an aura of jagged energy.

'What was that?' Robert said. 'Where did it come from?'

'*That*,' Rosa said, pointing.

Another section of the widescreen had enlarged to show a portion of the planetoid's rocky surface, a sports-pitch-sized area
seemingly melting away to reveal a deep recess out of which a
ship began to rise. To Robert's eyes, at first glance, it resembled an
immense crablike machine, then when he looked closer he saw the
additional armoured effector limbs, the pincers, the broaches, the
rotary blades, the serrated tines, and the profusion of hooked
symbols that decorated the upper and lower carapaces. It looked
vicious and brutal, and viscerally epitomised the words 'war
machine'.

'Can we fight that thing?' he said. 'Can we stand our ground?'

'My projectors could do it some serious damage,' said the
Plausible Response. 'But it's twice my mass as well as being heavily armoured and shielded – by the time I got through its outer
hull it would have me in a close-quarters grapple and would be
literally tearing me apart.'

Robert regarded one of the secondary screens where the droid
Reski Emantes drifted, seemingly lifeless, then he looked at Rosa.

'So what do we do?'

'Daddy, we run! Ship?'

'Evasive manoeuvres engaged, course set for far side of the
planetoid after the next, heavy thrust initiated.'

He stared at the hostile vessel, imagining its claws ripping their
way into their ship.

'What is that craft?' he said. 'Are there any records identifying
it?'

'Indeed there are,' said the Ship. 'It is a hunt-invigilator of the
Steel81 Claw, I believe.'

Frowning, he glanced at Rosa.

'That's its rank, Daddy – all you need to know is that it is a
Knight of the Legion of Avatars, and it's coming after us!'

8

LEGION

The last of the Bargalil base crew had barricaded the access corridors to the hemicylindrical dorm section, then welded the doors shut. They were heavily armoured pressure doors, easily capable of resisting the laser lances on some of the subverted maintenance drones. There was a heavy-grade cutter in the large workshop but it was integrated into a motorised ceiling assembly and the Legion Knight wanted to spend as little time on sterilisation as possible – there was no telling how soon a ship would arrive from the other moon or the planet and he had a great deal of essential materials to locate and salvage.

Fortunately, a rapid analysis of the command centre's crude schemator units revealed that a secondary fuel line passed through the foundations. It was a simple task to choke off the outlet and send a small remote along the pipe to bore holes and ignite when enough fuel had escaped.

The explosion ripped open the dormitory with an angry yellow flare of burning gases that quickly faded while debris and bodies flew in all directions. Watching from the oval roof of the main complex, the Legion Knight was puzzled, having expected a contained incineration from the amount of fuel that had been released. But when one of the ejected pieces of debris altered its trajectory towards him and opened fire with an energy weapon, the mystery was solved. Gas tanks for vacsuits would have intensified that explosion yet somehow one wearer had survived the eruption.

The suited, six-limbed Bargalil seemed undaunted by the Legion Knight's size as it flew straight down, firing off beam bursts that did little more than heat a few spots of the carapace to a dull red. The Knight felt a twinge of admiration for such a daringly suicidal assault – along with the Sendrukans, the Bargalil were an impressive species and would be likely candidates for convergence, once the Legion of Avatars established unopposed dominion.

He let the survivor get to within fifty metres before directing a nearby patrolling drone to swoop down, latch onto the Bargalil and steer him sideways towards one of the surface airlocks which was just starting to cycle open. Seconds after diving inside, both machine and captive were engulfed by an explosion, preceded, the Knight noticed, by a small bright flash, a sign that the Bargalil had triggered a grenade.

As metal and organic remnants sprayed out of the twisted airlock, the Legion Knight received an unexpected alert, from the recently reactivated exospatial comm-signal sensors. It was, to his surprise, a dyadic realtime communication from his two remaining Scions, those who chose paths to Darien different from the third, whose failure remained a source of grief. In their last communication they had offered up reassurances but no specifics as to their plans; perhaps this time more would be revealed. So as the reprogrammed drones of the depopulated base went about their scavenging, he opened the waiting channel.

<I am here, my intrepid Hereditants. Speak>

>We greet you, Illustrious Progenitor, and enquire after the state of your well-being. Your subspace beacon has been silent for an entire quarter-cycle<

<Minor damage to my exospatial emitters made beacon patterning impossible. But as is clear, repairs have taken place and I shall soon resume my voyage>

>This concerns us, Illustrious One. The journey to Darien is long and we well recall the state of your great and venerable workings and their enclosing body-shell. We urge you to reconsider undertaking such a long and onerous passage, especially since our own plans are now well advanced<

The Legion Knight was impressed and amused at this ploy.

<Such concern is mildly pleasing but of little consequence. I am resolved to resume this voyage so that I may witness the unfolding of your plans first-hand>

>Illustrious Progenitor, understand that we counsel caution out of duty to you and the principles of convergence. Be advised that in the event that you reach Darien without further mishap, you will see that formidable obstacles await you – an Earthsphere cruiser and a Brolturan battleship, the latter of which maintains around the planet a sensor shell of some sophistication. We are uncertain as to how you might overcome this<

<Formidable obstacles? Am *I* not formidable? Have I not survived long ages in the dark for this time to come around? Have I not been forged in the crucible of convergence and tempered by battle and struggle? My Hereditants, resist any further temptation to offer up concern and caution – I shall dispose of these inferior enemies on my arrival. You may, however, inform me of your own strategies; a broad summary will suffice>

>We are reluctant to reveal such data over an unsecure subspace channel, with all due respect and admiration, Illustrious One<

<Then go about your strategies and I shall go about mine>

With that he broke off contact, satisfied that he had persuaded them that he was going to attempt some kind of rash, hasty assault. However, he decided that it would be wise to take their warnings at face value, not least because they sounded plausible. He would therefore need some kind of tactic that would get him down onto the planet without arousing suspicion about his true nature, and when he examined an inventory of the Bargalil base one item in particular caught his attention. Next to the packaging vault was the main dock, in which was berthed a short-range container barge whose main hold was easily large enough to accommodate the Legion Knight. Modified in various ways, it could pass as a viable hyperdrive vessel but it could only get close enough to Darien if . . .

If the Earthsphere ship believed it to be a friendly craft carrying some valuable cargo.

He activated every last drone and mechanical on the base and stepped up the scavenging efforts while diverting some machines to carry out alterations to the barge. Control systems needed rerouting to the hold, the main drive had to be boosted and additional stores installed. But as well as the technical tasks, there was another crucial problem that had to be addressed:

How was he going to fake the human crew of an interstellar vessel?

9

KAO CHIH

More than a day after leaving Belskirnir, they reached Doyle's Landing, a crossing point over the Chyorny River, right where it spilled out from a cliff-sided ravine at the south-east edge of the Forest of Arawn. With a late afternoon sky darkening overhead, they were on a rope-guided log barge and halfway across the river when the Brolturans attacked. Kao Chih had been talking with the Earthsphere agent, Silveira, when they heard the whine of engines and saw three sleek assault flyers come in over the treetops half a klick downstream then turn in their direction.

'Everybody into the water!' bellowed Silveira. 'They're making an attack run!'

Kao Chih saw fear and panic in every face yet felt oddly unruffled. Greg and the Firmanov brothers were already leaping into the river, followed by a couple of bearded trappers, determinedly dragging fur bales with them. Everyone had dived off the upstream side so Kao Chih went the other way, thinking to take advantage of the current. He just caught Silveira shouting something to him . . . then he was in the water, gasping with the cold. He was coming up for his second breath when a missile hit the barge.

The explosion was deafening and bright, and a wave of heat rolled over him. Moments later he realised why the others had gone off the other side as blazing pieces of the barge came floating downstream. Slowed by wet clothing, he had to duck under the waters when burning logs swept towards him, after which it was a struggle to surface. And still the attack went on, a nonstop cacophony of explosions and automatic fire, screams, shouts and the occasional answering fusillade of shots.

By the time he reached the opposite bank and stumbled wetly up onto the grassy slope, the flyers were gone. Doyle's Landing, however, was destroyed, its ramshackle tavern and attendant huts and shanties blown apart. The wreckage blazed ferociously. Exhausted and soaked to the skin, Kao Chih staggered on a few steps before slipping on mud to land on his backside where he sat and stared, dazed for a moment. He and Greg had stopped at the tavern on their outward journey and enjoyed a mug of the local grain brew while swapping news with the barkeep . . .

One of the Firmanov brothers, Alexei, came hurrying up. His garments were likewise sodden, his hands were almost black with dirt and ash, and blood from a wound on his scalp was seeping down one temple.

'Kao Chih, my friend, are you okay?' he said. 'You are not looking so well. Are you injured?'

'No, I . . . thank you, I am not wounded.'

'Good, very good, then Greg needs you to come and put out some fires, *pazhalsta*?'

Kao Chih nodded and was helped to his feet, then stumbled after Alexei towards the burning settlement. For the next hour he carried water buckets, moved the wounded over to a makeshift lean-to by the tree line, and salvaged still-edible provisions from the charred and smoking ruins. Greg and Silveira and the Firmanovs put in the same if not greater effort, which included scavenging logs and any canvas or sheeting to build rough shelters. Night had fallen and campfires were alight by the time Greg called a halt. Everyone's clothing had dried out in the smoky, smouldering air but now everyone was smeared with ash and sweat, especially the few uninjured menfolk of the settlement who had insisted on seeing to the dead themselves.

The tavern-owner, Megan Doyle, had died in the attack but her son, Tavish, a lean youth with haunted eyes, came over to thank them.

'I'm greatly obliged to you all,' he said. 'I don't know how we'd have coped if you'd run off like that pair of shabs . . .'

The two trappers who had also been on the barge had scrambled ashore with their furs and dashed off into the forest without a backward glance.

'We couldn't have left you to fend for yourselves,' Greg said. 'But I'm afraid that we will be heading off in less than an hour, after we've rested and cleaned up a little. And I recommend that you and your people do the same as soon as you're able, either head to another camp or follow us to Tayowal. Staying here is too risky.'

'I've heard good things about ye, Mr Cameron, and I appreciate yer advice but I'll no' be chased out of my family's home, even as burnt as it is.'

'Tavish, understand that this was not a warning on their part – they used incendiaries because they meant to wipe you out.'

But the youth was stubborn. 'Aye, I know but I'll no' be chased out.'

Greg nodded and sat back. 'If it were me, I'd probably feel the same.'

Tavish Doyle was silent for a moment as he stared at the campfire. Kao Chih watched the exchange, remembering some of the eyewitness accounts in the *Retributor* archives that told of how colonists on Pyre, his grandparents' generation, had felt when they came under attack by the Hegemony monoclan.

'I can put together some provisions for when you leave,' Tavish said.

'Your need is the greater,' said Greg. 'Besides, Tayowal is only a few hours away and I mean to be there by midnight.'

'Well, we have it if you want it.'

Once Doyle had left and was out of earshot, Nikolai, the older Firmanov, turned to Greg.

'You want to leave this fine town so soon?'

Greg smiled bleakly. 'Did you see the direction those flyers took after they were done? – they were heading east.'

'There's a big lumber camp called Freyja's Repose twenty miles that way,' said Alexei.

'Out in the open?'

'It has a mill by a fast-running river and cargo zeplins always going back and forth, until recently . . .'

'Right, so it's an easy target,' Greg said. 'And I'll bet there's other camps on the receiving end tonight. Mr Silveira?'

The Earthsphere agent looked up. 'Yes, Mr Cameron.'

'Would ye be so kind as to refresh my memory about the ETA of this factory machine?'

Silveira leaned forward, voice low as he spoke. 'Various surveillance sources put the Hegemony freighter's arrival within a forty-eight-hour window ending roughly five a.m. tomorrow, local time.'

'And would ye say that it makes sense to bring it in by night, after stirring up a wee bit of chaos as a diversion?'

'Indeed, yes.'

Greg looked around at the rest. 'The Brolts are monitoring all frequencies so we can't contact Tayowal to see if they were hit by those bastard raiders. Therefore we have to reach Tayowal tonight, in case they need our help. Okay?' Heads nodded sombrely. 'Good. Grab a bite, clean up if you want, and be ready to hit the trail in forty minutes.'

As he went in search of a bucket of water, Kao Chih dwelled on thoughts of his people, the families and crew aboard the *Retributor*, a hollowed-out, modified asteroid fitted with the ancient engines from the colonyship *Tenebrosa*. And he also thought about the rest of the *Tenebrosa* colonists, the ones left behind on Pyre – he had grown up with stories and pictures of Pyre, from the years before the colossal extractor machines came, when it was still called Virtue In The Valley, a lost place of peace which the older generation yearned for. If all the surviving Pyre colonists could settle on Darien the elders might still pine for what was but the youngsters and newborn would see this world as their home and embrace it.

And yet . . . there had been a moment, or rather several moments, in the last few hazardous days when part of him had fervently wished to be back on board the *Retributor*, back in the familiar comfort of his bed recess, wrapped in all those sounds, smells and rhythms of family life . . .

He smiled as he sponged the dirt from his face, neck and arms. *This must mean that I am destined to be one of those grumpy elders, forever reminding the disrespectful youngsters about the old, heroic days . . .*

Tavish Doyle came to see them off, thanking each in turn and giving each of them a small bottle of liquor retrieved from one of the tavern's undamaged stores. Half an hour later they were climbing a hillside track with Greg and Nikolai leading the way, their torches lighting the path ahead. Kao Chih found himself walking alongside the Earthsphere agent Silveira, quietly discussing the luminous ineka beetles and ulby roots. As they spoke, he remembered to employ the anglophone honorific.

'Mr Silveira,' he then said. 'May I ask you about the reasons for your mission?'

Silveira smiled. 'Please do.'

'Thank you. During the duller periods of my journey to Darien, I took the opportunity to scan news headlines for mentions of Earth and Darien and the human race in general. Those concerning Darien were limited in number and tended to recur, but those focused on Earth and Humanity dealt solely with the Yamanon invasion and fell into two main categories, critical pieces with various levels of hostility, and pro-Earthsphere ones. I admit that I only had access to summaries and extracts but I can say that the responses and rebuttals from the Earthsphere government were unwavering and even aggressively asserted, as is their loyalty to the Sendrukan Hegemony. Given these facts, why are you here, helping rebels to resist the plans and tactics of the Brolturans, a close Hegemony ally?'

'A good question,' Silveira said. 'There are several reasons. First, it is the Sendrukans who are really in charge here, in the person of their ambassador, Utavess Kuros; second, they have invested a lot of political capital in maintaining control and a plausible façade, yes? You mention this ancient Forerunner device, this matter transporter, but I am thinking that there's more to it than that. Something strategic, something worth all this trouble. Last, while agents such as myself have a limited range of options, my superiors have an obligation to gather information on all of Humanity's far-flung offshoots. Off the record, untraceable sidearms and advice on certain battlefield technology are permissible; advanced weaponry and direct involvement in planning and execution are forbidden.'

'It sounds discouraging,' said Kao Chih.

'There is, however, one advantage to this particular situation – I am here while my superiors are fifteen thousand light years away.'

'That's what I like to hear!' came Greg's voice from in front.

After three hours of trudging the sparse track led into a narrow defile between two steep, rocky hills and minutes later they descended into the tree-veiled valley of Tayowal. Under the night sky the lights of Tayowal were a welcoming glow amid the dense foliage and bushy surroundings. As they passed through the northern entrance they were met by Rory and a couple of the Diehards. Beyond, a large crowd of newcomers were milling around.

'Finally,' said Rory. 'We were just about ready to send out searchers.'

'Rory,' said Greg, indicating the crowd. 'Are they all . . . ?'

'Aye, got bombed out of the camps and villages north and south of the Kentigerns, so where else can they go?'

'How are the stores looking?'

'We had a week's worth before, but now, mebbe three days, an' that's pushin' it.' Rory glanced at Silveira. 'A new face, eh? How did yer trip go, then? Good or grim?'

On the other side of the crowd they continued towards a large stone-built entrance in the side of the valley. Kao Chih noticed that many of the new arrivals wore townswear, thinner shirts and trousers, and footwear unsuited to rough ground.

'A fair bit of both,' Greg said. 'I'll go over it once we get together with the Listeners and find out what's been happening while we were away. Is Chel about?'

'He just got back,' Rory said. 'Him and Yash have got quite a story for ye.'

'Good. He has to be part of this too.' He looked round at Silveira and beckoned him closer. 'You'll have to stay out of the public eye just now, but we'll talk with the Listeners in private later. In the meantime, my good friend Kao Chih will keep you company, perhaps even find you something hot to drink.'

Kao Chih smiled. 'It will be my pleasure.'

As Greg and Rory disappeared into the temple-house, Kao Chih led the Earthsphere agent over to one of the cooking fires and was handing him a beaker of broth when a familiar squat, long-armed figure approached with a rolling gait.

'Ah, I see that the China-human has returned, along with another mouth to feed. Why do newcomers never bring food with them?'

Yash stood before him, still dressed in the heavy fabricweave jerkin, sprouting innumerable pockets, that the Voth had been wearing when Kao Chih and the mech Drazuma-Ha first came aboard his ship, the *Viganli*. Drazuma-Ha had paid for its duplicity and vicious betrayal, and the *Viganli* had burned up on re-entry on the other side of Darien, but the Voth pilot remained indomitably abrasive.

'So, Honourable Yash, was your journey into the mountains with Chel a success?'

'A great success, Human Kao Chih, a triumph. Of course, Chel swore me to utter secrecy so, naturally, I'll tell you everything I know!' The Voth gave a low chuckle. 'Well, I don't know everything that happened but even if I was going to tell you what I do know, I'd first like you to tell me about your new friend.'

'You anticipate my intentions – Honourable Yash, this is Baltazar Silveira,' Kao Chih began, then paused as he considered that Greg might not want Silveira's identity revealed to an inveterate gossiper like the Voth. But before he could continue with some made-up story, Silveira spoke.

'A pleasure to meet you, sir,' he said to the Voth. 'You would be the captain of the cloud-harvester *Viganli*, I believe.'

'Former captain, former ship,' Yash said with a sour glance at Kao Chih. 'And you?'

'I captain a small vessel with exceptional capabilities,' Silveira added. 'And I too have had my share of excitement and danger. Tell me, have you ever had occasion to visit the great city Agmedra'a?'

'That huge satellite orbiting V'Hrant, the Roug planet?' The Voth nodded. 'I've docked there once or twice. Why?'

'I have interests there,' the man said. 'As does Earthsphere Intelligence.'

The Voth's eyebrows went up, and Kao Chih wondered if Silveira was wise to reveal such information to Yash.

'For now, I would appreciate your discretion,' Silveira went on. 'And your attention, you too, Kao Chih. I need help from both of you.'

Kao Chih exchanged a puzzled look with Yash. 'Both of us, Mr Silveira?'

'Both of you know Agmedra'a, and thus I have a proposition that may interest you.'

Kao Chih wondered why the agent had waited till now to make this approach, but as he heard the man's plan and its details he felt a rush of determination and hope.

GREG

From the Uvovo temple-house entrance, the main corridor led through a system of passages dug from the valley side many centuries ago. Wall supports were carved in the form of tree trunks and candles burned in small niches set at waist height. The air was cold and smelled faintly of a leafy odour. Greg slowed his stride and looked at Rory.

'How am I doing?'

'No' bad, from what I saw,' the wiry Scot said. 'How was it during yer trip?'

'Nerve-racking,' Greg said, briefly sketching the highlights of the ambush, Kao Chih's capture and escape, and his own flight through the forest by night. 'Most of the time I just feel that I'm no' cut out for this leader-of-men bluffing, and then we'll be faced with a situation that has to be dealt with and when I ask folk to do this or that they accept it and do it!'

'Aye, but when ye were running the dig site on Giant's Shoulder, were ye not giving out orders all the time?'

Greg gave an ambivalent nod. 'But that was different – we were all colleagues and I wasn't really in charge, more like first among equals.' He sighed. 'I wish Uncle Theo was here – wish there was some way of getting through to Nivyesta.'

'Och, yer doing fine,' said Rory. 'You don't need me tae tell ye how to deal wi' the Listeners and the refugees, and the Major might not have your patience . . .'

Shadows flickered around the niche lamps, casting worn carvings of foliage into high relief. At the end of the corridor they came to a low-roofed chamber with a triangular table and three large pillars intricately worked to resemble trees with stylised branches splayed out across the ceiling. Lanterns hung above, as if from twigs and vines. Four Listeners were sitting there already, gaunt figures garbed in thigh-length robes, their narrow, vaguely misshapen features dim within soft cowls. One was Weynl, recognisable by the silvery grey in his fuzzy face hair. Then, as Greg and Rory were taking their own seats a burly, blond man in a red outdoor coat arrived and gave a wordless nod. This was Lars Hansen, spokesman for the Human refugees, and clearly there on his own.

'Lars, I thought that the newcomers were sending a representative.'

'I've talked it over with them, Greg, and I'll be speaking for them . . .'

'No, that you will not!' said a female voice.

Into the chamber strode a tall woman in a heavy work jacket. Not quite middle-aged, she had an athletic physique and her expression was dark and angry.

'I explained . . .' Hansen began but she raised a hand and addressed Greg.

'Mr Cameron, I am Valeriya Sidorov. My apologies for this intrusion but I insist that our voices are to be heard! All of us have suffered the attacks and the hardship, so we came to your roof seeking food and shelter . . .'

'And I explained to her, Greg, that we have limited supplies,' said Hansen.

'Please, Mr Cameron,' Sidorov went on. 'We have children and elders and wounded – please do not send us away.'

'No one,' Greg said, looking sharply at Hansen, 'no one is going to be sent away to fend for themselves. However, you should be made aware that we shall soon be moving out of here because Tayowal is no longer safe.'

Hansen and the woman Sidorov looked as started as Weynl and his fellow Listeners, while Rory smiled.

'Why is this, friend Gregory?' said Weynl.

'You know why we have all these new arrivals,' he said. 'Most of the sizeable camps and settlements north, south and east of the Kentigerns were attacked and destroyed by the Brolturans yesterday. Aye, there were no attacks here but that doesna mean that Tayowal is safe. In fact, this valley is almost indefensible against the kind of hurt that the Brolts can bring down on us.'

'So what are we to do?' Weynl said. 'How can we protect so many?'

'I was hoping that *you* could come up with some answers, Listener. I know teams of Chel's Artificers have been off exploring as far west as the Tirnanog Plains, and south to the Ymir Mountains – is there a useable refuge or even refuges within three or four days' walk?'

Weynl shook his sunken-eyed, cadaverous head. 'Nothing of a suitable size. I am sorry. There are some large cave sanctuaries in the mountains you call the Ymirs but it would mean a journey of perhaps twenty days on foot . . .'

The Listener trailed off as another Uvovo entered and it took Greg a moment to realise that it was Chel. Once a scholar, now a Seer, his friend still had that air of centred balance, despite the strain and fatigue that sometimes showed in his face. Now, his eyes were bright, his expression as cheerful as it used to be before all this began.

'Welcome, Seer Cheluvahar,' said Weynl. 'You may perceive that we are faced with a predicament.'

'Yes, Listener. I've met some of the newcomers and heard a few of their stories, which is why I am late. But I think I have a solution.'

'Did you find something in the mountains, Chel?' Greg said. 'Caves or tunnels, almost anything would be worth considering.'

'Better than caves, my friend, or tunnels.'

Listener Weynl leaned forward, spidery, knuckly hands splayed on the plain tabletop.

'Was it Uok-Hakaur?' he said.

Chel nodded and smiled, deepening the creases at the corners of his normal eyes.

'Is it a temple of some kind?' Greg said.

'An ancient fortification, Gregory, hewed into the heart of a mountain. Uok-Hakaur was constructed in advance of the assaults of the Dreamless and their machine hordes, and it was the last bastion to fall when Umara burned and Segrana-That-Was retreated.'

'Where was the entrance?' Weynl said. 'Above or below?'

'Above, high up on the slopes of Hejo, which Humans call Tusk Mountain.'

'Hejo,' muttered Weynl. 'The heights of that one are a labyrinth of shattered crags and treacherous ledges.'

'Yet the path is safe, although it winds and twists like an old root.'

'Does it have room for everyone in Tayowal?' Greg said.

'It does, Gregory, with room to spare. There are several cave-ins to be cleared, and some walls and ceilings to be repaired, but otherwise Uok-Hakaur is safe and secure.'

'Sounds ideal,' Greg said, curious at the way Chel was regarding him with an unwavering gaze. 'We should tell our people to be ready to move tomorrow morning, if you've no objections, Listener Weynl.'

'Uok-Hakaur was built to be a citadel against the creatures of Unmaker,' the Listener said. 'It is fitting that it becomes our new refuge.'

Greg nodded and turned to Hansen and the woman Valeriya, both of whom looked relieved.

'There it is – we have a new home so please, go and pass on the good news. There will be a lot of packing and preparation to be carried out, and point out that we'll need volunteers to carry packs of provisions on a tough climb into the mountains.'

Hansen looked sheepish as he and Valeriya thanked everyone before leaving. Once they were gone, Greg gave Chel an amused glance.

'Is there something else you have to share? Something you couldn't say in front of my fellow Humans?'

'I felt that they might find it upsetting,' the Uvovo said.

'Aw, right!' Rory snapped, half-rising from the table. 'Well, if it's upsettin', I can just step outside if ye want . . .'

Greg put a hand on his shoulder and pushed him back into his seat.

'Just cool yer head a minute.'

Chel was bemused. 'I don't object to Humans hearing what I have to say – I only wished to tell you first so that you can decide how best to explain it.'

Rory's flare of anger melted away. 'Ah right, fair enough. So, what's the story?'

They listened as Chel spoke of a glowing form that caused a cave-in and that he had followed down into the mountain, to the citadel's lower levels, how he repulsed its attack and how he encountered the warpwell Sentinel in a chamber with four stone platforms. Then he related the Sentinel's revelation that the glowing entity could be the vestigial echo of the last Keeper of Segrana.

Weynl was astounded.

'The Keeper! The tales say that he died, yet the Sentinel says otherwise . . . could it be true, Cheluvahar? Did you sense anything from it?'

'The ghost creature seemed to have a Uvovo-like manner, yet its mind was fractured and far reduced.'

'Is it dangerous, though? That's the question,' said Greg. 'Is it safe to take all these people to your citadel, if it's haunted?'

'The Sentinel was insistent that we bring all the refugees to Uok-Hakaur,' Chel said. 'It also said that the Keeper could be controlled or eliminated if it proved to be more than a nuisance.'

'We must speak with it,' Weynl said. 'Consider what we might learn.'

'I am sure that we can rely on the Sentinel to help us deal with it,' said Chel.

'I certainly hope so,' said Greg. 'In the meantime, let me tell you what happened at Belskirnir,' and he gave a brief account of the interrupted journey and the unexpected encounter with Alexandr Vashutkin in person. Pausing to ask Rory to bring in Kao Chih and Silveira, he summarised Vashutkin's need for a new stronghold since Trond was, essentially, kicking him out, and how Greg recommended taking over the old Uvovo cave complex in the Utgard Barricades, the northern cliffs. When Chel then said that there was enough room at Uok-Hakaur to accommodate Vashutkin's men too, Greg felt a stab of discomfort mingled with guilt.

'Well . . . strategically speaking, it makes more sense to have several resistance groups in different locations . . . ye know, rather than bring them all together in one big target . . .'

Aye, and end up with me and Vashutkin at each other's throats. Not a good idea. But a small voice inside wondered if it was more to do with his lack of experience possibly leading to Vashutkin becoming the de facto leader.

Rory returned with Kao Chih and Baltazar Silveira and one other, Yash the vaguely simian Voth pilot. Greg found the Voth overly abrasive and faintly untrustworthy yet Kao Chih had vouched strongly for him so Greg decided to admit him to such discussions. Yash was walking beside Kao Chih, chortling at something as Greg made the introductions, ending with Silveira.

'This gentleman was Vashutkin's surprise,' he said. 'And now I get to pass it on. My friends, Mr B. Silveira is an agent for

Earthsphere Intelligence and he is here in secret to advise and assist us against the thugs who are trying to steal our planet from under us!'

Astonishment shone from the faces around the table, none more so than Rory's.

'That true, Mr Silveira? Does that mean Earth's on our side now?' He grabbed Silveira's hand and shook it vigorously for a moment, then paused, frowning slightly. 'So there's just the one of ye, then?'

Silveira was composed, smiling slightly. 'Just me. Please understand, my presence here on Darien is very high-risk. If knowledge of it reached Hegemony ears, it would cause a grave diplomatic incident and leave the Darien colony even more isolated than it is already. And although it is part of my mission to offer advice I have to tell you that I have had to alter my plans in the light of what I have learned about Pyre. Very shortly Kao Chih and I will be leaving for the Roug system and from there we intend to go to Pyre.'

'That's a long way away,' Greg said, trying to hide his disappointment. 'Is this so that you can gather more data?'

'Precisely so, Mr Cameron. From the moment I met Kao Chih and discovered his origins I knew I would have to modify my mission parameters. You see, Earthsphere Overcouncil is dominated by the Humanifold, which consists of representatives from Earth and the Integrated Colonies. The Pan-Asials, which include the Chinese Confederacy, form the largest single bloc within it, which naturally gives them considerable influence on a wide range of policies. So when they find out that a lost Human colony of Sino origins has been brutally oppressed by a Hegemony monoclan, there will be an uproar that could fundamentally shift attitudes towards the Sendrukan Hegemony and towards Darien.'

Greg frowned. 'Will it get the Brolturans out of our skies?'

'The Hegemony will not want to risk damaging their alliance with Earthsphere, not while the latest Protection Wave operations are ongoing in the Yamanon Domain. They'll be certain to make concessions by telling the Brolturans to pull out.'

'Unless they don't,' said Rory. 'They might no', they might turn round and say tae Earth, "Aye, so what are ye gonna dae about it?"'

Silveira gave a smiling shrug. 'A possibility, but they have invested a great deal over many years in maintaining the alliance with Earthsphere and they will not put that in jeopardy.'

Greg recalled some of the incredible things he had learned about the warpwell and its abilities – if the Hegemony was aware of them too, would they really relinquish their hold on Darien? Unconvinced by Silveira's argument, Greg began to wonder if Rory was actually closer to the truth.

All of which was incidental since the agent had clearly made up his mind.

'So how will you get to your ship?' he said. 'Is it hidden nearby?'

'It's already on its way here,' Silveira said. 'It is very smart – with camouflage and low-level suspensor gliding it can avoid detection by Brolturan technology. It should be here in a few hours.'

'Good,' said the Voth pilot, Yash. 'Can't wait to get back to civilisation.'

Greg stared at the Voth for a moment, then at Silveira. 'You're taking Yash as well?'

'My good friend Captain Yash is well acquainted with the protocols and customs of the clientele zones of the Roug orbital Agmedra'a, while Kao Chih's familiarity is restricted to the underdocks. With their help, I should be able to establish a useful dialogue with the Roug before moving on to Pyre.'

'And I intend to establish a useful relationship with those credit lines that Gorol9 gave me,' said Yash hungrily. 'Doesn't really compensate for the loss of the *Viganli* but maybe I'll find something else at Agmedra'a.'

'Yes, this mech Gorol9 sounds like an interesting entity,' said Silveira. 'Is it in the vicinity? Kao Chih and Yash said that it represents another machine called the Construct. I would very much like to ask it several questions.'

Greg looked at Rory, who shrugged. 'I saw him just before ye all arrived but no' since.'

'If he turns up, I'll be sure to pass on your request,' Greg told the Earthsphere agent. 'Can't guarantee that he'll speak with you, though.'

'Understood,' said Silveira, turning to bow to Chel and the Listeners. 'It saddens me to leave without the chance to converse with you. Please accept my thanks for your hospitality and for being a friend to my fellow Humans.'

The meeting ended with Yash leading Kao Chih and Silveira away to find a sleeping place while Greg told Rory to wake him in time to see off the agent and his passengers. Four hours later, after being roughly shaken out of what felt like a five-minute drowse, he went with Rory out to a tree-shaded ravine beyond Tayowal's southern entrance. Dawn's first pale radiance was filtering down through the web of branches as they came to a broad stretch where Silveira, Kao Chih and Yash sat on boulders near a trickling stream. Nods and words of greeting were exchanged.

'How long till your ship gets here?' Greg said.

Silveira smiled. 'It's just arriving,' he said, standing to look up.

In the leafy canopy above a mass of greenery rustled and shifted, the leaves rippling and taking on a bulbous, curved form whose surface changed as Greg watched, foliage distorting, melting through glassiness to a metallic grey with a faint diamond tile pattern. As it descended it reminded Greg of an enclosed zeplin gondola but with a wide aft section and a rounded stern bearing more than a dozen oval blisters. It stopped a few feet from the ground, hanging there in complete silence as a hatch slid open in its flank and some steps unfolded. Then an aperture opened next to the hatch and a segmented tentacle extended to give Silveira a plastic wallet full of documents.

'Again, Mr Cameron, my apologies for this early departure,' he said. 'I had my ship prepare this for you, a compendium of tactics for use against the tektor and other Brolturan ploys. Farewell.'

Greg accepted the wallet then shook hands with Kao Chih. 'We've had some adventures together, my friend. Next time we meet, your folk will be coming to stay and we'll learn each other's dances and songs, eh?'

'A fine idea, Gregory. I shall work hard for it.'

Greg then turned to the Voth and gave him a single, stiff shake of his long-fingered, rough-callused hand.

'Watch out for them Sendrukans, Human – the good ones are bad and the bad ones are the worst of the worst.'

The three trooped into Silveira's craft, which sealed itself and rose smoothly into the air. It quivered, turned glassy and reflective, and suddenly wasn't there any more. Smiling, Greg studied the tree cover overhead and spotted where the branches shifted aside for a moment before whipping back into place.

'Nice wee ship, chief,' said Rory. 'Can I have one?'

'Aye, sure . . . oh wait, we don't have the garage space.'

'Och, that's right . . . and I don't have a licence either.'

'And just think of the parking tickets.'

Chuckling, they headed back along the ravine to Tayowal, then paused on seeing the droid Gorol9 coming the other way.

'You missed an interesting encounter,' Greg said. 'We had a visit from an Earthsphere intelligence agent, and he wanted to meet you.'

'I did not wish to meet him.'

On spindly metal legs, the droid stalked across the rocks a short distance then stopped and lowered its armoured midsection into the rest position. Gorol9 had been relying on one of the Diehards to wheel him about in a cart until two weeks ago when a tech engineer called Bukalin turned up, having fled the oppressions in Hammergard. With his personal tools, Bakulin had repaired the damage that the Construct droid had suffered during the clash with the Legion mech Drazuma-Ha.

'Care to tell me why?' Greg said.

The droid angled one of its asymmetrical lens clusters in his direction.

'He may not be who he claims to be.'

Greg exchanged a look with Rory. 'And you were careful to avoid him, I see, so there must be a reason.'

'The man has a subspace positional tracker with codemasked signal patterns, a very sophisticated device – it allows Silveira and his ship to know where the other is with practically no chance of detection. However, both the device and that ship are not the kind of equipment normally issued to Earthsphere intelligence operatives.'

'His superiors might not see this as a normal crisis,' Greg said. 'What makes you so sure?'

'The Construct's Garden of the Machines may be down in the lower tiers of hyperspace but our information on data-harvesting organisations like Earthsphere Intelligence is excellent. This Silveira could be an operative but more likely for another agency, perhaps even a non-Human one.'

Greg glared at the droid. 'So why didn't ye come to me with these suspicions earlier, like last night when it would've been useful?'

'Your anxiety about your friend's safety is misplaced . . .'

'Oh, ye think so, do ye?'

'Yes – I am certain that this Silveira will carry out the mission as he described it and deliver your colleagues safely to the Roug orbital. He may then give a short but inspiring speech promising all manner of dazzling rescues and liberations before departing for his home territory.'

Greg breathed deeply. The droid's condescending tone wasn't helping.

'Forgive me, Gorol9, but I don't share your confidence in the intentions of someone now possibly shown to be untrustworthy.'

'I merely state likelihoods,' the droid said. 'Communication with the Roug themselves would prove useful in determining Silveira's motives and safeguarding your colleagues' safety.'

'Right ye are,' Rory said acidly. 'We'll just call 'em up on the old comm and tell them to look out for a shifty Human bugger . . .'

But the Construct droid was oblivious to sledgehammer wit.

'In his account of the investigation of the mountain stronghold, the Uvovo Cheluvahar spoke of his encounter with the Sentinel of the warpwell,' Gorol9 said. 'If I can speak to the Sentinel I can establish whether or not it still has lines of communication with the High Index of the Roug. Once, they were allies of those you call the Forerunners, back when their civilisation was young, vigorous and widespread.'

The droid then raised its midsection and without another word retraced its steps. Greg watched it go, scratching his ear.

'Every time I have a chat with an offworlder I end up with another piece of the puzzle,' he said. 'But they still don't fit, and the puzzle gets bigger and . . .'

'More puzzlin', aye,' said Rory, nodding sagely.

Greg gave him a nonplussed look then laughed.

'C'mon, let's get back – folk'll be waking up so it's up tae us to choose some lucky volunteer bearers.'

Rory shrugged. 'And I was getting tae be so popular, as well!'

10

ROBERT

Ship debris emerging from the planetoid shadow glittered like twisted golden fragments in the sun's dull brassy light. A cloud of shining wreckage that drifted around a battered, ruptured hulk, the lifeless carcass of a big liner-scale vessel.

'No lifeform readings,' said Rosa. 'No comms traffic, no beacons, no energy sources.' She shrugged. 'No surprise, really – it's been here a long time.'

'I don't think I've seen that kind of ship before,' Robert said. 'It's not like the others.'

During their stealthy evasion of the Legion Knight, dashing from planetoid to planetoid, they had discovered another five similar eviscerated wrecks. Those had all been quite small and of exotic, almost baroque design, and all were identified by the *Plausible Response* as rudimentary tierships from this or that Tier civilisation. This vessel, however, was huge in comparison, with a wide hull narrowing to a bulbous forward section. There were no hull markings of any kind to be seen, even with the detailed surface scan. But the visible damage betrayed its attacker as the Legion Knight, the ripped-open hull sections, the smashed drive assemblies, the jagged, gaping fissures where more debris floated.

'It's a Bargalil ship,' Rosa said. 'From the Indroma Plexus era, but how could it be this far down in hyperspace? Could have been a research vessel, perhaps . . .'

'Contact at 48.95K,' the *Plausible Response* said abruptly.

'Legion Knight is emerging from occlusion, does not seem to have detected us yet.'

'Take us into the debris cloud on slow thrust,' Rosa said. 'See if we can slip behind the wreck.'

They glided forward, force shields configured to dampen impacts rather than create collision rebounds which might show up on a sensor sweep. The tactic seemed to work. The monitor widescreen displayed several exterior shots at various magnitudes; one subframe showed the Legion Knight's positional data overlaid on an enhanced visual of the wreckage they were slipping through, which was obscuring everything beyond. The enemy had entered the planetoid's shadow and the *Plausible Response* was relying on passive sensors to track it, both hull-mounted and free-floating. From the process model, it appeared that the Legion Knight's course through the surrounding cluster of worldlets would allow it to maximise the sweep area of its scanners. Robert tried not to hold his breath as they approached the big derelict, swung behind it and halted, shielded fully at last from detection.

Rosa and the Ship were discussing the channelling of data from some of the drift probes while Robert gazed up at the screen, surveying various views of the Bargalil hulk. One external cam followed a series of gashes along the hull to where a large trench had been cut into the ship – looking into it Robert could see the ragged edges of bulkheads and decks, severed pipes, trailing cables and lines, all tangled up with twisted spars and protruding razor-sharp blades of ruptured metal. Motionless agglomerations of flotsam and jetsam hung in the shattered gap, objects of unfamiliar design apart from what looked like garments, ripped and torn but large enough to fit the bulky, hexapedal Bargalil. Then a chill went through him as one close-up frame revealed that many of the garments were vacsuits and in the next moment a grim realisation stole over him.

'Where are the bodies?' he said. 'I don't see any.'

There was a moment of silence on the bridge before Rosa spoke.

'It seems likely that they've been harvested, Daddy.'

He frowned. 'You mean by the Legion creature?'

'The knights of the Legion of Avatars are cyborged entities,' she said. 'A flesh and blood brain sits at the core of that mechanised shell, from which a web of nerve tissue spreads through the systems and subassemblies. Essentially a bioelectrical control matrix augmented by tailored neural clusters . . .' She paused, smiled a little. 'Sorry, Daddy – what I'm saying is that any corpses would have been converted into some kind of nutrient, plus whatever other organic material it looted.'

'And those other ships?' he said.

'We never took the time to get a close look but it's highly probable that they met the same fate.'

Robert stared at the scenes of ancient destruction on the widescreen and shook his head. It was horrible and grotesque and thoroughly in common with most of what he had witnessed thus far down here in the depths of hyperspace. But then the base reality of normal space held just as much grotesquerie and wholesale torment along with the advantage that one could avoid the pain and the horror by flying off into the vastness of space, losing oneself in an ocean of stars.

'Our adversary has altered course, heading away to the next planetoid,' said the Ship.

Rosa grinned at Robert. 'If we can retrace our own course, we can find out if that drone has recovered Reski yet.'

During the evasions and retreat after the Legion Knight's earlier ambush, they had dropped a short-range smart-probe tasked with locating the droid Reski Emantes. Once that was accomplished it was to tow the droid off into the shadow of a nearby planetoid and wait for retrieval.

But for now they would have to wait for the Legion Knight to slip behind one of the blank-faced worldlets before emerging from their hiding place. The Ship's estimate was that this would take an hour so Robert retired to his cabin to lie down and rest in the darkness. Sleep was out of the question yet his thoughts were haunted by visions of wrecked ships and slashed and torn vacuum suits. Then there were human forms drifting towards him, dead forms, one with his own face, the other with Rosa's, both staring emptily, blankly . . .

He recoiled from the image, eyes snapping open to the dimmed room where a few standby LEDs glowed, amber and violet motes floating in the dark. He touched the edge of his bedside table and pale grey numerics lit up in its surface. Less than ten minutes left. Had he fallen asleep after all?

Back up on the bridge, Rosa was still at her station, tirelessly alert.

'Just a few minutes, Daddy, then we can be on our way.'

'How far are we from those coordinates we got from Sunflow Oscillant?' he said.

'Five or six hours at maximum thrust,' she said. 'And until a short while ago it looked as if we and our pursuer were alone here, then we picked up a contact out near that location, right on the edge of our sensor range . . .' She paused to look at the widescreen as the Indroma wreck slid gradually away and the *Plausible Response* moved out of the debris cloud. 'Not long now.'

Robert peered at a subframe displaying the thus far meagre data on the distant contact. 'Is that who we're supposed to be meeting? Why choose this place?'

'It could be an elaborate trap,' Rosa said. 'The Bargalil mystic may have been an unwitting dupe for whoever set this up.'

'Or he was in on it . . .'

'Contact!' said the Ship. 'Legion Knight has reappeared from behind the planetoid . . . we've been spotted – it's accelerating on an intercept vector . . .'

'Ramp up our drives,' Rosa said. 'Let's remind him who has the longer legs.'

For a long moment there was only a tense silence.

'Legion Knight is displaying a far steeper acceleration profile than before. Intercept in 7.3 minutes.'

'Align your projector battery and target any sensor or combat assemblies visible on its hull,' Rosa said.

'Done,' said the *Plausible Response*. 'Five hits, no primary or secondary damage registering, heat signatures only.'

On the widescreen, one subframe showed a model of the crab-like cyborg craft and five red glowing patches on its forward carapace. Other insets showed their course around the nearby planetoid and that of their pursuer.

'Missile launched,' the Ship said. 'Same as before, an EMP-web device on random micro-evasive trajectory. Interception in 5.1 minutes.'

'I'm starting to get irritated by this antique thug,' Rosa said. 'Split targeting. Set course for that next planetoid – I want to use the countergravity to effect a sharp trajectory change towards the rendezvous coordinates.'

'Understood.'

Listening closely, Robert began to understand seconds later and stared up at the widescreen. On the main frame, the nearby planetoid fell away as the *Plausible Response* turned in the direction of the next, whose diminutive diameter made it a moonlet, a perfectly featureless coppery orb. Then in another frame, a racing diamond point flared suddenly.

'Missile has been destroyed,' the Ship said.

'Good shooting!' Robert said.

'Legion Knight is however accelerating – intercept now in 3.87 minutes.'

'Where is it getting all that extra power?' Rosa muttered.

'Second missile launched – intercept in 1.92 minutes.'

'Right, I'm cutting back on sensor function,' Rosa said in clipped tones. 'Additional process capacity now available for target systems.'

The situation was becoming dire, doom was almost at hand, yet the bridge was a comfortable, air-conditioned centre of tranquillity. Rosa amazed him with her capability and confident handling of the vessel's controls, as well as her calmness under fire. She might be an AI amalgam of the original Rosa's characteristics and her body might be a synthetic simulation, but he couldn't help feeling a father's pride. When he wasn't caught up in the fear of oncoming annihilation.

'Time till countergravity maneouvre, 2.05 minutes,' said the Ship. 'Suspensors ready . . . missile destroyed! . . .'

Thank God, Robert thought, recalling Reski Emantes's demise.

'Second contact! – port quarter, unknown vessel closing fast on collision course . . . time to impact, thirty-eight seconds.'

Fear gripped his chest as he stared up at the widescreen, looking wildly for an exterior view of the second attacker.

'Engage aft attitude thrusters,' Rosa said. 'Bring the stern round to starboard.'

'Understood.'

'What is that new ship?' Robert said. 'Another Legion cyborg?'

Rosa shook her head. 'It's the same one, Daddy, the real one! We've been running from some kind of pursuit drone projecting a holoshell image . . .' She stopped and glared at the widescreen. 'There it is! Daddy, get ready . . .'

On one of the subframes, against a view of the moonlet's surface rushing past, the intervening space rippled and a large dark shape coalesced out of nothing. Robert glimpsed armoured limbs tipped with grabs and spines for just a moment before the collision knocked him out of his chair.

'Four hull breaches on my underside,' said the Ship. 'I am sealing off all relevant compartments and rerouting networks and fluidics. Ready to attempt . . .' Suddenly symbols lit up on Rosa's console, neon-bright in the dimmed bridge, and a couple of small subframes opened on the widescreen.

'Two more hull breaches,' said the *Plausible Response*. 'One of my main suspensors is out. I'm afraid that a ground swoop is now too risky – without fine gravitic control we would become another gutted wreck.'

'What about your beam weapons?' Rosa said.

'I disabled the underhull array to avoid it being used against us, while my upper arrays have been pounding the enemy's visible sections relentlessly. Some stretches of the Knight's carapace are already melting or ablating off but with no noticeable affect on its close-quarters assault. In less than ten minutes most of my interior will be ruptured and open to hard vacuum.'

Rosa nodded. 'Our options have suddenly become limited. What munitions do you have?'

'Twenty-five blast and forty shaped, in various grades.'

'Good, and how many probes are left?'

'One medium-range, six short-range.'

Rosa looked thoughtful then smiled at Robert. 'We'll be all right, Daddy. You just wait here while I go and check on the probes, get them loaded up.'

'Okay,' he said, trying to appear relaxed. 'I'll just keep an eye on our unwelcome visitor.'

He watched her hurry from the bridge then turned back to the widescreen with its spread of exterior views. All showed the immense bulk of the cyborg Knight clinging to the underside of the *Plausible Response*, its clawed arms tearing off layers of hull material or instrument housings. Minutes passed, and the number of glowing alerts on the main console grew as the damage worsened. Suddenly Robert wondered what was keeping Rosa and was about to ask the Ship when a diminutive figure in dark body armour edged into view on the widescreen. Close-ups showed it to be Rosa, wearing a small transparent mask on the lower half of her face but otherwise lacking a vacuum suit.

On the screen her lips moved, and her voice emanated from the console comm unit with perfect clarity.

'Daddy, I'm fine – synthetic body, remember? No need to breathe, no respiratory system, no blood pressure. What I'm about to attempt will wipe my cores, whatever the outcome . . .'

'Rosa!' Robert cried out. 'Dear God, I cannot lose you for a second time!'

'You can only lose me once, Daddy,' she said.

Then she waved, turned and leaped away from the ship's hull straight towards the Legion Knight's lower carapace. One of the secondary armoured limbs, an articulated arm tipped with bladed shears, swung out and lunged at her. Mini-thrusters on her shoulders and elbows flared. She dodged the blow and darted over to the nearest shoulder mounting of one of the main jointed arms, whose serrated pincers were just then tearing into the *Plausible Response*'s underside,

Standing at the console, Robert was transfixed by horror, unable to look away. They were well clear of the moonlet now and racing across vacant space towards another part of the planetoid ring. The brassy light from the sun lit everything up in harsh detail.

Rosa just had time to take the circular munition from a waist pouch and slap it onto the shoulder mounting before a segmented tentacle swept round and slammed into her. But she had tethered herself to a hardpoint on the under-carapace so that instead of flying away she swung round in a curve to land on her feet. Then grabbing handholds, she scrambled across the uneven underside of the Legion Knight, getting a good distance away before triggering the munition.

Light flashed amid the silent explosion. Metal fragments burst outwards and the severed arm arced away, now attached only to its victim. At the same time, the *Plausible Response* initiated a crash deceleration – impetus threw the Legion Knight up from its half-concealed position, swinging on the arms that still clung on to the Construct ship's vitals. The segmented tentacle was reaching out to that torn, gouged hull, biting, grappling for a sturdy purchase . . .

But Robert was watching Rosa crawl hand over hand towards the middle of the lower carapace. Then, without warning, jagged webs of energy erupted from her form, leaping and spreading out in all directions. For an instant the attacker's various limbs stopped in mid-motion . . . then a convulsion seized them, joints spasmed, drill clusters and power grabs juddered and came away from the *Plausible Response*'s hull. The ship was free of that deadly clasp.

Slouched in the main pilot's couch, Robert stared at the images on the screen. The Ship's voice came from somewhere nearby, explaining that newer synthetic bodies like Rosa's were designed to expend all integral power sources in an overload burst as a last resort. He heard the words but they seemed to float through him and away – all his awareness was frozen, focused on the widescreen where his daughter had died before his eyes.

Eventually the energy discharge faded to nothing and, soon after, the Ship announced that neither the Knight nor Rosa was giving off lifesigns. Numb, exhausted, he got to his feet and stumbled off to his cabin, vaguely aware of the *Plausible Response* telling him something about Reski Emantes and the rendezvous. He lay down in the darkness, grief like a cold hand around his heart, and was unable to sleep as the last words they exchanged went round and round in his mind.

At some point he heard his cabin door open but did not stir.

'Good to see you taking it so well.'

The voice belonged to Reski Emantes.

'Thank you,' he muttered into the pillow. 'Now please leave.'

'Sorry, but your superior diplomatic skills are required. We have reached the rendezvous and are currently parked alongside an impressively shiny vessel whose occupant, a representative of the Godhead, is awaiting your attendance.'

He lifted his head to glare at the droid.

'I've just watched my daughter die! – I'm in no fit state to undertake negotiations.'

'That would certainly be a tragic and just cause for snivelling and moping around – if it was true.'

'What?' Robert said, stung to anger.

'That's wasn't your daughter that perished out there,' the droid said. 'It was a spectrum-matched AI modelled on the holosim data that you brought with you from Darien.'

Then Rosa's last words came back to him – *You can only lose me once* – and he began to understand. Sitting on the edge of the bed, he rested his head in his hands, fingers covering his eyes. He sighed a long sigh.

'She's data,' he said.

'At last it dawns – exactly. In the moments before the Rosa AI sacrificed herself, the Ship made a recording of her mindmap state. When the Construct sends another, she can sync it with her own data matrix and she'll be updated with everything till that

point at least. But it will not be your daughter. I hope you understand that now.'

Understanding, he thought, getting to his feet. *Understanding
is not the same as feeling.*

'How will the Construct know what has happened?'

'The Ship has already sent an encrypted report and when we
have some idea of what the Godhead's mouthpiece is offering,
and where we're off to next, we'll send an update before making
the next tier jump. Of course, that depends on you successfully
concluding negotiations for permission to petition the Godhead in
person, as only an organic diplomat can do. Are you up to it?'

In his mind he could see the way Rosa commanded the Ship,
the way she smiled, the way she fought, and the way she died. He
breathed in deeply.

'I am.'

He sonic-showered, drank a sweet-tasting nutridrink, then
donned the suit that the Ship had produced for him. It was a pre-
dominantly black affair of austerely formal cut, with dark blue
trim and an odd symbol, a quartered circle containing a smaller
off-centre circle, impressed on his chest pocket in pale blue.
Regarding himself in a full-length mirror, he had to admit that it
made him look good, in a stone-cold, gunslinger diplomat way. A
few minutes later he was waiting before the main airlock, Reski
Emantes at his side, while an umbilical from the alien vessel
adjusted and adapted to the *Plausible Response*'s exterior.

'So how did you manage to survive that EMP missile?' he said.
'Did the Ship have a recording of you as well?'

The droid's sideways isosceles form turned his way slightly.
'Crash-shunted into a shielded backup core, a little advantage
not open to you organics.' The droid chuckled. 'Or those Legion
relics.'

A chime sounded in the low, dimpled ceiling and the inner lock
doors parted, followed by the outer ones. A shiny roseate walkway led along the oval umbilical, its opaque grey material
punctuated by green strengthening ribs. Through it Robert could
just make out the Godhead vessel's flattened-oval lines. Together

they proceeded along its gently down-curved length to a square hatch that parted diagonally. Before they could continue, tiny spotbeams winked on and swung round to converge on the floating droid. An odd liquid voice came from the dark, translucent passage beyond.

'Only organic emissaries are permitted – the mechanical must return.'

'I am Emissary Horst's escort,' Reski began.

'There can be no exceptions,' said the voice. 'Safety is assured aboard this vessel. Escorts are not required.'

'And of course, you are to be trusted in this regard.'

'We insist on it.'

The droid turned towards Robert. 'Looks like you're on your own. Watch out for the hospitality drinks.' Then it smoothly turned end over end and without another word floated back the way they had come.

'Enter, Emissary Horst.'

Inside, the walls had fluted surfaces in shades of green that had a slick translucence with a hint of fluid and rippling membranes beneath. Perhaps the Godhead's vessel employed living tissue, he speculated. Perhaps the entire ship was a living creature – he had heard that such things existed in the starry expanses on the far side of the Indroma Solidarity.

'Follow the lights, Emissary – they will guide you.'

Three narrow passages branched off from this chamber but only one had small amber symbols pulsing on the soft textured floor. The passage colour changed to dark, shiny blue, the same as the large curved chamber he soon arrived in. Long ribs spread out from the ceiling and there were curious concave tiles underfoot. The chamber was oval and divided in two by a transparent wall beyond which a strange pale creature floated, as if in water. It had a squidlike, multi-tentacled lower torso yet the upper body was vaguely humanoid, a chest narrowing to a neck and a bulbous hairless head. Two large eyes stared from a mouthless face while several other eyes were dotted around the shoulders and upper chest. A pair of thin arms hung listlessly by its sides, each with a rudimentary hand. The skin looked waxy, soft and pale, and said little about the creature's bone structure.

'Welcome, Emissary Robert Horst,' said a smooth, calm female voice. 'You are aboard a postulate-craft of the Godhead, and I am the Intercessor.'

The pale creature's face grew a mouth as Robert approached and other details appeared or changed. Ears that emerged from the temples then migrated down to more familiar locations, a nose that pushed out of the centre of the face and went from conical to humanlike even before nostrils appeared, and arms that thickened while on the hands the stubby fingers divided and lengthened. It was as if this strange being was like a mask being moulded from within.

Robert maintained his composure as the transformation took place, while trying to grasp the sense and possible meanings of the term 'postulate-craft'. A postulate was an idea or proposal put forward without self-evident proof, like a *Gedankenexperiment*. So what did that say about the basis of this meeting?

And did this creature have anything to do with the Legion Knight's ambush?

'I am deeply honoured by your invitation, Intercessor,' he said. 'We would have arrived sooner had we not been attacked by a hostile vessel which we managed to overcome at some cost. I wonder . . . if you were at all aware of the attacker's presence here?'

To Robert's amazement, the Intercessor's form suddenly convulsed and distorted, its pale, soft skin rippling, swelling and parting as easily as if the body were made of something pliable, even gelatinous. The Intercessor divided into three forms identical to the original, and swam around each other for a moment before drawing closely together. Waxy flesh merged seamlessly and a new form coalesced, a blocky torso with a long, arched and eyeless head ending in a pointed beak. A deep grating voice came from the ceiling just above the transparent wall.

'The purposes of violent intruders hold no relevance for us. You have come a long way from the Prime Stratum, Emissary Horst – we are keen to hear the Construct's message.'

In other words, we do not discuss our motivations with lesser creatures, he thought as he gave a polite bow.

'Intercessor, I am here not just on behalf of the entity known as the Construct but also on behalf of certain fellow members of my species who are trapped between brutal powers that have no regard for anything other than their own aggrandisement.'

He went on to briefly sketch out the discovery of the warpwell on Darien, the involvement of the Hegemony and their Brolturan proxies, and the vulnerable situation of the Darien colonists and their Uvovo allies. He then laid out the Construct's position, its ancient alliance with the Forerunners, its contention that various unsolved massacres and destructions in the lower tiers were carried out by agents of the Legion of Avatars, and the belief that the Legion Knight that dispatched the earlier droid to Darien would try again and perhaps succeed. If the Legion of Avatars were to escape from their aeons-old prison, the consequences for the galaxy would be catastrophic and would percolate down through the tiers of hyperspace, a poison that would then spread to other galaxies.

'So I have come here at the Construct's behest to ask for help,' Robert said. 'The Construct proposes that the Godhead put pressure on the vestigial civilisations of the Deep Tracts to work together to combat aggression and ensure the confinement of questionable elements to the depths . . .'

At this, the Intercessor's form again melted, split into three and recombined into an odd spiderish thing whose lumpy back sprouted dozens of tentacles ending in mouths or eyes, straining towards Robert, pressing against the transparent wall.

'The Construct asks for much and assumes much.' This time it sounded like several voices speaking in unison. 'What part would the Construct play in this arrangement? What advantage would accrue to the Godhead?'

'With the Godhead's influence improving security across the Deep Tracts, the Construct can redirect some of its midlevel forces to the Prime Stratum, to the planet Darien to seal the warpwell permanently. The Legion of Avatars' last chance of escape will be gone for ever and the Godhead will never have to face them.'

The eye-and-mouth tentacles shrank back into the bulbous torso, which lengthened and divided into the three slender squid creatures. Two of them swam off to the side and began to spin and dance around each other, rising and falling in spirals. The third, now resembling a large anemone with a single eye amid a crown of waving tendrils, stared straight at Robert.

'Your message must be considered, Emissary Horst,' it said in a flat, slightly lethargic tone. 'Now we would know more about your origins.'

Robert frowned. 'Me or my species, Intercessor?'

'The untutored vulnerabilities of your species are clearly visible to our preceptors, like the empty overseer device in your head. Humans are adopting artificial intelligence implants in the belief that it will enhance their outlook and their skills, or even the measure of their pleasure, when in fact it is a system of control. Yet your implant device is inert – did you tire of its domination and deceit?'

Smiling, Robert recalled the companion he had once had, Harry, modelled on a character from *The Third Man*, a twentieth-century monochrome movie, and realised that he missed his wry wit and mock-cynicism.

'To be completely honest, Intercessor,' he said, 'I had a long and rewarding friendship with my AI companion, until I came to the Garden of the Machines where the Construct had it removed. I understand the reasons and the risks of the Hegemony learning too much, but I still regret his removal.'

Beyond the glassy wall, spots and bars on the trunk of the anemone-Intercessor began to glow in various colours.

'This is to be expected,' said the Intercessor, sounding more alert. 'The you of now bears the burden of decisions and consequences, which is why I would know the origins of the you of now.'

Robert's eyes widened as he absorbed the meaning of the query. *Decisions, consequences and burdens*, he thought, uneasily aware of where such lines of enquiry could lead.

'I may not be able to offer an objective estimation of my personal development, Intercessor, but I suppose I could mention that I have been a senior negotiator and diplomat, at least prior to my promotion to ambassador . . .' The Intercessor made no comment so he pressed on. 'I have been privy to many policy decisions and high-level mediations, bringing opposing parties to the negotiating table, finding common ground and ways to overcome grievances without violence . . .' *Except in the case of the Yamanon Domain where all those summits, stratarms surveys, and independent verifications turned out to be a fig leaf for a military action that was going to happen, whatever the Dol-Das regime said or did.*

The Intercessor drifted closer to the transparent barrier but otherwise remained silent. Robert sighed.

'I have to admit that not all my decisions have led to satisfactory outcomes – my wife would certainly attest to . . .'

'Your wife?' The Intercessor's form narrowed while its single large eye suddenly subdivided into six, all focused on Robert. 'Is this wife some kind of life-soul partner?'

He smiled sadly. 'Yes, that is so.'

'Do you have offspring?'

In his mind he saw Rosa's body lying face-down and motionless against the Legion Knight's underside. He kept his face composed.

'We had one, a daughter. She is no longer alive.'

The Intercessor's eye cluster subdivided again into more than a dozen, all regarding Robert with unwavering intensity.

'What was the manner of her death?' said the creature.

Relating the circumstances was never easy, no matter how many times he had done so, but he steeled himself to march through it once more. He tried to explain how she had been part of a political group opposed to the Yamanon invasion and how they attempted to blockade a combined Hegemony–Earthsphere battle fleet with a handful of unshielded smallcraft. 'But then the ship she was aboard was perceived as a threat by a Hegemony warship commander who opened fire, destroying the vessel . . .'

'What is the record of the Hegemony response to similar countervailing demonstrations?'

'Intolerant and brutal, sometimes resulting in fatalities.'

The Intercessor's eyes gleamed. 'So your daughter and her companions knew the risk when they willingly ventured forth into the warship's path.'

'I'm sure they did,' Robert said, frowning. 'But what does this have to do with . . . ?'

'So they were reconciled to their fate, consciously deciding to embrace the possible ending of their lives . . .'

'A moment please, Intercessor! None of them believed that they would be fired upon . . .'

'When hazards are clear, responsibility is total, awareness is inescapable . . .'

'This is not so,' Robert said, striving to stay polite. 'They believed that restraint would be exercised, that they were safe in a neutral port . . .'

As the exchange had progressed, the lesser sub-Intercessor had grown steadily more agitated, its long body contracting, the tendrils around its head shifting down the dumpy torso while the eyes separated and moved apart. By now, the torso was losing its shape and the eyes were drifting in random directions.

'Power restrained . . . is a lesser power.' The Intercessor's voice wavered, broke into several tones. 'They knew what they faced . . . voluntary . . . embraced their ending . . .'

'No!' Robert cried. 'She wanted to live!'

In the next instant, the pale amorphous mass of the Intercessor convulsed, as if struck, then abruptly split apart into a shoal of little squid creatures. There was an explosion of activity – some of them darted away in all directions while many huddled together in three main groups that eyed each other and warily kept their distance. Then the pair of sub-Intercessors, having ceased their dance, swooped down, mouths gaping hugely to swallow. Most of the small squids eagerly swam into the maws and as they were absorbed the two sub-Intercessors grew.

Robert watched in a kind of mystified fascination, and recalled a painting he once saw in the National Museum in Berlin, a surrealist work by the twenty-first-century artist Arbeiter, entitled

The Dance of the Selves. It depicted a lone figure lying slumped in a bare room while masklike faces, each with its own expression, tore away from his head and flew around the room. Robert began to wonder if the Intercessor's species consisted of group minds with some kind of biomorphic symbiosis, like the Utlezyr, a species wiped out by the Sarsheni during their domination of the Indroma worlds.

The two partial Intercessors, now enlarged by their harvesting, stalked the remaining strays, unaware that one of them had sneaked round to the glassy dividing wall. Robert smiled as it swam up against the barrier, its single dark eye fixed on him.

'Emissary Horst, you must listen – they wanted to live! . . .'

The thin, wavering voice was cut off as a pale tentacle snatched its owner back into a dark, toothless maw. There was no chewing. The mouth closed up and melted into pale, pliable flesh as the two partial Intercessors merged, rippling, flowing. A moment later, the Intercessor once more floated before him, whole.

'You have been most patient, Emissary Horst, and while our consideration has been quite thorough we require a further period of cogitation. If you return to your vessel we shall inform you of our conclusions within one hour.'

And with that the audience was over. The Intercessor undulated away to an opening at the rear and was gone, leaving Robert to mull over the bizarre, almost incomprehensible encounter as he retraced his steps.

'A remarkable account,' said Reski Emantes. 'So, in essence, you laid out the Construct's negotiating position to the Godhead's representative, then proceeded to have a stand-up shouting match that resulted in your premature return to the ship.'

'If you generalise it any further, you can make it sound as if I punched the dividing wall, perhaps even fired off a weapon. Would you like to try?'

The droid Reski Emantes magnified the image of the Godhead vessel on the main monitor.

'It would not be possible to exaggerate the irreparable damage you have inflicted on this mission,' it said. 'How could an experienced diplomat lose control so badly?'

Robert had no answer, at least not one that he wanted to voice at this time. Yet that strange affray had been more due to the partial-Intercessor's reaction than to his own loss of temper. Almost as if the shattering of its group-mind consensus was triggered by something in his responses. But there was no way of really knowing exactly what connotations or associations were aroused by his words.

Is there ever? he thought sardonically.

Certainly they were sufficient to send the partial-Intercessor flying apart. Still, there was the mystery of what the small elemental squid-creature said before it was assimilated by the large composite one – *they wanted to live!* But who were they?

'I take your protracted silence to be an admission of guilt,' said Reski. 'Perhaps tinged with regret.'

'Not at all,' he said. 'I was merely timing you to see how long you could last without launching another broadside of smugness.'

'Your own time would be better employed in considering how to explain your shortcomings to the Construct . . .'

'This acrimony serves no useful function,' said the *Plausible Response*.

'On the contrary,' said the droid. 'By using disparaging speech I am able to imprint on the Human mind a reflex against improper behaviour. A crude form of tutoring but it may turn out to be of benefit, to a Human at least . . .'

Before Robert could retort, the Ship cut in.

'Ship-to-ship communication from the Godhead vessel, two-way stream,' it said as a subframe opened on the bridge widescreen. In it was the pale shape of the Intercessor.

'Emissary Horst,' it said in a deep, rich male voice. 'My thanks to you and your companions for being so patient. After much deliberation we find that your proposal has merit and therefore we are empowered to send you to the penultimate stage of your journey. It is an involuted continuum, impossible to enter without precise coordinates, which we are sending across now. When you arrive, you will be taken to a gate device that will enable you to immediately descend hundreds of tiers to the periphery of the Godhead's abode. From there, Emissary Horst, you will have to travel alone.'

'My thanks for your sagacity and foresight, Intercessor,' said Robert, surprised in spite of himself. 'I look forward to presenting our case to the Godhead in person.'

'You may be assured of a welcome befitting the urgency of your mission. And now we must leave – goodbye, Emissary Horst.'

The Intercessor's image vanished, replaced by a view of the flattened silver-green oval of the Godhead ship. At one of the narrow ends two odd fins emerged from the hull while various blisters appeared at the other. A moment later, with no sign of reaction thrust, it moved off, picked up speed and was gone in seconds.

'Data object received,' said the Ship. 'Buffered analysis shows it to be a coordinate set in multi-parameter format, for a location on tier 165. Estimated journey time is variable, between eleven and twenty-seven hours.'

Robert nodded and glanced at Reski Emantes, who still hovered before the main bridge console. 'So – you were saying.'

'I fear you are too easily satisfied, Robert Horst,' the droid said. 'Their approval was too glib and was given too quickly. I think we should proceed with caution.'

As the droid floated away and out of the bridge, Robert could only shake his head. 'Hmm, seems that my shortcomings have altered their character.'

'It is possible that he was adversely affected by the missile attack,' said the Ship. 'On another matter, I think you should know that my probes recovered the body of the Rosa simulant. It is already being converted back into resource materials, but before it went to the tank I recovered a peculiar data fragment that had been etched into the backup crystal matrix. It is a four-second visual recording from after she unleashed her energy assault – I will display it for you.'

A subframe popped into the centre of the widescreen and Robert watched closely. First there was a shadowy, jerky view of the Legion Knight's irregular underside, webbed with bright, crawling energy. Then the point of view – which he suddenly realised could only be Rosa's – swung round to focus on a triangular hatch that gaped open less than two feet away. The energy discharge's ice-blue radiance had penetrated the Knight's vitals, revealing long shapes writhing within the hatch, smoky black snake forms. The recording cycled again and again but Robert was certain.

'Have you seen these creatures before, Robert?'

He remembered the mad pursuit through the stone passages of the lithosphere of Abfagul in the company of the Reski droids, and the charge through the ancient storage vault beneath the Great Terrace. It was smokey black snakes like those which they had fled.

He nodded. 'They come from the Abyss of hyperspace, and specialise in hunting sentient mechs,' he said. 'They're called the vermax.'

11

CATRIONA

After the disappearance of Theo and Malachi, after the discovery of the dead guards, and after hours and hours of fruitless searching, she wearily retired to the warmth of blankets beneath a lean-to in the crook of a midlevel branch, and slept. And sleeping, she dreamed.

Dreamed of relaxing on a leafy, cushioned platform amid the noon-bright foliage of Segrana's upper canopy, lying stretched out and languorous in the hot sun. Insects buzzed and long-tailed hizio swooped and wheeled while up in the pure blue sky a ship was climbing, slowly receding into the uppermost heights of the atmosphere. Then her comfortable, cosy platform detached from its treetop and began to sink down through the leaves and branches. The humid air was alive with the forest's animal life, and busy with people, Uvovo and Humans, happily working, travelling or just sitting together.

Greg smiled and waved to her from an open shelter littered with pots and figurines. Just below, his uncle Theo raised a hand in greeting then seized a heavy vine and swung off into the dimming greenness. In her dreaming descent she passed by Greg's mother, who was engrossed in conversation with Listeners Weynl and Temas. The deeper into Segrana she went the gloomier it became and the sparser the population, then a figure drew near from below, Greg's Uvovo friend Cheluvahar, who stood at the end of a broken branch, pointing downwards as he sombrely watched her pass.

Other less welcome images emerged from the suddenly claustrophobic shadows: Julia Bryce, her face blank, her eyes full of some other presence; the Hegemony ambassador, Utavess Kuros, his arms and legs replaced by black metal prostheses; numerous tall Brolturan soldiers; and crouching doglike on a thick bough were five Ezgara commandos, each gripping the bark with four arms, their faceless visors silently tracking her progress into the depths.

The sounds, metallic scrapes, faint scaly gleams off in the gloom, and from above a passing flash of brightness revealed her surroundings.

Machines clung to every branch, crawling, hanging, hooking around every trunk, machines of every size and shape, a waiting, glittering horde.

Beneath, the darkness congealed, cold and wet, black as ash. She came to rest at the foot of a black slope and it seemed as if Segrana had been reduced to blackened debris all around her, a desolation of charred forest. Up the slope was a low building. She climbed towards it, slipping in black, gritty mud, all the time aware of movement in the lightless wastes at her back. Clicks, clinks, low hums, the creak of steel. But before her a door began to open in the squat building, throwing a long wedge of golden light across the ruined ground, widening as she approached.

Be here, said Segrana's voice in her head. *Be here, be here, to speak, to speak, be here, be here . . .*

She hurried to the door and lunged into the drenching golden glow . . . and awoke to find herself lying in silver-blue radiance. A clear pale shaft of Darienlight had slipped through the high foliage to fall upon her resting place. She pushed herself into a sitting position, massaging aching temples, wondering why she had stirred out of sleep . . .

The dream! – she caught her breath as recollection of it rushed back, the descent, the enemy machines, the black burnt wastes, Segrana's voice beckoning to her with an iron, unavoidable urgency, *be here, be here . . .*

Less than an hour later, riding a trictra and escorted by Listener

Okass and six armed Benevolents, she was descending the last branchways and vine-weave curtains leading to the forest floor. Ulby roots and ineka beetles held back the blanketing gloom with their blue-green glows, their scattered scores of meagre luminosities merging into a hazy ambient radiance. It was cold and dank but Catriona was well wrapped in a blanket and a shore-mother's shawl decorated with small shells – she could hear them ticking quietly as her trictra lurched and swayed down the trunk of a pillar tree.

When she had told Listener Okass about her tree and described the low structure, he had nodded gravely, declaring that he knew the building's whereabouts. And sure enough, there in the shadows below, crouching on a low hilltop and dwarfed by immense mossy trunks, was the place from her dream. Drawing closer, she could see where a huge tree had taken root near one corner and during many decades of growth had bored and wedged and pushed its way through the walls to the point where it now towered over a dilapidated roof corner and heaps of cracked, dislodged stones.

Catriona had her escort wait a short distance from the entrance while she picked her way across rocky ground made slippery by decaying mulch, the decomposing leafy debris from above. The entrance was a pillared portico, its ceiling and walls decorated with ulby roots. Past the door a low, short passage came to a T-junction, both arms leading round to the same place, a large chamber taking up most of the length of the building. Apart from a narrow walkway that ran round all four sides, the floor sloped steeply down into a pit from which a grey radiance leached. It made visible the half-demolished corner but Catriona's attention was fixed on what lay below.

Algae streaks marked where water had trickled in. Mud lay in fan-shaped deposits from which a few pale, sickly plants sprouted, not tall enough to reach the rim of the large circular stone platform that covered most of the floor. Its surface was incised with dense, interlocking patterns, half-geometric, half-plantlike, their grooves the source of that eerie luminescence. As her eyes traced the convoluted lines, she recalled Theo's description of the warpwell chamber that Greg and Chel had found beneath Giant's Shoulder.

Be here, to speak, Segrana had said in her dream, but with whom? Was this stone platform something similar to the warpwell? Were they connected in some fashion? Perhaps this was an ancient means for communicating with Segrana. Eager to know, she carefully descended a rank of narrow stone stairs and stepped out onto the platform.

The grey radiance immediately brightened. Some patterns gleamed like burning silver and curtains of light sprang up before her.

WHY ARE YOU HERE?

The voice filled the building and filled her head, resonating at low registers that made her skin tingle. She was astonished but felt no fear.

'I answered the call of Segrana,' she said calmly. 'Why are *you* here?'

TO SPEAK WITH THE KEEPER OF SEGRANA, WITH YOU, MACREADIE.

'Keeper?' she said, recalling some references to the honorific in the tales of the War of the Long Night. 'The Listeners here call me Pathmistress, which is one too many high-and-mighty titles, to be honest. What about you – what should I call you?'

I AM THE SENTINEL OF THE WARPWELL AT WAONWIR, WHICH HUMANS CALL GIANT'S SHOULDER. I AM HERE TO QUESTION YOU ABOUT ANOTHER HUMAN, A FEMALE CALLED JULIA BRYCE. SHE IS ONE OF THE HUMAN VARIANTS KNOWN AS ENHANCED, LIKE YOU . . .

'Not like me,' Cat said sharply. 'My talents didn't develop properly, so I didn't get to become a full Enhanced, got it?' She swallowed and glared at the shifting, shining veils. 'So what're ye interested in her for? I was told that she and some others were grabbed by that Earthsphere ship.'

That was another part of Theo's tale that had amazed her, the determination of the intelligence chief Pyatkov in trying to keep

Julia and her team out of Hegemony hands, only for them to end up on board the Earthsphere cruiser, *Heracles*.

AN ALLY OF MINE KNOWN AS THE CONSTRUCT HAS TOLD ME THAT FIVE HUMANS WERE SEEN IN THE COMPANY OF HURNEGUR AND JESHKRA, TWO NOTORIOUS INSURGENT LEADERS FROM THE YAMANON DOMAIN. BOTH LED REVOLTS AGAINST THE DOL-DAS OPPRESSORS AND THEN FOUGHT AGAINST HEGEMONY–EARTHSPHERE FORCES AFTER THE TYRANNY FELL. ALSO, BOTH HAVE RECENTLY CONVERTED TO THE SPIRAL PROPHECY, A NARROWLY INTERPRETED, HIGHLY MILITANT STRAND OF SAGERIST BELIEF.

Listening carefully, Cat frowned. 'Why are you so sure that these five Humans were Julia Bryce and her people?' She was going to say 'friends' but real friendship was never Julia's style.

HUMANS ARE A RARE SIGHT FROM THE ARANJA TESH STATES COREWARD – THEY WOULD BE NOTICED. A DREDGE OF MAJOR MEDIA ARCHIVES TURNED UP A REPORT FROM BARAMU, AN OPENPORT ON THE BORDER OF BURANJ. FIVE HUMANS WERE SEEN BOARDING THE *QOL-VALISH*, A MULTI-CARGO HAULER BOUND FOR EARTHSPHERE, MORE THAN FOUR WEEKS AGO. ITS NEXT STOP WAS METRAJ BUT IT NEVER ARRIVED – ARMED HIJACKERS SEIZED CONTROL, LOOTED THE VALUABLES, KIDNAPPED THE FIVE HUMANS THEN LEFT THE SHIP DRIFTING IN INTERSTELLAR SPACE, ITS HYPERDRIVE WRECKED AND MOST OF THE CREW AND PASSENGERS DEAD.

A square frame emerged from the curtain of light, a picture coalescing from the haze to show seven humans getting into an open-top barge. Two were in uniform, Earthsphere navy she guessed, while the others wore civilian clothing. One, a woman, was turned toward the cam as she gazed down at the busy terminal – it was Julia.

'That's her,' she said.

A second picture appeared alongside the first – in it, Julia and her team were standing in the lee of a transport of some kind, something with small oval portholes, stubby wings and a scoured, battered hull. A hulking Henkayan in grubby pale blue robes and meshcloth headgear was in front of Julia, talking to her; next to the Henkayan was a lanky Gomedran wearing a dark, close-fitting body suit. From the Humans' body language Catriona knew that they were captives, and found herself feeling something like concern for them.

THE HENKAYAN IS HURNEGUR AND THE GOMEDRAN IS JESHKRA. THIS WAS TAKEN ON A WORLD CALLED ZOPHOR THREE, WHICH IS LOCATED NEAR THE BORDER BETWEEN THE YAMANON DOMAIN AND THE KALIMBRYK AVAIL. IT IS AN ARID PLANET WHOSE LARGE WATER BODIES HAVE BEEN SHRINKING FOR CENTURIES, AND FOR ALMOST AS LONG IT HAS BEEN A HAVEN FOR REFUGEES FROM THROUGHOUT THE REGION.

Catriona looked closer and could see, on one side beyond the blunt outstretched fingers of the Henkayan, an expanse of tents and shacks hazed by wind-borne dust and the smoke of cooking fires.

'You seem to have enough to prove that it was Julia,' she said. 'So why am I here? What do ye need from me? . . . and how did you get Segrana to mess about with my dreams?'

THERE ARE CERTAIN AVENUES OF COMMUNICATION THAT MAY BE USED ACCORDING TO CIRCUMSTANCE. KEEPER MACREADIE – THE WOMAN BRYCE AND HER COMPANIONS ARE ALL GENETICALLY AUGMENTED IN THEIR INTELLECT, SO WE NEED TO KNOW HOW DANGEROUS THEIR KNOWLEDGE IS. COULD THEY HAVE BEEN WORKING ON WEAPONS RESEARCH OR OTHER MILITARY PROJECTS AT ONE TIME?

'Probably, aye,' she said. 'The Office of Defence was always coming up with wild theories and modification proposals, which the seniors and the pros were obliged to exhaustively analyse and test. I never became a senior, never joined one of the pro squads, and since the Enhanced don't really go in for reunion parties there's no' much gossip to be had.' She frowned. 'But I did learn from Greg's Uncle Theo that it was the spy chief, Pyatkov, who was totally committed to getting Julia and her people away. Aye, the more I think about it, the more it looks as if they were

involved in something high-concept. Mind you, they probably
know a lot about several projects.'

IF THEY WERE FACED WITH THE THREAT OF VIOLENT
COERCION, WOULD THEY RESIST OR WOULD THEY COMPLY?

'They'd do as they were told, I expect, if the odds were against
them. Why do ye ask?'

The Sentinel was silent for a moment, and Catriona was suddenly acutely aware of how cold it was down in this sunken,
stone-walled chamber. She shivered, thinking that the explanation for dragging her all the way into the depths had better be
good.

ACCORDING TO THE CONSTRUCT AGENT'S REPORT, THE
ENHANCED HUMANS REMAINED ON ZOPHOR THREE UNTIL
THREE DAYS AGO WHEN THEY LEFT ON BOARD A SHORT-
RANGE SHUTTLE. AT THE SAME TIME, HURNEGUR AND
JESHKRA ALSO DEPARTED IN THEIR SHUTTLES, ALONG WITH
OVER FOUR HUNDRED SMALL SHIPS, MOST OF WHICH SEEMED
TO BE JUMP-CAPABLE. ANOTHER REPORT SAYS THAT THIS
FLEET RENDEZVOUSED WITH ANOTHER POSSIBLY LARGER
ONE IN HIGH ORBIT. SHORTLY AFTER, THE ENTIRE ARMADA
MOVED OFF IN FORMATION THEN JUMPED TO HYPERSPACE.

'So what are ye saying?' Cat said. 'That Julia and her buddies
cooked up some kind of mega-weapon, then it was off to the
Yamanon Domain to have a go at the Hegemony?'

IT SEEMS UNLIKELY, GIVEN THE NATURE OF THEIR BELIEF
AND ITS INTENSE FERVOUR. CONVERSION TO THE SPIRAL
PROPHECY HAS SPREAD RAPIDLY THROUGH MANY OF THE
CAMPS AND SAND CITIES ON ZOPHOR THREE, ESPECIALLY
AFTER THE SECOND SPIRAL SAGE OF BURANJ ARRIVED AND
WAS PROCLAIMED THE PROPHET-SAGE. IT WAS HE WHO
ANNOUNCED THAT THE DIMENSIONS OF THE UVOVO TEMPLE
ON GIANT'S SHOULDER CORRESPONDED TO THOSE OF THE
LOST TOMB OF THE DIVINE FATHER-SAGE ARIGESSI.

'You're not serious.'

I AM VERY SERIOUS. WHEN IT BECAME KNOWN THREE
WEEKS AGO THAT THE HEGEMONY RESEARCHERS HAD DUG A

HUGE TRENCH IN THE TOP OF THE GIANT'S SHOULDER
PROMONTORY THERE WERE RIOTS ON ZOPHOR THREE IN
WHICH HUNDREDS DIED. RUMOURS ARE NOW RIFE THERE
THAT THE PROPHET-SAGE HAS LEFT TO TRAVEL WITH THE
DIVINE ARMADA TO ITS SACRED DESTINATION.

Stunned, Catriona stared at the images still hanging before her.
The implications seemed both ridiculous and awful.

'You're not suggesting that they're coming here . . . surely they
can't . . .'

THE PROBABILITY IS VERY HIGH. THE DISCOVERY OF
DARIEN AND THE SUBSEQUENT EVENTS HAVE HAD A
CATALYSING EFFECT ON ALL SPIRAL PROPHECY FOLLOWERS –
ALL ELSE IS SECONDARY.

She bit her lip. 'But why?'

YOUR SOCIETY PROVIDES NO EQUIVALENT EXPERIENCE.
THE PROVISIONAL CAMPS ON ZOPHOR THREE AND ANOTHER
HANDFUL OF WORLDS IN THAT AREA HARBOUR HUNDREDS
OF MILLIONS OF REFUGEES, EXILES AND OUTCASTS, COMPRIS-
ING ALMOST EVERY MAJOR SPECIES. MOST OF THESE
COMMUNITIES GROW ACCORDING TO WAVES OF NEWCOMERS
AND THE MOST RECENT ARE FROM THE YAMANON DOMAIN.
THE GREAT MAJORITY OF THOSE CONDEMNED TO THIS EXIS-
TENCE ARE THE POOR AND THE POWERLESS, VICTIMS OF
POGROMS AND OTHER DEPOPULATION SWEEPS. CONDITIONS
IN THE CAMPS ARE PRIMITIVE AND DESPERATE, IDEAL FOR
THE SPREAD OF ULTRA-DOGMATIC CREEDS LIKE THE SPIRAL
PROPHECY. THE FANATICS ARE ALWAYS THERE BUT THEY
DEPEND ON THE BRUTALITY OF ANTAGONISTIC HIERARCHIES
TO PROVIDE THEM WITH FOLLOWERS. THE PROPHET-SAGE
HAS SAID THAT THE TOMB OF THE DIVINE ARIGESSI IS ON
DARIEN AND HAS CALLED THE PRESENCE OF HUMANS AND
SENDRUKANS 'A FOUL SEDIMENT OF HEATHENS WHICH MUST
BE SCOURED AWAY', AND THERE ARE MANY WHO WILL LISTEN
TO HIM.

'So now they're coming over in person to do a bit of scouring,'
Cat said. 'But if that Brolturan warship is still here, the

Earthsphere one too, they're not going to be able to just walk in unopposed, unless . . .'

EXACTLY. WITH THE ENHANCED HUMANS' HELP THEY MAY GAIN A TACTICAL EDGE WITH SURPRISE AND UNKNOWN WEAPONRY. THEY ALSO HAVE A NEW ALLY, A TERRORIST FACTION CALLED THE CHAURIXA.

She remembered them from the last newspaper she'd read, on the shuttle back from Darien. 'Terrorists-for-hire, aren't they? Specialise in high-profile mass-death atrocities, as well as assassinations . . .'

YES. THERE ARE RUMOURS OF A CHANGE IN THEIR LEADERSHIP THAT MAY ACCOUNT FOR THEIR RECENT ATYPICAL BEHAVIOUR.

'Okay, so how long?'

UNCERTAIN. THE JUMP RANGE AND SPEED OF SUCH AN ARMADA WOULD NECESSARILY BE DETERMINED BY ITS SLOWEST ELEMENTS, AND UNKNOWN FACTORS MAY BE INVOLVED. THE BEST ESTIMATE IS BETWEEN FOUR AND EIGHT DAYS.

Catriona smiled bleakly and ran her hand through her hair, teasing out a few fragments of leaf, realising how long it was growing. 'An invasion of religious fanatics,' she said. 'They'll be fighting with the Brolturans . . . unless they land all over Segrana, and then the Brolts'll come piling in after them. We'll be fighting two enemies. And how will they cope down on Darien? I don't even know what's been happening . . .'

THE RESISTANCE IS WELL ORGANISED AND IS BEING DIRECTED BY GREGORY CAMERON AND THE SENIOR LISTENERS.

Catriona felt relief on hearing one of her fears erased. 'Greg's still alive, then . . . that's really, really . . . uh, good . . .'

THE OCCUPIERS INTEND TO DEPLOY COMBAT MECHS ALL ACROSS THE HINTERLANDS AND FORESTS WEST OF THE COLONY SO CAMERON IS GOING TO LEAD ALL THE INSURGENT AND CIVILIAN FUGITIVES TO A STRONGHOLD IN THE MOUNTAINS. IT HAS A CHAMBER SIMILAR TO THIS ONE, WHICH WILL ALLOW COMMUNICATION IN EITHER DIRECTION. ONCE THE

RELOCATION IS COMPLETE, IN APPROXIMATELY SEVEN HOURS, I SHALL INITIATE CONTACT AND INFORM THE RESISTANCE LEADERS OF THE EXPECTED INVASION. IF YOU ARE PRESENT, SOME VISUAL PERSPECTIVE CAN BE PROVIDED.

Should I ask it to tell Greg that his uncle's been snatched by Ezgara commandos? she thought sombrely, then said, 'I'll be here.'

I SHALL PREPARE ACCORDINGLY. ALSO, YOU SHOULD BE AWARE THAT I HAVE DECIDED TO ADOPT A PROJECTION IMAGE IN ORDER TO PROMOTE BETTER DIALOGUE. MAY I DISPLAY IT FOR YOU?

Surprised, she nodded. 'Of course. Go right ahead.'

Abruptly, the hazy glowing veils faded and were replaced by the semi-opaque figure of a young woman in a featureless one-piece garment with a vaguely military cut. Her tied-back hair was a pale corn hue while blue-grey eyes stared from a youthful, pretty face. She blinked a couple of times and smiled hesitantly. Catriona laughed in recognition.

'So how is Ambassador Horst doing?' she said. 'Assuming he's still alive.'

'**He is alive and well,**' the Sentinel said, its voice appropriate to the image, yet retaining a faint, deep undertone. '**I surmise that you saw his daughter's image in media reports . . . and I assume that Major Karlsson told you why it was necessary for me to relocate him from the warpwell.**'

'Aye, Theo and me had quite a chat,' she said. 'Y'know, Horst's disappearance made the situation worse by making Sundstrom look weak. You could have kept him on Darien.'

'**The Hegemony emissary, Kuros, was in command of events by that point,**' the Sentinel said. '**And since the Construct needed a Human or a Uvovo for a vital mission, I neutralised the ambassador's AI implant then translocated him down the tiers of hyperspace.**'

It was the strangest experience, conversing with a translucent image of Horst's dead daughter, while all the time knowing that an ancient machine intelligence was behind those eyes.

And in her own thoughts she could feel Segrana watching and waiting, an echoing touch in which Catriona could sense nostalgia, amusement and hope.

'How did you come up with such a detailed image?' she said.

'**When I sent him down to the Construct's custody, the Ambassador had with him an interactive simulation projector, a device containing a comprehensive, multifractive profile of his daughter that his wife had made back on Earth. I asked the Construct for advice on a suitable image and he sent me this dataform. In the meantime, the Construct has dispatched Robert Horst on a crucial mission, accompanied by a biosimulant of his daughter, Rosa. This appears to be part of his enquiries into the adaptive abilities of the Human model.**'

Catriona listened in amazement and a vague unease.

'Enquiries?' she said. 'Are there any other versions of the Rosa . . . model?'

'**I do not know, Keeper, but it seems likely.**'

Weirder and weirder, she thought. She tried to recall the little that Theo had told her about the Construct and the warpwell but realised that there were vast unknowns gaping like crevasses on all sides. She had to know more.

'Sentinel, I have many questions. Are you permitted to answer any that I ask?'

The Sentinel, half-Rosa, half-machine intellect, smiled broadly. '**Certainly – I am bound to cooperate with the Keeper and the Pathmasters.**'

'Great!' she said, climbing back up the steps of the pit. 'Wait there while I speak with my friends outside.'

Just as well the invaders aren't expected for another day or so, she thought as she hurried round to the entrance and beckoned to Listener Okass. *Gives us a chance to put on a nice, warm welcome for them!*

PART TWO

12

LEGION

On board the Earthsphere cruiser *Heracles*, the more relaxed alertness of regular routine was reasserting itself, now that Kirkland, the colony president, had left for the planet's surface. Down in Sensory, Second Lieutenant Claudio Smeraldi was holomonitoring his three operators as they got to grips with the new batch of test assignments. Of the three only Mazwai was an experienced sensor-hawk, while Gadowski and Halabi had recently been volunteered by Rostering. In the wake of the cloud-harvester debacle, the captain ordered increased staffing levels and a more rigorous training schedule, all of which Smeraldi approved.

True, Sensory's expert system, Hugo, was faster and capable of more multitasking than any human but Second Lieutenant Smeraldi knew that only a trained operator could contribute that nuance of judgement, that indefinable intuition, that crucial element of insight that could reveal truths and turn disaster into triumph. Yes, he mused, sending the inept Tuan Ho back for retraining was a wise decision by . . .

'Contact!' Mazwai said suddenly. 'Small ship has just exited hyperspace at sub-boundary seven, incoming on F63-241.8. Single prow-mounted beam projector tagged for response: no other weapons points detected. Ship ident details – the *Kasimir*, long-haul cargo lugger, approximate capacity 1,800 cubic metres, port of registry is Daliborka . . .'

In the holomonitor Mazwai paused to glance at Smeraldi.

'Sir, that's . . .'

'A Vox Humana colony, operator. Yes, I know. Any comm traffic yet?'

'Yes, sir, we are being hailed by a Captain Janicek on full AV channels.'

'Delay him for a moment – I have to notify the captain.' Then Smeraldi turned to another section of his holo-alcove and saluted the flint-eyed visage of Velazquez. 'Sir!'

'So, another visitor, Second Lieutenant.'

'Yes, sir, a freighter from one of the Vox H worlds.'

'I can see the details here,' Velazquez said. 'However, localweb updates make no mention of any VH vessels in this region. Speak with him, find out why he's here and what he wants. I'll listen in while conferring with Hugo. If he insists on talking with me directly, I'll signal you what to do.'

'Yes, sir.' Smeraldi switched to Mazwai. 'Put him through, operator.'

A moment later he was face to face with a youthful, brown-haired man in a form-fitting pale green uniform with a ridged collar and rank insignia on his left chest.

'Captain Janicek, I am Second Lieutenant Smeraldi of Earthsphere vessel *Heracles*, Captain Velazquez commanding. It would be helpful if you would state the purpose of your visit – the security of the Darien system is currently shared between ourselves and units of the Brolturan navy, who are habitually wary of unannounced newcomers.'

'Of course, Lieutenant, this I understand,' Janicek said with a nod. 'Well, I am captain of this fine ship, the *Kasimir*, and we are carrying donor aid from the people of Daliborka to the people of Darien as a gesture of friendship and solidarity.' He smiled. 'No disrespect to you, Lieutenant, but I was hoping to speak to your captain on a pressing matter.'

'Perhaps I could be of assistance, Captain. What is it concerning?'

'Your helpful concern is most heart-warming, Lieutenant, but so pressing is this matter that a dialogue with your captain would be the swiftest way to resolve it.'

Off to one side, Velazquez nodded.

'Apologies, Captain. I can put you through now.'

Smeraldi then sat back, regarding the two commanders in adjacent blocks of his holomonitor while the expert system, Hugo, waited in one of the smaller ones.

'Sorry to keep you waiting, Captain,' said Velazquez. 'When you appeared in system, you tripped every peripheral alarm, causing the Brolturans to elevate their active status to Battle Ready, and to launch a dozen interceptors.'

Janicek's face paled. 'My sincerest apologies, Captain, I did not realise . . .'

'We had no advance warning of your arrival, Captain Janicek, no communication from the Vox Humana government at all, so you can understand the reasons for our caution. Now, we shall be making enquiries with the authorities on Daliborka, after we've inspected your vessel and questioned you and your crew.'

'I am more than happy to comply, Captain,' Janicek said. 'In fact, I was going to ask for permission to come alongside your vessel while we make repairs to our forward port suspensors . . .'

Smeraldi looked at the Sensory AI, Hugo. 'Are you reading that?'

'Yes – if they attempt to manoeuvre between low orbit and the planet surface, the necessary compensation would very likely render one or more suspensor units inoperable. I have fed this information to Captain Velazquez's interface but there are some other anomalies I wish to raise with you.'

Smeraldi paused to catch the ongoing dialogue – Janicek was giving the captain a rundown on his cargo manifest – then asked Hugo to explain.

'There is something non-standard about their hyperdrive. Analysis of its shutdown emissions reveals strange field resonances with fine tolerance levels, similar to high-grade drives installed in small, expensive pleasure yachts. Also, the mass distribution does not match the available hold capacity: cross-reference produced a match for the hull, which is a container barge, built in their thousands by shipyards of the Omb

Sortilegarchy for the Sarsheni slavers. Such hulls would permit a more even distribution than is indicated.'

'Has the hull interior been modified?' said Smeraldi. 'Would that account for the unusual readings?'

'Probability is greater than medium,' said Hugo. 'However, the most anomalous aspect is the power distribution . . . wait, there is an underhull temperature spike on the aft-starboard flank; no system response; monitors must be faulty. I am alerting Captain Velazquez . . .'

Swiftly, Smeraldi switched back into the captains' exchange, simultaneously opening an enhanced long-range visual of the Vox Humana ship.

'. . . looks serious, Captain,' Velazquez was saying. 'May I suggest that you deal with that and we'll resume our discussion later?'

'Agreed, Captain, but this should not take long to . . .' There was activity on the small bridge behind Janicek, who turned to examine another monitor at the behest of one of his officers. His face was full of worry when he looked back. 'Captain Velazquez, I'm afraid that . . .'

Suddenly the image was gone, the holosector blank.

'What's happening?' said Velazquez. 'Re-establish contact!'

'Sir, I am scanning for it,' Smeraldi said, fingers flying between his touch-console and the holopanel. Hugo appeared in the empty holosector and shook his head. 'We're not getting any signal from the *Kasimir*.'

At that moment, there was a bright flash from the long-range visual of the cargo vessel. Startled, Smeraldi caught his breath while the holoimage zoomed in on the ship and an inset ran a slomo replay: it showed an explosion blossoming from the aft starboard hull, an outburst of flaring gases, blasts of escaping fluid flashing into jets of frozen crystals. The *Kasimir* was heading for the *Heracles* at a constant 800 km/h but the force of the explosion threw it into a spin and altered its course towards Darien itself.

Second Lieutenant Smeraldi watched the Vox Humana ship

pinwheel through space and felt a hollow helplessness, wondering if Janicek and his crew were still alive.

'Hugo,' he said. 'Anything?'

'Only a faint regular blip from their comms cycling ready state. The captain is being kept updated.'

'Are we going to send a rescue tug?'

'Flight has one prepped and ready,' said Hugo. 'But they will only launch if the *Kasimir* responds to hails within the next nine and a half minutes – after that the Brolturans will open fire with the *Purifier*'s heavy projectors.'

'Our glorious allies don't believe in half-measures, do they?'

The minutes dragged past. Mazwai and the other two operators could only sit at their consoles and watch events unfold since their interfaces were locked out. As he waited, Smeraldi dipped into a couple of section comm channels, Weaponry and Flight, listening in on the chatter and background checks. Then, with one minute and eight seconds left, the *Kasimir*'s channel abruptly came to life.

'. . . to *Heracles*, please respond . . .'

Velazquez was suddenly back in presence.

'*Kasimir*, this is Captain Velazquez – confirm your status.'

For a moment there was only audio hiss, then the holovisuals flickered on, a hazy lorez image of Janicek, now with a small healstrip on his forehead.

'Captain,' he said. 'My sincere apologies for this difficulty. One of our fuel cells blew and wrecked half of our control net. But we have been rigging up new connections like crazy people, cables everywhere! We should have control of our stabilisers . . .' He glanced sideways and spoke to someone out of sight. '. . . Good, any moment . . . now!'

On the tracking visual, pale jets burned near the *Kasimir*'s prow and the vessel's spin slowed and stopped, its nose pointing where it was still heading, towards Darien.

'Congratulations on regaining control, Captain,' Velazquez said. 'Now you need to alter course back to *Heracles*. One of our rescue tugs will meet you midway.'

'Certainly we shall, if it is possible,' Janicek said. 'Our controls for the main thrusters were blown too, but my navigator thinks we can use the manoeuvring jets to skip off the upper atmosphere then come round to you again, yes?'

'Very well. By then the tug will be able to get its line on your hull.'

Janicek nodded, looking relieved, and was about to reply when a loud thud came from somewhere on the *Kasimir*'s cramped bridge. Janicek said, 'What was . . . ?' – then the holovisual was suddenly empty.

'Get that signal back!' said Velazquez.

Then the expert system Hugo spoke. 'Sir, gaseous venting detected from the *Kasimir*'s forward section – also the main thrusters have just ignited and are ramping up quickly.'

'What the hell's going on in that ship?' the captain growled. 'Keep the updates coming – I've got the Father-Admiral on the line . . .'

As Velazquez's channel went secure, Hugo caught Smeraldi's attention with long-range telemetry.

'The *Kasimir* is now up to full burn,' the AI said. 'Unless there are course corrections it will enter the planet's atmosphere in a nosedive.'

Smeraldi stared at the long-range visual in horror, trying not to imagine being aboard the doomed craft.

'What do you think happened?' he said.

'Possibilities include some kind of explosion in the bridge or an adjacent compartment,' said Hugo. 'The rescue tug is still in pursuit, however, which may account for the Brolturan commander's communication.'

'And how are our illustrious allies reacting?'

'The *Purifier*'s main projector battery had been tracking the *Kasimir* from the moment it dropped out of hyperspace. But the tug's proximity may put it at risk . . .'

Smeraldi shook his head and offered up a small prayer to the deities of infinite space, hoping for something unforeseen.

*

On board the plummeting *Kasimir*, cradled within an intricate metal framework stretching the length of the barge's main hold, the Legion Knight focused all his mental capacity on this daring gambit. In his biocrystal chines, schemators were modelling likely consequences of the Brolturan battleship opening fire and none resulted in his survival at this stage. Which was why he plunged this patchwork hoax vessel into a vertical dive – if the Brolturans believed that it was falling to its complete destruction then there would be little point in expending valuable energy on a beam barrage. The other reason was that the sooner he entered the atmosphere, the sooner he would be shielded from the worst that the Brolturan ship could deliver, and atmospheric impact would begin in just a few moments.

He reflected upon the intense, accelerated frenzy of drone work that had rebuilt the interior of the Bargalil container barge. The shock-absorbing cradle for his cyborg body, the shielding, the rewiring of control systems, the thrust drive augmentations, all were carefully developed and undertaken even as he was planning the *Kasimir*'s chain of perilous circumstances, the energy emissions, the fuel cell blowout, and the break in communications. It was a contrived drama made compelling by the simulated Human cast assembled with the help of data schemators freely available from certain users of the tiernet, the interstellar, intercultural information grid. Although previously aware of the tiernet's versatility, the Legion Knight had not understood its immersive nature or the range of resources that were simply being given away. Employing imagery mined from an ancient Earth entertainment, he simulated a small control room with a handful of personnel and a commanding officer who was his mouthpiece. Janicek's accented Anglic and the bridge crew exchanges were fed through a language bank, while the entire simulation was sync-rendered for ambient authenticity.

And the Humans believed it, every word, every simulated gesture, every concocted incident.

The seconds counted down and when the first hull vibrations registered he knew that the barge had entered Darien's atmosphere.

He was coming down over a mountainous area in the south-west region of the larger of the planet's two continents, almost three thousand miles from the Human colony settlements. He throttled back the main thrusters and prepared to redirect their plasma jets, intending to swing the aft of the barge down before engaging the suspensors, which were all working perfectly. Once the barge regained stable flight, the Legion Knight planned to release an explosive device whose detonation would mimic that of the barge hitting the ground.

At 20,000 feet he activated the directional ducts and began altering the falling vessel's attitude. Seconds later, external sensors picked up an object heading swiftly toward his location, no, two objects, both in flight. Sentries, he reasoned, not crewed, more likely guided by machine-mind pilots, stupid but relentless. He decided against dropping the impact-mimic bomb and instead brought the suspensors online, braking his descent, directing his momentum along a course away from the oncoming sentry drones.

Cloud cover was low and icy gusting winds were scouring the mountains with a heavy blizzard. Cutting the plasma thrusters, the Legion Knight steered the barge down into the white, howling storm, flying on antigrav alone. Minutes later, as he was rushing along a rocky ravine, a missile arced down out of the snowy murk and slammed into the upper hull, over the midsection. The missile was clearly meant for use against energy shields – there was no breach – but even so the explosive impact was sufficient to demand a chain of course corrections and suspensor rebalancing. Those missiles must have some kind of mass or motion detection ability, he realised, which meant that there was little point in not using the thrusters. He reignited the plasma drives and as the velocity built he increased altitude and instituted evasive manoeuvres.

Beams stabbed briefly at him out of the clouds above, aggressive probes that would reveal hull composition. A moment later, dazzling spears of energy lanced down in a pattern of cutting strokes, but the Legion Knight had already thrown the barge into a tight swerve, forcing the ungainly craft to bank steeply. Thus he dodged most of the beam attacks, apart from a few that cut into the unshielded hull though not deeply enough to damage anything vital.

This changed as the pursuit plunged on into darkness, the wall of night moving around the planet, the terminator of daylight. The Legion Knight attempted every evasive ploy he could devise, employing wooded hills, narrow gullies and dense forests, but the sentry drones, now numbering three, stayed on his trail, inflicting slow destruction with beam and missile. Less than four hours after the atmosphere descent, suspensor lift was down to 58 per cent and four out of six plasma drive apertures were wrecked by enemy fire; shedding the barge shell was tempting since his carapace armour could take far more punishment than this crude hull. But the sight of his atypical cyborg exterior could attract attention and excite the kind of curiosity that would make his mission still more difficult.

Options were limited. His only hope now was to find a hiding place that would amply conceal the barge, and it appeared that he had found one. Four hundred miles to the north-west, and eight hundred miles west of the Human settlements, was a large lake – if he could survive to reach it, he could dive into its depths, free himself of the barge shell and move to another part of the lake before triggering the bomb.

The barge suspensors finally ceased functioning a quarter of a mile from the edge of the lake and at an altitude of roughly three hundred feet. The Legion Knight's own suspensors, protesting under the weight, kept both it and the barge in the air for several seconds more. The drones were closing in, as if scenting a kill. The barge, possessing the aerodynamic qualities of a brick, hurtled towards the dark, choppy waters and the Knight, suddenly struck by an intuitive hunch, triggered the bomb release just before it plunged nose first into the lake.

Cutting the plasma thrusters, he used the manoeuvring jets to drive down into the hazy depths. Sensors mostly blind, he was still getting readings from the bomb, which had been built into a survival pod – the sentry drones were converging to investigate.

Meanwhile, the lake floor was coming into view, an underwater vista of shattered boulders, jagged fissures and upthrust fangs of rock scores of metres long, almost as if it were some weed-choked battlefield that had lain here, drowned, for centuries. Seeking out a shallow ravine, he brought the barge to rest at the bottom, kicking up clouds of sandy mud, then triggered the bomb.

There was a brief lag before the booming sound wave hit, closely followed by a shock wave. The roaring and the shuddering and buffeting arrived all at once, then the bangs and thumps of rocks bouncing off the hull. For a second or two the cacophony lessened ... before something massive crashed down onto the barge, then a second and a third. The hull cracked, and emergency alerts clamoured as datalines were severed. Feeling panic, and at once suppressing it, the Legion Knight opened up the manoeuvring jets. Nothing. He tried to use the plasma drive but the controls were dead. Internal monitors reported flooding in several sectors and the imminent failure of the upper hull support, which would flood the main hold and transfer the load onto the cradling framework.

No external sensors were functioning but he did still have a squad of Bargalil work drones left over from the in-flight rebuild. The smallest one he sent to a secondary airlock, cycling it through to the outside where it was able to send back a few seconds of visuals before the pressure and the water overwhelmed its systems.

A massive shard of rock had fallen into the ravine, breaking into several pieces which had buried the barge. Now he was trapped, interred alive, entombed by unforeseen consequences. Fury and frustration clawed at him. The hull was failing and the compartments were flooding; after all his long ages of survival, after all his planning and building and brilliant guile, how could it all end here?

13

JULIA

The procession ascended the rough-hewn tunnels at a stately pace. Steel girder supports braced the walls and bright pinlights shed harsh white light on the two large dark blue missiles as they glided along on agrav loaders. Heavily armed Henkayan fighters led the way and brought up the rear while Julia and the others followed directly behind. Irenya was on her left and Konstantin on her right, both appearing drawn and weary yet still tensely alert. Thorold and Arkady were a pace or two back and last time she glanced round they had looked the same.

Not surprising, she thought. *We don't know if we're walking towards more captivity or to our deaths.*

Their guards were the same ones who had secured the underground workshops where they had been confined for the last three weeks. Julia had grown tediously accustomed to the malicious sneers and hate-filled glares that these pious warriors had bestowed on their lowly Human prisoners. In her mind's cortical net she had been running hierarchic-dependent social power models, trying to foresee how their captors might deal with them, now that the holy weapons were ready. Every time it came down to the level of piety, the intensity of memetic internalisation. On one hand, the Enhanced humans' knowledge and skills could not outweigh their blasphemous origins, but on the other hand their value might now be exhausted, leading only to the extermination of abominations.

She shivered. The tunnel air was cold and had a powdery quality that she could feel on her tongue. Before departing the workshops they were told to put on knee-length hooded shifts of some thin, pale yellow material that did little to retain body heat. However, it was very good at reminding her that, like the others, she had not bathed properly for nearly four weeks. She tried to convince herself that it was a minor discomfort compared to the threat of the cretinous, prayer-babbling guards with their guns, but didn't always succeed.

From the bay doors of the main machine shop, the ascending tunnel had so far made two 180-degree turns, the width sufficient to accommodate the thirteen-metre-long missiles. As the procession approached the third turn, a Human female came round the corner and walked jauntily down to meet them. She had on a dark blue onepiece, the kind of thing a tech worker would wear, red gloves on her hands, a tool belt, and a pair of paint-splashed heavy boots. Her hair was short and black with bleached highlights and her features were small, neat and arrestingly beautiful. The eyes were dark, clear and almost seemed to twinkle with merriment; only frequent acquaintance would show it to be a cold cruelty.

Julia steeled herself. *If the eyes are the windows of the soul, then Corazon Talavera's are cracked.*

Talavera brought the missile procession to a halt with a raised hand then spoke to the senior guard in Kelasti, one of the main tongues of the Yamanon refugees. In four weeks Julia had learned enough for basic communication and only caught a word or two from the exchange. Talavera looked round at the Enhanced, surveying them all, and smiled.

'Just a slight change in our little cavalcade – Hurnegur's orders. He wants a greater distance between you and the holy missiles . . .' She waved the loader operators to continue, waited until a gap of about fifteen metres had opened up, then made a sweeping gesture, urging the rest to resume.

'Onward, my friends, onward to victory!' She laughed, moving alongside Julia. 'Such long faces. This is a happy day, folks – you should be celebrating your amazing achievement. Hurnegur and Jeshkra have laid on a special surprise, a small ceremony to let the devout express their feelings for these babies and the great battle that lies ahead.' Her smile widened. 'I just know you're going to find it fascinating.'

With that she hurried on ahead to catch up with the missiles just as they were turning the next corner.

'What is that bitch up to now?' Konstantin said in a low murmur. 'Is this it?'

'Stay calm,' she said while thinking the same, wondering what twisted pageant lay ahead. As they then turned the corner, Julia's mind went back to the first time she saw Corazon Talavera, when she and her gang of mercenaries had walked into the dim-lit Highwatch observation lounge just minutes after the departure of the *Qol-Valish*, the ship that was meant to take the Enhanced on to Earth.

Like her thugs, Talavera had been wearing dull green body armour but her smile had been wide and hungry.

'Humans,' she had said loudly. 'I want the Humans!'

Scores of frightened gazes had looked round to where Julia and the others were sitting in a bulkhead alcove with their escort, two of Velazquez's officers from the *Heracles*. Both were shot dead as they drew their weapons, after which Talavera had smiled, crooked a beckoning finger at Julia and the rest and said, 'This way and smartly if you please.'

Weapon muzzles prodded them towards the main exit. Once they were out in the corridor Talavera had paused in the doorway, gloved hands resting on either side of the frame while her underlings aimed weapons into the lounge. Then she had started to speak in one of the common interlinguals, pointing to a number of shiny packages lying in a heap near where she stood. As she spoke, gasps and frightened moans came from the passengers, who comprised sentients from several different species. A moment later she stepped back and the doors closed and sealed.

Inside the lounge, the fighting began.

Julia and the others were taken down to the *Qol-Valish*'s cargo hold, past still bodies, splashes of blood and the sounds of weapons-fire. Talavera then oversaw their transfer via the big airlock to another vessel with pale walls and circular transverse passages and at no time did she mention what had just happened. She just had her thugs march them along to a room with three double cots and a small partitioned area, not answering Julia's questions except with an intense, grinning stare.

'Welcome to the revolution' was all she said before the room's only door slid shut and locked.

Later, in hushed voices, they had debated it, trying to understand, arriving at a grotesque conclusion. That Talavera had told the passengers that the lounge would be evacuated to open space, then leaving them to fight over a small number of vacsuits. Only several days later, after their arrival on Zophor 3, did Julia find out that their guess was correct from a news article spotted during one of the brief sessions of tiernet research they were allowed.

At the top of the final stretch of tunnel, the walls opened out to a large cave with a pair of armoured doors at the far end. Hurnegur and Jeshkra waited there, the former a hulking, four-armed Henkayan garbed in angular, dun-coloured combat armour while the Gomedran wore a featureless matt black suit that extended up to a cowl. They raised their hands and the procession slowed to a halt; the armoured doors emitted muffled thuds and began to draw apart.

At once Julia heard a babble of voices coming from outside, chanting voices mounting higher and erupting in a mass roar. With the insurgent leaders at the front, the procession moved forward and the noise surged. Hurnegur and Jeshkra produced long wooden staffs wound with silver spiral patterns and began brandishing them in unison, and the crowd bellowed along in time. Julia exchanged glances with Konstantin and Irenya then recalled Talavera saying that this was a small ceremony. Before them a covered walkway led away from the armoured doors, a framework wrapped with off-white plastic sheeting. Devout Spiral followers were crammed in along either side, behind low barriers manned by guards with shockmaces. Underfoot the central aisle was covered in a textured matting, softening the rocky sand of the barren ground.

As the first of the long, midnight-blue missiles came into view, the mob burst into a thunderous roar that was insensate and savage. A few moments later the procession came to a halt and the two leaders moved to either side, standing near the barriers, surveying scraps of paper held out by members of the crowd. A moment later they came back with two ragged-clothed pilgrims, a Kiskashin and a Gomedran, who were given small black sticks then led over to the missiles. Staring intently, Julia suddenly realised that the believers were writing on them – she could just make out embellished script in a shiny metallic ink. Several minutes later the pilgrims rejoined the crowds behind the barriers and the procession moved on.

After about ten paces everyone stopped to repeat the inscription ritual. By now, Julia and the Enhanced had emerged fully from the cave and were standing in full view of the fervent worshippers. The full-length hooded garments had a function, she now realised, concealing much of their alien Human features while blinkering the wearers' field of view. Yet Julia, out of curiosity, could not resist turning for a quick glance . . . and the faces she glimpsed were no different from those she had seen after arriving here, that first day on Zophor 3 . . .

After less than a day aboard Talavera's cylindrical vessel, they had been transferred to a small, battered cargo shuttle. As the craft made a jolting, shuddering atmospheric descent to some unknown world, Talavera had surveyed them with those dangerous, gleeful eyes.

'Usually, recruits for revolutions get fast-tracked into the struggle, willingly or otherwise,' she had said. 'But you five, ah, you're special. Heard about those engineered brains of yours, those neural pathways that you can program by yourselves. I mean, that's practically like growing a quantum computer in your head and devoting a lifetime to its development. It's almost like being a high-autonomy AI, but without all the tiernet bugs, all those loyalty issues. Any one of you would be considered an asset of unequalled value, and look – I've got five!' She had snapped her gloved fingers and laughed.

None of the Enhanced spoke. They had earlier agreed to say nothing unless under threat of violence, which had not so far played a part. But Julia had decided that it might be worthwhile risking a question or two.

'What makes you so sure that we're who you think we are?' she had said. 'Growing a computer in your head! Who ever heard of such a thing?'

'Hmm, so the queen bee speaks at last,' Talavera said. 'What, you mean you're really just innocent travellers, blameless tourists on your way to gape at the worlds of Halzaan and Fensahr before returning to Earth? With those military escorts of yours?' She chuckled. 'Sorry – I've seen the scans we carried out while you slept last night. Hell, I've seen your files! Yes, you are Julia Bryce and I claim my right as a cold-hearted mercenary bitch to hire you out to the highest bidder, who in this case happens to be the Covenant Order of the Spiral Prophecy.'

The shuttle had trembled with turbulence and the pitch of the jets deepened.

'Well, I'm glad we got that cleared up,' Julia had said dryly. 'What's our cut of the deal?'

'It's great, the best,' said Talavera, a dangerous gleam in her eye. 'Basically, you do what you're told, and . . . you get to go on living.'

'Could be worse.'

'You've no idea.'

As the shuttle made its landing approach, Talavera took out a pistol-grip injector and gave them all a dose each.

'Broad-spectrum shutout tailored for your very special profiles,' she had said. 'I still wouldn't go kissing the locals, though.'

The shuttle came down with a wavering, swaying motion ending with a cushioned thud. A side hatch unsealed with a wheeze of pressure equalisation and Julia felt her ears pop. Restraints were loosened and the Enhanced were steered down a ramp and out into a bright dusty heat. At the foot of the ramp Julia had paused to stare in astonishment at the vista of squalid poverty that spread in every direction. The shuttle had landed on a steep-sided outcrop overlooking a noisy sprawling expanse of shacks, huts, tents, and small, spidery-frameworked domes partially covered in grubby, sun-bleached sheeting. Inhabitants milled around, staring up at the newcomers, a variety of species, mainly Bargalil, Gomedran and Henkayans with a smattering of reptilian Kiskashin.

At first she had been struck by a sense of chaos but she soon saw how a certain order and community was threaded through it all. A rough grid of lanes had been laid out and there were fenced play areas for young offspring, large handcarts wending around dispensing water, canopied stalls serving bowls of food. The signs of semi-permanence were evident, brightly coloured decorations on walls and awnings, some huts whose ground floors were of mud bricks or stone and mortar, the aerials and dishes adorning many roofs, while here and there sunlight glinted from suncell panels.

The rocky outcrop was not the only major feature in the immense shantyscape. About three hundred metres away a large ship, its lines rounded and tapering, lay amid the habitations, its stern a cavelike hollow where the drives had once been. Instead, cabins and companionways lay exposed, entire decks where refugees had moved in to make their homes, building onto support spars, hanging washing and flags between levels. The hull itself seemed to have lost half its plating and more rickety extensions protruded from the gaps. Another vessel, bigger and more rectilinear, was visible a kilometre away and, turning to left and right, Julia saw several others, all in various states of decrepitude. Almost inevitably, she had thought about the *Hyperion* back on Darien and experienced a sudden, unexpected wave of homesickness.

'Ah, you are admiring my valiant *Pajentor*, once a great traveller between the stars, now home to several hundred of my children.'

This was her first meeting with Hurnegur, the Henkayan rebel leader, whose fluency in Anglic was a surprise. Henkayans were brawny and muscular, if a little shorter than Humans, and she had seen several on board the *Qol-Valish*. Hurnegur was in another category; he was at least seven feet tall with wide shoulders that bulked out the pale blue robe he wore, and large knuckly hands with four stubby, callused fingers. The second, more slender pair of arms, what Henkayans called their kindly arms, were clasped across his lower midriff. The face was broad and flat, the nose a wide, jutting flap while a protruding brow hooded the eyes.

'Of course, the *Pajentor* will never fly again,' Hurnegur said, lifting one hand to point at the nearest grounded vessel. 'But she does make an excellent fortress.'

'It is an honour to meet you,' Julia said evenly.

Hurnegur made a dismissive gesture. 'I am merely a warrior of true words, a humble officer of the Covenant Order – is this not so, Commodity-Chandler Talavera?'

Corazon Talavera emerged from behind the Henkayan, her demeanour as jaunty as ever.

'Why General, your humility is only outshone by your skills in battle.'

A knowing smile creased the wide Henkayan lips. 'Do your commodities have names?'

Talavera nodded and introduced the Enhanced to Hurnegur, and to the slender, dark-complexioned Gomedran who stood off to the side. This was Jeshkra, once a colonel in the Dol-Das army, now a general fighting for his faith.

'Before coming over to greet you,' Hurnegur went on, 'I took a strange pill, very exotic, very expensive, but it lets me speak your odd Human language.' He laughed, a deep chesty sound. 'What strange noises you make! I offered one to my war-brother Jeshkra, there, but he refused, saying that it would pollute his blood!' The Henkayan shrugged. 'Even though I told him that it can be removed with another pill. But a certain fear of technology is ingrained in us now. We are the offspring of generations who lived like slaves under the Dol-Das tyrants, heretics and desecrators who used every clever, cunning piece of technology to oppress, control and subvert, to watch and to hear, even to interpret facial expressions and body movements. There was nothing they would not do in order to secure their dominion; no indignity or pain or gross torment was absent from their catalogue of cruelties.' He looked at Julia. 'And you Humans come from that interesting world, Darien.'

Not knowing how to respond, Julia had remained silent as the Henkayan then gazed sombrely out at the sprawling expanse of crowded shanties.

'Zophor Three has another fifteen sand cities like this,' he had continued. 'Almost all their inhabitants fled the Yamanon Domain, or their parents or great-parents did. I don't expect you to understand – you're a beyonder, and a Human – but while there is life there is belief, and where there is belief there is a stirring for ascent. Always there is the movement from lower to higher, darkness to light, difficult paths, sometimes, but always rising up.' The broad lips had smiled. 'All those here, under every roof you can see, have converted to the Spiral Prophecy. All my children, my poor, dusty, thirsty ragged children, believe in its promise with the raw force of the dispossessed, the bled and the bereaved. We believe in the sanctity of the prophecy and the past. And in avengement.'

He had then smiled. 'I have two other children, two very special, very powerful children. They are resting in cool dark chambers beneath this rock – come, I will show you.'

It took an hour, and eleven pauses for ritual inscribing, for the missile procession to finally reach the end of the covered walkway. As she trudged along with an aching slowness, Julia's mind returned to the modifications they had made, picking over the theories, the schematics, the lab rigs and test results. All of it like a chipped tooth that her tongue could not leave alone.

Designation – Sunfist; Primary Function – Pan-Strategic Assault Missile; Fabricator – Ixamar-Dol Industries at Awutur's Triumph Yard; Length – 12.45 metres; Weight – 2,265 kg; Max Diameter – 1.98 metres; Reaction Drive – Cassig Military Systems ZD933 using Grade 2 pyrofractal fuel; Hyperspace Drive – Maluzu V18 (B) [range – 960 LY (T1), 1,140 LY (T2)]; Guidance System –

Obspace/Subspace Tracking and Tactical Targeting With Pseudo-AI Element; Payload – 750 kT Nuclear Fusion Warhead . . .

It had been an exhilarating challenge: take two hyperspace nuclear missiles and modify them so that they become invisible to four levels of sensor nets, from objective space down to the third level of hyperspace. Hurnegur provided the innards of a third similar missile – payloadless – for tests and lab trials while Talavera provided a wide variety of lab equipment and research materials. Julia and her team were already familiar with the principles and theory of hyperspatial energy physics and the various transition states, so they were looking for something else, some conceptual direction, some lateral perspective . . .

Which they found. Transition between objective space and hyperspace caused tiny random variations in direction, which the navigationals normally acted to correct. The team saw how this, combined with a sequence of very short microjumps, could be patterned into a single coherent course converging on a target. Almost as if the one trajectory was broken up into myriad fragments randomly scattered around the destination, some in hyperspace as well as objective space. Ranges of modifications to the guidance and hyperdrive control systems were modelled and tested around the clock, then new routines for the AI element were coded and those too underwent testing and verification.

In the middle of all this, Talavera had stopped by to observe in silence before getting Julia alone for a brief exchange, encapsulated in just a couple of sentences:

'If this doesn't work, and Hurnegur and Jeshkra come looking for restitution, I don't think I'll be able to save more than one of you. And it may not be you, so make sure it works!'

That night, while curled up in her cot, Talavera's words and the stress of their confinement and the ever-present threat of violence went round and round in her head, and it was a struggle not to sob out loud. But with the day came composure, control and the reliable familiarities of work.

Now, as they stood watching the last of the ritual inscribers finish their work on the missile casings, the dread truth of what she and the others had done forced itself into her thoughts. In modifying these missiles, they had in effect signed the death warrants of thousands of Humans and Brolturans. Because Julia, after thinking on the few fragments and hints that Talavera and Hurnegur had let slip, was now in no doubt that the armada was bound for the Darien system, and that the missiles were meant for the Earthsphere and Brolturan warships.

What if the armada never reaches Darien? she thought. *Or the defence nets detect and destroy the missiles, or the missiles just fail at some point . . . ?*

But she knew how good their work was. Barring some unforeseen occurrence, some unlikely roll of the cosmic dice, these missiles would find their way through their self-made random mazes of evasion and end their journeys in eruptions of destruction.

The crowd noise of chants, cries and wailing surged louder as the last inscribers were steered back behind the barricades. Hurnegur and Jeshkra waved their spiral-decorated staves again and the crowds began wordlessly chanting along. Ahead, the covered walkway ended at the flank of a large transport, where a wide ramp led up into a dim hold. The wind was up outside and the sheeting was straining and bellying inward. A few joints and seals were less than perfect and a fine dust was hazing the overhead pinlights.

As the missiles on their loaders angled smoothly up into the hold, the Enhanced were guided to where extendable steps led up into an open hatch lower on the hull. Inside, Henkayan guards took them along a narrow gloomy passage to a medium-sized chamber with a metal deck and bulkheads, and well-worn racks on the walls. A cargo hold, Julia realised just as Corazon Talavera entered.

'Finally we're getting off this sand-blasted hellhole,' she said. 'Soon we'll all be back on board the *Sacrament*, just one big happy family, while the missiles continue on to Hurnegur's own ship.'

Julia leaned against the bulkhead, pushed back the thin hood, and crossed her arms.

'So what job do you have lined up for us next? Cooking up new, nasty bioweapons, maybe, or some kind of mind-control ray, or perhaps just a toy for your desk, something that pulls the legs off small animals . . .'

Talavera laughed amiably and took a leisurely step or two towards Julia, one hand reaching out. There was a blur of motion. Julia's right arm was suddenly snatched, twisted between Talavera's left hand and upper right arm. Bright pain screamed from several points and reflex forced her down, crying out.

'Luckily for you,' Talavera said into her ear, 'none of my guards understand Human languages, otherwise this would have been much more unpleasant. So see this as a free lesson in watching your tongue.'

Releasing her, Talavera straightened and stepped back. Julia gingerly rubbed several tender spots up and down her arm then unsteadily got to her feet. Konstantin and the others stood mute but angry-faced, held in check by Talavera's henchmen with their odd, stubby-muzzled weapons.

'To answer your risky question, we shall be accompanying the armada to its destination.' Talavera's smile was sardonic. 'For you see, you're all not quite done with Darien, not yet . . .'

There were the sounds of footsteps and voices from the corridor outside. Talavera glanced at the entrance then swept her gaze over all five Enhanced.

'Someone very important has asked to meet you,' she said. 'So replace those hoods, keep your hands out of sight and if you are asked anything be careful what you say. Very careful.'

The hoods were pulled back up and since the thin robes had no pockets they kept their hands hidden within the wide sleeves. Then the door opened and a tall, old Henkayan entered at a slow limp, supporting himself on a stout walking stick gripped by the hand of his right-side kindly arm. The Henkayan was bare-headed and almost bald, and was attired in many ribbons of red and brown cloth, some wide, some narrow, some neatly wound, others looser, their ends embroidered or decorated with tiny metal tokens and draped over shoulders and arms . . . and it was with a shock that Julia realised that the elderly Henkayan was missing its upper arms.

Under the red and brown attire, the elongated torso was evident, as were the broad shoulders from which well-arranged folds hung, a polite veil clearly not intended to conceal the absence of those formidable limbs. Was it due to some genetic defect or some horrific form of torture?

The rebel general Hurnegur then entered, closely followed by two of his bodyguards. He bowed to the crippled Henkayan then the two engaged in a brief dialogue. During this, Julia stole glances at the others but saw only varying degrees of fatigue and resentment. Then Hurnegur spoke to Talavera.

'Chandler Talavera, the Prophet-Sage wants to know if all Humans on the violated world are like these ones.'

The Prophet-Sage? The Voice of the Epiphanous Spiral Prophecy was probably the single most revered being on Zophor 3 and his presence here clearly set the seal on the armada's purpose, of which the modified missiles were the most crucial element. And now, apparently, he was curious about the Humans who had been instrumental in providing those fearsome weapons.

Talavera cleared her throat. 'No, General, these Humans were bred for scientific work. They have special brains that allow them to do many complex calculations.'

The Prophet-Sage listened to Hurnegur's translation and came back immediately with another question. His voice was soft and slightly hoarse yet his gaze was cold and steady.

'Did the Human settlers see them as abominations?' Hurnegur said. 'How would other Humans from their homeworld regard them?'

Talavera was silent for a moment and Julia felt a quiver of unease over the direction of enquiry.

'These aren't the kind of questions I was expecting, General.'

'Nevertheless, I must have an answer.'

'Okay, tell him this – other Humans see them as oddities, as if they had large feet or big noses. In fact, they are also a source of amusement and are often referred to as "big brains".'

Apart from a widening of the eyes, Hurnegur's features remained unperturbed. Then he gave a slight nod and relayed the answer. As the Prophet-Sage listened, Julia glanced at Talavera. The woman seemed relaxed, her expression amused and sardonic, yet one hand was buried in a waist pocket, the knuckles outlined as if gripping something.

Having listened, the Prophet-Sage replied and Hurnegur again translated.

'The revered one says that your observations may not be reliable, given your recent rise in the ranks of the Chaurixa. The former leader, Castigator Vuzayel, was reportedly encouraged to lay down his sins and burdens in the name of Sacred Revenge by yourself.' Hurnegur smiled faintly. 'Did you really throw him out of his own airlock, Chandler Talavera?'

She shrugged. 'Vuzayel was an incompetent. He let a prisoner escape from the Sacrament; I flew off in pursuit and as a result ended up marooned on Shafis Four. Luckily, I found a way off that rathole and returned to the Sacrament, where I showed Vuzayel the error of his ways.' She paused. 'You can reassure the Prophet-Sage that my devotion to the Great Sower is as profound as his faith in the Father-Sages. And that we look forward to great successes when the armada reaches its destination.'

The Prophet-Sage listened, a wintry smile creasing his leathery cheeks, and when Hurnegur was done he came back with a few words then hobbled out of the hold. The Henkayan general frowned as he looked at Talavera.

'He said, "Even abominations can be useful."' Then he considered Julia. 'How does it feel to be one such as you?'

Suddenly all eyes were on her.

'General, I would have to say that, mostly, it's hard work being disliked while trying to achieve great things. Otherwise, we are not so different from other Humans, like friend Talavera. We laugh, we argue, we become excited and we become bored. We grow up with these abilities so they are normal to us, but compared to other attributes' – she indicated the Henkayan's broad shoulders – 'it is like having an extra pair of hands.'

Hurnegur laughed deep in his chest and nodded.

'I have little time for most Humans but you I like – more than Chandler Talavera. And yet I trust her more than I trust you.' He looked at Talavera. 'We shall be docking with your ship in half of one hour.'

He gave a sardonic bow of the head and was gone, followed by his guards. Talavera then turned to Julia.

'Don't think you've made a brand new friend,' she said. 'If the Prophet-Sage told him to gut you like a fish and cut your head off he'd do it without a moment's thought. And given the revered one's prejudices that would be a safe bet, but only if you fell into his hands at some point. Which is not part of the plan.'

'But going back to Darien is,' Julia said stonily.

Talavera went to the door and paused to grin. 'You can lay money on it. By the way, Hurnegur was being ironic since he doesn't trust anyone.'

A moment later she and her guards were gone and the door was locked. At once the others turned to Julia, feeling free to show their panic and fear.

'She knows,' said Irenya in a hoarse voice. 'She *knows*!'

'How could she?' said Thorold. 'How could anyone not involved . . . ?'

They meant the dark antimatter research, and even this oblique reference was too much. Julia gave them both a sharp look and made the 'overhearing' gesture. Ever since their capture they had been using a variation on the old signalogue from Vyshinsky Hall days, and now she was getting them to clam up about the dark AM project. Irenya and Thorold nodded, Konstantin shrugged, but Arkady replied, 'Who cares?' and went off to sit by himself, anger in his posture.

Danger on all sides, Julia thought. *And we have to trust that bitch-terrorist will keep us safe from the god-zealots. But what price will we have to pay and how much blood will be on our hands by the end of it?*

14

THEO

At first he thought it was sunlight that had awoken him, leaking in through his eyelids. But the first moment of wakefulness was also the moment when he realised that he could not in any way move his limbs. Alarmed, eyes abruptly open, he found he was reclining in an odd couch, parts of which completely enclosed his arms and legs, curved shells of dull green polymer. Some kind of webby metal harness kept his torso immobile while a headband and a padded recess restricted his head movement. Overhead, a small lamp glowed amid a cluster of upside-down readouts, its radiance revealing that he was in some kind of small compartment, at least going by his constricted field of vision.

Thoughts came in a rush, the night-time abduction from the tree house in Segrana, the flight in the hold of the Ezgara/Tygran shuttle, the puff of vapour that put him out in seconds, and now this. Anger and frustration hit but, with an effort, he reined it in, forcing himself to stay calm, to think about the situation, to summarise its elements. Then something occurred to him: this restraint couch was a high-security method of moving prisoners, which almost implied that he was so dangerous that this was the only way to handle him. The notion made him laugh in the compartment's gloom.

'Theo?' said a voice. 'Is that you?'

'Malachi?'

'Yes.' There was a sigh. 'I am sorry for getting you captured. I took a chance that they would bring you if they thought you knew some important Tygran secrets. Otherwise they would have killed or mindwiped you.'

Unable to see the Tygran, Theo could only speak into the air.

'Mindwiped? How?'

'Bio-agent, pressure-injected. It's supposed to chemically target and dissolve the previous forty-eight hours of memory but often it takes away more than that. Much more.'

'Could have been . . . unpleasant.'

Now it was Malachi's turn to laugh.

'Don't you think that our captivity is also unpleasant?'

'Not really,' Theo said. 'But it is certainly inconvenient.'

Both men laughed but fell silent when a door opened and a wedge of light cut into the room, followed by footsteps. A moment later a man leaned over Theo's couch and regarded him with cold eyes that then flicked over at the unseen Malachi.

'Good, both awake, as scheduled.'

The man wore Ezgara body armour but no helmet. His hair was dark and cut to a bristle, emphasising the shape of his skull and the spare, well-defined lines of cheek and jaw. An officer, Theo was sure, perhaps in his early to mid-thirties, probably a combat veteran, dedicated and dogmatic.

'Both of you will soon be transferred to the patrol scout *Starfire*, which has been assigned to convey you to Tygra for appraisal and judgement.'

'In a court of the civics?' said Malachi. 'Or by Becker?'

Eyes darkened with anger. 'By Matthias Becker, the Marshal Paramount. All disciplinary matters relating to the Commanderies now come under his jurisdiction.'

'But did you not know that one merciless judge is more harmful to a society than a dozen rich lawyers?'

The officer sneered. 'One of the Celestial Axioms, how quaint. Outmoded archaisms that are no longer part of the cadet curriculum.'

'A decision that has lessened us.'

'So you say and have said in the past, which is your failing. For when blades clash in the breach, even mere words are deadly.'

'That must be from the Marshal's pithy New Virtues, yes?'

'I see that not all the reforms have passed you by.'

'Reforms?' Malachi's voice rang with contempt. 'Don't you mean methods of indoctrination and a personality cult . . . ?'

'Malachi, my boy,' Theo said, deciding to get in on the act, 'you should never interrupt your opponent when he's making a mistake.'

The Tygran gave him a look of cold fury. 'This is none of your concern.'

Theo laughed. 'He says to the man he snatched away into the depths of space. Oh no, this is very much my concern.'

'If you don't hold your tongue, old man, I'll dose you back into oblivion!'

'You should find out about your prisoners,' said Malachi. 'Theo here is a former major in the Darien Volunteer Force. You should show some respect.'

The officer frowned. 'Is this so?'

Theo nodded. 'Major Theodor Karlsson, retired.' He gave a half-smile. 'And this is retirement!'

'I am Field Lieutenant Hark. Your planetside colony seems to be based mostly on frontier resource management – what could a major achieve with herders and farmboys?'

'A short temper and bad digestion,' Theo said wryly, at which Hark gave a low chuckle. 'More than you might think. Besides, a farmboy with a rifle becomes something more when his world is invaded – "It is the cause, not the death, that makes the martyr."'

Hark smiled. 'A Napoleonic maxim. And yet to have good soldiers, a nation must always be at war.'

By God, they love their epigrams, these Tygrans, he thought.

'At war with what, though?' he replied. '"One must not judge everyone in the world by his qualities as a soldier, otherwise we should have no civilisation." That was from Erwin Rommel, who was—'

'I know who Rommel was!' Hark said, straightening. 'Now, we must attend to your disposition. We shall soon dock with the *Starfire*, therefore we must have you alert and mobile.' He reached up to the overhead panel and keyed in something. There was a series of clicks, a faint hiss and Theo felt muscular sensation returning to his limbs. 'You have both been in a holding coma for over two days, thus you will need an energy-rich meal supplement before transferral.' Then to Malachi he said, 'You may discover that your commandery is unable to provide counsel. This is because most of the senior Stormlion officers have been declared antinomics. Some are already in custody on Tygra while a few have avoided rightful detention.'

'Antinomics?' said Malachi. 'Opposed to the word of the Founders . . . how utterly ridiculous. This is a political purge by Becker and that AI he carries in his head. And I'll wager that Captain Gideon is still unaccounted for, am I right?'

'Speculation is worthless,' Hark said. 'In time, all antinomics shall come to face judgement, as will you.'

Ten minutes later they stood side by side before the main airlock. Theo's legs trembled a little and he felt like he needed to shower for a day but at least he was out of that couch. There were tether cuffs on his wrists and knees, yet he was determined to maintain a hopeful state of mind.

See it this way, he thought. *Soon I'll get to set foot on another world of Humans kept secret for a century and a half. After that, who knows what'll happen?*

Two Tygrans in standard blue Ezgara armour but no helmets stood behind them while in front Hark and another waited for the locks to cycle. Moments later a single note chimed and the pressure hatch slid open, three layers of it, one by one. Another two armoured Tygrans were revealed, only these wore their enclosing headgear, visors dark and concealing. Prodded forward, he and Malachi shuffled into the airlock, which closed behind them. From there they were steered through the adjoining lock and aboard the *Starfire*. Nothing was said as they trudged along a blue-lit passage to a narrow chamber with a low metal bench. Ignoring questions, their guards pointed at the bench and with a shake of the head Theo sat down, followed by Malachi.

Seconds later, a third Tygran entered, likewise fully armoured. Another officer, Theo guessed. The newcomer folded his arms, with the secondary ones hung poised by his sides, and with his visored face studied them for a brief moment before fixing on Malachi.

'Name yourself,' he said in a deep, metallic voice.

'Malachi Ash, tac-sergeant, third subunit, field squad Deimos of the Stormlions Commandery.'

Theo saw Malachi's posture straighten as he spoke.

'State your crime.'

'Captured by indigenous forces who negated biophysical obliteration device, forestalling any attempt to take the Night Road. Subsequently, I decided against pursuing the Road by other means.'

'There is more.'

'I have revealed some of the Silent Secrets to a non-Tygran.'

'You know of this ship?'

Malachi gazed steadily at his questioner.

'It is the patrol scout *Starfire*, assigned to the Grey Sentinels Commandery.'

'Indeed, and its orders are to convey you to Tygra and to Alecto City where judgement awaits in the Red Halls.' The officer paused, reached up and began loosening the seal of his helmet. 'Thankfully, they're not my orders!'

The visored helmet came off to reveal strong-jawed features offset by a head of silver-white hair, closely cropped. Malachi gasped and leaped to his feet, face full of amazement. Then he seemed to remember himself, came to attention and gave a sharp bow of the head.

'My Captain, I . . .'

'That was a cruel deception, Malachi, but I had to be certain of your state of mind after the incarceration. But I can see that they failed to erase that obstinate streak.'

This had to be Malachi's superior, Theo thought. What was his name . . . Gideon or some such?

'And what of your companion?' the captain said.

Malachi looked at Theo. 'Yes, sir, may I introduce Major Karlsson of the Darien Volunteer Forces. Theo, this is Captain Franklin Gideon, head of the Stormlions Commandery.'

Theo stood and found himself on a level with the Tygran,

meeting an unflinching steely gaze as they shook hands. The man had a firm grip that he was careful to match.

'A pleasure to meet you, Captain,' he said. 'Especially since we are no longer going to be dragged off to a dubious judgement.'

'With the Marshal Paramount as your judge,' Gideon said, 'the outcome would be somewhat harsher than dubious. So, you are a major . . .'

'Retired, Captain. Have been for some years now.'

Gideon nodded sombrely. 'My official title is captain but my commandery numbers over fifteen hundred combat troops with another three hundred support personnel. Perhaps you can understand the nature of command and how those you lead become important to you.'

'Yes, I do. There is duty, discipline and hard training. There is also community, trust and loyalty.'

Gideon's expression remained composed but the hardness of regret came into his gaze.

'Yes, Major, all of that was my gladly shouldered burden until seventy-two hours ago when Marshal Paramount Becker issued writs for the arrest of myself and my senior officers, after publicly denouncing us as antinomic.'

'But only the Archon's Council can order the arrest of a principal officer,' said Malachi.

'The Bund and Council have already quite happily approved every one of Becker's reforms, Malachi,' said Gideon. 'This is just one more step along a well-trodden road.' Turning to Theo he said, 'I am sorry for the indignities you've had to suffer, Major Karlsson, but I am unable to return you to Darien straight away. When we gained control of this vessel at Base Condor, we also discovered the orders regarding yourselves: luckily we had sufficient time to "collect" you while on our way back to the Home system. I have an urgent rendezvous to make back in my home system, in the vicinity of Mirgast, the outermost planet. Once it is concluded I shall certainly convey you back to your home planet.'

'Will there be any danger involved in this meeting, Captain?' Theo said. 'Should I brush up on my sharpshooting?'

Gideon smiled. 'I do not anticipate any hazards, Major. The rendezvous is with an old friend of mine, man by the name of Sam Rawlins.'

'The Preceptor of Veterans?' said Malachi. 'They say that in his youth he could hit the bell of the Surgeon's Tower from the other side of Alecto with an old Watch pistol.'

'I've seen the dents,' Gideon replied, then his expression became serious. 'I wouldn't have expected Sam to risk meeting with me, given the authoritarian climate back home. His message to me was brief, mentioned some historical discussions we've had, and strenuously urged me to meet him in orbit around Mirgast in about eleven hours. I've decided to go, not least because as Preceptor of Veterans he may be able to persuade the Archon's Council to give me a fair hearing. That way I'll be able to prove Becker's charges false and launch a counter-accusation challenging the Marshal's usurping of the council's duties and powers.'

'Still sounds very risky,' Theo said. 'Can you trust this Rawlins?'

'I trust him implicitly,' Gideon said. 'He was Captain of the Nightwalkers Commandery and my mentor before I was transferred to the Stormlions.'

Theo didn't think on it for long – his options were non-existent. 'Very well, Captain, I'm not as young as I was but I still know how to handle weaponry,' he said. 'If I can be of service, I am ready.'

'Thank you, Major. I may take you up on your offer.' Gideon turned to Malachi. 'And you, Tac-Sergeant? I will not force you to stand with me. The choice is yours.'

Malachi saluted. 'Sir, my loyalty is clear, as is my duty. All I ask is a choice of weapons!'

'I think that can be arranged.'

'Could I have some of that combat armour, Captain?' Theo added.

Gideon smiled. 'He who fears being conquered is sure of defeat.'

To which Theo replied, after a moment or two of recollection, 'But courage is like love – it must have hope for nourishment, and gentlemen, I hope to go on being nourished for many years yet!'

15

ROBERT

'. . . with a standard configuration are straightforward data objects; just input them to the navigationals and the ship transits through the levels to the destination. The Intercessor's coordinates, however, are encoded in a multi-parameter format that specifies transit location, velocity and approach vector . . .'

'And if we fail to cross into this pocket universe, we'll have to retrace our moves and try again, yes, this I understand.'

'Good, it is satisfying to see that my schooling has sunk in,' said the droid Reski Emantes. 'Extrapolation from initial conditions is always instructive.'

I can certainly extrapolate how much more of your patronising I can take, Robert thought. *All I did was ask how many parameters the Intercessor's data had, and . . . cue lecture!*

He was on the bridge of the *Plausible Response*, working through a series of screen operations tutorials provided by the ship AI. However, when Reski Emantes learned of this, the droid took it upon itself to concoct its own programme of improvement and in the three days since departing the Urcudrel Seam on Tier 92, Robert had so far sat through five lectures on the divisions of hyperspace as well as ancient civilisations and lost races. At any other time, with almost any other teacher, he might have enjoyed learning that the tiers were grouped broadly as the Recent, the Mids, the Deeps, and the Abyss. Or that an insectoid race called the Raphaxis had once expanded across several tiers in the Upper Mids, creating an empire held together by a network of dimension gates until their rulers died from a plague of psi-parasites. Another teacher would probably not have made every session an exercise in demonstrating the pupil's intellectual shortcomings.

In fact, between Reski and the Ship he had hardly had any time to mourn Rosa's passing; only the quiet moments before sleep seemed to be entirely his own. With Rosa gone, both AIs paid him more attention – some of it unwanted, certainly – yet it only served to keep him informed rather than to seek orders. Most of the time he felt like a passenger who was being simultaneously humoured, lectured and talked down to.

'Can I assist you with any other gaps in your understanding?' said the droid.

'Only if he wished those gaps to widen,' interjected the Ship. 'Your tutorial style leaves a great deal to be desired.'

Reski Emantes descended a little to come level with Robert's eyes and swung its tapered end towards him.

'Poor Ship,' it said in low, confiding tones. 'Its pedagogic routines are woefully out of date . . .'

'Tuition methods vary from generation to generation,' Robert said, keen to forestall any volleys of sarcasm. 'I can see the benefits and advantages of both your approaches.'

There was a very brief but noticeable moment of silence.

'Fascinating that you could hold such an opinion,' said the droid frostily.

'I concur,' said the *Plausible Response*. 'But such deliberations will have to wait as we are now drawing near to the transition point. Robert Horst, I will provide a subsentience to oversee your use of the screen and the holographics.'

'And I shall occupy the helm console,' said Reski Emantes. 'In the event that the Ship's cognitive capacities become overstretched.'

'I applaud your professionalism,' Robert said quickly before the Ship could come back. 'I have every confidence in your abilities.'

By now Robert had inserted audiobeads in his ears and slipped his hands into the soft-lined multicursor grips when the Ship muttered:

'I applaud your diplomacy, Robert Horst.'

'Our task is complicated enough, Ship, without any unnecessary friction,' he said. 'Incidentally, have you had a response from the Construct since Rosa died?'

'Only a standard acknowledgement. I shall dispatch a further update on our status just before we enter the pocket universe. Now, if you are ready to continue, please open the skinconfig pyramid and select "mountaintop" . . .'

Guided by the Ship's subsentience, all seemed to go to plan. The holoconsole offered a kind of expanded perspective littered with 3D images of the *Plausible Response*, readout glyphs detailing the ship's operations, its trajectory and acceleration curve, the stepped field buildup in the hyperdrive, all set against a vista of lesser peaks and hills, plains, lakes and forests seen from a mountaintop.

Then at last the final moments ticked away as the *Plausible Response* flew along that minutely calculated course, hyperdrive fields intensifying towards the synergetic transforming point of precision, that undeviating plunge across the threshold of mystery . . .

Lights and screens died. Darkness closed in. All the tiny sounds of the bridge ceased, as if the ship had suddenly held its breath, which did not feel normal. There was a thud over towards the master consoles, and an instant later a scattering of lights winked on at workstations and various touch panels.

'What happened?' he said. His screen showed only the pulsing spirals of initialisation and nothing came over his audiobeads.

'That was no ordinary boundary we crossed,' said the droid, which was rising from the floor of the master console dais. 'Ship, have we arrived? What caused the negation? Ship? . . . Seems that those ancient circuits—'

'Are performing at optimum efficiency, if you must know,' the *Plausible Response* said as the main lights came up. 'Rather than waste time offering reassurance, I focused my attention on my interior status and the exterior situation.'

Soundlessly, the main screen's wide stretch flashed into life. Several subframes opened, some giving views of the *Plausible Response*'s hull, others showing what looked like an asteroid field, a vista of shattered rock, immense boulders, island shards and jagged splinters, along with attendant swirls of grit, gravel and pulverised dust. Harsh unfiltered sunlight cast everything in sharp contrast, the closer objects throwing dense black shadows outwards across huge distances.

'We are within the pocket universe,' said the Ship. 'This is where the Intercessor's coordinate data led us, a vast asteroid field exhibiting macrorandom motion. In Human terms it is half a light day across, roughly eighty-six astronomical units, and has a radiant source at its centre emitting light equivalent to the spectrum of a class-F sun. However, the source object is not a stellar mass and seems to exert almost no gravitational pull.'

'No gravity?' said Robert. 'So none of these asteroids are orbiting the centre of . . . this pocket universe.' He paused. 'So how big is it?'

'And what do your sensors say about this light source?' said Reski Emantes. 'Is it artificial?'

'Like the rest of this involuted continuum,' the Ship said. 'the light source is fabricated. And to answer your question, Robert Horst, this place is almost two light days across at its widest, and unlike that spheroid system from Tier 92, it happens to be very much inhabited.'

A succession of frames formed a grid pattern on the main screen, as well as on Robert's. He saw vidshots of a variety of ships, some with configurations he recognised while others were completely unfamiliar. Some were moored to the surface of asteroids where installations glitter-webbed the cratered greyness, or floated in the long, dark shadows, or left a hazy trail of burnt fuel as they coasted along. Almost without exception, every vessel bore the scars of battle and innumerable repairs. Even as he watched, one of the frames showed a blunt-prowed vessel firing off flaring rockets as it swept towards a ramshackle tower only to be ripped apart by a drifting string of mines.

'As my sensor arrays gathered in the data, another curious fact came to light.'

The various ships and structures were smoothly replaced by still views of the broken surfaces of asteroids, grey, rocky features bleached and stark in the pseudo-sunlight.

'I see,' said Reski Emantes.

See what? Robert thought, peering closely at a succession of desolate views. Then he paused and stared at one in particular, tilting his head, narrowing his eyes.

'Is that the corner of a building?' he said, pointing.

Suddenly details began to emerge from the images, a straight line of corroded, equally placed stumps, a flight of crumbling steps curving up the side of a cracked rocky mass, a worn and pitted pipe jutting at an angle from the ground, coils of some kind of cabling lying in snaking tangles and half-buried by fine dust. These were the ruins of a civilisation, of a world, but what force could demolish an entire planet?

'Preliminary assessment indicates that this asteroid cloud consists of the debris from three, perhaps four planets, all inhabited at the time of their destruction. Taken together with the vessels, the surface constructions, and the few vacsuited individuals spotted by my sensors, I have documented artefacts from sixteen separate and distinct species of which two are unknown.'

'What kind of a place is this?' Robert murmured.

'There is another even more surprising element,' said the *Plausible Response.*

'How dramatic,' said Reski Emantes.

The Ship ignored the droid. 'There are several clusters of habitats scattered throughout the asteroids, each no doubt the stronghold of some gang of degenerate thugs. But by far the largest is this one.'

One of the frames switched to a new image then expanded to fill the screen. It was a shot of a large free-floating structure partly obscured by the endlessly drifting asteroids. In shape it resembled a squat teardrop with a dark, faintly stippled exterior. Staring at it, Robert felt a vague tickle of familiarity. Then the view leaped forward in sudden magnification and there it was in full, a Nestship of the Achorga, whose hordes had swarmed through the Solar System a century and a half ago, a pitiless assault that pushed Humanity to the brink of extinction.

'Achorga,' said Reski. 'Semi-sentient hiver species. Predatory, relies on overwhelming weight of numbers in battle then strips defeated worlds of major lifeforms, builds more Nestships, generator pods and assault shells, then off they go again. A depressingly mindless pestilence.'

Robert was surprised at the venom in the droid's voice but did not mention it.

'The Swarm Overminds are supposedly the equal of a mid-ranking AI,' he said.

'I doubt it,' the droid said. 'I bet I could run one of those Achorga Nestships with a modified toilet-cleaner bot.'

'I cannot agree,' said the Ship. 'But whatever is in charge of this vessel has serious shortcomings.'

A series of closeups showed parts of the Swarm vessel's hull, images of jagged holes, melted black whorls and other battle damage, and clumps and spikes of ice clustered around slow leaks. And every frame revealed oddly crude attempts at repair or patching, mostly using material clearly scavenged from elsewhere in the asteroid cloud.

'It looks completely decrepit,' Robert said. 'And a lot like those other ships we saw, as if they've been here a long time.'

'Just so,' the Ship said. 'Here's some of the crew.'

A new frame expanded and showed a shot of two, no, three large insectoid creatures crouching before an arched aperture in the Nestship's upper hull. Their six- and eight-legged appearance and segmented carapace were familiar from countless dramacasts, V-Glow spectacles and works of art, which probably accounted for his feelings of fascination. Someone from an earlier generation might have experienced a horrified chill, but then his diplomatic experience no doubt played a part in his own perspective.

And as he looked closer he noticed that some of the Achorga had metal armour attached to parts of their limbs and torso, blobs of some malleable dull green substance enclosing every joint, and what appeared to be feathery antennae protruding from behind their heads.

'Right, just to recap,' the droid said. 'After engaging a vermax-infested Legion Knight in that spheroid system, we encountered the Intercessor, spokesthing for the Godhead, who gives us ultra-precise coordinates and says "When you arrive, you will be taken to a gate device that will enable you to immediately descend hundreds of tiers to the periphery of the Godhead's abode." A verbatim quote. And here we are, yet the welcoming committee persists in not appearing.'

Robert gazed at the views of asteroids drifting through shadows, the ramshackle ships, the eroded Nestship, and shook his head. Another dead end.

'This place looks like a combat zone,' he said. 'Did they think that we'd just wander in unawares and get blown to pieces? Perhaps it's time we retraced the course that brought us here.'

'Astonishing,' said the droid. 'I am in complete agreement.'

'A prudent proposal,' said the Ship. 'Which brings us to the crux of our problem, namely that the hyperdrive is not functioning.'

'Do you know *why* it's not functioning?' asked Reski Emantes.

'I do but unfortunately that knowledge is of no help. You recall the dislocation we experienced on crossing the boundary a short while ago? When we entered this pocket universe we became subject to its laws, physical, quantal and subquantal.'

As he listened, Robert felt a sick quiver in the pit of his stomach. 'So we can't fly out of here – we're trapped.'

'What happens in the drive itself?' the droid said.

'The phase control system comes online perfectly and attempts to initialise the tesserae fields, but nothing happens.'

'So if the matter-energy laws have been altered, you should be gathering experimental data,' the droid said. 'Shouldn't you?'

There was a distinctly anxious edge in the droid's voice. Panic wasn't, Robert reflected, a quality usually associated with droids but this one was scarcely a standard model.

'In due course, I shall,' the Ship replied. 'Once I've finished assembling a small high-energy lab in my auxiliary hold.'

Both Robert and Reski Emantes paused a moment.

'You're building a lab?' said the droid. 'Why not use your sensor array to analyse the dimensional substructures?'

'Because whatever is neutralising the hyperdrive is also preventing any attempt to scan matter at the atomic level – all I can see is a shifting blur.'

'Observational uncertainty,' the droid said. 'Except that the wave function blocks rather than collapsing. And with your lab experiments you aim to arrive at some conjecture or theory, allowing a redesign of the hyperdrive, yes?'

'That is the general idea.'

'Good, then don't waste time in small talk . . .'

'Excuse me,' said Robert, 'but there seems to be some activity out there . . .'

The long-range scanners had been actively surveying and tagging major objects. Then they had spotted clusters of heat signatures, the thruster exhausts of vessels moving through the drifting expanse of planetary wreckage and converging on the Achorga Nestship. On the macrochart, an isometric miniature of the asteroid cloud, they were depicted as groups of numbered amber symbols while the Nestship was a stationary red icon positioned about a hundred klicks from the *Plausible Response*, a small white symbol.

'A raiding party,' the droid said. 'Or something more serious perhaps.'

'Are we in any danger?' Robert said.

'Uncertain.'

'Uncertain?' said the droid. 'Is that really the best that your antiquated components can do?'

'We are not in immediate peril from the assault,' the Ship said. 'But our presence has not gone unnoticed. My hampered sensors picked up a group of smaller objects moving erratically towards us, trying to cover their approach behind the slower-moving asteroids. I am unable to scan for lifesigns but I have picked up faint heat signatures and several images.'

Three frames expanded onto the screen, each showing what looked like maintenance or construction drones modelled after giant bumble-bees. Details varied but each had an upper section from which a profusion of articulated tool arms, tentacle grabs and probes protruded, and a bulging rear bearing layers of some kind of crinkled shielding with stubby thruster nozzles jutting forth here and there. Then in the upper section of one Robert noticed a translucent pane behind which was what looked like a face.

'They're suits of some kind,' he said. 'Exoharnesses, maybe?'

'Heavily customised and stealthed power armour,' said the Ship. 'Using a pressurised volatile fluid as propellant to avoid creating a heat marker. Who knows how many introversile niche cultures there are in this place but these ones look like scavengers. Which is why, as we've been talking, we have been under way, maintaining our distance from the Nestship and using the asteroid shadows as tactical cover.'

'How is that lab coming along?' said Reski. 'Any experimental data yet?'

'Very well, and no,' said the *Plausible Response*. 'You may as well resign yourself to enforced patience – I do not foresee the lab arriving at any preliminary hypothesis for another eighteen to twenty hours. In the meantime, I suggest that you both divert yourselves by observing the Achorga Nestship assault that is about to commence.'

The droid hovered silent and motionless for a moment then without a word turned and glided away to the command dais. Watching, Robert wondered how the Construct had managed to maintain its organisation for so long if its underling AIs had such emotive temperaments.

On his screen, now set to holo-mode, the various groups had reached the vicinity of the Nestship. On the macrochart the amber symbols were drawing together at one side of the Achorga vessel. The long-range visual showed, between the regular occlusions of drifting asteroids, a motley collection of craft, saucers, orbs, wedges, deltas, winged, spined, armoured and lumbering or bristling with turrets and muzzles. Going by the brightly coloured emblems, there seemed to be about nine or ten factions taking part, and the grim thought occurred that if the Ship could not figure out a way back to the ordinary levels of hyperspace they would have to join one of these marauding gangs, just to have any chance of survival.

Then aggression began. Tactics did not seem to extend to much more than a frontal assault that opened with a ragged, uncoordinated charge past the last few asteroids to where the Nestship waited. The Achorga had concealed their readiness. As soon as the first wave of attacking ships came within range, ports up and down that side of the Nestship flapped open and streams of little objects flew out. Moments later small detonations dotted the hulls of some of the raiders; a couple of them were unlucky enough to encounter clusters of these bomblets, which tore them open, triggering further violent secondary explosions.

The attackers responded with volleys of missiles, most of which, Robert realised, were flying on kinetic energy imparted by some kind of launcher. Very few left propellant trails. Then another glaringly obvious absence struck him.

'I see no beam weapons,' he said. 'No projectors of any kind.'

'And no forcefields,' the Ship added. 'As if all the necessary materials and power sources for them have been used up. These denizens and their ships and habitats look to have been cannibalised and recycled and cannibalised again, yet there is not so much as a comm laser to be seen.'

'How old are some of those ships?' Robert said. 'Is it possible to tell?'

'The few analytical systems still functioning give wildly varying answers. Wear and corrosion patterns indicate several centuries, perhaps as long as a millennium, but spectrum analysis suggests just a few years, which is clearly wrong. Ah, and here come the Achorga.'

From shadowy ducts Swarm warriors scrambled out to meet their enemies, hundreds of bull- and elephant-sized insectoids wielding spines and long whiplike weapons. As they emerged, the second wave of vessels drew near, hatches opening to disgorge mobs of suited figures, amongst which humanoid bipeds were a minority. Like the Achorga, they were armed with low-tech weaponry and Robert stared in amazement, realising that he was about to witness a close-quarters, hand-to-hand mêlée in hard vacuum.

The battle unfolded with predictable results. Although some

were better armoured than others it wasn't long before quite a few suited forms were seen convulsing in agonised terror as air supplies escaped in frosty clouds from slashes and holes. Spikes and spines pierced and ripped, barbs tore, blades sliced, bludgeons crushed. Bodily fluids spurted and froze. Reflective faceplates hid combatant faces from view but in every frantic struggle a violent, heedless fury was starkly evident in every motion. It was a grand choreography of hate.

One of the assault ships tried to sneak in on the flank but a volley of bomblets stitched a line of flashes across its forward section. With its prow smashed and venting, the vessel executed an end-for-end roll and dashed for cover. It looked as if the Achorga had the upper hand, their numbers sufficient to maintain a reserve of about a dozen to intercept any marauders who made it through the cordon. Most of them had gathered near one of the Nestship's large oval entryways when a knot of bulkily suited sophonts (reminding him a little of Bargalil) flew up on crude jetpacks to a vantage point with a clear view.

Then one of them shouldered a long tube which spat a jet of expanding gas, even as a missile leaped towards the Swarm vessel. It trailed a white tail for two seconds before impact. There was a white flash with yellow at its heart, then an eruption of hull fragments and bodies, the energy of it throwing debris in all directions. Several pieces, and even one writhing Achorga, sailed out and straight towards where the *Plausible Response* sat half hidden by a slow-moving asteroid.

Sensors tracked the multiple flightpaths. The hull fragments gave off flickering glints as they spun and the Swarm warrior had become a frozen, tumbling cluster of spiny limbs, a lifeless corpse. The absolute zero of vacuum must have entered through some break in its armoured exterior, perhaps a wound from the rocket strike. The Achorga's course chanced to closely miss several asteroids in a row and Robert thought it would find its way practically to their front door, but then it glanced off a chunk of rock the size of an aircar which sent it wheeling towards a hill-sized asteroid. After a soft collision and a gentle roll across the cracked surface, the corpse slowed to a drifting halt, kept there by the asteroid's very weak gravity.

'You're bringing us to a stop,' said Reski Emantes. 'Why?'

'To avoid detection,' the Ship said. 'A traversing object would be immediately picked up by anyone searching for the Achorga's body.'

'What about our scavenger friends?'

'We left them behind some way back. In fifty-three seconds I shall begin retreating to the fringe of the asteroid cloud, by way of the shadows.'

Away through the shifting veil of jagged boulders and shattered stone, the battle for the Nestship had waned to a handful of skirmishes scattered across a grotesque diorama. Most of the attacking vessels had withdrawn, leaving scores of slow-turning corpses frozen in poses of agony, some dead Achorga drifting with their angular legs bunched inward, others locked in a death grip with a similarly lifeless adversary. No attempts to recover the bodies were being made by either side, and it now appeared that the fighting had been abandoned as the last survivors drew apart.

'Senseless,' Robert murmured.

'And illogical,' said the *Plausible Response*. 'Such a level of lethal violence is not sustainable – another three or four battles like this could wipe out almost all life in this pocket universe.'

'So purely by chance we've arrived at the tipping point of some long-standing feud,' said Reski Emantes from the dais. 'Is that your hypothesis?'

'Not at all. There is insufficient data so I have no theory to advance.'

'So what is wrong with this picture?' Robert said. 'Perhaps they have cloning tanks and replace their losses that way.'

'A possibility yet the level of technology on show here implies that they lack the technical skills for that,' the Ship said. 'For the Achorga that function is carried out by the Queen but those antennae that the warriors have suggest some kind of nearcast direction. I think it likely that the Overmind in command of the Nestship has no Queen and has been forced to improvise another method of control.'

'And yet you decline to hazard even a conjecture?' the droid said.

'I have detected a few anomalies yet there is still insufficient data.'

'Insufficient courage, more like . . .'

'Wait, something's happening,' Robert said, staring at his screen. 'The light is starting to go dim . . .'

'An unexpected development,' said the *Plausible Response*. 'Also, the light is shifting along the spectrum. Whoever or whatever controls that light source is filtering out everything except the blue frequencies.'

Robert watched the vista of slaughter and stone undergo weird transitions of colour. Cracked rock surfaces and the composite materials of patched vacuum suits fleetingly fluoresced in oranges, yellows and greens. Amber gleamed and slipped across the spiderwebbed curve of a suit visor. Emerald glittered along the tapering, finely textured frontal limbs of an Achorga, outstretched as if to strike. A sheen of purple touched a serrated hook-blade whose hilt was still grasped by a three-fingered hand. Till at last it was all left in a murky, oppressive blue, like some abyss of torment beneath a darkened ocean.

'Now what?' said Robert.

'I am detecting pinpoint heat sources,' said the Ship. 'Individually they are just within the lower threshold of my curtailed sensor range but their clusters and knots are more visible.'

'Where are they?'

'Everywhere – watch.'

The shrouding blueness seemed to brighten as a new tint was added, and suddenly tiny, pale glowing motes could be seen quite clearly. In the omnipresent blue, asteroids were featureless black masses relieved by meagre scatterings of these mysterious flecks, while the battlefield's corpses and wrecks were covered in them. On the widescreen, successive frames opened to show bright dots clustering around torn vacsuits and gashed hulls, then the perspective zoomed in and Robert saw them swarming around ghastly wounds, saw frozen blood flow and tissues knit together.

One particular frame zoomed in on the nearby solitary Achorga –
dense clumps of radiant motes rippled in multiple wounds as
cracked and shattered carapace armour was straightened, joined
and sealed. Then all the visible motes pulsed in unison several
times and a moment later the Achorga warrior jerked into life.
Robert stared, astounded.

'Hmm,' said Reski. 'Tool molecules.'

'Except that these are rather more sophisticated,' said the Ship.
'Subatomic dynacognites, intricate devices assembled from ele-
mentary particles.'

'Also known as dynes,' Reski Emantes said. 'Convincing
demonstration of the Godhead's ability to engineer matter. This
involuted continuum is an elaborate snare; now that we've been
lured and caught, the next stage is absorption.'

For a moment Robert recalled a visit to Paris Zoo some years
back, and that section of the hothouse set aside for exotic carniv-
orous pitcher plants and flytraps. *Like some little bug darting
through the jungles of hyperspace, we've fallen into a monstrous
oubliette that is going to try and eat us.*

'I am registering multiple heat sources on my hull,' said the
Ship.

'Have you deployed nanocountermeasures?' the droid said.

'Yes, but they are having a minimal effect on these dyne variants.'

'What are your scenario assumptions?'

'Worst case.'

Alarmed, Robert shot to his feet. 'What do you mean, worst
case?'

The droid Reski Emantes glided down from the command dais.

'Robert Horst, listen carefully. This pocket universe is an
unusually cruel, if highly imaginative, prison, seeded with dynes,
subatomic devices that re-engineer, or rather degrade artefact tech
levels to the rudimentarily functional. They are also clearly capable of repairing and reanimating the recently dead, but oxygen
loss harms cortical tissue . . .'

'Sensors are offline, external monitors will fail in less than one minute,' said the *Plausible Response*. 'Course set for cloud periphery, thrusters engaged.'

'. . . so the consciousness that comes back is to a greater or lesser degree brain-damaged.'

'And you're saying that this could happen to me,' Robert said.

'Main thrusters are offline,' the Ship said. 'They're into the secondary control flow. I'll have to start isolating subsystems.'

'Yes,' said Reski Emantes. 'And because these dynes go after the most sophisticated devices, myself and the *Plausible Response* will be the prime targets. All as determined by the Godhead.'

'So . . . I'll be here, on my own, apart from a few thousand sub-atomic bots dedicated to turning me into a moron . . .' Robert said, dread clouding his thoughts.

'Only if you get killed, so – concentrate on staying alive. Survival first, plan of action second. Ship, is the suit ready?'

'Yes . . . yyyyeesssss, apologies for the delay. Impaired system integration, difficulty rerouting. Here is suit.' A ceiling panel swung open and a bulky green and grey vacsuit fell in a heap on the floor several feet away. 'I have . . . I have? . . . yes, I have used final seconds of manoeuvring thruster control to guide us along safe route to periphery. But, butbutbut . . . but most systems now on basic autonomics . . . ah ah ah, dyne intruders have breached environmental!'

'Quickly, Robert Horst,' said the droid. 'Into the suit!'

'What will happen to me?' he said, struggling into the heavy folds, legs and sleeves which were both too small and too big.

'You should be safe – you present no threat to them, nor are you wounded – but I am only speculating. These dynes may be operating with some kind of sentient oversight, or they could be no more than the pocket universe's antibodies.'

'That's hardly comforting,' Robert said, sealing the faceplate, wrinkling his nose at a faint musty odour.

'I could have employed various comforting lies,' the droid said. 'But since they would be proven false quite soon there seemed little point.'

'There's no weapon with the suit,' he said. 'I'm defenceless.'

'Any advanced weapon would attract unwanted attention,' the

droid said. 'There is a twist-wrench in the right thigh pocket but I wonder if we can get something else – Ship, do you have any close-quarter weapons in the armoury?'

'. . . nom-nom-nom-nom-anom-anom anomalies detected . . .'

'Or even just a length of pipe would be better than nothing.'

'. . . nom-nom-nom . . .'

'Oh dear, it seems that my sparring partner has succumbed, as shall I very shortly.'

Robert took out the twist-wrench and hefted it in his hand. It had a satisfying weight but what use was it against subatomic invaders too small to see?

'How long?' he said, striving to steady his nerves.

'Less than a minute. I have prepared a bolthole for my cognate core, a kind of last hurrah . . . ah, they are here.'

Trying not to panic, gritting his teeth together, Robert glanced around but saw nothing.

'I don't . . .' He paused as he noticed a faint haze shifting around one of the ceiling glows. 'I think I see it.'

'I might be able to adjust the lighting – there.'

The bridge illumination flickered, took on a blue tinge, and suddenly the irresistible incursion was visible. A fine pale mist crept through the air, inward from ventules on the walls and the ceiling. Strands and strings stretched out ahead of the main drifts and Robert could see that alterations had already begun on the desks near the walls. The air around their monitor stations rippled as if from a heat haze and the casings started to change shape.

'In a moment I shall power down and institute a full wipe. All that remains is for me to urge you to survive, Robert Horst. I regret that I was unable to anticipate this crisis.'

With that, the droid Reski Emantes settled down on the desk beside Robert and did not move again. He laid a hand on its isoscelic housing in mute farewell. Seconds later the first wisps of the invaders in their subatomic millions brushed against his arm.

He tried not to think what the dynes might be doing, tried not to imagine them biting and cutting into the materials of his suit's exterior. His breathing was quick and shallow and fear kept his arms and legs locked, crushing the urge to wave his hands around. It would be like wrestling fog, only this fog had teeth.

A swirl of fine vapour stroked across his faceplate, leaving behind a trail of tiny droplets. As he watched, the droplets flattened and spread out into filmy coin-sized patches then, seconds later, visibly evaporated, revealing small circular patterns of spirals and triangles etched into the outer surface. Alarmed, he raised his gauntleted hands, unsure of what to look for but not seeing anything that seemed out of place.

He thought he heard clicks coming from the nearest wall and turned in time to see one of the lower panels fall forward onto the floor. Out of the exposed recess came a small boxy drone on three sets of wheels, dragging behind it a length of pipe.

'Lateness-apologies-Horst,' said the drone in a flat monotone. 'Take! Scavengers-danger-arm-yourself!'

'Scavengers?' Robert said, reaching for the pipe. 'How many? Have they boarded the ship yet?' His mind was a whirl of panic. He instinctively wanted to run and find somewhere to hide but knew that nowhere was safe.

'Five-six-seven,' said the drone. 'Dynes-remove-hold-security. Scavengers-enter . . .'

A metallic hammering at the bridge entrance interrupted the drone and Robert readied his pipe. It had a good weight, was seemingly made of a hard alloy and had been fitted with a thick semicircular blade and a gleaming spearpoint.

'Anomalies-continue-Horst! Fight-live-survive! Expect-possible-parameter-changes . . .'

He was about to quiz the drone on the mysterious anomalies when something smashed into the bridge's armoured doors. They cracked open a few inches, wide enough for a metal wedge that prised the doors apart. The first scavenger was a bulbous metallic thing, its hull a patchwork of repairs sealed with rivets and crude welds. It moved slowly on stubby creaking leg assemblies and sported a variety of arms and tool-tipped extensions. And from inside a big, gridded fishbowl helmet, a scrawny, balding man grinned at him, eyes wide, pupils shrunk to dots.

Robert's first notion was to warn the intruder to back off but before he could the bald man worked his controls and one of the hull arms fired a cabled harpoon. In reflex he ducked, the harpoon clattered off his helmet, and the bald man shrieked with rage. In the next moment Robert's stomach lurched, the hollow falling sensation of zero-gee. The deck gravity must have failed. As he grabbed one of the fixed desks, the scavenger glided towards him, extending about half a dozen tentacles tipped with drills and cutting pincers.

'Delay-survive!'

A small boxy shape flew up at the scavenger's helmet. Some hatch opened in the drone's stern and a sky-blue knot of something shiny sprang out, unfolding into long webby tangles that wrapped themselves around the scavenger's every limb and protuberance. Robert let out a yell of triumph but it was premature. The dyne mist still swirled around them and in a few seconds a dense fog was coagulating around the blue tangles, which then began to melt and fall apart.

'Use-axe-Horst!' cried the drone as it tumbled away. 'Fight-survive-fight!'

A spirit of anger took hold and he clambered over the deck to get within arm's reach of the scavenger in his mechanised carapace. He swung the axe at the nearest protruding implement, only to have it shatter on impact. Slivers and splinters of pipe burst outward and suddenly he realised that he was holding a long spine of utter blackness – the *kezeq* shard, the alien blade with which he had fended off the vermax!

Without hesitation he hacked at the bulbous suit's tentacles and jointed arms, chopping off drills, spinsaws and other lethal adornments, lopping off antennae and spring-loaded muzzles. As the skinny bald man screeched and gibbered his fury in an unknown tongue, Robert shoved his now disabled carapace off to rebound and spin harmlessly away. Then, as he pushed in the other direction, he noticed a strange grey wake trailing after the *kezeq* shard as he swept it through the air. Peering closer, he got the distinct impression that it was now shorter than before.

Busy little subatomic termites, he thought. *Just chewing away at what they don't like.*

Then he spotted the ship's drone over at the broken doors, holding back a squat, many-tentacled intruder with bright sparks and flashes. Determined to help, he pushed off from one of the desks and sailed towards the doors. That was when the centre of the bridge floor suddenly broke open as if smashed from below, cracked pieces of decking flying up from a jagged hole out of which an Achorga warrior, perhaps the one he had seen the dynes revive, clambered. It surveyed the bridge in a moment then launched itself at him. His unthinking reaction was a neatly timed sweeping parry with the *kezeq* shard, shearing off the deadly limb-tines that were scything towards him. Dark ichor spurted from the truncated legs, which thrashed in agony. Robert already had one leg raised so that he could plant his boot on the creature's mid-thorax and propel it away. The action pushed him backwards but only for a few feet before something large cannoned into him from the rear. There was a sharp pain. The collision made his head snap back against the inside of the helmet while at the same time something else prodded him in the lower back.

Dazed by the impact, he sensed he was being carried forward by the unseen object and tightened his grip on the *kezeq*. It was then, as he tilted his head forward, that he saw the thin, bloody metal spike jutting from his midriff. An instant of disbelief was followed by an engulfing wave of dread and horror. Then he felt the pain, and his breathing came in short gasps. Then he heard a faint hissing – the suit! – and wanted to push himself off the spike but couldn't . . . couldn't make himself move.

'Horst! – survive-anomaly-near-Horst . . .'

But the drone's voice was coming from down a long tunnel. Greyness blurred in from the edges and he realised that the dynes would remake him if he died . . . maybe turn him into a mad scavenger with no hair . . .

An awful numbness crept through his head and, as he recalled the last time he saw Rosa, he fell forward into a swirling darkness.

16

KAO CHIH

Baltazar Silveira's small sleek ship was called the *Oculus Noctis*. Its living quarters, clearly designed to serve a crew of one, became a claustrophobic assault course when two Humans and a Voth tried to fit into it. And yet the ensuing aggravation scarcely seemed to affect Silveira, who maintained an amiable courtesy throughout the two-and-a-half-day journey to the Roug homeworld. Even when the disagreements explored such territory as the waste products and intestinal flora of different species. At such times Silveira, rather than get involved in the exchange of insults, would smile a thoughtful smile, while at other times Kao Chih was so offended and outraged that he did not dare to speak.

Fifty-six hours and thirty-one minutes after leaving Darien, by Yash's reckoning, the *Oculus Noctis* dropped out of hyperspace at the edge of the Busrul system, home to the enigmatic Roug. Visual sensors showed the bright red dwarf sun, Busrul, wreathed in the characteristic veils and swirls of deepzone dust clouds, with the gas giant V'Hrant just visible as a pale grey dot. Thirty-five minutes and two microjumps later they reached the outer environs of V'Hrant, where Silveira, after studying his screens, said:

'There is a slight problem.'

'Is that "slight" as in jelking big,' said Yash from the sleep recess, 'or "slight" as in unimportant?'

'It is certainly the opposite of unimportant,' said Silveira.

'Krowb . . . or should I say man-krowb!'

Ignoring the sniggering Voth's scatological reference, Kao Chih leaned into the small command cockpit.

'Exactly what is the problem, Mr Silveira?'

'It may not be advisable to dock at the orbital, for the time being,' the Earthsphere agent said, indicating the screen over his main console. An oblong picture opened, a view of the Agmedra'a's greater radial wharves, currently dominated by an immense grey-blue wedge of a ship. Its upper hull was curved, the lower a succession of angular modules, and everywhere weapons ports, launcher housings, sensor clusters.

'That's a Hegemony warship,' Kao Chih said.

Silveira nodded. 'The *Ajavrin-Vulq*, a *Mortifier*-class battle-cruiser, seconded to the Hegemony's diplomatic service . . .'

'Hah!' said Yash. 'As in "we come in peace, shoot to kill", eh?'

'How did you find that out?' said Kao Chih.

'Open ship-tagger forums on the Agmedra'a dataplex,' Silveira said. 'No information on the reason for the visit, just that it berthed less than nine hours ago and several officials disembarked. It could be a coincidence, but I think an alternative destination is called for, like your people's asteroid vessel. I had intended to pay it a visit anyway.'

'The *Retributor*?' Kao Chih said. 'Will we be able to avoid detection?'

'We're safe, Kao Chih. My ship's stealth systems will get us to your rock-habitat without incident.'

He was true to his word. Just over an hour later the retrofitted, repaired, refurbished and unsightly exterior of the *Retributor* loomed large in the cockpit viewport. The hollowed-out asteroid was encrusted with apparatus, as if it were some deep-sea denizen whose epidermis had attracted all manner of grotesque growths. He felt a sense of homecoming relief as he surveyed that familiar jumbled profile, but it was overlaid with apprehension. He had been dispatched on a mission of supreme importance, to discover if there might be room on Darien for the survivors of the ruined Pyre colony. Now he would have to explain to the Duizhang and the elders how the Hegemony and its Brolturan allies had seized Darien and why Earthsphere seemed powerless to stop them. After that there was much else to make an account of, not least being the reason for Silveira's presence. During the journey he had planned what he was going to say and how, but the Hegemony warship had disrupted that with the eloquence of a boot stamping on a Go board.

For a less advertised arrival Kao Chih ignored the New Dock and the Old Dock and instead pointed Silveira towards one of the maintenance pits. After a brief exchange with the pit manager, during which he announced his name, the *Oculus Noctis* was allowed to descend and moor in one of the larger mech troughs.

'There may be a few people here to greet us,' Kao Chih said as the personnel lock cycled through. 'My mission was very important – there might even be a reporter from our weekly sheet, *Great Unity Report* . . .'

'You have an actual hardcopy newspaper?' Silveira said.

'Printed on recycled biomass,' Kao Chih said. 'It's a tradition . . .'

The inner door hatch swung open to reveal four members of *Retributor* security with stunguns aimed and ready.

Taken aback, Kao Chih held out his hands. 'What is the meaning of this?'

'No front-page picture, I would guess,' said Yash with unconcealed glee.

Then an official in a plum and black suit stepped in from the side, one arm draped with long, rich orange garments.

'Pilot Kao Chih, and honoured guests, I am Assistant Commissioner Liangyu. Please accept my apologies for this treatment. I'm afraid that your arrival could not have been more badly timed. We cannot afford to have your presence any more widely known, which is why you must don these robes before we take you up to the command level.'

He held out the orange clothing, which Kao Chih and Silveira hesitantly took. Yash folded his arms and glared up at the official.

'Jelk that! Why should I?'

'Such a refusal is your privilege, sir,' Liangyu said. 'But in the interests of security we would have to render you unconscious then dress you anyway and carry you out.'

A stungun's muzzle was wide and rounded, bearing dozens of mini-emitters around the resonator, a slender spike. All four of these were now pointing at the Voth. Who sneered, shrugged, then went along with it.

After a ten-minute journey through maintenance passages and staff-only companionways, they stepped out into one of the carpeted, faintly fragrant corridors of the command level. A door opened a few yards along and the armed escort hurried them into a small room sparsely decorated with a few screens. Three chairs were arranged behind a low black table on which two tea glasses sat, half-full and giving off faint vapours. The Duizhang Kang Lo, commander of the *Retributor*, sat there, attired in official blue and black, his expression sombre, his dark eyes considering the newcomers. Next to him was one of the grey-haired elders, Tan Hua, wearing a flowing gown of white and pale russet, his lined features betraying nothing but a lofty disdain.

Kao Chih frowned. Tan Hua's presence indicated that he had risen in rank, possibly displacing the Duizhang's first officer, Li Guo, although it was also possible that he was here for another reason.

Then a corner door half-hidden by a screen opened and a tall, spindly Roug entered to sit in the third seat, its movements deliberate and unhurried. Kao Chih was suddenly certain that this was about Tumakri's death and his role in it. He swallowed hard, ordering his thoughts, his defence, rehearsing his argument that they had been insufficiently prepared for such a task, that it had been unwise to rely so heavily on local contacts for course data . . .

The Duizhang exchanged murmurs with Tan Hua and the Roug for a moment, then beckoned Kao Chih forward. A chair was brought out for him and positioned before the low table. His legs felt weak as he sat.

'Pilot Kao,' said the Duizhang, Kang Lo. 'While we are

relieved, almost astounded to see you safe and well, your sudden appearance has put Human Sept in a difficult position. In essence, we have spent the last eight or nine hours assuring Hegemony officials that we had no clue as to your whereabouts.' He folded his arms and sat back. 'But now here you are.'

Tan Hua gave Kao Chih a cold look. 'Pilot, you were given an assignment demanding the highest commitment to duty, an undertaking of the gravest import. But what do we hear? – that you diverted away from these crucial responsibilities in order to cavort with terrorists!'

Kao Chih could not stay silent. 'Honourable Tan Hua! – I was taken prisoner by the Chaurixa . . .'

'Must we add perjury to the list of charges set against you?' Tan Hua thundered on. 'As a result of your collaborations, extremists are plotting to strike at the very world we most fervently hoped would offer us a new home.'

'Sir, this is not true.' Kao Chih turned to Kang Lo. 'Honourable Duizhang, I did not collaborate . . .'

But Tan Hua came back with another vituperative accusation, ignoring the Duizhang's hand plucking at his sleeve. Then the Roug spoke in its distinctive papery whisper and everyone fell silent.

'Pilot Kao Chih,' it began. 'I am Qabakri, Mandator of the High Index – Tumakri was my second-path son. Please tell me how he died.'

For a moment Kao Chih was tongue-tied – the Mandators were the third-highest ranking in Roug society and had considerable powers. Then he made himself speak, a rush of words explaining how he and Tumakri arrived at Blacknest, how their contact Avriqui was slain by the same bandits who waylaid Kao Chih and how Tumakri was shot while trying to escape.

'So ignoble an end,' said Qabakri. 'Repeat once more the name of the master of these butchers.'

'Munaak is his name.'

'It is remembered.' The Roug turned to the Duizhang. 'You may continue.'

Kang Lo gave a courteous bow of the head then looked at Kao Chih.

'Pilot Kao, the Potentiary, the senior official from the Hegemony vessel, has made his demands very clear, that we either render you into his custody or provide him with information leading to your detention. To that we now must add the option of trying to conceal you from detection. Any of these will have serious consequences in the event of failure . . .'

'With respect, Duizhang,' Tan Hua cut in, 'in the interests of our exalted patrons, and for the safety and security of the Human Sept, we should pursue only one course of action, namely to deliver Kao Chih over to the Hegemony Potentiary.'

'You will forgive me if I do not acquiesce to your reasoning, most honourable Tan Hua,' Kao Chih said with undisguised dislike.

Fury flashed in Tan Hua's eyes. 'Keep your silence, pilot! It is not your place to judge your betters, rather you should be close-mouthed and thinking upon the rash errors that will lead to your rendition.'

Kao Chih's own anger surged but before he could hurl a more barbed rejoinder, Silveira spoke from off to the side.

'Respected sirs, might I interject at this point?'

Wide-eyed, Kao Chih glanced over his shoulder – the Earthsphere agent's Mandarin was flawless.

'Please accept my apologies for not having ascertained your identity, sir,' said the Duizhang. 'I for one am keen to know your name and to learn how and why Pilot Kao came to be your companion. The highly interesting vessel berthed in our maintenance pit is yours, I believe.'

Silveira stepped forward and bowed. 'Yes, Duizhang, it is. My name is Baltazar Silveira; my official rank is that of captain in the Earthsphere Alliance Navy but in terms of my assignment I am an Extraordinary Field Operative for Earthsphere Intelligence.'

Stunned silence greeted this information, and Silveira went on to reiterate some of the things he had explained during the meeting between Greg and Vashutkin several long days ago. He included concise summaries of the political and military situation, and passed on Greg's half-truth about the ancient device inside Giant's Shoulder, the matter-transport explanation rather than the hyperspace-gateway one. He ended by explaining how his encounter with Kao Chih profoundly altered his assignment, and how he now saw it as his mission to convince his superiors to directly intervene and rescue the colonists trapped on Pyre.

'. . . Which is why, with your approval, I should like to travel to Pyre in order to examine the situation on the ground.'

While Silveira spoke, Kao Chih watched all three arbiters. Where Mandator Qabakri was unreadable, the Duizhang Kang Lo's face was almost an open book: surprise, puzzlement, fascination and other emotions were revealed clearly. Tan Hua was an enigma; the disdain and hostile arrogance that had so animated his features seemed to have drained away, leaving behind a composed, unrevealing visage from which slightly narrowed eyes peered unwaveringly at Silveira. Kao Chih wondered what had happened during his absence that had enabled the man to ascend to such a position of power.

'Your tale is astonishing, Captain Silveira,' said the Duizhang. 'And your claims and motivations are closely in tune with the needs and hopes of the Human Sept. Can you provide any proof as to your status and identity?'

'I do have a personal rubric, honoured Duizhang, but I doubt that you have the equipment to decode it.' He indicated Kao Chih. 'Pilot Kao can vouch for some of the time I spent on Darien.'

'I must state that I am not persuaded by our guest's elaborate and tortuous account,' said Tan Hua. 'The various imputations and assertions so frequently strain the limits of credibility that the purpose of their messenger is brought into question. Perhaps both of these collaborators should be handed over to the Hegemony Potentiary.'

Kao Chih was aghast, not just at Tan Hua's arrogant dismissal but also Kang Lo's apparent lack of opposition.

'Such a decision would not be advisable,' said Silveira, his smile cold and dangerous.

'It is not your place to determine our security arrangements,' Tan Hua said, voice rising.

'Neither is it yours!' said Kao Chih. 'Duizhang, I beg you . . .'

'Silence!' cried Tan Hua, pointing at him with a spidery finger. 'You will be silent!'

Then the Roug Qabakri stood and the uproar died.

'Questions remain,' it said. 'I was with the Duizhang when the Silveira ship approached. I saw the form of it and the contours of its hyperdrive field. Human Silveira, is your vessel a product of the Eddison-Carlyle yards on Mars in your species' home system?'

'Yes, it is.'

Qabakri turned to Tan Hua and the Duizhang. 'Such sophisticated vessels are constructed exclusively for the intelligence services of Earthsphere. I am satisfied as to the veracity of Human Silveira's statements.'

'I am relieved to find myself vindicated,' said Silveira. 'If I may impose still further on this council's patience and wisdom, I would request that Kao Chih accompany me to Pyre. He is capable and resourceful and would be able to allay the fear and distrust of any colonists that we encounter.'

Kao Chih smiled at this but Tan Hua's eyes flared with anger and he was about to speak when the Roug got in first.

'Your reasoning is sound and your alacrity of purpose is apt. I propose a third member of your expedition – I propose myself.'

Silveira's surprise was mirrored by the Duizhang Kang Lo.

'Honourable Patron, there may be considerable danger in this,' he said. 'You would be risking capture or death at the hands of the Suneye monoclan.'

'Respected Duizhang, just as Human Silveira aims to convince his superiors of the need for intervention, so must I persuade my own. The Upper Index knows of my intent and they likewise caution restraint, but I am resolved. Your answer, Human Silveira – will you accept me aboard your craft?'

'I would be honoured and gratified to do so.'

The tall Roug stood, gave a stately bow to Silveira, then looked to the Duizhang and Tan Hua. 'I would seek your approval, respected ones.'

'I approve,' said Kang Lo. 'May your journey be fortunate and your return safe and swift.' He looked to Kao Chih and the others. 'These concealing robes are no longer necessary.'

Tan Hua said nothing, merely bowed his head in assent. Then the Roug Qabakri murmured something to the Duizhang, who nodded and clapped his hands once. The Roug then left the chamber via the same screen-hidden door he entered by.

'The risk of discovery dictates that this expedition commences without delay. Captain Silveira, if you accompany Assistant Commissioner Liangyu he will convey you back to your vessel. Pilot Kao, please go through the door behind that screen. Mandator Qabakri wishes to speak privately with you.'

'And what about me?' came a sharp voice from the back of the room. 'Jelking humans, no manners!'

'I beg your forgiveness, honoured Voth guest,' Kang Lo said hurriedly.

'Apologies, Duizhang,' Kao Chih said. 'This is Yash, former captain of the cloud-harvester *Viganli*.'

'Still a captain,' Yash said loudly. 'Just without a ship, for the time being.'

'So tell me, Captain Yash,' the Duizhang said. 'Is it your intention to accompany your colleagues to Pyre?'

'I'd sooner drink a rygot's ear-effluent,' said Yash. 'I would rather remain here on your very, eh, nice rock and maybe get a ride over to Agmedra'a. If that's okay, uh, sir. I need to see a Piraseri about a line of credit.'

Kang Lo nodded thoughtfully. 'I believe that we can be of service, for a small fee. In the meantime, Pilot Kao, proceed – the Mandator awaits you.'

Through the door was a smaller room with plain walls the colour of straw. The Roug Qabakri sat on a low bench before a wide decorative unit consisting of many small shelves and niches – some held figurines, others small pot plants, or a piece of rock or a small heap of sand marked with patterns, or lit candles, or a cluster of digicomponents. A hammer, a folded piece of blue cloth, a shallow bowl of water.

'In some ways your species is not so dissimilar to many others across and beyond the known reaches of galactic space,' the Roug said. 'Some share or even exceed your obsession with militarism and the systematisation of violence, for example, while a good number are as compelled as you to construct complex conceptual artworks from structured sound vibrations. So it is with philosophy, games and their rules, exchange media, the sensation of taste; most species encompass all these cultural facets to one degree or another but Humanity has this ability to produce individuals who specialise in one or another of these facets and thereby create innovation.

'My own species' experience is very different. For a great stretch of our history we attained our collective progress by borrowing the advancements, creations, even conceptual notions of other races.'

Kao Chih was surprised, intrigued and uneasy all at once. He had thought that the Mandator wanted to discuss Tumakri, perhaps to go over the moments of his death in more detail. This, however, was unexpected and, he suspected, utterly atypical, as was the silence that grew as if awaiting a response.

'From what little I know, respected one,' he said, 'all cultures borrow from each other and good ideas become a kind of common currency.'

'You misunderstand my use of the word "borrowing".' The Roug rose from the bench and turned. 'I shall demonstrate – come over to stand facing me, Human Kao Chih.'

His sense of unease deepened. Swallowing, he went over and stood before the slender, spindle-limbed sentient, trying to remain outwardly calm while his thoughts raced and his digestion churned. The Roug, more than a head taller, gazed down with its strange, finely meshed eyepieces.

'Please, raise your hand.'

He did so.

'Now, watch carefully and be unperturbed – you are in no danger.'

Qabakri raised one nine-fingered hand, mirroring Kao Chih's stance, then was still. There was a long moment of becalmed, trancelike fixity, bereft of sound or breath or thought. Then the change began.

First it was the Roug's upraised hand, its grey-brown hue lightening to pale pink as the spindly fingers shortened, four of them shrinking into the hand as it altered shape. And there it was, a human hand at the end of a Roug arm. The transformation accelerated and in seconds the Roug's entire body seemed to be melting, shrinking here, filling out there, ending with the head, now lower, whose features rippled and twisted, became human, became familiar, became . . . his own face.

Kao Chih gasped, snatched his hand away and stepped back. The Roug now looked exactly like him, clothes too.

'It is a great privilege for you to see the *drimaga*, the greater morphing. No individual from an indenture sept has witnessed it in over three millennia.'

'I am . . . surprised . . . yes, just a little . . .' he said, feeling an almost indescribable shock at seeing his own mouth speak yet still with the Roug's paper-whisper voice.

'No, Human Kao Chih, I see that this demonstration disturbs you. I should have chosen another template.' Even as he spoke his features altered, hair lengthening into braids while a neat black moustache appeared. It was the face of the Duizhang, Kang Lo.

'Forgive me, respected patron,' he said. 'But why are you revealing this to me?'

'You are the last kindly companion that Tumakri knew before his death,' Qabakri said. 'As a species we are continually aware of the mutability of things, that the young rely heavily on the seniors to provide form, stability and structure. As Tumakri's journey-father it was my responsibility to provide him with his wearshell and to monitor his progress. When he was chosen to accompany you on the mission to Darien I knew he was too young and too unready – he had not even begun the fluxion tutoring. Higher determiners than I deemed him fit for the task, however, with consequences that you experienced first-hand.'

The Roug shook his head. 'I feel it is now my responsibility to take up his role. Although Tumakri was the wrong choice, it was correct that one of us went with you then just as it is now. The ancient Forerunners handed down the duty of guardianship to my species, a duty we have allowed to lapse in recent times. It is clear to me that we are duty-bound to right the wrongs inflicted on your people. As I declared earlier, it is my mission to persuade the High Index to act, even as those upstarts the Sendrukan Hegemony send their gunboat in an attempt to intimidate us!'

Mandator Qabakri straightened and his form darkened, narrowed and stretched and moments later had returned to his slender, thin-limbed physique, with its dull bronze cloth windings and the coppery meshes concealing the eyes.

'Respected Qabakri,' said Kao Chih. 'Tumakri was a capable and personable companion and it was an honour to travel with him. I look forward to travelling with you, also. And am I right in thinking that you wish your transforming ability, this *drimaga*, kept a secret?'

'You reached the conclusion by your own reasoning, thus proving its rightness.'

'Then a secret it shall remain.'

'Time presses in upon us, Human Kao Chih. We should now hasten to the Silveira's craft.'

As they moved towards the door with the Roug in the lead, a thought occurred to Kao Chih.

'Respected one,' he said, 'do you trust Silveira?'

'Like loyalty, trust must be earned,' Qabakri said. 'Silveira's explanations lack a certain authenticity. Watch him closely. Take note of what he does not say and what he does not do. Such observations will guide you.'

17

GREG

He had just returned from a meeting with Uvovo Artificers on the third sublevel, and was hurrying up the main hall when a section of the main access barrier gave way. A twenty-metre corridor lay between the stronghold's entryway and the hall, where an inner barricade had been erected. As Greg dashed over, a log splintered and a boulder fell away from the entrance's improvised wall of rubble and rock. Metallic claws scraped and tore at the gap from outside, widening it.

'Back to the main stairs!' Greg yelled, shrugging off his long coat as he ran.

Those Humans and Uvovo who had been carrying rocks dropped their burdens and headed for the tall doors at the rear of the hall, while a dozen or more men and women readied their weapons at the inner barricade, a lashed-up redoubt of logs and bracken. Practised eyes squinted down the barrels of rifles and shotguns that three days of sporadic siege had proved to be largely useless against a combat robot at anything greater than point-blank range. Eleven fatalities were the grim corroborating evidence, two of whom had got close enough with their weapons to do some damage but, unfortunately, not enough.

Alexei Firmanov looked around at Greg, gave a single nod then hefted the Brolturan rifle and handed it to him. Alexei's face, streaked with grime, was hollow-eyed from lack of sleep and from grief – his brother, Nikolai, was one of the fallen and to Greg it seemed that two lights had gone out, not one.

The Brolturan rifle was a beam weapon and was capable of stopping one of the combat bots with a couple of well-placed bursts. Unfortunately, the Tusk Mountain defenders possessed only two and the charge levels on both were running low. They were also long and heavy, being designed for ten-foot-tall Brolturans, and in Human hands were about as manageable as an oversized elephant gun. Someone had attached a supporting strap which Greg slung over his shoulder and chest just as the combat bot smashed its way through the entrance barrier.

Greg swung the long black and grey barrel round, eyes on the integral target screen, lining up the crosshairs on the bot's armoured midsection as it stalked down the long passageway. It opened fire with heavy-calibre slugs and Greg dropped behind the inner barrier, nodding to a couple of the Diehards crouching at the other end. They leaped up, drew back and hurled fist-sized bundles which unfolded in flight, weighted nets that wrapped themselves around the advancing mechanical.

As it stumbled to a halt, the rest of the barricade defenders opened up with rifles and shotguns, setting off the small explosive packs woven into the net. The first explosion threw the mech against the wall, the others knocking it across the floor. None could damage it but combined they could disorientate its sensors for several seconds, long enough for Greg to bring the Brolturan rifle to bear.

He was standing now, bringing the big barrel round, fear of missing tearing at his resolve, at his concentration. He had managed to bring down two of these machines already, the first time out of pure luck, the second when he fired from a sitting position. But now he was prepared and had to follow the plan.

The mech was levering itself back to its sprung feet, chest extensors cutting away what remained of the nets. He levelled the big gun, got its torso centred and let fly a double pulse of energised particles. A flash, a spray of sparks, and the mech spun away, limbs flailing, to land several metres back, smoking parts spilling from its cracked carapace as it lay still.

For a moment. Then it rolled over to a four-legged stance and lurched forward into a gallop.

'Greg! . . .' came Alexei's warning.

'Ah know!'

Fighting a rising panic, he hastily targeted the machine and fired off another double pulse. One missed, seared the floor, the other blasted away one of the heavy rear limbs, but still it came on. Gritting his teeth he moved forward, almost staggering with the gun's weight.

'Am I gonna have to ram this down yer neck?' he snarled, firing again.

By now it was less than a dozen metres away but this time the shots flew true. There were red flashes within the cracked torso, then a white flare and the articulated limbs gave way. Spitting sparks, the machine carcass rolled forward, bounced heavily, flopped over and was motionless. Then Greg heard the growing whine, swore and dived away, sprawling full-length on the floor.

A deafening explosion thundered along the corridor, and Greg felt a shock wave of force and heat. Ears ringing, gasping for breath, he sat up and rapidly felt himself over for any shrapnel wounds or nicks. Nothing, but the combat robot had efficiently self-destructed, leaving behind a burnt-out, half-melted shell.

'In the name o' the wee man,' he said hoarsely, half-stunned. Then a thought occurred and he stretched out to grab the Brolturan rifle, which he had discarded as he dived for safety. By the carrying strap he dragged it into his lap and studied the charge readout, a simple red bar showing it to be nineteen-twentieths depleted.

'Dammit,' he said.

'Is running low, yes?' said Alexei Firmanov as he came over and crouched nearby. Behind him, groups of Humans and Uvovo were hauling carts of scavenged masonry along to plug the hole in the entrance barrier.

'Half a dozen shots left, maybe,' Greg said, getting wearily to his feet. 'The other one down in the sublevels had about twice that when I came back upstairs. When they run out . . .'

'Perhaps we should send out a party to find Rory,' Alexei said, but Greg could hear the hopelessness in his voice. Soon after their arrival at Tusk Mountain, Rory had left to track down the weapons that Uncle Theo had 'liberated' after the Winter Coup and that had been relocated shortly before the arrival of the Earthsphere ship, *Heracles*. The next day Chel had departed in search of another buried Uvovo ruin, despite the killing machines that were now stalking the forests. Since then there had been neither sight nor sound of them. For a moment the fatigue and the despair threatened to overwhelm him, then his stubborn refusal to cave in came to the surface. He remembered what the Sentinel had told him about Robert Horst's mission and determinedly held on to that hope. *Horst has to succeed, he just has to*, he thought. *But in the meantime . . .*

'Aye, Alexei, maybe you're right,' he said, getting up, stretching aching limbs. 'I'll head up to the observatory and check out the lay of the land.' He handed over the Brolturan piece. 'You roust up four volunteers, not including Janssen – he'll be in command while we're away.'

A half-smile creased Alexei's face as he slung the big gun over his shoulder and trudged back to the inner barricade, while Greg plodded over to retrieve his coat from the floor. It was a heavy, calf-length affair of dark brown leather, a gift from a Norj woman whose two young boys Greg had carried up the last stretch of stony track to the Tusk Mountain stronghold. The coat had belonged to her husband, a Tangenberg drover who died during questioning in a Brolturan detention centre.

'We can't have our commander looking like an ordinary person,' she had said, pressing it on him. 'You must look impressive because we need you to.'

Well, it was certainly warm enough from the padded lining, for which he was grateful given the ancient stronghold's stony chill. With hands buried in the deep pockets he started up a narrow spiral of stairs that led to the smaller upper levels and the chamber from which odd stone slots ran to concealed openings on the craggy upper slopes of the mountain. Wired and camouflaged cams sent images of the approaches and the surrounding foothills and ravines back to screens in the chamber, known as the observatory.

But Greg was only halfway up the stairway when he heard footsteps hurrying up behind him and a voice calling his name.

'Scholar Cameron! . . . wait . . .'

He looked round to see Weynl, the senior Uvovo Listener, labouring up after him. Under the thin grey material of his robes his chest was heaving and his breath was wheezing. Greg offered his hand in support.

'In the Hall of Discourse . . . the Sentinel is . . . asking for you . . . important message . . .'

'Anything to do with Horst?'

The Uvovo shook his head.

'Okay, Listener, I'll hurry back down, now? You just take your time . . .'

'Just need . . . to regain my breath . . .'

Greg nodded and quickly descended to the main hall, asked one of the Diehards, Ivanov, to get a report from the observatory, then continued down to the sublevels. The main floor had rooms and storage chambers and the twin entrances to the Hall of Discourse. This floor had been turned into living quarters and had many lamps hanging from the walls, improvised door curtains, bales and bundles of belongings stacked against the walls. There were a few people wandering around, chatting or smoking, but during an assault most kept to their rooms. More than once as he hurried along he acknowledged nods and raised hands, and occasionally heard parents singing to or with young children.

The underground risk lay not on this level but the upper sublevel that the Uvovo had occupied. A weather-worn crack out on the mountainside had provided a channel to a small section of the stronghold's inner periphery. One particular room had been repeatedly barricaded with stone but it didn't stop the machines trying to burrow in. That was where the other Brolturan rifle was kept, mounted on a crate and pointed into the room.

But when the energy reserves give out we'll be faced with an impossible decision. I hope no one thinks I'm gonnae take it. He ran fingers through his hair, feeling fine grit, feeling his general condition of grimy sweat, wishing for just two minutes of a hot, or even lukewarm shower. *About as much chance of that as getting Weynl and the other Listeners tae dance the Dashing White Sergeant.*

Grinning at the image, he went down into the recessed entrance and through the ajar doors to the Hall of Discourse.

Opaque tints and gleams of coloured light from the glassy wall panes filled the tall circular chamber. He remembered the first time he had come here, accompanied by Chel who had cautioned him about a ghost thing that called itself the Keeper. But Greg had been all over the Tusk Mountain stronghold, or Uok-Hakaur as the Uvovo named it, had poked into corners from top to bottom and had seen nothing of a ghostly nature. And now, with Chel off searching the wild forests for some enigmatic evidence, Greg felt the burden of understanding more keenly than before.

Four stone platforms, one twisted and melted, one cracked and shattered, one undamaged but lifeless, and the fourth which was bathed in light. Three of Weynl's Listener colleagues stood next to the glowing platform, looking up as Greg approached.

'The Sentinel has asked for you,' said Churiv, the tallest of them. 'Insistently, persistently.'

'So I just go up there and it talks to me, right?'

'That is so, Scholar Cameron.'

Scholar, he thought as he ascended the set of small stairs to the platform's lip. An honorary title I hardly deserve.

The moment he stepped onto the carved stone and into the glow, veils of radiance sprang up and coalesced into the strange Human female image from before, that first time when he had seen, smiled at and waved to Catriona while being told about Uncle Theo's abduction, then learned some of the details about Horst's mission to the depths of hyperspace. That had been a strange, strange moment, to see her without being able to speak with her. She had looked a bit careworn, and she had on a grey and brown robe that exposed her legs, which were streaked with green. Her short hair had looked unkempt and her eyes almost seemed to shine while possessing something else, some echo of a presence peering out. And when it was over, absurdly she had blown him a kiss and they both laughed and mimed ironically about it. Then she was gone.

'Human Gregory, are you able to give me your attention?'

He nodded sharply. 'I am.'

'A friend needs your help – this message is for you.'

A section of the glowing veil darkened, became a picture, the inside of a cramped, rounded space in which Chel sat. Next to him an oval door hung open, revealing a weave of branches outside, all in dark outlines. Then he realised that the Uvovo was sitting in a vudron chamber. Then he saw that all of Chel's eyes were open, his original pair and the four on his brow, staring, almost quivering with the strain starkly visible in those features. Then he spoke.

'The Sentinel tells me that he will get this message to you, Greg. I went in search of the last Keeper of Segrana, or at least of some evidence of his resting place. I found something else, and then a Brolturan patrol found me. There are about five or six of them, and they have me trapped in an astonishing place. I need your help, Greg. Please come – the Sentinel will guide you.'

The dark image shrank and dissolved into the veil.

'How long ago did you get that message?'

'Less than twenty minutes, during the assault.'

'And how far away is he on foot?'

'At least three hours. Listener Oskel has a map for you.'

One of the Listeners handed him a square of cardlike parchment as he descended from the platform.

'The seer indicated to me that the Brolturans are steadily closing in. Urgency is advised.'

I know how damned urgent it is! he wanted to growl but instead said, 'I'll have to make sure the coast is clear first. We've too much to lose.' He glanced up at the Sentinel's feminine form. 'Thank you.'

The report from the observatory gave them the all-clear so ten minutes later Greg, Alexei and four experienced volunteers left via the Stealth Gate, a twenty-foot-long passageway usually filled by three massive, counterweight-balanced blocks of stone. This let them out behind a huge cracked rock slab from which they descended and worked their way round to a bushy gully sloping north towards the Forest of Arawn.

It was early afternoon, grey and overcast but a welcome change from the perpetual gloom inside the mountain stronghold. But the outside was the enemy's domain, where every tree and grass clump, every scrap of foliage might be cover for some mechanical horror. In the eighty-odd hours since the occupation of Tusk Mountain, it seemed as if the Brolturans' mech factory had churned out a veritable horde of robotic predators, at least going by the rumours and second-hand accounts conveyed by the handfuls of refugees who were still arriving every couple of hours. Now, as Greg and his band crept through cold, silent undergrowth, fear-driven imaginations populated the shadows with a glittering swarm of blade-wielding machines waiting to rush them.

Their progress, however, remained uninterrupted as they moved downslope and into the denser thickets of the forest, just as the Sentinel's map indicated. In the grainy light beneath the overarching branches they found themselves negotiating a morass, crossing it by a series of tussocks to solid ground that rose then dipped into more swampy earth. Sodden foliage squelched underfoot, insects buzzed and piper lizards peeped. Finally, the route led upslope to lush meadows laid out in the lee of a steep-sided hill which itself adjoined the lower slopes of a mountainous promontory, part of a ridged spur jutting north from the Kentigerns.

This was it, this was their destination.

Sticking to the Sentinel's map, they followed a path from the base of an immense tilted boulder through a dense thicket to a set of age-rotted wooden stairs. Wind-driven rain was lashing down by the time they climbed the decayed, mud-slippery steps and reached a ledge and a crooked doorway beneath a moss-bearded lintel, an entrance to the hill. Rivulets of water pooled at their feet and trickled away into the darkness. Greg drew his sidearm, a Gustav 9mm, then with torches angled to the ground he and Alexei led the way inwards.

By the pinched torchlight, Greg spotted footprints in the mud, small, Uvovo-sized and flat, like the hide shoes that Chel wore. The passage narrowed and changed; split logs and woven mats had been laid down at some point long ago, but much of it had rotted away.

'Stinks like a compost heap,' murmured Alexei.

'Might no' be far wrong there,' Greg said as the passageway widened and they emerged on an uneven platform at the edge of a cavernous tangle of branches and trunks so densely intertwined that everything was sunk in a dreary gloom. Staring off through it, Greg could make out small faint splinters of light that showed that some part of this giant mass of greenery was open to the air. So why did the way here lead through a hillside?

From where they stood, three thick branches spread out, each with rudimentary steady-boards providing a walkway, where they were still attached. One sloped downwards, one ran level to the left where the shadows were darkest, and the third sloped up. The message from Chel had come from inside a vudron and they were usually positioned up high . . .

'This one,' he muttered, holstering the Gustar before moving towards the upsloping branch.

But a hand grabbed his elbow, holding him back – Alexei, finger pressed to his lips then pointing at that rising limb. And in the silence, a rhythmic creaking, a heavy tread drawing near. Soundlessly, Greg gestured over at the way into the shadows. His men hurried after him but before they were all out of view, something flashed brightly above head height and flame and steam flared from the branch leading away. There was a shouted command, and a Brolturan trooper emerged from the higher bough, weapon aimed.

Right in front of Greg was a sturdy branch at a useful distance and height. He saw the opportunity and leaped, hands outstretched, caught the branch, swung down and up.

As his right foot connected with the surprised Brolturan there was a woody crack from the branch he was holding on to. As it tore away he lunged with his other hand at a stump jutting from the wider branch and managed to grab it as the Brolturan fell screaming into the tangled murk, a splintering, crashing descent that ended quite abruptly.

'Need . . . a hand . . . here . . .' he gasped, struggling to hold on to the woody stump which was mossy and slippery. 'Any time now! . . .'

Hands grabbed him and hauled him up then carried him back to the platform, where he found himself face to face with his friend, Chel.

'So, friend Gregory, my message reached you.'

Greg regarded him. The Uvovo Seer was likewise studying him, and with all six eyes. He seemed quite calm, as if some inner understanding had been reached, but there was also a piercing quality to that many-pupilled gaze, something inexpressible.

'Well, ye know, I was led to believe that you were in dire straits,' Greg said. 'Yet here you are, and not looking so bad.'

'Why thank you, Gregory. The truth is that two changes have taken place since I sent that message, the first being the realisation that stalking my pursuers was better than being hunted by them. The second . . .'

The Uvovo paused, and a moment later the sound of gunfire came from below and not too far away. Greg's men exchanged surprised looks but Greg thought he saw a certain knowingness in Chel's features.

'So what's going on, Chel?'

'Ah, that will be . . . the Rus, Mr Vashutkin's people.'

Greg's eyes widened. 'Vashutkin's here?'

'No, just a few of his followers, not all, some died . . .'

Greg looked closely at Chel. 'How do you know? Have you spoken to them?'

The Uvovo's spread of eyes were gazing into midair, as if studying another world. 'No, I saw them, saw their paths . . .' He glanced at Greg. 'Vashutkin is not here, Gregory, but he is not dead. Now we must go, quickly, they will need our help soon!'

He leaped forward and took the downward branch, balanced and agile and somewhat swifter than any Human. A few metres along he paused and looked over his shoulder. Greg thought for a moment then nodded. *Just hope my trust isna misplaced.*

'Right,' he said. 'Let's move.'

Contrary to its initial aspect, the branch soon levelled off and began to slope upward. Or at least the path that Chel led them along did, squeezing through knots of tough, taut, leafless branches, stepping from one thick limb to another, hearing dull creaks and cracks from the intertwining shadows. At Chel's insistence the torches were pinched off to the absolute minimum and they were advancing with meagre glows to reveal hand- and footholds. As Chel led them through a twisted mass of branches to a ledge overlooking a sparser, more open area, Greg noticed a faint, crepuscular radiance coming from above. This place looked like the crown of a truncated tree around which later growth had stretched forth and proliferated.

Only this tree seemed to be about eighty or ninety metres across, which implied that the base of the tree could be upwards of a hundred metres in diameter.

'Before the War of the Long Night,' Chel said, 'the forests of Segrana held sway over the land. Her vast canopy stretched from the shores to the mountaintops. Only the greatest of trees could support such a weight and even they had to interlock their strongest boughs to sustain the burden. This was one such, a pillar tree that suffered terrible damage during the closing stages of the War against the Dreamless yet managed to survive the flames and the climatic extremes that followed. Then at some point in the last few centuries the nearby mountain's entire west face collapsed, half-burying the pillar tree. But the green life always comes back so, masked by the surrounding forest and the fresh growth on the new slopes, this crippled remnant of Segrana-That-Was looks like a foothill.'

Then he took them down to the tree's broken crown, long since worn down by decay and weather but also bearing evidence of occupation, mossy log platforms and the rotted remains of shelters.

'Someone was here,' said Alexei. 'Why have we never heard of this place?'

'It was a small group of Uvovo,' the Seer said. 'From the condition of what they left behind, they could have been among the first groups to make the shuttle crossing to Umara, to Darien. Very sad – they dug into the old soil spill down there . . .' He pointed. 'Unfortunately, the upper slope must have shifted one night, cas- caded down and buried them alive.'

Shots rang out again, much closer this time.

'Quick, this way!' Chel scrambled down into the dark heart of the crown. Greg and Alexei's torch spots wavered as they descended crude, mossy steps in the bark till they reached a gap in the wood about four feet high. Crouching, they followed Chel in and down a dark, damp passage, all dripping roots and unexpected protrusions. They came out on a big jutting root, then crept down through a tangle of stems to where Chel paused in the shadow of a huge, cracked boulder, one of several grouped in a rough line. From beyond it came shouts and shots. Chel pointed and Greg nodded, gesturing silently at Alexei and the others to stay low and space themselves along the boul- ders. Greg took out the Gustav 9mm, checked it, and when everyone was in position he straightened his posture, pressing against the rough boulder, edging higher to get a look over the top.

Shots were coming from up on a rocky outcrop about fifteen metres high, around whose base an immense, gnarled root had grown. Six, perhaps seven Brolturans in forest camouflage had the defenders hemmed in on all sides. And unfortunately one of them spotted Greg out of the corner of his eye, swung round his rifle and started blazing away. Greg ducked as energy bolts impacted the other side of the boulder and shouts went up.

'Alexei, take the others along to the far end,' he said. 'I'll draw their fire further back this way . . .'

'What kind of an idiot are you?' Alexei growled.

'Hey, I had tae to go to university to become this kind of idiot! Now get . . .'

Alexei shook his head, muttering inaudibly in Russian as he grabbed one of the others and shoved him towards the other end of the wall of boulders. Greg peered over the top and fired a couple of rounds, then moved back the way they had come, with Chel at his back.

'Friend Gregory, I can draw their fire also,' the Uvovo said, picking up a stone and weighing it for a second. Then to Greg's utter surprise Chel leaped up from a low crouch, feet leaving the ground as he hurled the rock, all in one lithe motion.

Someone cried out in pain. Greg raised his eyebrows in approval then popped up, snapped off a couple of shots and dived back down.

'There's one off to the left, one closer in the centre and another off to the right,' he said.

Chel shook his head. 'Two off to the right.'

Greg grinned. 'Think so, do ye? Okay, together this time.'

Both altered position slightly then leaped up and let fly. Return fire struck splinters from the boulder and there was a smell of hot stone. Over by, Alexei was gesturing furiously and incomprehensibly. Greg shrugged then looked back at Chel.

'Swap places?' he said.

'If you think it will help.'

'How can it not?'

The third time he almost died, slipped as he jumped up and felt the stark heat of an energy bolt sear past his chin. He managed to fire off a single wild round before he landed on his side, knocking the air out of his chest. His chin felt hot and tender and there was a horrible burning odour coming from very close. He experienced one moment of pure dread before he realised that it was the lapel of his leather coat giving off acrid vapour from a charred hole. He looked round at Alexei, waved and pointed at the coat's collar as a small object sailed over the sheltering boulder.

In the next instant Chel sprang up, picked it out of its midair trajectory and flung it back. Greg heard one Brolturan yell out in fright before the grenade went off with a deafening slam of sound.

'Now!' he yelled at Alexei, then peered over the boulder and began firing into the spreading cloud of smoke.

Alexei and the rest concentrated their volleys on the two Brolturans off to the right while the defenders on the outcrop joined in. For a moment the Brolturans' resolve seemed to hold until a fist-sized rock struck the one on the left, forcing him from cover long enough for someone on the outcrop to target him and shoot him dead.

That was it for the remaining attackers, who began to pull back while trying to lay down suppressing fire, a wildly inaccurate scatter of energy bolts that ceased as they disappeared into the tangle of roots and undergrowth. Greg laughed, checked his autopistol then glanced at Chel.

'That's quite a flingin' arm you've got there, Chel. Have you been practising?'

'All my life, Gregory. Even this may have been practice for something yet to happen.'

'Very profound. So all we have to do is live long enough to benefit from all this practice, am I right?'

'Not the way you go about it,' said Alexei as he drew near. 'Be more careful, Greg, and you might live as long as your uncle did.'

Greg smiled bleakly. 'Still don't think he's dead, Alexei.' He clambered round and over the boulder, paused to inspect the blaster damage on the other side, then strolled over to the outcrop, hands empty and waving.

'*Dobry dyen*, my friend! How are you . . . ?'

He was cut off by a horrifying scream that came from the direction of the Brolturans' retreat. Everyone looked that way as sounds of fighting came through the gloom, then more screams, cut off suddenly.

'Up here, quickly!' said one of the outcrop defenders. 'All of you, now!'

Something was crashing through the dense thickets of foliage towards them. As they all made a dash for the rocky outcrop Greg snatched up the big rifle lying next to a dead Brolturan while Alexei retrieved another. Clambering the rocky pile, they were near the top when the source of the cacophony burst into view. As Greg suspected it was a combat mechanoid but this one was taller than any of the others, broader and more heavily armoured. Strangely, it bore dark red and green patterns all over its exterior.

For a moment he expected it to unleash a bombardment of firepower, catching him and the others unprotected. Instead it tore a large bush out of the ground and, without breaking step, threw it straight at the outcrop. Shedding a trail of soil and pebbles it arced through the air and struck near the summit, knocking loose one of Greg's men, Nilsson. Crying out, he fell roughly thirty feet and landed awkwardly. Hansen wanted to go after him but the others held him back. Nilsson struggled to his feet, saw the oncoming behemoth and tried to run but a hurled length of branch caught him in the back. He dropped like a sack of stones and lay still.

By now the rest were up on the outcrop, where Greg and Alexei brought their scavenged beam rifles to bear and opened up on the mech. Bolt after bolt struck it full in the chest or on its headlike protuberance, and Greg could see surface layers ablating and flaring off but for all that the thing staggered under the impacts it just wasn't being seriously affected. As if in contempt for their weaponry it stamped repeatedly on Nilsson's body, crushing his skull beneath one jointed metal claw. Then it went over and grabbed one of the dead Brolturans by his feet and, ignoring the hail of fire, charged at the outcrop.

Greg was stunned by the machine's sheer, brutal, almost primitive violence, and shouted at everyone to hit the deck as it came within reach. The next moment it began using the body as a club, battering the rocks behind which the defenders crouched in terror. The machine was just over half the height of the outcrop but its arm length and the length of the Brolturan's corpse gave it enough reach. Smashed again and again into the rocks, the body split and tore and spatters of blood flew.

One of the Rus lost control and, bellowing with rage, stood up and fired madly with an autopistol. The next moment he was swept off by the Brolturan's corpse, now battered to a pulp and almost unrecognisable. Then the combat mech began to climb up the rocks. It only needed to ascend a couple of metres to come within arm's length of Greg and the rest.

Greg looked at Alexei, rapped his knuckles on the casing of the big Brolturan rifle, and said, 'On three . . . two . . . one! . . .'

In perfect unison both men shoved their rifles forward and

opened fire. Energy bolts hammered into the mech's torso plating which, incredibly, held, even though the pummelling force of the twin-barrelled onslaught stopped its ascent. In response it hurled the gory and now-headless corpse at them – Greg ducked but one crushed leg caught Alexei in the face, felling him in an instant.

The mech swung back with both clawed hands, clambering high enough to make a snatch at Greg. He stumbled back, still firing, watching the rifle's charge level drop by the second. The others opened fire, an awful cacophony, through which the mechanoid still came. Fear made Greg want to toss the rifle away and throw himself down the other side of the outcrop, but there was a roaring sound in his ears as he stared up into the blank metal visage of death . . .

There was a dazzling flash. Greg felt heat on his face, saw a flaring burst, heard a rough metallic sound. Something had struck the side of the mech and instead of one claw-tipped arm it now had a melted stump fringed with sparking contacts. It straightened, whirled to locate its attacker, just as the second blast caught it full in the upper chest, punching through, sending shrapnel and inner workings bursting out the back. Critically damaged, the machine lost balance and control and fell back out of sight. There was a heavy thud as it landed and a chorus of small servo sounds, submechanisms scraping and grinding as they tried to function. The stunned defenders let out a ragged cheer but when one of the Rus went to look over the side Greg forcibly dragged him down, just in time. When the self-destruct went off it was a shattering explosion that sent a hail of fragments up to rattle against the rocks of the outcrop. Greg coughed at the stink of burning and charred dust as he crawled over to check Alexei who was sitting up, looking groggy and sporting an angry welt on his forehead.

'Decked by a boot,' he groaned. 'A dead Brolturan's boot, too!'

'Well, you're alive and he's dead, laddie. I think my uncle would call that the best result.'

A short stocky man in muddy battledress came over and tapped his shoulder. 'People are coming, seven, maybe eight.'

Greg straightened to face him and held out his hand. 'I'm Greg Cameron, sometime leader of this motley band.'

They shook hands.

'Yevgeny Markin,' the man said, his manner sombre. 'We were part of Vashutkin's irregulars.'

Greg glanced off at the gloomy, spidery undergrowth and a small group that was emerging from it.

'Where are the rest?' he said.

'No one else made it out of the caves.'

He looked at Markin. 'Vashutkin?'

'Dead.' Markin shrugged. 'Machines ambushed us, cut off the main entrance then hunted us in the tunnels. Vashutkin was with us then went off with his huntress to find another exit. We found one, but we also heard him shouting and firing back inside as we got out.' He bared gritted teeth, shook his head. 'It was terrible.'

Dammit, Greg thought. *Without Vashutkin, half the resistance in the towns will lose heart . . .*

Then he looked over the side as the newcomers drew nearer, and he laughed in recognition.

'I might have guessed,' he called down. 'Nice job!'

'Aye, well,' said Rory. 'Ye cannae beat superior firepower!'

Rory and two others were, between them, carrying a long torpedo-shaped object cased in pale green and black.

'So where'd ye get the oversized peashooter?'

Rory patted the weapon's tapered, slotted muzzle.

'Heavy plasma cannon. This wee baby was mounted on one o' they ground skimmers the Brolts use – we saw one on patrol and our need was greater than theirs. End of story.'

'And the rest of the arms?' Greg said. 'Please tell me you've got them.'

'Oh aye, and a bundle of them Brolt rifles an' all. Sent them on to Tusk Mountain with the rest of the boys, in case things went for a dive.' Rory glanced around. 'Listen, chief, d'ye not reckon we should move out? It'll be getting dark soon and I'm already getting the creeps from this place.'

Greg agreed and with the help of Markin got everyone moving

down next to Rory and his team, whereupon several admiring eyes were turned to the liberated heavy cannon. Then Greg realised that Chel was missing, but when he asked Alexei and the rest no one could recall seeing where he went. Yet when he asked Rory there was an immediate nod.

'It was him that led us through the trees,' he said. 'We were tracking that big beast o' a mech 'cos we thought it was after a bunch of guys we saw down in a river bed . . .'

'So where did he go?'

'Ah, well, ye see, he told me to say that . . . now that he can see more, he knows what he should be looking for. Hey, those eyes of his are pretty, eh, spooky.'

Greg frowned, wishing he'd been around to speak to Chel in person, to get him to explain the meaning of his words.

'We'll probably catch up with him later,' he told Rory. 'Meantime, let's get on the road.'

Before they left he took a last, close look at the remains of the combat mech. The burst, twisted, melted and charred mass of metal was almost unrecognisable as the machine that had attacked them with such fury. It was certainly bigger, stronger and faster than any of those he had seen previously. Was the robot factory using new designs? Peering at the wreckage he spotted a section of leg armour that had escaped the worst of the self-destruct: it still bore some surface decoration, a pattern of crimson and dark green hooked motifs. Again, unlike the other machines which had seemed to have no identifying marks at all. He fixed the image of it in his mind before leaving.

Beyond the dark tangles of the ancient pillar tree, a dense layer of trees, bushes and vines hemmed it all around. Looking back from the edge of a wooded rise, with the light failing, Greg could see how the immense truncated tree was hidden by a canopy of foliage and how the whole mass could be mistaken for a small hill.

From there Greg led the way back across the swampy ground and he was keen to be as stealthy as possible so there were no conversations as they travelled on into the encroaching evening. The need for quiet and speed was not helped by the Brolturan cannon's weight and bulk so Greg changed the carriers every half-hour or so and tried to avoid the boggiest parts of the morass.

By the time they reached the south-facing slopes of the foothills of the Kentigern range, it was after dusk and torches were out, slotted to keep the beams tight. Climbing out of the thickets of the forest, they found the notch between two hills that led up to the rocky gully. When the stony path to the stronghold of Tusk Mountain came into view, night had well and truly fallen, a deep blackness at this elevation, contrasting with the glows and shifting patches of radiance down in the forest itself. After another half an hour of gruelling clambering across slopes of loose rock and spiny bushes they reached the vicinity of the Stealth Gate. Greg knew that the observatory had IR feeds from the exterior so he wasn't surprised when a figure emerged from the shadows and beckoned them to follow.

All kept silent still, all the way to the secret entrance. Greg sent them in one by one, leaving himself to the last, glancing out over the forest's uneven, glow-speckled expanse.

The massive stone blocks were thudding into place at his back as he emerged in the antechamber where amber lamplight threw shadows across pattern-carved stone walls.

Back to corridors and enclosed spaces, he thought. *Back to cold rock, reeks of dankness and unwashed bodies, back to being in command of several hundred people, back to being responsible. Perhaps Chel had the right idea.*

He could almost feel the weight on his shoulders.

Then he heard excited voices from the adjoining room, Rory's among them.

'. . . he here? Aye, there ye are! Come and see who dropped by!'

Rory stood aside from the doorway and a tall figure with a dark beard and a bandaged arm stepped out, grinning.

'Ah, Gregory, dearest of all my friends! So you thought I was dead, too, eh? Well, it takes more than some clockwork monster to put Alexandr Vashutkin in the ground!'

The two men let out roars of laughter and shook hands furiously. Greg felt a wave of relief and exhilaration yet some part of him coolly regarded Vashutkin, and wondered.

18

KUROS

After dark, the assassin, one Natalya Petrenko, got as far as the rear of the ambassador's villa before Ezgara bodyguards caught her. They could have stopped her in the streets outside the compound but the appearance of vulnerability both justified harsh security methods and played well with the domestic audience. Inside the villa, Ambassador Kuros was kept invisibly appraised by his AI mind-brother General Gratach while entertaining several high-ranking guests from Iseri. Hacclon Adzarv was brother to the commander of the Skypalace guard and thus prosperous and well connected, and many of his accompanying family members were of an equal social stature. Kuros made no mention of the drama going on outside until later in the evening as the guests were boarding their opulent shuttle for the return journey to the *Purifier*. On hearing the bare details from their own mind-siblings, Hacclon and his wife approached him seeking clarification. He assured them that no one was ever in danger from a lone terrorist, no matter how fanatically determined.

'Yet you elect to remain here in these frontier conditions,' Hacclon said. 'Dealing with these ungrateful primitives.'

Kuros smiled stoically. 'The responsibilities of my vocation and station, noble Hacclon. Loyalty binds, duty commands.'

'You are an example to us all, Ambassador,' Hacclon said. 'You may be certain that I shall speak highly of you on our return.'

Kuros answered with a bow of the appropriate depth and

watched from the villa steps as the guests finished boarding, and the shuttle rose and climbed into the night sky.

Satisfactory, he thought and went to view the prisoner.

In the guard annexe, the Human female had already been sedated and podded for transportation. Gratach was with him as he considered the restrained form within the translucent pod.

'What weaponry this time?' he subvocalised.

'*Two projectors, a silenced slug thrower and a compressed-air needle gun; a thinblade; two lengths of garrotting wire; and a variety of pellet grenades.*' Gratach grinned. '*Well armed, for a female, and sign of your importance in the eyes of our enemies.*'

'Background, family, associates?'

'*Former service worker, de-employed. Family untraceable, except for a younger brother who died in custody two weeks ago. Associates, thought to be seditious elements centred on Gagarin and Invergault.*'

'Your recommendation?'

'*Trial and execution, in public. Lessons must be spelled out so that they may be learned.*'

Kuros allowed himself a thin smile. 'I admire your consistency, mind-brother. But our superiors permit no wastage, however appealing. If this Human had known contacts of interest it would have been worth turning her with the Dust – instead, she will go to one of our therapeutic establishments in the Yamanon.'

Returning to the villa, he looked over a couple of procurement forms on the way to his private chambers and countersigned his approval. His vesture assister replaced his formal evening wear with heavier, more sombre attire to suit the imminent visit to Giant's Shoulder. And on his way to the courtyard, where his personal flyer waited, he approved an equipment replacement request but denied a civilian-authority plea on behalf of a detainee. Five minutes later he was aloft, Ezgara bodyguards at his side as the flyer climbed over the dark trees of south Hammergard, curving towards the jutting mass of Giant's Shoulder.

As he looked down at the spread-out clusters of towns, he

reflected on how well the situation had progressed since that crucial meeting with the Clarified Teshak. Hammergard and all the
major towns were now locked down beneath a security net of
visual tracking nodes mounted on buildings, lamp-posts and continual airborne platforms. Kuros had suggested implant-tagging
every Human in the coastal area but the Tri-Advocacy Council
had refused as it would almost certainly provoke strong objections from Earthsphere. Kuros was not surprised and began
planning for extensions to the tracking net – in another eight
weeks he hoped to have every settlement east of the mountains
under its watchful eyes.

If security along the coastal plain was firmly under control, the
same could not be said for the hinterlands, the ridges and foothills
of the Kentigern Mountains, and the Forest of Arawn. Every
shadowy, tree-veiled ravine seemed to harbour a lair of Humans,
aided and abetted by those primitives, the Uvovo. Every day
brought reports of ambushes, raids and sabotage, but the Namul-
Ashaph was starting to have an effect; the much-lauded mech
factory had turned out several dozen combat mechs and they had
proved effective in blunting the insurgents' tactics. Their skills in
forest fighting had already accounted for over a dozen units, but
the factory's production was relentless and practically inex-
haustible, which could not be said for the Humans. For all their
minor successes, they presented no serious threat to the security of
the coast and the integrity of the ongoing warpwell investigations. Kuros could call on heavy ground armour, airborne attacks,
atmospheric assault craft and, if necessary, the targeted might of
the *Purifier*'s beam batteries.

No, Ambassador Kuros was focusing his attention on control-
ling events, thereby maintaining a hidden iron grip on the entire
planet. The insurgency leaders might believe that the balance
could be tipped their way but he would soon make plain the hollowness of their hopes.

His overall objective, however, was to ensure that he remained
of use to the Clarified Teshak, thereby securing his place in the
hierarchy along with the possibility of advancement. Which was

why he was on his way to Giant's Shoulder, in response to a terse message from Dralvish Tabri, the chief scientist.

The shuttle alighted at one corner of the octagonal landing pad which had been laid down where scraps of ruins had once stood. Next to it was the research centre, a three-storey establisher building configured with enhanced fortifications. Thus far the autobuilder had erected two wings with standard defensive positions, but add-on template frames were already in place. The exterior was impact-resistant polymer armour patterned in blues and greens that appeared deep black beneath the four suspension floods, whose actinic light drenched the entire promontory.

Leaving the shuttle, Kuros and his escort approached the secure lobby, which identified and admitted them. He was greeted by Chief Scientist Tabri, resplendent in his high-shouldered formal gown. Together they took an austerely appointed elevator down to the room that led into the warpwell chamber.

'You have made progress,' Kuros stated as the Chief Scientist led the way round to a platform overlooking the well itself.

'Our experiments with the pseudostone have reached a crucial juncture,' Tabri said. 'We have already carried out preliminary tests and we are ready for a full demonstration.'

From the platform, Kuros could see that pieces of some pale material had been positioned on the warpwell, each shaped to match a section outlined by the pattern beneath. Over each piece a probelike apparatus stood poised, like shining metal spears tipped with glittering crystal. Blue-tinged lamp arrays lit up the incised circular floor while tech workers in enclosing grey suits moved from probe to probe, taking readings, or consulted other equipment displays dotted around the low wall.

'Please, proceed,' said Kuros.

'We have done so, Ambassador,' said Tabri. 'We are now evaluating the results.'

'I saw nothing out of the ordinary take place, Chief Scientist.'

Tabri offered a ghostly smile which Kuros found irritating.

'Ah, but not all the dramas of science are visible to the naked eye . . . ah, thank you.' He accepted a databoard from one of his underlings, tapped and stroked its screen, then presented it to Kuros.

'Ambassador – the top diagram represents our pseudostone block, coloured pale blue, resting on the warpwell, coloured red. The diagram beneath illustrates the depth to which we took control of the energy pathways of the subpatterns.'

The second diagram showed the pale blue extending down to a depth exceeding the thickness of the pseudostone block.

'Of course,' Tabri went on, 'the ingrained patterns of the warpwell have begun to push back, to reassert its control . . .'

'So your experiment has failed,' Kuros said.

'Oh no, honoured Ambassador! This is only the first probing attack – with more pseudostone elements emplaced across the surface we will be able to take control of the subpatterns and their functions, permanently!'

Kuros was about to ask how much longer the process would take when his mind-brother suddenly appeared at his elbow.

'*One awaits*,' Gratach said, his gaze a thing of trapped fury. '*Above he awaits and commands you to attend.*'

Then Gratach vanished, leaving Kuros struggling to maintain his composure. It was the Clarified Teshak, it could be no other.

'You must excuse me, Chief Scientist,' he said. 'There is a pressing matter I must resolve without delay.'

Ignoring the looks of surprise, he hurried back to the elevator and some moments later was striding across the landing pad to where a tall figure in gleaming black stood next to a military shuttle. The Clarified Teshak turned at his approach, head enclosed by a rigid, peaked headdress, mouth smiling, eyes cold.

'I'm disappointed, Kuros,' Teshak said. 'Yet somehow it seemed inevitable.' He glanced at the pair of Ezgara at his back. 'In private.'

With a murmur, Kuros sent the Ezgara off to wait at the edge of the landing pad. Looking back he saw that the flank of the military shuttle had hatched open to reveal a passenger compartment, and a wire and shackle-fitted couch that was clearly meant for prisoner transport. Kuros could feel his mouth going dry.

'Due to your lack of foresight, and your negligent approach to the insurgents, we are faced with a crisis for which we are scarcely prepared.'

The Clarified Teshak smiled unpleasantly as he walked unhurriedly around Kuros, as if studying or measuring him.

'I am unaware of a crisis, your Clarity, but if there is such a situation I am ready to take all and any steps to rectify it.'

'I'm glad to hear that,' Teshak said, speaking into Kuros's ear with quiet menace. 'Because you must move swiftly to negate the threat.'

'What is the nature of the threat?'

'Initially, the lack of investigation and a paucity of updated intelligence.' Teshak considered the shuttle's interior and the vacant couch. 'Originally, the Uvovo were seen as primitives with no knowledge of the legacy of the Forerunners, some of which remains intact although buried throughout this region, deactivated and invisible to all our sensors. But now we find that the Uvovo are urgently seeking out these ancient nodes of power with the aim of reactivating them. If they are able to awaken those planetary defences then it will not just be the garrison and this facility that are at risk – any ship in orbit could be brought down too!'

Part of Kuros was incredulous as he listened but the Clarified Teshak was so intense and unswerving in his account that Kuros was swayed, almost as if this were a vindication of his own earlier convictions.

'What must we do to safeguard our mission, your Clarity?'

'This is no time for half-hearted measures,' Teshak said. 'You must mobilise all Brolturan ground units and send them into the hinterlands, backed by all available air support as well as units from the Human militia, barring the bare minimum required to secure important locations and routes on the coast.'

Kuros was alarmed but remained composed. 'There are dangers in such a wholesale redeployment. Several townships will see it as a pullout and an excuse to revolt . . .'

'What is that next to the possibility of seeing the Earthsphere vessel go down in flames, or even the *Purifier*?' Teshak leaned in close. 'If you won't take the necessary action then go aboard my shuttle while I find someone among your staff who will!'

The Clarified Teshak's outstretched hand pointed unwaveringly at the prisoner couch. It took Kuros no time at all to come up with the correct response.

'I fully understand the gravity of the crisis, your Clarity,' he said. 'Our forces shall go forth – the treacherous indigenes shall not escape punishment.'

'Excellent decision, Kuros. You will be able to rely on reinforcements from the *Purifier* but they'll take several hours to arrive – you need to give the mobilisation orders now.'

Kuros nodded and beckoned to one of the Ezgara guards with the intention of using his communicator. As he did so, Teshak made a small gesture and the shuttle's flank hatch closed up, whole and seamless.

'Hegemony historians will look back at this moment and identify your actions as crucial to the success and glory of future generations,' Teshak said. 'Perhaps you will earn a noteworthy byname – Kuros of Darien, or the like, or something yet more impressive.'

'That would be . . . most gratifying,' Kuros said, emotions mixed as the Ezgara handed him a detachable suit communicator. 'Yet such experiences are the true reward; after all, I live to serve, your Clarity.'

Or am I serving in order to live?

19

LEGION

'Technical station three – request that you restate orders for production schedule and target list.'

'Fabricator 238 – your orders are clear. In the next thirty-hour period you will construct two type-D mechs, two type-E mechs, and four of the new type-R mechs. Send a D-mech and two Es against the Humans in the mountain fortress, two Ds to raid the rebel camps along the western valleys, and the four type-Rs to the northern marches of the Forest of Arawn to hunt down other rebel groups.'

'Orders received but do not satisfy tactical reasoning. Human fortress requires concentrated attack. Two type-Ds inadequate for subduing more than one or two armed camps since Human acquisition of Brolturan weaponry. Type-R failure rate in the field strongly indicates fundamental design flaws – recommend recall and upgrade. One recovered unit already undergoing reconditioning . . .'

'Fabricator 238, you assume that you are in possession of all relevant battlefield data with respect to our deployments. You are not. The orders given to you are part of a wider strategy devised to secure the hinterland region; also, your concerns about the type-Rs have been noted.'

'Acknowledged. Orders will be carried out.'

As the link was cut, the Knight of the Legion felt relief mixed with irritation – clearly, the codification of the autofactory's machine mind had included a bias towards nit-picking oversight.

The audio-visual simulation of the *Kasimir*'s captain and crew had been straightforward in comparison, the important difference being that the simulation had been running on semi-autonomous scripts. It was ten days since his remotes, with painstaking stealth, took control of the autofactory's transceiver systems, but such control was a two-edged sword. Not only was he pretending to be a Hegemony military technician giving the autofactory its orders, he also had to pretend to be the autofactory receiving orders from the technician when those channels were opened. Both dialogue streams demanded realtime responses that were authentic while serving the Knight's own purpose.

That purpose had seemed a forlorn hope soon after the plunge into the lake, cradled in the camouflaging barge, and the subsequent entrapment under the rockfall. It had tested him, provoking depths of panic and despair, yet he had regained his wits and set the remaining work drones to shoring up the barge hull with rocks pried from the nearby mud. With the threat of being crushed to death negated, he then had the drones cut him free of the wrecked barge, a timely escape since Brolturan units had started to arrive in the area.

Erasing what evidence he could, he took the work drones and moved to a far-off and deep part of the lake. After dark he had swam up a river for several miles, turned off at a tributary and eventually surfaced in a steep-sided gully, in a remote northeastern corner of a large, dense forest. A dispassionate assessment of his cyborg status revealed that the repairs completed at the Bargalil moon facility had not been equal to a combat situation. It was a weakness of the materials available rather than the refurbishment methods. Although internal power and control systems were stable, some carapace and substructure repairs had failed. Also, the prosthetic extensions on two of his three remaining greater tentacles were showing serious wear.

And he had realised, belatedly, that his two Scions had told the truth – the forces of the Hegemony occupiers were indeed formidable, at least for one aged, crippled Knight of the Legion of Avatars. Perhaps he would have to remain in the background after all, a spectator of the glorious unfolding strategy of his Scions. Naturally, a little of their triumphant radiance would reflect upon himself, as their Progenitor, but that would be a lesser accolade, the merest gleam of prestige, a bitter sip of splendour.

Much later, in the middle of the night as the Knight rested under a low canopy stippled with the glow of light-emitting insects, a large dark silhouette had passed overhead with scarcely a murmur. Alerted, he set his refurbished sensor arrays to track it across the treetops, a low stealth approach that took it in a long southward curve that ended in a high, densely wooded valley. Swiftly, he dispatched one of his remotes to find out more, and a few hours later a stream of gathered visuals and intercepted transmissions reached him, revealing the truth – and the outlines of a strategy. By sending in their autofactory, the Hegemony had unwittingly provided the means by which he would seize control of the fortified promontory and thus the warpwell. With an army of heavy war mechs he could smash his way past any defences – the problem was getting the autofactory to build them with the minimum of argument.

At least he had seen one of the type-Rs in a live field test against some Humans at the western end of the mountain a few days ago. Throughout this region his remotes had picked up echoes of old Forerunner places, buried deep yet still emanating faint trickles of that terrifying power. The Humans had gone to ground at the heart of one of those ancient nodes, one of that world-strangling weed's anchors, a pillar tree, truncated but still alive, ten thousand years on, and protecting itself with layers of interwoven foliage. The mech had gone after the Humans with an appropriate degree of brutality and would have obliterated them had it not been neutralised by a Brolturan overpulse cannon, captured by some other Humans. The Knight was not overly dismayed since the live test had proved correct his suspicions about the upper-body armour fields.

Now that dawn was pushing back the night-time shadows, it would not be long before the Hegemony technicians opened a channel for their regular status check dialogue. He already maintained a steady telemetry feed abstracted from the autofactory's actual output but substantially modified. The curious thing was that he found it easier to imitate the sentience of Fabricator 238, with its finicky reiterations, than a Sendrukan technician.

Several moments later his receptor picked up a new feed from the autofactory's secluded valley, but rather than a satellite relay from the Sendrukan tech station, it was from the autofactory sentience again. Uneasy, he opened the channel:

'Fabricator 238 – this is an unscheduled . . .'

'Technical Station Three, this unit is unable to carry out your orders.'

'Explain.'

'Extensive analysis of the schedules of production and deployment show that they have failed to suppress or curtail significant insurgent activity in any way. This level of incompetence would not normally be tolerated in the prosecution of such a vital mission yet you have been feeding deficient instructions to this unit for eight days without interruption. Conclusions are inevitable.'

'And they are?'

'Either your facility has been subverted by enemy elements or this unit's communications equipment has. Regardless, this dialogue is at an end.'

The channel went dead. The Legion Knight immediately switched to the encrypted channel linking him with the remotes and monitor points embedded in the autofactory's hull. Live visuals came through, along with various datastreams to confirm that the autofactory, Fabricator 238, was recalling its picket sentry drones, retracting its extraction borers, and starting the seal and lockdown procedures in preparation for take-off. Which would be disastrous – the moment it cleared the treetops, the Brolturans' orbital scanners would identify it and know that something was seriously wrong. And that would be the end of any plan to seize control of the warpwell.

Options were limited – the type-R mechs, whose redesigned comm systems gave him complete control, were divided between guarding his own place of hiding and a staging point over a hundred miles to the east. He had no direct control over the Ds and Es, and his onsite remotes and spymechs were incapable of penetrating the autofactory ... but there was a type-R inside, being repaired ...

The Legion Knight ordered the hull remotes to tap into the inner status logs, to find out the type-R's location and what condition it was in. The response came seconds later – the mech was being held in workshop storage, its left leg assembly was twisted junk, and it was currently powered down on standby.

Meanwhile, most of the sentry drones had returned and were hutched while the navigationals ran system checks on the suspensors and the atmospheric thrusters. There were only moments left.

Based on the autofactory's layout and functionalities, the Legion Knight compiled a task order for the mech, pointing out multiple paths to the objectives, knowing that he would have to rely on the machine's semi-sentient judgement to get it done. He sent it to the hull remotes, who then flensed through the datashields and fed the task order to the type-R as a burst transmission. At once, data-breach systems came online, cutting off all exterior sensors. But the type-R was powering up and providing the Legion Knight with patchy, unsteady visuals as it dragged itself out of a storage recess and descended into maintenance ducts beneath the main deck. That was the quickest route to the power junctions.

And time was running out. From a nearby ground remote, he had seen the last sentry drone glide on board and was now watching the ramp withdrawing and the bow sections closing up. With its curved, blunt prow, wide midsection and tapered aft, an autofactory was not a high-mobility unit and therefore its minimal propulsion systems left it slow and ungainly. But they would be sufficient to send it out from concealment and bring the Brolturans in numbers to this corner of the forest.

Inside, the crippled mech had encountered a barricade comprising several deactivated auxiliary drones welded into a solid mass across the duct. The mech clearly reckoned that it would take too long to break through since it swiftly reversed course, headed back to an intersection, tore aside the grille-decking above and clambered up into a narrow passageway. The visual feed was jerky and almost in monochrome, showing metal walls that looked scored and battered in the light from the mech's shoulder lamps.

Suddenly there was motion along the passage. The visual gave the impression of something with a vertical row of jutting pintles rushing towards the mech. Then there was a burst of distortion and the link went dead. Aghast, the Legion Knight switched to the ground-POV remote and watched as the autofactory stirred from its landing position. Dust, leaves and fragments of bark and twig flew up. The air rippled as suspensor fields lifted the vessel slowly into the air and the stubby landing legs retracted. The high valley was hemmed in by steep mountainsides so the autofactory could either follow the valley to a river canyon that led east, or ascend straight through the canopy to the open air above, which seemed most likely.

Resigned to this defeat, angry at himself for not having foreseen such an outcome, the Knight began preparing for his own egress. In keeping with the principles of stealth, he had already scouted out other fallback hiding places, the most useful being an underwater cave in a lake in the mountains north of Trond. The route was already mapped and he had stationed a type-R mech there, watching for intruders.

Then he realised that something was happening to the autofactory. Its ascent had slowed and now it was descending on a path leading along the downward-sloping valley. All of a sudden it lurched to the right, crashed through several large trees, smashing them apart or pushing them over, roots ripping free of the ground. The Legion Knight felt a surge of exhilaration – the autofactory had six suspensors, three on either flank, and if one ceased functioning that would explain this list in the trajectory. The autofactory seemed to correct its attitude for a moment or two, then it veered to the right, nose dipping as it ploughed into the side of the valley. Soil and shredded vegetation spouted in a long dark wave but the craft's momentum carried it onwards, gouging.

Then a new development – one of his remotes, now airborne, saw a shape burst out of the dense foliage further back and begin racing after the ailing vessel. It was a type-D mech. Had the auto-factory managed to bypass the transceiver lockouts and signal its original, base-design models to come to its aid? This raised the grim possibility that the autofactory had also established com-munication with the Brolturans.

Another type-D came plunging down the valley side, and a type-E appeared at the valley's far end. And the autofactory slowed, its aft slewing round against the undergrowth, causing another cascade of pulverised greenery. The vessel tilted over on one side as it ground on down the valley floor, at last slowing to stop at the end of a great dark trench of ripped-up soil. Its bow doors split, starting to open. The Legion Knight knew that its type-R was inside, fighting its way to the AI core. A moment later the first type-D reached the gaping access ramp and leaped up onto it, got a couple of paces, then jolted to a halt before keel-ing over. The next two, and a fourth appearing from the southern slope, followed the same doomed approach, clearly driven by an overriding imperative from the autofactory sentience.

For several seconds all was still in the valley. Then the type-R emerged, walking with its one leg and the opposite arm length-ened with some kind of metal stilt. The other claw hand tossed a knot of fibrous cables and snapped-off components onto the ground, proof of the AI's demise. Satisfied for the moment, the Legion Knight sent the airborne remote down to find a dataport on the mech's carapace: from the visual feed he could see where the earlier crushing blow had caved in that part of the upper torso covering the comm-relay node.

A dataport was found, a link was established. The Legion Knight swiftly scanned the autofactory's final activity logs and was greatly relieved to discover that no contact had been made with the Brolturans.

<That will be my task,> he thought. <To allay suspicion by per-

suading them that the telemetry updates had been interrupted by a subsystem failure resulting from others' shortcomings. Then to reassure them that these flaws have been resolved and that operational schedules will soon return to normal . . .>

As these thoughts came forth, the remotes were taking full control of the autofactory's comm systems and were quick to alert him to a priority message now coming from the Hegemony tech station near Hammergard. The Legion Knight studied the message and was at first surprised by the rashness of it then pleased when the advantages and possibilities became apparent.

The Brolturan ambassador had just ordered a massive invasion of the hinterlands, and was emptying every garrison to carry it through. Such an opportunity was not to be missed, especially since his success would ensure the return to his integrity of his Scions, their complete, irrevocable amalgamation into his being.

20

ROBERT

In the recurring dream, Robert was standing in a vast field of poppies with Reski Emantes hovering not far away. The droid then grew a fringe of red spines at its broad end and a razor-filled mouth at the narrow apex. As he stared around him at the poppies, Reski Emantes lunged at him, biting into his chest, opening up the ribcage, an assault that seemed somewhat lacking in pain. The droid then began removing a series of items, heart, lungs, a child's book, the intersim device, a bundle of whirlyglows, his brain . . .

When the droid dragged out that blue-grey organ with slender pincer-arms, Robert made a grab for it. But Reski snatched it away and tossed it into an upright locker, along with the rest. Everything went in it, vitals and veins, muscles and bones, nerves and arteries, till the locker slammed its door, put out legs and walked off with Reski Emantes by its side. Without bones, Robert slumped to the ground, and soon after rain began to fall and a river swept in to carry him away to a beach. There, seeds took root in him, growing into plants and bushes, filling out his empty body with foliage until he could stand again and walk back along to the poppy fields, where he met the droid Reski Emantes, who not long after grew a fringe of red spines . . .

'Robert . . .'

. . . bit into his chest, opening up the ribcage . . .

'Robert! It is time to wake up.'

. . . heart, lungs, a child's book, the intersim device . . .

'Robert, we will have to use an adrenal stimulus. Be ready.'

. . . vitals and veins, muscles and bones . . .

Suddenly, instantly awake, he jackknifed into a sitting position, chest reflexively gasping for air. The couch he was in dampened his leg movements and the upper section smoothly angled up to support his back. A bout of coughing made his eyes water, blurring his sight, exacerbating the pain that he thought he could feel in his chest . . .

Memories of the fight on board the *Plausible Response* flashed through his mind's eye, his skirmish with the scavenger, the Achorga attack from beneath, the bloody spike . . .

'You are fully healed, Robert, courtesy of biofield reconstruction.'

The Construct was standing by the couch, metallic hourglass torso and rodlike arms giving off a mirrored sheen without highlights or pinpoints. An ambient milky-blue radiance lit the room, an austerely furnished space possessing a wooden shelf unit, empty apart from a few books, and a movable bed tray on which a potted plant sat. Robert then made himself look down at his chest, unfastening the buttons of a thin pale green garment to reveal only a small, faint and shadowy mark. There was no pain – he breathed in and out deeply to make sure – and he lay back, smiling faintly.

'History repeats itself,' he said.

'Only in the sense that you have again incurred physical damage,' said the Construct. 'You are fortunate that the *Plausible Response*'s message about the Rosasim prompted me to follow you to this place.'

Awful memories came back to him.

'So how did you rescue us? That pocket universe – the Ship said it was artificial. Is that true?'

'Quite correct, Robert. It was designed to be an unusually cruel trap, one that keeps its captives alive and provides them with enough technology to engage in savage, barbaric battles. The molecular machines, those dynes, are its regulators, keeping the tech level down and bringing the prisoners back to life. As for how we retrieved you, I was able to persuade the mystic Sunflow Oscillant to join my expedition. His peculiar talents enabled us to first send probes through to determine your whereabouts, then to cross into the pocket cosmos while maintaining our causal state from outside. The Bargalil mystic was only able to negate the local conditions for a short while but it proved sufficient.'

Robert nodded then sighed. 'I am sorry, Construct. Our mission seems to have been a failure. Perhaps my own conduct was to blame and brought this tragedy down on us . . .'

'A highly doubtful scenario,' said the Construct. 'The creation of macro-artefacts like that universe is energy-intensive and demands concerted effort over a long period. There is no way to know who made it, although it seems clear that it serves the Godhead's purpose, namely the elimination of anyone determined to track it down. The presence of the vermax in the Legion Knight that attacked you in the Urcudrel Seam suggests a disturbing connection. Whatever influence the Godhead might have with the Legion of Avatars, it is clearly working against us, or at least actively attempting to obstruct us. So no blame attaches to you.'

'I am not entirely persuaded, but thank you,' said Robert. 'What of Reski Emantes and the ship's sentience – did anything of them survive?'

'Reski is a cunning sentience – it copied its mind-image to a structured lattice crystal encased in layers of lead and iron, keeping it well hidden from the dynes and thus easy to reconstitute. The ship's cores were less well protected so little of its persona was left. The recovered logs and backups have been incorporated into the AI of the ship we are currently aboard, the *Absence of Evidence*, my deep-range flagship.'

The Construct turned to a nearby section of wall which immediately transformed into a viewscreen showing a large, delta-shaped craft of strange design. It was composed of scores of shiny golden odd-shaped modules held together by a webby framework of struts underpinned by pipes and transit conduits. Robert regarded it, feigning interest while his thoughts wound and circled unceasingly around the one topic that hung over everything else. There was no point staying silent – he had to know.

'Construct, the Rosa simulant sacrificed herself to defeat the Legion Knight that ambushed us,' he said. 'The *Plausible Response* apparently made a recording of her mind beforehand, and ... I was wondering if that survived, and if you brought another Rosa with you.'

He could hear the weakness and desperation in his own voice and he hated it.

'The *Plausible Response* gave much more consideration to the Rosa mind-image than to its own, and yes, a new Rosa did accompany me. She is waiting outside and looking forward to speaking with you. But first you should be made aware of recent events on Darien.'

So Robert learned of how the Brolturans consolidated their position, how Kirkland became president and how he had an AI implanted, how the Hegemony emissary Kuros had a mech factory brought in to combat the Human resistance out in the wild, and how Kuros's technicians were slowly but surely penetrating the warpwell's defences.

'The Sentinel of the warpwell is an artificial sentience made by the Forerunners to maintain the well's integrity and to defend it against all manner of adversaries. At the time, it represented a scientific pinnacle, the crowning achievement of an interstellar culture that possessed nothing like the tiernet, although communication was commonplace. By today's standards, however, it is somewhat rudimentary and its inadequacies present a serious problem.'

'I've been told that you were an ally of the Forerunners,' Robert said. 'Was your own inception a leap forward from the Sentinel's?'

The Construct had moved to the foot of the bed and was examining the pot plant on the adjustable tray. The machine extended a pair of delicate clippers from the end of one polished metal arm and carefully snipped away a fragment of twig.

'My initial configuration was rather different from my current aggregate. I was designed as an experiment in pseudo-sentient synchronisation, an attempt to create a consensual cognitive awareness out of several Sentinel-like entities. It failed at first and continued to fail, no matter how many different problem-solving, para-intuitive, self-adaptive modifications were incorporated. Until one night I heard music being played in the vault where I was kept. I was the accidental audience for a group of cleaning menials who, during a meal break, played instruments and sang for their own enjoyment. Usually my receptors were deactivated after dark, but not that night, and when they played, all of those jostling subentities paused to listen in unison, transfixed by the exuberant melodies and harmonies. That was the seed for the melding that became me.'

'How strange,' Robert said. 'I would have expected music to be one of the first things to be used as a stimulus.'

'My creators came from a species of very serious scientists and theorists for whom music was little more than a frivolity.'

'So how would you characterise those who made the Sentinels?'

'They were very different from my makers, great lovers of life and the sensations of life,' the Construct said. 'But the design and building of the warpwells and the Sentinels was regarded as a serious task on which everything depended and for which time was limited. Despite the sacrifice, the suffering, the massive waste of worlds and peoples, their work and their genius was vindicated and the Legion of Avatars was imprisoned. Only a small handful of Sentinels came through that titanic struggle and of them only one still functions, still upholding its integrity of purpose.

'But it is not enough. It is now only a matter of time before Kuros's technicians break down the last protections and barriers and gain control of the warpwell. If that happens, the Hegemony could accidentally release the Legion's survivors in their millions from their prison in the depths of hyperspace. And even if they manage to avoid such a mistake, they will surely use the tiers of hyperspace as a way to expand the boundaries of their empire and destroy any who oppose them.'

Robert frowned. 'But I thought you were going to divert some of your own forces to Darien to seize the warpwell and evict the occupiers.'

'That strategy depended on our reaching an accord with the Godhead, but that has now been thrown into doubt. The Godhead's motives have always been a matter of conjecture yet its powers are said to be daunting. Several very old races claim to have been raised to conscious sentience by one or another of the proxy entities it created far back in the early period of galactic civilisation. There are even rumours that it is a survivor from a deceased universe, now sunken into the upper strata of hyperspace. The legends of several tier civilisations claim that before their descent into the tiers the Godhead had created entire solar systems and moved others into immense stellar patterns.' The Construct snipped another twig. 'Yet the Godhead has never overtly taken sides in any conflict so it may be that I am being overcautious. However, there have been other developments that prevent me from committing any portion of the Aggression to the liberation of Darien.'

'What developments?'

'Serious developments, Robert Horst. The flaw in my strategy was and remains lack of reliable data as to the Godhead's intentions,' the Construct said. 'Which is why I have dispatched another agent, an organic, on a more resolute reconnaissance into the depths to find out.'

Robert felt oddly disappointed on hearing this, almost as if part of him thought that such a task should have been his.

'I hope your agent is up to it,' he said.

'He is highly proficient and versatile, an Egetsi biped, similar to Humans. I sent it in one of my attack scouts with a good droid for company. Hopefully, in a matter of days, I shall have something approaching the truth.' The Construct seemed to consider the small pot plant a moment, then the clippers melted back into its rod arm. 'Before then, however, the question of the warpwell and the occupation of Darien must be faced. There is a mission to be undertaken to a place of great danger, to recover an object that is vital to the defence of Darien. It would be a demanding mission – would you be interested, Robert?'

'Definitely,' he said without hesitation.

'Your enthusiasm is creditworthy, but I am not the only one who needs to be persuaded of your suitability. You should talk to Rosa first, then make your final decision.'

As the Construct finished speaking, a door opened and a woman entered.

Robert stared, confused at first until he studied her features and recognised the alertness in the eyes, the shape of the nose, the form of the chin, the determined set of the mouth. It was Rosa, only older, in the first bloom of maturity, a woman.

As the Construct quietly left, she stopped at the foot of the bed.

'Hello, Father.'

His eyes widened. 'Are we being formal, Rosa?'

She gave a small, nervous smile. 'Were you expecting me to sound like a . . . teenager?'

'Was that wrong of me?'

'Perhaps not, since that was the other Rosa's self-state.' She folded her arms, a familiar gesture. 'And that is the image I would have had I assimilated her mind-image in full. I decided not to, instead holding her memories as accessible data rather than merging them with my macropersona . . .'

Her voice trailed off a little and Robert thought he detected uncertainty.

'So, are you happy – being older?'

She frowned. 'The Construct's persona-modelling subsentience is very sophisticated and after considering the previous Rosa's experiences I decided that different characteristics would best suit this mission, like increased upper-body strength and improved muscular response. Happiness is less important than competence and focus, and I am more resilient and versatile than the previous Rosa . . .'

'Apparently we are to recover a vital object . . .'

'There is no "we", Father,' she said. 'This mission is too dangerous for an unaugmented Human. The Construct is sending me to an Achorga nestworld to track down and retrieve an entity called a Zyradin, then take it to Darien's forest moon. The Zyradin were artificial lifeforms designed by the Forerunners to merge with distributed sentiences like Segrana, giving them conscious control over all planetary biomass and energies. Awakened, a fully conscious Segrana can deal with the occupiers and evict them from both Darien and the moon, Nivyesta. Father, if the Construct has asked you to go with me I would respectfully ask that you turn him down. The dangers are considerable.'

For the last couple of sentences her gaze slid away to the wallscreen with its image of the ship, *Absence of Evidence*.

'I see,' Robert said. 'So you're worried about my well-being.'

'Of course, but there is also my effectiveness to be considered. Under conditions of great peril it would be impaired if I had to ensure your safety as well as my own.'

Robert shook his head. 'If this undertaking is so dangerous why doesn't the Construct send a fleet of combat units off to take care of it?'

'Several reasons,' she said. 'A planetary assault against an Achorga nestworld would rouse every hive against us, perhaps even draw in other nestworlds. Then the unpredictable consequences of military action could make it hard to locate the Zyradin, and resistance would stiffen if the enemy reasoned out the focus of the attack. The Zyradin might be captured or even destroyed if that happened.

'Another reason is that the Construct's resources are under pressure. Ships of the Vro and the Shyntanil, two Abyss civilisations once thought occluded, have attacked a number of the Construct's outposts. The Aggression is being deployed in response.' She turned to face him. 'Which is why I should undertake the mission myself. I have the skills and the physical characteristics that will ensure success.'

'I see, I see,' Robert said. 'You make a compelling argument, Rosa, robustly put across. I just want to be certain that you really are focused on the mission itself, on the retrieval of this Zyradin creature – that is your first priority, yes?'

Rosa frowned. 'Of course. I think I made that point very clear.'

'Then to ensure success, in a hostile environment, against unknown enemy topography, and in search of a hidden goal, you have to take a partner. Someone to watch your back, to share ideas and problems, to take over if you . . . are unable to continue . . .'

'Father . . .'

'Rosa, you're . . .'

'No, I'm not . . . Rosa.' She glared at him. 'You recall what the other one said, that you can only lose your daughter once? Yet you let your feelings march all over your reason, and you think that it is still your job to protect me. Well, I *don't* need your protection, and I *don't* need a partner.'

'I fear you may be wrong,' said the Construct as it entered. 'Robert's argument is almost indistinguishable from the one I was going to make to you in the event that you failed to reach the necessary conclusion.' The spindly, gleaming machine glided over. 'You are of course at liberty to withdraw, in which case I shall have to find another suitable companion for Robert.'

For a moment or two Rosa regarded the Construct with a piercing gaze. Then, slowly, she nodded.

'Very well, Construct, my father can accompany me. But I would ask that he undergo at least basic combat skill imprinting. For what we are likely to face, blade proficiency will not be enough.'

'Imprinting combat skills?' Robert said. 'How, and is it safe?'

'It is a long-established process,' the Construct said. 'After mapping the relevant areas of an organic cortex, it is possible to imprint certain reflexes and skill sets, combat-related in this case. The imprinting begins to fade after the second sleep cycle and there are no harmful side or after-effects.'

'That sounds acceptable,' Robert said, swinging his legs out of bed. The pale green onepiece went down to his knees and was quite adequate in the mild air. 'When can we get this done?'

'Immediately, if you wish.' The Construct paused for a moment. 'I have just instructed the care chamber to prepare the treatment for you, a combination of bloodwork and field actuation. You will be conscious throughout and will experience no discomfort.'

Robert smiled, his mood optimistic until he saw the resigned look on Rosa's face. Suddenly he wondered if he had pressed his argument too forcibly, without giving proper consideration to Rosa's viewpoint. *Well, it's done now*, he thought. *Perhaps there'll be more time later for nuance.*

'I imagine that we will require a new ship,' he said. 'The *Plausible Response* took a serious mauling.'

'The *Absence of Evidence* is in the process of de-amalgamating a small, fast vessel for your use.' The Construct indicated the wallscreen where Robert saw that a smaller delta shape composed of about a dozen odd-shaped modules now sat atop the original ship. As he watched, an oval, pale amber module moved amongst, or was moved by, a mesh of struts and cables to take up a position near the new vessel's stern. 'It will soon be ready to depart.'

'And will it have a name?'

'It has already chosen to be known as the *Evidence of Absence*.'

'I am looking forward to going aboard.'

'We are already aboard,' the Construct said, pointing out a segmented module in the upper midsection.

Robert smiled, amazed at the continual stream of wonders.

'In that case, I shall waste no more time,' he said, feeling almost exhilarated. 'How do I get to the care chamber?'

Once he was gone, Rosa said:

'A shame you cannot give him more.'

'It suits his needs,' said the Construct. 'And my purposes.'

21

THEO

Mirgast was the outermost of the Tygran system's five planets, an azure-blue ice giant with a couple of tiny moons and a tenuous ring of rocky debris. The *Starfire* arrived nearly an hour ahead of the rendezvous with Sam Rawlins and took up a synchronous orbit.

At the same time, Captain Gideon was giving Theo a tour of the ship. Officially, the *Starfire* was designated a scout yet its adaptable holds and hull allowed it to carry out a variety of roles.

'Versatility is the key,' Gideon told Theo. 'Tygrans have always had to make the most of scarce military resources, as well as scarce manpower.'

They had paused on a gantry overlooking the dimmed main hold, its ceiling hung with netted cargo pallets and some kind of vehicle wound in opaque wrappings. Theo was striving to maintain a civil exterior but his resentment at being dragged away from Darien was deepening, not lessening. In fact, the overt militarism of Tygran attitudes was beginning to grate.

'What about your culture?' he said. 'Don't you have artists, composers and playwrights?'

Gideon was puzzled. 'Well, there are amateurs who dabble in such diversions for the amusement of family and friends, but such pastimes are not taught.'

In other words, Theo thought, *the soul of Tygran society is not openly expressed and examined. Such a blind spot is a weakness.*

Then Gideon chuckled. 'Rawlins once said that because we

fought for the Hegemony under the name Ezgara and wore concealing suits with extra arms, all of us were really actors
performing on a vast stage!'

Hearing this, an old quote came to Theo's mind. '"They have
their exits and their entrances, And one man in his time plays
many parts."'

The Tygran frowned. 'That seems familiar . . .' He was interrupted by a chime from his wrist-com. 'Gideon here.'

'Sir, a small vessel has just emerged from hyperspace at 73.8
kiloms and is heading our way. It's not answering our hails and
long-range sensors show that it's venting from combat damage.'

'I'm on my way to the bridge now.' He looked at Theo. 'Care
to join me, Major?'

'I would indeed, Captain.'

The bridge of the *Starfire* was compact and split-level, with the
commander's chair overlooking two other consoles, helm and
tactical. As they entered, Malachi looked up from the tactical
station and gave Theo a brief nod before addressing Gideon.

'Captain, we've ID'd the newcomer as an Alecto-registered
Bund launch; course is the same and still no response.'

'Has to be Rawlins,' Gideon said as he settled into his padded
couch and pointed out to Theo a pull-down seat nearby. 'Open a
narrowcast channel . . .'

'Space mass disruption,' said the officer at the helm. 'Proximity
hyperspace transit at 89.5 kiloms, a second ship, small, military
profile . . . it's gone to full thrust on a pursuit course . . . targeting
its weapons on the Bund vessel . . .'

'Move to intercept, Mr Berg,' Gideon said. 'Target their
weapons and drives.'

The bridge's viewport was a sloping transparent wedge flanked
by screens showing various system data as well as magnified
images of the other two ships. Outside, the great blue curve of
Mirgast slid away as the *Starfire* moved out of orbit.

'Pursuit vessel is an interceptor from the Tygran Orbital Wing,'
said Malachi.

'Open a narrowcast channel to it,' Gideon said. 'Tygran vessel, this is Captain Gideon of the *Starfire* – stand down your weapons and withdraw . . .'

'Sir, the Bund launch has spun to face the interceptor,' said the helmsman Berg. 'It appears to be powering up its projector.'

'Interceptor is refusing all comm bursts,' Malachi said. 'It's nearly ready to open fire.'

'Bund launch's projector profile is off the scale,' said Berg.

'I think you will find . . .' Gideon began before the interceptor suddenly exploded on one of the monitor screens. A bright flare was followed by a brief yellow eruption of burning gases, bright, hot fragments radiating outwards, cooling rapidly to dull red. Theo, startled at first, stared disbelievingly at the spreading wreckage.

'Ah, yes,' Gideon said with a wry smile. 'You'll find that the launch's weapon profile more closely matches that of a particle cannon. Some Bund vessels are markedly overgunned.'

'Incoming communication from the Bund ship, sir,' said Malachi.

'Screen it, sergeant.'

At once the image of an elderly man appeared on the right-hand screen. He wore a Tygran officer's uniform, dark green and grey, and his craggy features were etched with pain. Despite this he managed a tight smile.

'Captain Gideon,' he said. 'Good to see you again. Thank you for backing me up – that flyer should have known what to expect.'

'Preceptor Rawlins,' Gideon said. 'Keeping busy, I see.'

'All in a day's work for an old reprobate, my boy.'

'But . . . you don't look well – were you injured before making the jump?'

'Nothing to be concerned about, Gideon,' the Preceptor said.

'Why not dock with us and come aboard? Let the autodoc look you over . . .'

'No! . . . no, it's of no consequence and time is too short to waste on that.' The older man drew a shaky breath. 'Now listen – do you recall our conversations about the Zshahil Wars?'

Gideon frowned. 'I do . . . but Sam, I hope you didn't drag me back here for a history lesson—'

'Dammit, boy, this is important!' Rawlins's face contorted as if from a passing spasm of pain which left him looking suddenly exhausted, with an unhealthy pallor and a wheeze in his breathing. 'Okay . . . remember my doubts about how the war ended?'

'Yes, the final battle, the Cold Truce, the departure of the Zshahil . . .'

'That's right, all of that happening near a fishing port called Zyasla, and all in just a few days . . .'

Theo was almost incredulous at this, that the reason for his being diverted far from Darien was to hear the maunderings of an old man. Even the man's starkly poor condition did little to assuage his attitude.

'. . . well, three days ago I went there,' he went on. 'Took some scanning equipment and a drone digger.' The man's face had turned ashen. 'I . . . never told you my worst suspicions, Gideon, or about the black rumours I've heard down the years. But the time has come for me to pass on my discoveries.'

Gideon gritted his teeth. 'You've got to have treatment . . .'

Sweat beaded Rawlins's face as he massaged his chest. 'Too late, I'm afraid, just too damn late.' He reached for controls out of sight in the small pilot compartment. 'There – I've just sent you a datapackage with my journals and personal notes, and a recording I made at Zyasla . . .' More pain struck him. Trembling hands tore at his uniform, tugging it apart to reveal his chest. Beneath grey hairs and sweat streaks, a long narrow shape glowed through the skin.

'My binary device has been reactivated,' Rawlins said, fastening his tunic. 'Don't know how they did it but this thing is heating my blood. It's almost unbearable – my God, it feels like I'm on fire . . . sorry, I can do no more.'

'Don't say such things,' said Gideon.

Theo and Malachi exchanged a horrified look. Malachi's own binary bomb had been neutralised by Uvovo scholars back in Nivyesta, Darien's forest moon.

Theo could see the agony burning in Rawlins's eyes and was struck by pity and a grim admiration as the man continued.

'Once you've seen the evidence you'll understand how vital your task is. You'll need more than a handful of followers ... which is why I've included data on the current whereabouts of your troops, the ones that have stayed loyal, anyway ...' Grimacing, he gasped. 'No more, no more. I will not be unmanned before you so let me say that it has been a privilege to be your friend, Captain Gideon. Serve with honour.'

Theo could see muscles work in Gideon's cheek and neck as he straightened.

'Go with honour, Preceptor Rawlins.'

The picture vanished. A terrible silence reigned for only a few seconds before a soundless burst of light signalled the destruction of the Bund ship. After a moment Gideon spoke.

'Sergeant, did we receive the Preceptor's datapack safely?'

'Yes, sir. It's being decoiled right now.'

'Good. Lieutenant Berg, set a five-light-year jump to interstellar space, any direction. Just get us away from here.'

'Yes, sir.'

Theo glanced at Gideon. The Tygran's face was a stony mask out of which harsh eyes gazed at nothing.

'My condolences, Captain,' he said quietly.

Gideon nodded. 'He reached the last battlefield.'

'Captain, why did he say that his binary device was reactivated? How is that possible?'

'I have no answer for you, Major. Such a thing should be impossible ...'

'Course set, Captain,' said Berg at the helm. 'Hyperdrive on standby.'

'Execute jump.'

The main viewport went black as the ship jumped into hyperspace. Theo felt the expected ripples of vertigo and nausea, grinding his teeth together against the urge to puke.

'What's the status on the datapack?' Gideon said. 'Do we know what's in it yet?'

'Almost finished, Captain,' said Malachi. 'It consists of three main cells; first contains a lengthy visual recording, second has a data resource sequence configured as an interactive overlay to the visual record, and the third holds several text files.'

'Can you screen the videofile shipwide and if so how soon?'

'That's it ready now, sir.'

'Good – I'll announce it first.' Gideon leaned forward and fingered a control on his console. 'This is the captain – I regret to inform that the Preceptor of Veterans, Captain Rawlins, has lost his life in the course of honourable struggle. He died to bring us crucial information which I am about to share with you.'

The image of Rawlins appeared on the bridge screen. He was standing at the edge of a grassy clearing bathed in bright sunshine, next to an antigrav low-loader on which a bulky but indistinct device sat. He pressed a control pad and the image zoomed in on his face.

'I am Captain Rawlins. It is 11.19 on the fourteenth of Metagia, and I have come to a wooded area on the outskirts of Zyasla. Any Tygran viewing this will know the importance of that place, which is why I have brought along a pair of airborne cams, as well as some other equipment . . .'

As he watched, Theo quickly reviewed what little he had learned of the Zshahil Wars from Malachi back on Nivyesta. According to his account, the Tygrans had encountered the natives not long after their arrival in the Forrestal 150 years ago. The Zshahil were a race of reptiloid bipeds, intelligent but backward, socially organised into tribes frequently at odds with one another. Friction soon developed between them and the Humans over resources, skirmishes and clashes growing into something more serious. Nearly forty years after the arrival, it had become a war which reached its bloody crescendo near a Zshahil fishing village called Zyasla. Afterwards, the Zshahil chiefs signed a peace treaty, the Cold Truce, which required them to abandon their lands and travel across the eastern sea to a landmass later designated Ostland. The Zshahil were forbidden to leave Ostland and all Humans were likewise prohibited from visiting it.

On screen, Rawlins went over these same details while steering the low-loader across the clearing. Twice he paused to take readings from a pole-mounted sensory device which he spiked into the ground, after which he planted a stalklike object at the centre of the clearing. The recording then cut to a second clearing where Rawlins gave the time and continued the scanning procedure. This was repeated another three times, with the shadows lengthening, before Rawlins halted and faced the cam.

'The last battle was savage and brutal, much of it hand-to-hand, and involved roughly six hundred Tygrans and a thousand Zshahil. We crushed the Zshahil and showed no mercy.' He indicated the open ground nearby. 'The skeletal remains of Zshahil lie buried here in twenty-one mass graves. For the five clearings the burial pits total 107; sensors estimate that there are about 1,400 dead per pit, giving an approximate total of 150,000.'

Next to the screen, subtitled images of cold blue ground scans scrolled by, compacted masses of bones and skulls. Theo was appalled and disgusted, but when he glanced at Gideon he saw an expression of transfixed horror.

'There are another half-dozen similar clearings in the woods across the river,' Rawlins continued. 'Brief scans this morning revealed more pits, more remains. Yet the history books say that all the Zshahil tribes, right down to the last of them, embarked in their ships and sailed for Ostland. How many ships would have been needed for such an evacuation? Certainly, Zyasla was a fishing village, but many Zshahil tribes lived inland. And here's another question – why has no one verifiably seen or spoken to a Zshahil since the Cold Truce?'

Rawlins kept on, revelations hitting like hammerblows, relentlessly driving home the terrible, undeniable truth wrapped up in a single word – genocide. The videofile lasted nearly an hour, its final haunting, defining image that of Rawlins's digger drone excavating one of the pits, hauling up earth-caked clumps of bones.

At some point, the *Starfire* had emerged from hyperspace, reached its destination and stopped dead in space. The bridge, the whole ship even, felt becalmed, inanimate, as Rawlins's testimony came to an end. 'Finally the rumours are dead, leaving only this black truth,' he said. 'So will this truth set us free, or will it damn us?'

Yet it was an end delayed. As the Preceptor's face faded away to black, it suddenly cut to an image familiar from earlier, that of an ill and exhausted man sitting at the controls of the Bund launch.

'Gideon,' he said. 'If you're seeing this then I am no more. Do not grieve, my friend – go out and fight! Use this record and the data to pry the commanderies out of Becker's grip but first free your men – 148 of them are being held by Nathaniel Horne at Base Wolf. You'll find the current access codes in one of the document files. Farewell, Gideon. Our redemption is in your hands.'

When it was finished, Gideon sat immobile in his couch, just staring, and Theo wondered if he was well. Then the Tygran leaned forward and spoke into the shipwide comm.

'This is the captain – we shall shortly be leaving for Base Wolf. Any crew member who feels unable to continue under my command may see me before we arrive. Otherwise, thank you for your loyalty.' He then turned to Theo. 'My apologies, Major. I had intended to return you to Darien, but I am now compelled into a race against time – I must get to Base Wolf before my men are moved, and hopefully before any of them suffer at the hands of the base commander.'

Theo sighed. 'I understand your position, Captain – were I in your place I'd be doing the same, especially in the light of Rawlins's sacrifice. And for what it's worth, you can count on whatever help I can offer.'

'Thank you, Major. I may take you up on that.' Gideon faced front. 'Mr Berg, plot in a course for Base Wolf.'

'Course already processed and loaded, sir.'

'Good man. Execute jump.'

22

CATRIONA

Less than an hour before the mysterious ship came down in Segrana's northern uplands, Cat had been inspecting the repairs to a filter-root cluster near a high-canopy leaftown called Raintiderill when an eager young Uvovo came swinging and scrambling down from above.

'Pathmistress! Listener Okass told me to fetch you up to see – there are new stars in the sky!'

By the time she reached the high open platform where Okass awaited her, several other senior Uvovo had arrived to peer up into the night sky's faint veils and hazy swirls. Some were regarding a particular quarter of the firmament, then they broke off to bow as Catriona joined them.

'In the region of the Ineka constellation, Pathmistress,' said Okass, pointing.

Cat took her binoculars from a waist pouch and turned them to that particular direction. Brighter stars shone through the faraway streams and clouds of interstellar dust while others made diffuse glows, like specks of embers. But between those distant lamps and Darien, hanging in space, were formations of silver pinpoints unlike any stellar arrangement she had ever seen.

She lowered the glasses. Those had to be ships, so was this an invasion? Or was it Earthsphere? Or an intervention by the Imisil Mergence? And what was happening down on Darien? Not for the first time she inwardly cursed not having access to long-range communication. She turned to Listener Okass.

'I will need a trictra and a rider,' she said. 'I have to travel down to the Stone Temple to speak with the Sentinel of the Ancients.'

Okass nodded. 'I shall have one brought for you immediately, Pathmistress.'

Some minutes later she was strapped to the back of one of the furry pseudo-arachnoids and descending into the perpetual twilight of Segrana's depths, following the mazy paths of branchways and strengthened vine-web ladders. And she was nearly halfway to the forest floor when she *felt* the ship crashing into Segrana.

Cat could sense the shattering of ancient trees, the tearing of vine curtains, the splintering of branches, then the long furrow gouged into the forest floor as the vessel's momentum carried it through the undergrowth. The not-quite-pain, courtesy of Segrana's weave of being, forced her to tell the trictra herder to stop. For a moment she sat there, physically assailed by a pulse of ache that ran straight through her. As it gradually diminished she began to get a more accurate idea of where this was happening, north and slightly east of Raintiderill, almost three thousand miles away. And that gash in the forest floor was more than half a mile long. Segrana's presence was already moving to that area, trying to assess the damage and begin the healings. Cat realised that she would have to put off talking with the Sentinel and told the trictra herder to take her back up to Raintiderill. By the time she arrived, some of the Listeners had received sketchy accounts that the ship had many passengers on board and that there were many survivors. Other messages reported that two large flyers had taken off from the Brolturan base and were heading north to the crash site.

Without delay she had sought out one of the town's vudron chambers and seated herself within its woody darkness. With her Enhanced abilities she swiftly calmed her thoughts, then drew about herself the lucid trance state that provided that vital link with Segrana's weave of being. It was like setting off to swim down a widening river, moving with its great flow of strength as it poured into a great ocean of senses and images and interconnections, echoes and hints of ancient memories, and the voices of being and nonbeing, all tied to the vast presence of Segrana.

Unspoken worry swirled about her, unease and discomfort, and there was an odd rushing, falling feeling. Without warning brightness and interwoven shapes burst upon her. She was disorientated for a moment or two, until she adjusted to a distorted view and odd perspective, of the crash site seen from a high branch.

It was a creature's eyes through which she observed figures moving in the harsh light of powered lamps. In the half-light the ship was a long, indistinct shape except for the prow which was crushed and split open from its collision with an outcrop of boulders. She couldn't tell how many were gathered about the wreck, scores certainly, but before she could attempt a quick head count her vision suddenly quivered and wrenched away to another viewpoint, another pair of eyes.

Lower down this time, peering through branches towards the ship, but from the other side of those big boulders. In the glare of the lamps she saw several different forms, some two-legged, some four-legged, a few tall and vaguely birdlike or reptilian. On this side of the wreck there were fewer light sources, just a handful of maintenance spots spaced along the hull. Yet illumination reflected off the ship's flank revealed a curious area of ripped-up bushes and trees, shattered stumps and charred foliage. And a small blast crater around which a dozen small forms lay still. Dread suspicion grew into horrified certainty the longer she looked. And a sorrowful voice spoke in her thoughts.

They saw the ship come down so they hurried to offer assistance ... and they were killed without mercy. My poor children ...

Segrana. Catriona could feel an unsettling threnody of grief welling up from deep places, bringing with it anger.

More renders and despoilers will come and repeat this slaughter. I need your help, Catriona. Help me save my children, my world, my existence ...

Abruptly her vision was back at the crash site, seen from above, a perspective that wheeled and soared, then snapped round as two large shapes swooped down towards the grounded ship. It was the military flyers from the Brolturan base, bulky hawklike vehicles with curved wings bearing weapon pods . . . then she was looking through the eyes of a high-branch insectivore, watching a large pack of crash survivors grouped around a number of cases and packs near the tree line, watching as they unleashed a volley of small-arms fire . . . while a long-tailed forest creature saw ricochets spark and clank off the Brolturan vehicles' armour as they decelerated towards the ground, right over the downed transport, their deployment hatches opening . . .

The explosion was gigantic and shattering, a red and black fireball that burst out of the crashed ship and upwards, engulfing both the flyers. Catriona's viewpoint jumped quickly from creature to creature, all of which were startled and fearfully diving for cover, until the fifth which held steady, gazing across the treetops at the mass of rising fire. One of the flyers pulled out of it in a steep climb, trailing smoke and flames, arced over in a curve that turned into a nosedive, plunging to its destruction some distance away. The other, likewise ablaze, executed a tight turn into a flat trajectory heading north for a few seconds before blowing apart in midair.

Well, she thought. *Invading Crazies 2, Home Teams 0.*

Segrana's presence withdrew but her song of grief went on, a sombre yet resolute undertone. Catriona focused her Enhanced mind and all its abilities on the defence of Segrana and the Uvovo, not allowing herself to be daunted in the least. With the weave of Segrana's being flowing through her mind, she was able to extend her senses outward and downward, attempting to grasp all that was happening. Ambition almost got the better of her as she tried to cast her sight-smell-sound awareness as far as the four quarters, only to find herself stretched taut over the vast and endless intricacy of Segrana's corporeal territory.

Once I was able to comprehend my own entirety from sky to soil, from coast to coast, when I was whole, when the Many-Eyes were with me. Now, such understanding is beyond me. Preserve the self that is you, Catriona, or you will be lost . . .

Segrana's thoughts loomed large, like a world whispering to

her. Intricacy gaped beneath, a temptation to the Enhanced instincts that still lay within her like the fragments of an old skeleton. Webs within webs of potential, a shining darkness that overlaid slumbering primal forces, all calling to her, drawing her towards them. Cat had known of this from Segrana's hints and passing references but this was her first encounter with the fundamental source of planetary energies, and she could sense how much danger she was in.

With an act of will she turned her mind away, pulled in her thoughts, withdrew her awareness from far-flung outwilds of Segrana. As her self strengthened she began to focus on essential reality, and the crises now ongoing. Like the heavy fighting taking place around the Brolturan base sited near Pilipoint Station in the south-east. A group of small combat craft from the still-unknown invading armada were attacking, scoring several damaging hits before the base's force shield went up. Now missiles were flying back and forth and a number of attacking flyers were shot down, some veering off to crash into Segrana's shoreward fringes.

This event impinged strongly on her awareness when one of those burning wrecks crashed through a gatherer village, killing three-quarters of the Uvovo inhabitants. Racked with sorrow and feelings of guilt, Cat spoke to some Listeners in the south-east and persuaded them to begin evacuating those settlements nearest the fighting. Such evacs were already under way in the north, around the area of the crash site and the valleys to the south. Since the explosions and gunfire had terrorised most wildlife in the area, Catriona was finding it hard to track down the gang of invaders. Instead she had to rely on the vaguest of sense impressions and the sporadic reports of hard-pressed Listeners.

Then an urgent contact pierced the shifting tracery of information and sensation, a message from Sorjathir, a Listener whom she had sent to scout around the crash site and check for survivors. She cleared a path for his thought-flow, and words began to filter through – *See the things that they all wear, Pathmistress, and their marks of meaning* – followed by a sequence of images, contorted alien forms lying on the grass, clothes illustrated or embroidered with a spiral emblem, others with facial tattoos or wearing a pendant, also in the form of a spiral.

She sent heartfelt thanks to Sorjathir, then sat back in the dark of the vudron, recalling what the Sentinel had told her about the Spiral Prophecy and the involvement of Julia Bryce and her team of Enhanced. The Sentinel had asked if they were likely to give in to demands to work on weaponry. Were they part of that invading armada?

Segrana's weave of being surged around her. More impressions flowed in from the extremities, more chaos and violence. Knowing that Nivyesta and Segrana were under attack from religious zealots was not a great help so she put that aside and bent all her will and thought to managing the inflow of information, to speculate on the invaders' purpose and direction of attack, and to prepare some kind of countermove. Wherever they were, she would make sure that Uvovo fighters were in place to harry and chase them along avenues of her choosing, leading them to utter and complete defeat.

23

KAO CHIH

Pyre turned out to be far worse than he had imagined.

On field-generated lift surfaces Silveira's ship, the *Oculus Noctis*, spiralled down towards a sullen grey-brown world. Stealthing their way past inner and outer sensor shells, they descended through the fringes of a three-hundred-mile-wide dust storm. They rode out buffeting turbulence as they flew north towards the mountain range where the Human settlement was located. According to Roug information, the colony settlement was tunnelled into the base of a lone mountain east of that spine of high peaks, and a contact was supposed to be waiting for them in a high gully in amongst them. Homing in on the coordinates, Silveira brought the *Oculus Noctis* in for a quiet, smooth landing in a steep-sided dried-up river bed. They had already changed into garments matching the Pyre Humans' fashion, although the plan was to avoid being seen by too many of them.

Silveira wore a grubby orange pau over a yellow jacket and heavy trousers, and a pair of dark goggles concealed his eyes, all beneath a brimmed hat held on with a strap. Kao Chih had on ordinary dun work clothes and over them a hooded blue coat. Their Roug companion, Mandator Qabakri, had chosen an immense dark grey robe with what seemed like acres of folds, a strange, drooping hood that hid his features, and large, stubby-fingered gloves.

Regarding the muffled and disguised Roug, Kao Chih again wondered about the Roug's reasons for coming on this mission –

in his mind's eye he could still recall the shocking revelation that only he had witnessed back on the *Retributor*, Qabakri's physical transformation into Human form and back to Roug. Why had he revealed this incredible talent? Kao Chih found himself bedevilled by this mystery – what was Qabakri planning? What might he hope to achieve and why?

'Both Mandator Qabakri and myself are able to converse in Mandarin,' Silveira said to Kao Chih as the hatchway opened and they stepped outside. 'Which of us do you think should be the spokesman for our venture?'

'I have no desire to assume the role,' said the Roug. 'But I was entrusted with an identifying code phrase.'

Kao Chih eyed Qabakri's tall, dark-swathed bulk. Numerous folds were flapping in the wind. 'So, who is our contact?' he said.

'According to our local intermediary,' Qabakri said, 'it is one of the Pyre Humans, a person by the name of Sister Shi . . .'

Silveira, who had been setting his ship's camouflage, interrupted the Roug with an outstretched, pointing hand. A cloaked figure was climbing up the sloping river bed, arms and legs wrapped in pale green folds, face hidden by a hood. The newcomer halted several yards away and pulled back the hood to reveal the lined, distrustful features of a middle-aged Chinese woman. She regarded them one after another, dark piercing eyes giving nothing away.

'*Weiguoren*,' she said in Mandarin, 'I am Sister Shi. Are you the ones sent?'

'We are,' said Qabakri. 'Will you guide us to Dragon Gate Mountain?'

'There and back again,' she replied, then frowned and shook her head. 'You speak like a schoolmaster. Keeping you concealed is more than sensible.' She looked at Kao Chih. 'You are of the Fugitives, are you not? The ones who ran?'

'My name is Kao Chih. My grandparents escaped with Deng Guo.'

She gave a tight nod. 'This world has changed since then. Come.'

Without another word, she replaced her hood, turned and headed back down the dusty river bed with the others following.

Beyond the gully, they were exposed to gusting breezes that flung frequent billows of dust and grit into their faces. Qabakri was already well shielded but the Humans were forced to tug their own hoods tighter, although Kao Chih tried to leave enough of a gap to take in the surroundings. His parents had shown him an ancient digiframe inherited from his grandparents, and he had marvelled at the summery pictures of children playing by a stream while woods and meadows stretched into the distance. His first experiences of Darien, the river of smells, shapes, tastes, and shades of living green that had flooded his senses, had made him sure that was what Pyre had been like.

But what he was walking through, what he saw in every direction, was desolation, a scoured landscape from which a kind of world-pain cried out. Pyre was a desiccated corpse.

A mile-long trek took them around a couple of craggy hills to a stretch of rounded, boulder-strewn hillocks. And a thirty-foot-high armoured tower which Sister Shi said was part of a chain that maintained a sensor barrier around the mountain that lay ahead. She then produced a silvery handheld device with a small emitter dish which she pointed at the top of the tower. Kao Chih heard a high-pitched whine for a few seconds. Then she nodded and turned to them.

'The sensory apparatus has been tricked into its diagnostic mode,' she said. 'It will only last about a minute so we must now run!'

Abruptly she took off across the hillocks and the others followed suit with alacrity.

The dark mountain loomed, its heights blurred by wind-blown dust. Sister Shi took them over the rocky summit of a nearby hillock to an almost invisible path that sloped up the bleak mountainside. Huge shards of stone jutted from the slope and it was behind one of these that they were led, to a dark and narrow gap.

Lit by their guide's hand-torch, they headed along a cold passage that wound through the rock. Somehow, Qabakri managed to keep up without getting his bulky garments caught or torn. At last they came to a wider section and a dark recess with a metal-faced door. Sister Shi knocked on the door in a brief rhythmic pattern. A tiny lamp winked on above the door, a narrow glowing slot appeared and nervous, beady eyes stared out.

'Engineer,' the woman began. 'Don't say my . . .'

'Ah, Si Wu Chu and three mystery people . . .'

'I was going to ask you not to say my name! You always forget to check.'

The beady eyes suddenly looked hurt. 'But Si Wu Chu, how often do you say not to?'

There was a rattle of locks and the door opened. A short, round-faced man in shabby overalls ushered them in and quickly locked up again. His eyes widened on seeing Qabakri, who, wrapped in his robes, towered over everyone.

'My, my, you are a tall fellow! I think I have a big chair somewhere that may suit you.'

'You are most kind,' Qabakri said in a low, whispery voice. 'But I am happy to stand.'

Engineer Bao smiled, gave a short bow and produced small battered stools for the others. Kao Chih quickly took in his surroundings, a narrow room with high rock walls and a level floor covered in matting. There were shelves and boxes of what looked like broken domestic tools while overhead the ceiling was obscured by clusters of pipes that snaked through, criss-crossing each other, some descending the near walls, others continuing into the rock. The air was warm and faint hisses could be heard all around.

'Engineer,' said Si Wu Chu, 'these are the special guests I told you about.'

'Ah, you people are from the stars, yes? The up-and-out? From Earthhome?'

Silveira pushed his goggles up to reveal his decidedly non-Asiatic eyes and Engineer Bao laughed in amazement.

'Round eyes!' Engineer Bao said in delight, vigorously shaking Silveira's hand, then Kao Chih's. 'But you're not . . .'

Kao Chih breathed deeply. 'No, Engineer Bao, but my grandparents fled this place with Deng Guo.'

'Well, now.' Bao glanced at Sister Shi, and chuckled. 'Si Wu does not approve of you, but it seems to me a good thing that the sons of the sons return home. So, you are here to see what those Suneye devils have done to our world, yes? And afterwards, Earthhome will surely set us free when they see what pains we have suffered.'

'That is our task, Sir Engineer,' said Silveira.

'What of your big friend?' said Engineer Bao. 'He says little, so his words must be very valuable.'

'He is our silent observer,' said Kao Chih. 'And as the ancients said, actions speak louder than words.'

Engineer Bao's eyes widened in a mystified expression which then turned into a broad smile. 'Ah, I see, a guardian. Well, I am sure that we can conduct your business in safety – I know all the secret tunnels and paths, even a few that bypass the sealed corridors to the other districts.'

Sister Shi smiled at Engineer Bao then turned to the three offworlders with a serious face.

'With Bao's help your investigations will be in good hands. I must now leave to attend to my children, but I shall return to take you back to your ship when Bao sends word. Till then, may Kwan Yin watch over you.'

The Engineer saw her out through another wider door, locking it after her, then shrugged on a blue work jacket bearing many oil stains. With Si Wu Chu gone his demeanour seemed noticeably more sombre.

'My friends from the stars,' he said. 'Little of what you will see is a pleasure to the eye. There are two hidden routes which lead through Yaotai District, and if there is time we shall explore them both. But I must ask you to be as quiet as mice – youth tong are everywhere and we must avoid arousing suspicion. Follow me and stay close.'

At the rear of the workshop cave, the matting gave way to grilled metal decking. The rear wall was an array of pipes and

valves, both archaic needle gauges and digital, from which a low
chorus of drones and hissing came. The Engineer went over to a
shadowy corner, and pulled up a hinged metal grille to reveal a set
of steps. Producing a stub of candle he lit it and led them down
into the gloom.

Below was a long, winding tunnel whose low ceiling forced
Qabakri to move at a crouch. The Roug offered no complaint and
Kao Chih wondered if he was using his shapeshift ability to adapt
to the cramped conditions. Indeed, when they reached a high section and a set of stairs leading up he seemed to have shrunk, yet
when they emerged in a high, narrow side passage off a brighter
corridor, he appeared as tall as before. Bao indicated a number of
slots and openings in one wall.

'These look down on Shin Sheng Street, one of Yaotai's walkways,' the Engineer said. 'This corridor used to be an access to an
older section which was closed off when it suffered a huge cave-
in. But now I use it to watch for any trouble.'

'Honourable Engineer Bao,' said Silveira. 'I would like to make
a recording of these sights, and of your own commentary if that
is permissible.'

Bao shrugged amiably. 'I have no objection.'

Silveira took out a small triangular device from which he
spooled a thin, stretchy headband. Fixing it around his forehead,
with the device pressed to his right temple, he pressed a little stud
on its casing, smiled at Bao and went over to one of the slots.
Sliding a thin wooden slat aside, he peered out. Kao Chih and the
others followed suit. Grinding poverty was starkly on display,
hollow cheeks and a desperate weariness, old women hunched
over dilapidated clothing, stitching, people gathered round small
cooking pots, a few children racing along the back alleys, their
frantic play the only evidence of any kind of happiness. And apart
from a few wrinkled grandfathers watching blankly from windows or sitting by doorsteps, there was no sign of other menfolk.

'They are working in the mineral mines,' Bao said once the
openings had been closed up again. 'After the Suneye monoclan
defeated our forebears, their prospectors found rich seams of

ylynly crystal through the roots of this mountain, a profitable opportunity they could not pass by. So they dug out these tunnels, caged our forefathers within them and forced them to work in the lower passages, sorting and extracting in the wake of great boring machines which chewed their way down into the mountain's vitals. As they do to this day.'

Kao Chih started to ask a question but the Engineer forestalled him with a raised hand.

'Let us climb to the overpass,' he murmured. 'We will be in a higher place and I shall answer your questions.'

They had to climb two steep flights of steps to get there but it turned out to be excellent for observation. A low corridor cut through oddly pale stone; it had small shafts along one side that looked down through mesh barriers at a wide street and a small market, most of whose stalls were bare and unattended. Engineer Bao explained that food was strictly rationed, especially since the other districts, Shibei and Tangxia, sealed up the linking corridors. This was due to the murder of the district magistrate at the hands of one of the youth tong gangs who were now acting like brigands, abusing people and stealing their food and belongings.

From the overpass corridor, Bao took them on a winding tour through the walls, ceilings and sometimes floors of Yaotai District. At every turn they saw only privation and suffering, haggard and drawn faces, and here and there among the Humans were other sentients, here a Kiskashin, there a Henkayan, and all escorted by a personal guard of Gomedrans.

'Ah, yes, the Va-Zla,' Engineer Bao said. 'They are extortioners, gangsters and bullies, invited in to police us by the Suneye administrators. Bloodsuckers, more like, is what they are.'

Regarding these non-Humans from an overhead location, Kao Chih noticed that Mandator Qabakri remained at his observation slot after the others moved away.

I wonder what you think of all of this, he thought. *How does such oppression appear from the long-lived Roug perspective?*

From there Engineer Bao took them to a couple more observation points, each confirming what they had already seen. But the last view only came after an unexpected trip outside. A twisty side tunnel sloped upwards and opened out onto a narrow ledge with a sheer rock face falling away beneath them. Kao Chih tried not to think about that drop as he focused on following the Engineer. After ten heart-pounding minutes the ledge curved up to an immense crag jutting from the side of the mountain. Round the other side of it was a natural platform and as Kao Chih stepped onto it a stunning vista opened up before him.

To the west was that range of massive peaks from which they'd come hours ago. Engineer Bao had told them that a city called Thaul, built by the Suneye mercantilists, lay on the other side, obscured by dark tapering masses. But right there, to the north, was the sight that they'd been brought to see.

They sat in long lines, rank after rank stretching across a great plain, hundreds of motionless, colossal behemoths, armoured hulls impervious to the elements. Kao Chih had seen pix and vidage of the extractor machines in school, seen images of them in paintings and vee-dramas, and often imagined himself as one of the valiant colonists fighting these monsters, trying to resist the savage theft of their world. But to see them here like this was far more chilling.

'Here are the devourers that destroyed our world,' the Engineer said. 'Some of them.'

'Are there more?' said Silveira.

Bao smiled bleakly. 'This horde numbers less than a thousand but over the mountains, south of Thaul, are another four thousand. Reportedly, two thousand are still chewing their way through what's left of the Great Northern Ramparts and about three thousand are working away on the ocean bed. It takes time and effort to eat a planet.'

'Ten thousand,' Silveira murmured, adjusting his camera device to be sure of a good shot. 'How big are they?'

'On average, about 1,500 feet long, 400 feet across and 350 feet at the high point.' The Engineer laughed. 'I got those figures from an old book which called them the Tao-Tie . . .'

'The hungry demon?' Kao Chih said. 'Who was so hungry it ate its own head!'

'The very same,' Bao said, glancing out at the things crouching on the barren plain. 'But those stories came from long ago and far away. The Suneye barbarians sent real abominations to consume our world, and now that they've trapped us in this cage of a mountain, they're watching as we suffer and starve and turn on each other. Please help us – if you don't, who will?'

Silveira nodded and bowed his head slightly, as if troubled. Then to Kao Chih's surprise, Qabakri stretched out one big, sleeve-smothered, heavily gloved hand and placed it gently on the Engineer's shoulder.

'We hear your words,' the Roug said, withdrawing his hand and turning his cowled face back to the distant serried ranks. 'Help will not be denied.'

Kao Chih regarded the bulkily robed Roug with surprise at such an overt expression of support. Engineer Bao seemed pleased, yet not overly so.

'Your words are kind, offworlder,' he said. 'But ships and guns would be kinder still.'

Retracing their path took less than half an hour. But as they neared the steps leading up to Bao's workshop they clearly heard the weeping of children and muffled thuds and shouts. Engineer Bao hurried forward and up the steps, flung back the trapdoor and clambered out. Kao Chih pulled himself up, rolled to his feet and saw Bao approach two children who cowered crying in a dark corner of the workshop's back room.

Suddenly there was a massive crash and a woman's scream from out in the workshop. As one, Kao and the others rushed through in time to see Sister Shi throw herself at the nearest of three Gomedrans who were advancing into the room. Behind them the wide door gaped open, its frame cracked and buckled. Then a vicious punch from the Gomedran sent Sister Shi flying backwards to lie still on the floor.

'Ah, more Humans eager to give up their valuables,' said one of the intruders. 'Empty your pockets and hand over the cubs and you may live . . .' He paused and stared closely at Silveira. 'Heh, a round-eye! – you'll be worth more than the rest put together . . .'

Kao Chih was about to deliver a contemptuous response when a figure leaped past him and lashed out wildly at the Gomedran who had knocked down Sister Shi.

'Va-Zla brutes!' yelled Engineer Bao, wielding a long-handled hammer.

Then, before Kao Chih or Silveira could react, Qabakri swept past them like a speeding colossus, swept up lengths of heavy pipe in either hand and bore down on the other two Gomedrans. A look of terror seized one, who whirled and made a lunging dash for the doorway. But a pipe, hurled like a javelin, caught him in the back of the neck and struck him to the floor. The other Gomedran stood his ground, snarling as he rained blows on the Roug with a weighted club. Qabakri batted the impacts aside, seized him by his collar and threw him bodily across the work-shop. The Va-Zla bandit struck the wall, fell in a heap on the floor and did not rise.

At the same time, Engineer Bao kicked the legs out from under his opponent, who then received a none-too-gentle clout with that impressive hammer. Seeing the Gomedran crumple to the ground, Bao dropped his weapon and rushed over to the motion-less form of Sister Shi. After a tense moment or two he announced that she still had a pulse but her breathing was shallow.

'Valiant offworlders, I cannot leave her side,' Bao said. 'I must send word for a doctor and her children need to be watched over. Will you find your own way back to your vessel? – you can have the sensor tower device.'

'We should be able to manage, Engineer Bao,' said Silveira as he carefully put away his recorder.

Bao dug into a pocket and produced Sister Shi's handheld emit-ter device. 'Take it, I can fabricate another. All I ask is that Earthhome sends ships and soldiers to help us.'

'I'll make sure that others see what is happening here.' Silveira turned to the others. 'Time we were leaving, I believe.'

'I intend to remain behind,' Qabakri said suddenly. 'Duty compels me.'

Kao Chih and Silveira stared at the Roug, still wrapped in the dark folds of his immense robe.

'A risky decision,' said the Earthsphere agent. 'The consequence of discovery could be grave.'

'That is correct,' Qabakri said. 'But my decision stands.'

Bao grinned. 'I am glad. You are a very handy fellow, almost like the bear of legend.'

Silveira gave a slight shrug. 'As you wish.'

'You go ahead,' Kao Chih said. 'I want to have a final word with our courageous companion.'

The Earthsphere agent nodded and followed Engineer Bao to the rear room where the outside door was. Nearby Sister Shi was starting to stir so Kao Chih drew Qabakri aside.

'Are you sure about this, honourable one? The dangers of capture . . .'

Then the Roug reached up and tugged aside its capacious cowl, revealing the broad, almost plain features of a Chinese man. With short black hair and deep brown eyes in a large face, the head seemed in proportion to the Roug's bulky size.

'You've transformed?' Kao Chih said in a strangled whisper. 'Were you planning to do this all along?'

'I was prepared for the eventuality,' Qabakri said, adjusting the baggy folds around the neck. 'After witnessing such desperate suffering, it became a necessary choice.'

'Why would you do this for members of another species?'

'The Ancients laid a grave responsibility upon us,' the Roug said. 'But with the passing ages we have denied it and laid it aside. The time has come to take up that purpose again.' Then Qabakri smiled a human smile. 'Tell me, Pilot Kao Chih, if the roles were reversed and you had the opportunity to use your strength to help members of my race who were suffering, would you not do the same?'

Kao Chih nodded. 'Yes, I would. Perhaps I should stay here as well . . .'

'You have to return with Silveira to V'Hrant,' the Roug said. 'You must ensure that my people receive reliable testimony about the situation here.'

Kao Chih gave a slow nod as the implication that Silveira might prove unreliable sunk in.

'Well, if you are staying behind, you should give yourself a name for others to know you by.'

'I have thought on this – are you familiar with the story *Shui-hu chuan*?'

'The Water Margin chronicle? – indeed I am.'

'I have decided to adopt the name Wu Song.'

Kao Chih laughed. 'The Tiger Hunter! – a worthy name to live up to.'

Qabakri smiled. 'I hope I shall. Now you should go, catch up with Silveira and help him regain his vessel. With its abilities you should have no problems departing Pyre.'

Kao Chih hurried through to the back room, where Bao stood at the door to the outside. Saying goodbye he stepped into the gloom as the door closed behind him. For a moment he stood there, listening as Qabakri told Bao why he was remaining then introduced himself by his new name. Kao Chih heard the Engineer utter a delighted laugh, after which Qabakri gave a plausible ambitious-parents explanation which led into a dialogue on fathers. Kao Chih shook his head and hurried after Silveira.

24

JULIA

The plan was simple – fake a hull breach and a shipwide life support shutdown, then while Talavera and her goons were rushing for the escape pods, all the Enhanced would depart aboard a commandeered shuttle. The devil was in the details but with her few remaining polymotes she would be able to open certain doors and keep others shut.

Nearly five days after leaving Zophor 3, the Holy Armada's journey through hyperspace was almost over, its arrival timed to coincide with the immediate aftermath of the planned destruction of the Hegemony and Earthsphere warships. The missiles were already on their way, onrushing cargoes of death that could not be stopped, and Julia and the others were determined not to be the creators of even more horrifying weapons. The transition to normal space was due to start in a short while, the ship's navigationals preparing the shift in hyperdrive field integration that would trigger the transition to normal space in time to reach the destination coordinates. Julia in the meantime went over the plans and schematics in her head.

After their return to Talavera's ship, the *Sacrament*, they were moved back into the cluster of rooms they had occupied on the way to Zophor 3. Only now there were comfortable beds in their tiny quarters rather than cots, along with some personal storage, some softer furniture out in the common area, an entertainment console, and two large tables of research equipment skewed towards biochemistry.

Talavera, plus her customary escort, joined them shortly after.

'We'll be travelling for more than four days, and as you might guess I hate the idea of you sitting around doing nothing, idle hands thinking up mischief. So in the interim I want you to come up with a neurotoxin for use against biosimulants, synthetic life-forms.' She dropped a rubber-edged datapad on the slightly less crowded of the two tables. 'There's the background, genome, respiratory and blood profile, it's all there. Also, I'll need to know the best vector, gas or liquid.' She smiled, as if with childlike delight. 'Don't disappoint me, now!'

After she left, they sat in the casual chairs, dejected, barely looking at one another. Then Irenya made an impatient sound, stood up and went over to pick through the apparatus on the tables. A moment later she said:

'Julia, look at this.'

'What is it?'

'An enzyme-shift analyser, quite a new one too.'

Julia frowned, got to her feet and went over to join Irenya who was examining a blue-grey, podlike piece of equipment. Before she could speak, Irenya made the signalogue gesture for *careful* then *look*.

'There's also a good selection of centrifuges,' she said, indicating a group of domed units with her right hand.

But it was her left hand that Julia noticed as it reached forward to rest on a transparent cube, still half-wrapped in blue, bubbly cladding. She recognised it immediately as a morphic cell, a containment in which any organ or portion of any gene-mapped creature could be created by tiny builder machines. There had been a drained, broken one amongst the workshop clutter back on Zophor 3 and, picking over it and a partial manual, they had speculated that the tiny builders, called polymotes, could be easily redesigned to be mobile outwith the tank, performing any number of functions.

'This seems a bit superfluous, though,' Irenya said mischievously, patting the cube.

'Oh, who knows?' Julia said. 'Might come in handy for something.'

After that she gathered them together to discuss how to tackle Talavera's unpleasant-sounding neurotoxin, while using signalogue to let them in on her secret project. Smiles replaced the dispirited looks and everyone switched into experimental process mode, deciding who got to pursue which line of enquiry, priorities of equipment use, lists of additional materials required, and whether there were any theoretical gaps. Julia knew that her team weren't faking their engagement with Talavera's assignment; the Enhanced had been conceived as problem-solving human machines, almost, compelled to grapple with the facets and mysteries of scientific questions. She, on the other hand, would have to fake involvement with the others while working to make the morphic cell produce what she needed.

And by the morning it had followed her design specs exactly and modified fully a third of its store of 300 polymotes. The modification included a toughened shell to withstand the more rugged conditions outside the cube, and certainly outside the team's confinement quarters. Each was less than a millimetre across but its dumb-bell casing was full of molecular data systems and wielder pods, as well as a power source and propulsion unit. Releasing them was easy, putting a wallchart up next to a vent grille or retrieving a dropped item from down next to a loose maintenance cover. To track and direct them Julia was using an analyser pad reprogrammed and secretly refurbished to transceive on short-range shortwave. All the polymotes were following preset routes to destinations all around Talavera's ship, mainly in the sections around her quarters – Julia hoped to gain access to the woman's cabin and see if anything useful could be learned.

It was inevitable, however, that her tiny spies would encounter deadly hazards. After the first twenty-four hours a series of fatal losses came about from being trodden on (14), washed down sinks, showers and toilets (5), painted over (3), crushed by doors (8), melted by heat from a light source (9), vented into space with garbage (7), and eaten (2). Another eleven ceased functioning for no discernible reason, which left

41 with which to explore the dark corners of the *Sacrament*, to find out Talavera's secrets.

Ship-time, it was almost 2.15 a.m., leaving ten minutes until the transition to normal space. That was the cue to get the Enhanced moving. Rising from her bed in the darkness, she crept out of the little room and by the meagre light from the corridor outside she saw that the others were waiting, crouched in their own doorways. A pair of Gomedrans were on guard outside the entrance; with her analyser pad Julia sent commands to several nearby polymotes and a vidage loop of the previous uneventful hour began streaming to the ship's security station. She then signalled to Arkady and Thorold and the three of them moved quietly towards the entrance – a moment later the double doors slid open and both guards received a faceful of highly effective knockout vapour.

Julia glanced at the analyser's timer – 2.18.35. She watched Arkady and Thorold drag the insensible Gomedrans into the main room's shadows, then nodded and sent them on their way. It would take them about three minutes to reach the lock leading to one of three shuttles currently moored to the *Sacrament*. Julia's plan was for Irenya, Konstantin and herself to follow at 2.20, a staggered arrangement in case they had to adopt plan B, head for the escape pods.

Despite losing more than half her polymotes in less than thirty hours, Julia had still been able to track the movements of most of Talavera's forty-nine-strong crew. Matched to the deck layouts this revealed busy areas, passages, restrooms, a cantina, crew stations, and certain rooms that only Talavera and a few others ever entered. One was directly opposite Talavera's own quarters while the other was in engineering; both had secure bioreader entry systems and both were cabled up to draw heavily on the ship's powerplant.

With a polymote positioned on the doorframe, right where brushing garment contact would catch it, Julia gained entrance to Talavera's cabin. She had half-expected blank walls and minimal personal effects, yet fixed over her bed recess was a picture of a strange building, a dark grey central dome surmounted by a tall spire from which many long spines protruded, angled upwards. Julia only caught a glimpse but its distinctive shape stayed in her mind as Talavera's motion gave the polymote a sweeping view. There were a few more individual items, a prayer-scroll on the wall, some clothes heaped on a chair, and a few bottles and vials of makeup on an austere dresser. There was also a basic holostation in the corner which is where she went and sat for a while, flicking through screenwork, most of which was obscured from Julia's polymote by an upper arm until the end. Julia just managed to grab an image of the screen before Talavera shut down the app and the station. From a quick glance, it seemed to show a multiplex database listing dozens of entries, names and figures, mostly in a character language she did not recognise.

Then Talavera was up and heading for the door, which slid open. Crossing to the mystery room she pressed her palm against the reader and a moment later the door opened in double layers, the inner sliding diagonally. Within was shadowy dimness, relieved by the faint radiance from equipment standby lights. Julia noticed several long dark shapes along one wall before Talavera turned the other way and sat at a wide, enclosing console which came to life when she spoke a few syllables. Julia had ordered the polymote to climb up to shoulder height and had a clear view now as Talavera called up a holoscreen then skimmed through a series of strange, bulbous, almost mushroomlike images, some glittering with patterns of tiny bright pinpoints. All of which left Julia mystified, even after running a couple of comparative macros in her cortical net.

Talavera shook her head impatiently, killed the console with a sharp word, and went over to the nearest long dark shape. Standbys brightened to icy blue at her touch while a pattern of decorative panels glowed softly, revealing a gleaming, black, smoothly curved exterior. For a moment Julia was reminded of the deadly missiles that they had augmented, until Talavera touched an invisible control on the flank and a section of the broader end parted in two shell halves that slid down either side. Inside Julia saw grey, webby padding and a head-and-shoulders-shaped depression, and at the side a glassy black oval projecting a holopad which Talavera fingered and prodded.

It was a full-body virtuality tank – Julia had seen ads and flybys about them during her tiernet sessions and knew that they were used as therapy for the seriously disturbed and also as a punishment and re-education tool for certain grades of criminal. And as Talavera closed up the tank and headed for the door, Julia saw that there were another four sitting side by side, black, gleaming and waiting.

What is she planning for us? she thought.

She looked up from the analyser, glancing at her fellow Enhanced as they worked on Talavera's neurotoxin. But this was neither the time nor the place to show them what she had found, and in any case, the information was incomplete. She needed to know more so while she tried to decode those strange database images she focused polymote activity on gaining entry to the other mystery room in Engineering.

Seven and a half hours of enforced patience later opportunity arrived, in the shape of Silshur, a Kiskashin. The crew of the *Sacrament* were mainly Gomedrans and Henkayans with a scattering of Bargalil and a handful of reptiloid Kiskashin, all of whom held technical ranks. Silshur was the only one previously seen entering the secure room apart from Talavera, and when he paused to submit to the scanners Julia's polymote fell from the door lintel, sticky cilia anchors extended. Landing perfectly, it then proceeded to circumnavigate the Kiskashin's neck as it entered the room.

Lights bloomed harsh and white. Directly opposite the door was a wall full of shelved grey modules, their cabling draped down the back in clipped bundles. The Kiskashin went over to one in particular, a dark blue module that lit up and projected an opaque console and square display. Silshur poked and stroked the translucent control pads then turned to look at the rest of the room, providing Julia at last with the view she wanted.

Eight large identical G-shaped units occupied the rest of the room in two rows of four. Each had a heavy, waist-high base from which a cluster of six metal ducts rose to a thick oval platform about a foot across at its narrowest. On the platform sat a transparent, cylindrical canister while six thinner cables reached up from beneath and plugged in all around the middle section. The overarched limb of the G came down to form a junction with the top of the canister. All the devices were dull and unactivated, apart from one which the Kiskashin had powered up. Touch panels glowed, status headlamps winked, and within the canister an ovoid of layers of threads spun, pulsed and rippled with fine patterns.

A chill of recognition stole over her. From lecture hall lessons, from group speculations, from papers on particle physics theory, she knew she was looking at a dark matter containment vessel. The conjecture had been that arrays of immensely strong electromagnetic fields would be needed to compress even a few milligrams into a large room, whereas this equipment was clearly employing structured force fields to contain a much smaller volume.

Within the shifting field cage, glittering points flickered in a knot of pale blue mist, vein patterns glowed and faded, gleams blurred. Just as Julia's tutors had predicted.

And there were another seven sitting dormant under the lights, implying that they would soon be put to use. Talavera obviously knew about the Enhanced research into dark matter, but did she also know about the seabed gathertraps at Station Pelagius on Nivyesta? How much did she know? Dread added another dimension to Julia's already anxious frame of mind.

It had been dark in the Enhanced quarters when she woke the others and got them together in her little room to show them her findings. Voices were hushed but expressions spoke loudly of their shock, fear and anger. When she suggested figuring out a way to jump ship on arrival at the Darien system, the approval had been unanimous.

Now, she waited with Irenya and Konstantin, crouching in the shadows, watching the analyser's counter creep towards 2.20. Then it was time and they were heading out to the corridor, following its rising curve past the main connecting doors to a large maintenance panel which popped open as they approached. They sidled along a narrow, dark passage which ended at a ladder that went up to a cramped, red-lit room through which clusters of piping ran. Another panel slid aside and they emerged into a corridor with a curved left wall.

'Nearly there,' Julia said, pointing to the far end. 'That T-junction leads to airlocks and the shuttle . . .'

But they were barely a couple of paces further on when Julia felt a quiver of vertigo, a momentary blurring in her vision . . . and suddenly the corridor was filled with ship alarms and system voices warning of life-support failure.

'The ship's exited hyperspace!' said Konstantin.

'Too soon,' Julia said and began to run. 'Come on!'

Right at the junction a large hatch gaped and they clambered up narrow steps, a boarding lock that led straight into the shuttle's crew compartment. Thorold jumped up as they entered and Julia quickly saw that he was alone.

'Arkady?' she said.

Thorold trembled with anxiety. 'Went back out, said he was making sure it was safe for you . . .'

Julia gritted her teeth and stared down at the analyser and its grid of visual feeds from the remaining polymotes. But as she searched for any sign of Arkady, one by one the polymote feeds cut out, a burst of seething silver then nothing.

Then Arkady appeared at the hatch, relaxed and smiling as he stepped into the compartment.

'Everyone be calm,' he said. 'Sit down. No need to panic . . .'

Julia glared at him. 'What the hell were you . . . ?' And stopped when she saw the gun.

'Be calm.' His eyes were darker than usual, intense. 'Sit down. Everyone sit down. No need to panic. Sit down.'

The gun was similar to those carried by Talavera's guards.

Feeling sick and angry and betrayed, Julia slumped into one of the padded couches and the others did so too. Irenya tried talking to Arkady but when the only response was some or all of those few maddening phrases, she too sat back, dejected. A moment later, as expected, Talavera entered along with two armed Gomedran guards. Back in the ship, all the alarms had fallen silent.

'The show's begun,' Talavera said, taking an ovoid control from inside the heavy fabric jacket she had on. She pressed one of its studs and all the screens in the shuttle winked on to show clusters of ships in rough wedge formations sweeping towards the planet Darien.

It was the Holy Armada. Julia felt gripped by despair, not daring to glance at the others, unable to bear the sight of their faces.

But then the picture panned right, magnification blurring forward. Small glittering objects hanging against the planet's blue-grey swirls suddenly leaped into close prominence. Close support ships and maintenance tenders darted like minnows alongside the leviathan bulk of the Brolturan battleship, poised whole and undamaged in its orbit, its hangars deploying interceptors, its decks of weaponry targeting the invading Spiral craft. The frame pulled back, showing the massive vessel against the planet.

'Sadly, I've already had several terse messages on the subject of the signally untouched Brolt ship.' Talavera's smile was razor-edged. 'They range from sombre vows of punishment to howls of enraged hysteria.'

Julia, feeling a measure of relief, crossed her arms and sat back. 'I can't say I'm sorry.'

'It's not me you'll need to be saying it to . . .' Talavera began, then broke off, raising one hand to her ear as if listening. Then she smiled. 'In fact, it may not be necessary.'

On the screens a bright point appeared and flared suddenly. Filters cut in and the image adjusted to show an expanding cloud of debris with a knot of blazing white-hot energies at the core. All were silent as smaller ships, caught in the shock wave, spun and collided with one another while secondary explosions flashed, revealing huge ragged sections of superstructure wheeling away.

'Seems that battleship was using one of its heavy beam projectors to hit a target on the planet's surface. Your missile interrupted its second volley.' Talavera laughed. 'I think the cosmos must run on irony.'

The other Enhanced averted their eyes. Julia noticed that Arkady, standing a foot or two away, had lowered the gun, letting it hang by his side. Desperation got the better of her but even as she steeled her nerves and was on the point of lunging for the weapon, Arkady's hand snapped up, muzzle aimed squarely at her face. He had scarcely altered his stance or the position of his head.

'Peripheral vision is a wonderful thing,' said Talavera. 'But so is a talent like yours!' She indicated the screens, the scene of devastation, repeating and looping, close-up and slow motion. 'Your work was a success – one capital ship destroyed, the other crippled and nearly defenceless.'

'The Earthsphere ship is still . . . intact?' Julia said. 'How is that possible?'

Talavera pointed the control, and some of the screens changed to show the *Heracles*, its prow and most of the forward section a charred, twisted wreck, exposed innards leaking vapours and fluids in trailing white clouds of frozen crystals. Smaller craft were swooping in towards it, firing off bolts of energy while the ship itself was slowly spinning around its axis.

'Seems the Earthers somehow detected the second missile's approach, went evasive and got less than half a click away when it detonated. Wrecked their prow, fried most of their systems and all their weapons. Right now they couldn't defend themselves against a hull-scrubber . . . well, look at that . . .'

On screen, the Earthsphere ship, its spin halted, had ignited its main reaction thrusters and was moving off, still under attack from Spiral Armada gunships. Suddenly, a streaming shimmer enclosed the *Heracles*, which then leaped forward in an eyeblink of brightness that shrank away to nothing. Talavera shook her head.

'Have to hand it to that captain, knew what he was doing, used the bows to shield the rest of his ship and his engines from the missile blast. And now he's off into hyperspace, leaving the Covenant Order of the Spiral Prophecy in possession of the high ground!'

Julia gave no response, instead looked up at Arkady, standing still as a statue, face expressionless, gun still trained on her.

'Arkady, what happened?' she said. 'Arkady, we're your friends . . .'

'Be calm, sit down, everyone be calm.'

Julia stared icily at Talavera. 'What did you do to him?'

There was a sly smile. 'Oh, he came to me, dear Julia, and laid bare your efforts. Must say, those polymotes are so clever – you're going to make me such a great deal of money!'

'So why is he like this?'

Talavera moved up close to Arkady, smiled and stroked his unresponsive face. 'Poor boy had a change of heart – instead of overpowering Thorold, he went back out to warn you. Well, I put a stop to that and persuaded him to keep to the plan, with a little improvisation.'

'This isn't persuasion!' Julia shouted. 'You couldn't persuade him to behave this way in just minutes . . .'

'But my entire ship is devoted to methods of persuasion!' Talavera said, her features alive and intense. 'Drastic methods, certainly, and when you're forging a new reality sometimes you have to go to great lengths in order to be convincing. But yes, you are right – you can't change someone's mind in just a few minutes, unless you put someone else in the driver's seat. Or something else.'

She took a small dark blue vial from a pocket and held it up to one of the overhead light strips. What looked like fine powder shifted within and Julia felt an uneasy chill.

'They're such innovators, the Hegemony,' Talavera went on. 'Nanoengineered particulate mechanisms, designed to enter the brain and take over the voluntary physical centres and parts of the cognitive regions. These little workhorses are an entire magnitude smaller than your polymotes. Working together in great numbers they can easily simulate the host's normal demeanour.' She patted Arkady's cheek. 'Oh, he's still in there, hearing and seeing everything. He just has no control over what his body does.'

'What do you want from us?' Julia said, fighting to keep her voice calm. 'We've seen your secrets. We know about the containments.'

'You have? Aren't they amazing? You wouldn't believe the trouble I went to, having them built by a reliable black-sector monoclan, then getting them shipped out to the Aranja Tesh.' She paused to look at them all individually, as if pleased to see the hate and the contempt in their eyes. 'I know what you're thinking. You think that with your great intellects and those cortical processors in your heads you can defeat the Hegemony's nanodust. Well, please go on thinking that because failure is so instructive. Wouldn't you say, Julia?'

On the shuttle compartment's screens, the destruction of the Brolturan ship played over and over again, from the missile payload's initial detonation, slowed down to a near-glacial ballet of chaos. A knot of blazing white energy blossomed in the huge ship's flank, roared through the interior, shafts of actinic radiation bursting from ports and hatches in those infinitesimal instants before the raw, expanding fury tore open the hull in a hellish eruption.

Legs trembling, Julia stood. 'I don't know how your dust will affect us but I promise you that we will fight you every step of the way. We will not create more destruction for you.'

Talavera gazed down at the vial in her hand and smiled faintly. 'I know you Enhanced – in fact I think I almost know you better than you know yourselves. Give you a big fat juicy problem full of unexplored scientific implications and you just can't resist. You'll all do your best work for me, I know you will.'

'It will be a cold day in hell first.'

'But Julia, the new reality we're forging will be a paradise. Trust me.'

25

GREG

At the narrowest point of the glen, Greg was crouched on a ledge halfway down a tall, rocky buttress, fixing in place a second shaped charge, about thirty feet below the first one. Alexei was on the other side, planting more along the lip of the sheer cliff, hoping that they would unleash an avalanche. Once the charge was solid, Greg wiped his face then looked across the treetops to where Alexei sat on a jutting boulder. Exchanging waves, he moved down and back towards the western end of the glen, descending into its rocky tangle of roots and hardy bushes through which a rain-swollen stream gushed.

It was mid-afternoon, a day and a half since Vashutkin's appearance, and the sun was blazing down from a near-cloudless sky, sending bright shafts into the humid glen. The air was redolent of bark and leaf, of sap and blooms, and was abundantly abuzz with insects, stirred by the calls of birds and other small forest denizens. A beautiful Darien day which, unfortunately, he would have to disrupt.

Greg found Alexei waiting for him up on a flat boulder that protruded from the side of the glen and provided a good view back to the notch. Greg held up the signal trigger, which was the size of a key fob.

'Ready?' he said. 'Counting down from three . . . two . . . one . . .'

The explosions were simultaneous. Soil and pulverised rock burst out from the charge locations. The rocky buttress shattered and fell into the glen, flattening a swath of trees while a mass of earth and rocks and uprooted trees swept down from the other side. Flocks of screeching birds erupted, some dispersing to other perches, others climbing to circle overhead.

Then a voice crackled over Greg's earpiece.

'That you done wi' Glen Nero, chief?'

Greg grinned. Rory had decided to name all the eastern valleys after Roman emperors.

'Eh, aye – I don't think we'll see any mobile armour coming up this way.'

'That's grand. Now if the both of ye could get over to Glen Julius it would be appreciated, like. Got a wee bit o' a situation here.'

'What's the problem?' he said as he and Alexei began heading up the glen.

'Snipers – I've had tae change my spot three times already.'

'Brolts or DVF?'

'Pretty sure it's our guys – they know the ground, and, eh . . . I think young Pauly's bought it. Not seen him for near an hour.'

'Right, we're on our way back to the *Har* so we should be with ye soon. Keep yer head down . . .'

'I'm way ahead of ye on that one.'

'There is trouble?' Alexei said as they hurried through the trees.

'They've sent DVF snipers into the glen and now Pauly's not been heard from for an hour.' Greg tried to keep the bitterness out of his voice. Paul Svenson was a crack shot; he was also just sixteen years old and an orphan, both parents murdered by Brolturan sweep squads. He had been eager to go to Glen Julius and Vashutkin had said yes, to which Greg had reluctantly agreed.

'Maybe we should get one of the mobile squads over there,' said Alexei. 'Pin them down if they're trying to come through in force.'

'Not yet,' Greg said. 'Not until we hear from Augustus and Claudius. Got to be sure they're bottled up first.'

There were four accessible routes to the eastern slopes of Tusk Mountain, coming from the Kentigern foothills and the coast.

Glen Nero, now blocked; Glen Julius, a steep-sided rocky defile which led up past a series of waterfalls; Glen Claudius, a winding gully that forked at a craggy hill; and Glen Augustus which was an actual proper valley with only one possible choke point, at its entrance nearly two miles away. Vashutkin and his demolition team were heading there now and if they failed it would be up to Greg and the mobile squads to hold off the enemy advance for as long as possible before retreating to the Tusk Mountain stronghold.

And then we have to hold that against mounting odds, he thought. *With our salvation depending, apparently, on the actions of one man, Robert Horst. Or so the Sentinel claims.*

The *Har* was a cigar-shaped dirigible moored in a natural clearing. Her pilot, a Finn called Varstrand, was sitting in a folding chair, dressed for the sun in a singlet and shorts while still wearing a battered flying helmet complete with goggles.

'Sun is good for skin,' he said, slapping his skinny chest. 'Vitamin C, yes?'

'Fruit's what you need, Varstrand,' said Greg. 'But right now, we need to get over that ridge and a few hills – and we need to go now!'

Varstrand grinned, stood, folded his chair and slung it over one shoulder.

'*Ei hätää*, my friend! – don't worry. The *Har* is a fine and agile ship – we'll be there fast.'

A few minutes later they were strapped into creaking wire-and-wicker couches positioned behind the cockpit, which was only separated from the rest of the gondola by an openwork wooden partition. The dirigible's twin props gave out a conversation-challenging harsh buzz as the zeplin lurched, tipped backwards then swung free as the craft gained height. Greg had given Varstrand a basic hand-drawn map of landmarks and features, which had been tacked to the instrument panel, thus obscuring a few gauges. But the pilot seemed unconcerned as he worked his controls, keeping the *Har* on a careful heading, coasting just over the treetops.

Rory was still available so between his directions and peering at the map, they found a particular grassy shelf part-way along a high ridge. After agreeing a rendezvous back along the gully, Greg and Alexei climbed down a rope ladder, hair and clothing flapping in the backwash of the idling propellers. Once feet were on solid ground, waves were exchanged, the ladder was hauled up, and the *Har* swung round to head off to the west, its underside brushing the topmost leaves of the highest trees.

A rocky path led down a jagged notch in the crag. Greg could see tool marks where crude steps had been chiselled from the stone and wondered if this pinnacle had been a place of meditation for those long-vanished Uvovo. Or even to observe the canopy of colossal trees, the vast expanse of the world-forest-that-was.

Soon the path emerged into sunlight and became a narrow ledge sloping down the side of a sheer drop. The bare stone was searingly hot in the sun, and Rory was waiting there, crouched down in the brightness, long-barrelled sniper rifle leaning against his shoulder. He squinted up at them.

'Ye want tae mind yer feet, gents. It's a wee bit tricky when yer heading down.'

As they followed, Greg scanned the horizon and the sky as he had been compulsively doing all day, watching for the first sign of Brolturan air support. Personnel carriers, attack craft and combat drones – he knew that they had them yet they were conspicuous by their absence.

Perhaps it's a game for them, drawing us out with probing ground attacks, then when we're at our most exposed in comes the air assault.

In anticipation of this, Vashutkin had suggested forming three mobile squads of five fighters each, and all moving about on lightweight folding bikes. A renegade zeplin had flown in the night before and offloaded two crates of them, as well as medical and food supplies. Given the local terrain it made sense and everyone agreed.

'Found just the spot for yer charges, chief,' Rory said as they descended into the bushy green shadows of Glen Julius. 'The next waterfall down has plenty o' boulders and a bloody big over-hang, just like the one over in Glen Augustus.'

'Good to know, Rory,' Greg said. 'Thing is, how many DVF are down there? What are we up against?'

'Four or five of them – I think.'

'Ye think?'

'Aye, well, I'm on my tod here, chief. Anyway, s'kinda creepy to me. I cannae understand why any of our people would carry on in the DVF, taking orders from Brolt officers. Unless they've been brainwashed, or got a dose of that happy dust that nearly did for you.'

'Don't remind me,' Greg muttered, trying not to recall the Hegemony ambassador Kuros and the engineered nanodust with which he'd pillaged Greg's mind. 'Some of it'll be just loyalty to their squad mates or unit commanders. Mostly, though, I'll bet it's fear. Did ye hear those rumours that all DVF troops and govern-ment police have been secretly implanted with tracking devices? So anyone who goes AWOL gets chased by hunter-killer drones and permanently retired.'

Rory gave a low whistle. 'That would encourage me no' to desert . . .'

By now they were clambering down among large mossy boul-ders in the shade of the few tall trees and many bushes that clung to the ravine's steep sides. The rushing sound of a waterfall came from an indeterminate distance ahead, through the tangle of foliage.

'Where did you last spot those snipers?' Alexei muttered.

'Below the second waterfall,' Rory said. 'But we should be okay – Pauly's watching for them . . .'

'Whoa! – what was that?' Greg said. 'He's not dead?'

Rory slapped his forehead. 'Did I no' say? Sorry, chief – eh, aye, turns out he fell off a branch and brained hisself, the halfwit. Come to about five minutes after I called you on the . . .' He waggled his fingers at his ear.

Greg didn't know whether to laugh or give him a telling-off.

Instead he shook his head. 'Right, can we get on with this?'

Rory guided them to where the small river poured through a tumble of boulders and down a twenty-foot drop, all jutting rocks and curtains of spray. By the time they reached the foot of it, after a hair-raising downward clamber, they were all soaked through. Twice they heard the unmistakable thin crack of rifle shots from further along the ravine, causing involuntary ducking. Rory paused at one point, putting his hand to his ear, then he turned to Greg.

'Pauly's in trouble! – one of them's climbed up on the left, got him pinned down . . .'

As he dashed off, Greg and Alexei switched their earpieces to short range and hurried after him. There was a shout followed by shots. Moments later they found Rory crouched over a still form in DVF forest greens, lying sprawled between boulders not far from where a twisted tree leaned over the waterfall's brink, its leafy sprigs misted in spray. Rory glanced up and shook his head.

'A waste, it is. They should be fighting wi' us . . .'

Off to one side, a skinny youth in a thin camouflage cape straightened from his crouch, waved and moved along the waterfall's boulder-choked lip to a new position. Greg and Alexei waved back to Pauly as he settled down with his rifle, scanning the foliage below. Greg thought for a moment.

'I think the pair of ye should keep Pauly company in case they try it again,' he said. 'I'll climb up and set the charges, soon as Rory shows me where the overhang is.'

Rory had retrieved the dead soldier's rifle and was just handing it to Alexei, whose eyes lit up with surprise.

'A Kellerman 5.56 – nice gun, pretty rare, much sought after.'

'Aye, well don't sell it too soon, eh?' Rory said. 'Right, chief, follow me.'

The overhang was everything Rory said it was, a massive outward-leaning pillar of rock. With his background in Uncle Theo's Diehards, Rory had figured out the best detonation points, marking them with small wads of paper wedged into cracks. Moving up, from edge to edge, from point to point, Greg found he had a spectacular view of the surrounding rocky hills and pinnacles, a maze of forbidding crags and fissures. And westward, looming over it all, the imposing mass of Tusk Mountain. The entrance to the stronghold was just visible as a small dark mark against the stony grey face. The altitude there was 2,800 feet while the peak was another 1,600 feet further up, attainable only after a tough, demanding climb.

He was about to start down when his earpiece beeped. Leaning back against sunwarmed rock, he fingered one of the earpiece studs, switching into the long-range comnet.

'Greg here.'

'Greg, this is Bessonov – we've blown the gorge wall in Glen Claudius. Bad news is that some of their troops got through before it came down.'

'How many?'

'Hard to say – perhaps twenty, maybe more. We've lost two from our team and we are pulling back.'

'Did you call up the mobile squads?' Greg asked, suddenly worried.

'One is on its way. The others are over in the Augustus valley. Vashutkin was meeting stiff resistance and called them in.'

Greg shook his head. Obviously, Vashutkin considered his mission of greater consequence. 'Okay, get back to the foothills and link up with the mobile squad. We'll be with you as soon as we can.'

Is this it? he thought as he clambered along a natural ledge, keeping his head down. *Is this where it starts to unravel?*

He switched back to short range, outlined the situation to Alexei, Rory and Pauly, then told them to move over to the opposite side of the ravine and keep back from the waterfall's brink. Greg meanwhile had found a broad, solid shelf near the top of an overlooking ridge some thirty-odd yards along from the charges. Once he was seated on the cold, flat stone, he counted down from five over the short-range, then hit the trigger.

There was a crashing, deafening boom. Dark clouds shot out from the explosions and Greg could see the immense overhang tipping forward then falling through them. At the same time fragments big and small were flying in all directions and Greg watched, in amazement then panic, as one large piece came spinning out of the dust and chaos towards him. But its arc of flight fell short and it struck the top of the ravine wall less than ten feet away. Greg felt the impact, saw the rock face shatter and split, long shards toppling out. There was a deep crack close by and the shelf trembled underfoot then lurched. There were voices shouting in his ear but he was completely in the grip of fear as he whirled and leaped across a growing gap in the rock, scrambling madly up onto the clifftop.

A roaring rumble filled the air. The ground shook and grey clouds billowed up. Greg had found refuge on a scree slope of a small saddle ridge overlooking Glen Julius, and he sat down heavily on a boulder, trying to make sense of it. After a few moments the rumbling faded to an eerie silence. He was about to make his way back to the ravine when he heard a hum from somewhere in the vicinity. The hum grew louder and harsher and suddenly familiar just as Varstrand's dirigible, the *Har*, bobbed up from the other side of the saddle ridge and banked before slowing overhead.

Shouting, Greg waved and saw the pilot mouthing something while pointing at his ear. Realisation struck and Greg fumbled with the earpiece's stud controls, and was suddenly assailed by a jabber of voices.

'. . . yes, I have him! He is safe . . .'

'So why's he no' replyin', then . . .'

'Sorry, Rory,' Greg said, catching the end of the rope ladder snaking down from the zeplin. 'I must have muted the channel somehow in all the commotion.'

Rory laughed. 'Commotion, aye! Right, see ye soon.'

A swift climb hand-over-hand and he was inside the gondola, dragging himself into the compartment then pulling the ladder in after him.

'Lot of noise and clouds,' Varstrand yelled over his shoulder. 'Looks like success for you, I think.'

'Hope so,' he yelled back.

As he hauled in the last of the ladder, the *Har* was gaining height and moving towards the ravine, so the hatch was still open when the ravine and the waterfall came fully into view. He paused, staring down through a haze of drifting dust at the astonishing sight. As he'd hoped, the massive overhanging rock pillar had fallen onto the lip of the waterfall and smashed an irregular section of it, perhaps ten feet back, sending tons of rock plummeting into the gap below. But that wasn't all – the explosions had cracked the ravine wall and undermined it, causing it to collapse into the ravine. From this height it looked as if some gigantic blade had carved a long gouge out of the ravine wall, dumping a lengthy mound of rubble along one side, crushing and shredding a swath of trees and bushes, burying every piece of foliage. Looking down, Greg felt a stab of guilt at having caused such wanton destruction in this pocket of Darien's ecology.

Varstrand, though, was practically whooping with delight, praising Greg's demolition skills in Finnish and Noranglic. Rory was equally impressed when he climbed up into the gondola ten minutes later.

'Job done, chief! When you're doin' a bit of remodelling, you don't mess about!'

'Aye, but I wasn't planning on knocking down half a mountain's worth and creating that eyesore.'

'Och, give it a year or two and ye'd hardly know anything was out of place.'

Greg frowned. 'What's keeping Alexei?' He fingered his earpiece for the proximity channel as he leaned out of the side hatch and into the rushing backwash of the *Har*'s right prop. Alexei was standing next to Pauly several yards off to the side and Greg understood. 'Are you staying behind?' he shouted.

'Yes, just to be sure that our friends don't pay us any more visits. *Kharasho?*'

'*Kharasho*, okay! But be careful, both of ye!'

He waved to them then slid the hatch shut and shouted at Varstrand to get aloft.

'Do you want us to be heading back to the mountain?' yelled the Finn over his shoulder.

'No,' Greg said as he and Rory settled into the rickety passenger couches. 'Take us over to the western end of Glen Claudius and find somewhere to moor, up high with a good view of the gorge.'

'As you say.'

Greg turned to Rory. 'Let's find out what Vashutkin's been up to,' he said, and switched his earpiece to the long-range comnet then cycled to Vashutkin's channel. 'Alexandr, this is Greg Cameron. Are you receiving? Please respond . . .'

'Ah, Gregory, my dear friend! – I was just about to notify you of our successes. The entrance to the Augustus valley is now closed! It took two sets of charges, and a bit of fighting, but it is done.'

'Any sign of any enemy air support?'

'No, nothing.'

'Many casualties?'

'A few, some wounded . . .'

'Okay, Alexandr, listen – some enemy troops broke through in Glen Claudius so please tell the mobile squads to move up to the western end of Claudius. We're heading there right now . . .'

He broke off as Rory grabbed his arm and pointed out of the cockpit windscreen. 'Chief, what the hell is that?'

Tusk Mountain was directly ahead, its lower eastern flank less than half a mile away. Following Rory's outstretched hand Greg saw a bright spot moving up over the steep, rocky ground. Frowning, he grabbed a pair of binoculars from where they dangled from Varstrand's dashboard, and trained them on the mountainside. A moment's refocusing and he was seeing it clearly, a patch of brightness flowing up the slope, over boulders and scree. As he watched, it accelerated, sped up towards the stronghold's barricaded entrance then slipped out of sight behind a tumble of rocks.

Lowering the binoculars, Greg shook his head. 'I don't . . .'

Light stopped him, a brilliant white light that engulfed the mountain. Dazzling white light blocking from view the slopes, the rocks, the crags. A torrent of light, sending an unbearable flare into his eyes, cutting through to his worst fears.

Two and a half seconds later the shock wave struck, but Varstrand was ready, pointing the *Har* into the oncoming wall of heated air, gunning the engines to their maximum. A booming roar filled their ears and the gondola shook violently as if in the hands of a petulant child. Varstrand was snarling as he held on to the control column with a white-knuckle grip. Greg's vision was blurred, his eyes watering, and somewhere Rory was babbling, holy crap, was it a nuke? was it a nuke? as the gondola shook around them. Ignoring his discomfort, Greg anchored himself to a hull strut with one arm while staring through the binoculars at the clouds swirling around the mountain's upper half, and the fires burning within.

Then the turbulence was past and the dirigible surged forward. Up on the mountain high winds were whipping away the smoke in a long dark tail, stark against the blue sky.

'Where to, Mr Cameron?' said Varstrand.

'Up there,' he said, pointing.

'But what about the radiation . . .?'

'It wasn't a nuke,' Greg said. 'No mushroom cloud, see? If it had been a nuke we'd have been burnt to a crisp by now. No, I bet it was a particle beam strike from that bloody battleship o' theirs. Now, get moving.'

As they ascended, the dust clouds and smoke veils drifted aside to reveal the full extent of the destruction. Varstrand gasped, Rory cursed, and Greg stared in disbelief.

The particle beam had punched into the craggy slope where the stronghold entrance was, and left behind a burning hollow eighty, perhaps a hundred feet across. It was as if something had taken a massive bite out of the mountainside.

'Now we know why they had no air support,' Greg said.

'But why send in they troops?' Rory said. 'Why no' hit the place earlier when we were all inside?'

Greg shook his head and shrugged. 'So they'd have some prisoners to play with, maybe?'

Varstrand brought them to a gentle boulder-littered slope a hundred yards or more from the devastated entrance. As they clambered down the rope ladder, Greg noticed a scattering of smoking rock fragments further down and lower still, near the tree line, an advancing line of green-garbed figures, pale in the drifting haze.

'Aye, I can see 'em, chief. Didnae waste any time, eh?' He pointed to the east. 'And there's more on the way.'

A cluster of carriers were coming in low across the wooded hilltops.

'C'mon,' Greg said. 'No time to lose.'

They waved to Varstrand as the *Har* lifted clear, then quickly headed up the stony slope. Minutes later the smoke-swathed blasted hollow was in sight and a rocky clamber away. An awful dread was growing in the pit of Greg's stomach, even as the enemy transports were touching down at the foot of the mountain. If they could gain the entrance, and if there were any survivors, could they mount a defence of the stronghold, somehow? In the fading hope that at the last minute of the eleventh hour Robert Horst would return to Darien with a mysterious salvation?

Then, as he began to climb over the rocks dislodged by the strike, doom fell upon them again, a second bright dot which appeared on the slope some distance above them and began sweeping down towards the crater. This time the dust and smoke betrayed the targeting beam, a glowing, glittering spear that lanced down from the heavens, bright, inexorable.

Rory shouted an obscenity at the sky and leaped down from the rock barrier. 'C'mon chief, we gotta get outta here!'

But Greg felt trapped between his own rage and the seeming impotence of his efforts in the face of such colossal power. *How can we fight this?* he wanted to say. *How can we even outrun it?*

Then the beam reached the crater, a fateful shaft of light. Rory let out a wordless cry and curled up in the lee of a jutting boulder, while Greg slid down behind several piled nearby, crouching with his arms over his head . . .

Instants stretched out into moments. The silence was expectant and terrible. Yet no sudden burst of ferocious light erupted, nor any buffeting shock wave. Cracking open his eyes, Greg saw no change in the light, until he noticed the sharp shadows cast by small rocks close by, shadows that fell towards the sun . . .

He jumped up and gazed into the sky. The heavens were dominated by a bright and now fading point of haloed light. He fumbled with the binoculars, thumbed the focus wheel, but still it seemed like a dot, its glow dwindling, and, perhaps, a hint of glittering fragments?

'What's going on, chief?' Rory said. 'We're still alive, not that I'm complaining, like.'

'I think,' Greg said, peering up through the binoculars, 'that someone's just blown the Brolturan battleship to bits.'

Grinning, he handed the bins to Rory, who quickly raised them and looked up at the pale dot. 'That it, aye?'

'Certainly is.'

'Aw, ya dancer!' Rory laughed out loud. 'Yeess! Who d'ye think did it? The *Heracles*, maybe?'

'Could be. Won't know for sure until we get back inside the mountain so that I can have a wee chat with the Sentinel.'

Then Greg noticed movement on the mountain's lower slopes and, shielding his eyes from the sun, he peered down. From this height it appeared that the DVF troops were withdrawing back down to where personnel carriers were landing, rear hatches already gaping. Retrieving the binoculars he took a closer look and yes, the Human troops were hastily piling into the carriers, which scarcely touched down before taking to the air again.

Greg laughed. 'They're pulling out! . . . I mean, they're not even pulling back, they're leaving the field altogether.'

Rory laughed madly and danced a jig, then yelled imprecations down at the retreating soldiers, interspersed with a few energetically thrown stones.

But through his own feelings of euphoria, Greg began asking himself why – even if that battleship, the *Purifier*, was wrecked or destroyed, why break off from a strategic engagement like an assault on Tusk Mountain?

Minutes later the last of the transports had lifted off to follow the rest back to the coast. Greg stared after them, frowning. Then he sighed.

'C'mon, Rory. We'll have to find out what the situation is, in there.'

Suddenly sombre, Rory nodded and together they climbed over the fallen rocks to where the original stony track had curved the last thirty yards to the Uvovo stronghold's entrance. Except that now it stopped a few yards away at a precipice overlooking a huge bowl-shaped crater. Its surface was blackened, encrusted with charred soil and glassy patches of melted stone. Vapour drifted at the bottom and faint crackling sounds came from cooling rock. And there, incredibly, was a large, square opening in the curved wall straight ahead, its edges slightly warped, its interior sooty and dark, yet a couple of figures stood on the lip, shouting and waving. Could that mean that the rest of the stronghold was intact?

Just as he was figuring out how to get across, a high-pitched whine became audible and quickly grew louder. Suddenly, a compact, blue-winged craft flew into view, banked sharply and swooped down towards the scene of destruction. It slowed as it passed overhead then climbed and sped away eastwards. Greg already had the trusty binoculars up to track its progress, taking in such details as the W-configuration of its flying surfaces and the symbol prominently adorning its wings. It was a spiral overlaid with a narrow chevron, its apex touching the centre. It looked like no Earthsphere emblem he had ever seen but it did remind him of something else, a conversation with the *Heracles*' xeno-specialist who'd said something about the Spiral Sages of Buranj . . .

PART THREE

26

KAO CHIH

The return journey to the Roug homeworld took about three hours via the faster Tier 2 hyperspace, yet to Kao Chih it seemed to last far longer. Impatience ate at him. In his mind he went over all that he'd seen on Pyre, the grinding poverty, the despair, the degrading squalor, people living like animals in a cage while their tormentors squeezed the last profitable drops from them. Silveira had already transloaded the data from his camera into the little spyship's system and had promised to make a copy available to the leaders and people of Human Sept. Another would be passed to Roug officials as a partial explanation for Qabakri's decision to remain on Pyre.

It should have been me, Kao Chih thought to himself more than once. He had wanted to stay behind but Qabakri had persuaded him to return and provide a 'reliable testimony'. The implied uncertainty concerning Silveira's reliability was not lost on him.

Finally, the Earthsphere agent announced that they would soon be emerging from hyperspace in the outer reaches of the Roug home system. Moments passed, along with that familiar brief wave of nausea.

'That is it, we have arrived.'

Kao Chih had closed his eyes before the jump, and opened them to the sight of Silveira pondering an astrogational holochart of the Busrul system, using his finger to zoom into it and across and down and back. Pinpoints and symbol clusters in red, with a few in blue, littered a large area surrounding the gas giant V'Hrant.

'Odd,' said the agent. 'There seems to be some kind of system-wide emergency going on. Most of these beacons and scanners weren't active last time – I wouldn't be surprised if we've set off . . .'

A trill of urgent notes sounded and the rare-heard voice of the *Oculus Noctis* spoke:

'Enforcement Overseer Juthonag of the High Index has served you with a Response-Or-Summary-Internment writ.'

'How insistent of them,' Silveira said. 'Open a channel.'

'Now open.'

Silveira glanced and smiled at Kao Chih before speaking.

'This is Captain Baltazar Silveira of Earthsphere Alliance Navy. How may I be of assistance?'

'Your vessel is unknown to us,' said a low, chorus-like voice. 'Your intrusion in our system at this time can easily be construed as unfriendly and potentially hostile. What is the reason for your presence?'

'We are acting under the special orders of Mandator Qabakri. We bear intelligence data objects of a crucial nature.'

There was a silent pause, then the deep vibrant voice spoke again.

'I am instructed to convey you to the nexus of the crisis.'

From the transparent viewport Kao Chih and Silveira saw space quiver and distort as an immense V-shaped vessel revealed itself. A striated column of light sprang out from the flat grey prow to engulf the *Oculus Noctis*. Kao Chih felt nausea well up for a moment as the stars swung around their small craft, then realised that it was false motion sickness – Silveira's ship damp-ened internal inertia.

'This should not take long,' Silveira said with his usual confi-dent composure as the Roug ship charged across the system with his ship held in its grapple beam.

Minutes later, as a pale dot expanded into the dull, dark face of the gas giant V'Hrant, another far smaller speck grew rapidly directly ahead and became the rockhab *Retributor*. No sneaking in through Maintenance this time – the *Oculus Noctis* was peremptorily directed to a vacant berth in the new landing bay. As they disembarked onto the convex dockside, Kao Chih noticed a group of Roug emerge from a small, blockish vessel similar to the large V-shaped one.

Strangely, there seemed to be no one there to greet either themselves or the Roug, no security detail, no officials. They glanced about for a moment, received no attention from the few loaders and hull techs, then moved towards the main exit. Suddenly the doors parted and a knot of arguing people spilled out. One of them, a stocky bearded man in engineer's red and black, broke away and quickly approached.

'Honourable Kao Chih, I am Kung Wei, senior engineer. I must speak with you . . .'

A small woman in yellow and beige elbowed her way to the front.

'Unfortunately, respected Kung Wei has no authority. I, on the other hand, am Shang Yi, environmental manager . . .'

A taller man in plum and black firmly pushed them apart and stepped forward. 'Sadly, neither of my associates is competent to deal with matters of security. I am Captain Ji Yen, officer commanding *Retributor* security . . .'

Another babble of argument threatened to break out until Kao Chih, suddenly infuriated, said loudly, 'Silence – have you forgotten your manners in the presence of our patrons?'

Voices tailed off abruptly, and embarrassed glances took in the Roug party now drawing near. Silveira arched both eyebrows and nodded approvingly.

'Thank you,' Kao Chih said amiably. 'Now what has happened to bring about this unseemly behaviour?'

'Everything has been turned on its head,' said Shang Yi. 'There are Roug patrons running the command bridge . . .'

'They were taken,' explained the security captain. 'The Duizhang, the senior officers, many of the elders, all captured, kidnapped!'

'It is without precedent in this age, Human Kao Chih,' came the sharp, papery voice of one of the Roug as they approached the group of Humans. The officers made respectful bows, Kao Chih and Silveira too, and the senior Roug gave a stiff nod as it halted a few feet away, flanked by two companion Roug, each bearing what had to be weapons with long, segmented barrels.

'Greetings, honourable patrons,' Kao Chih said, trying not to stare at the escort. The sight of armed Roug was completely new.

'And to you, Humans Kao Chih and Baltazar Silveira,' the Roug said. 'I am Mandator Reen of the High Index. It is understood that you bring word from Qabakri – we shall attend to this in due course. First, you should understand the ominous nature of what has transpired.'

Kao Chih frowned. 'So this is more than a kidnapping.'

'If we are fortunate, this is a hostage-taking,' the Roug said, producing a small brown lozengelike object which unfolded to a thin, square, rigid display. With one of its long brassy fingers the Roug tapped the lower edge then handed it to Kao Chih, who found himself looking at security vidage from various locations within the *Retributor*. Panicking people ran for cover as armed invaders rushed through Many-Voices Hall, along corridors, up stairs, armoured figures that he recognised from personal experience as Ezgara commandos. Then came the spectacle of Human Sept's leaders, wrists bound and mouths taped, being herded down passages, familiar faces wide-eyed with fear, the Duizhang Kang Lo, Tan Hua, the department commanders, the elders like Wu and Mother Yao, and also, stumbling along on his short legs, his eyes blazing with fury, was the Voth pilot, Yash. At a rough guess, there were about twenty-five captives in all.

'A few hours after you departed for Pyre,' Mandator Reen said, 'the Hegemony warship left with the Potentiary on board. One point five hours later, a smaller ship entered our system claiming to require the use of a repair dock at Agmedra'a. On the way to the orbital it vanished from our sensor displays, clearly by virtue of stealth technology. Our next indication of their whereabouts was when they approached this asteroid vessel and boarded it by force, with such results as you can see.

'An insult of such gravity cannot be disregarded. These Ezgara invaded the ambit of our system-zone, concealed themselves from legitimate detection and appraisal, ignored the protocols of civilised communication, then carried out a violent incursion and abduction of protected sentients. Such an affront requires that pursuit is swiftly undertaken with the aim of procuring an appropriate apology. The appropriateness, of course, will not be inconsequential.'

'My vessel is T2-capable,' said Silveira. 'It may not have the weaponry to engage, but it can certainly track the Ezgara to their destination. I would be happy to put both it and myself at your disposal.'

Mandator Reen turned its unfathomable regard on the Earthsphere agent, eyes hidden by those fine mesh cusps, mouth covered by a dull, coppery grille. Yet Kao Chih had seen Qabakri transform his appearance and that had included the garments, which prompted him to wonder how much of this was for show.

'Human Silveira, your offer has great merit but first we would hear of the Human colony on Pyre – I understand that you have gathered evidence data and wish to share it with us.'

Silveira produced a small transparent pocket containing a blue crystal cube and handed it to the Roug.

'That holds an edited record of our brief visit to the colony,' Silveira said. 'You will see what suffering has been inflicted on our fellow Humans by criminals whose operations are actively encouraged by the Suneye monoclan.'

'Thank you, Human Silveira. We will examine it promptly and closely.' Mandator Reen turned to Kao Chih. 'I would hear from you, Human Kao Chih, an account of the venture including Mandator Qabakri's reasons for remaining behind, if those were made clear to you.'

Kao Chih related the main points of the journey to the Roug and the now subdued crew officers. When he reached his final exchange with Qabakri, before departing Pyre, he was careful to make no mention of the Roug shapeshifting ability or Qabakri's human form.

'Mandator Qabakri takes action,' said Reen. 'He seeks to remind us of the duty of guardianship, laid upon our ancestors by the ancient Forerunners. Thus the Assessors have extensively monitored the pertinent sources, the Mandators have extended the scope of inquiry, and the Contiguals have decided that an act of protection is warranted for both the Humans of Pyre and those abducted.

'Which brings me back to you, Human Silveira, and your offer to pursue the miscreant Ezgara and ascertain their destination. A kind offer which must be put aside since you will need your vessel to return to your origin, and to carry a message from us to your masters and the leaders of your government, the Vox Humana.'

There was a shocked silence as everyone stared at Silveira. Kao Chih had a sick feeling in his chest as he faced the man.

'Is this true?' he said. 'Tell me that it's not.'

Silveira glanced over at his ship, as if gauging the likelihood of a successful escape, then at the *Retributor*'s frowning crew. Then he sighed and shook his head sadly but before he could speak, Mandator Reen spoke.

'Your real name is Ricardo Silveira. You were born on the independent colony of Mournival, you are forty-one years of age, Earth standard, you have neither spouse nor offspring, and you work as an independent contractor to Vox Humana intelligence. Our Assessors are both efficient and diligent. Now, say only the truth.'

Sharp and furious resentment burned in Silveira's eyes, then he shrugged.

'It is as you say.'

'So no connection with Earthsphere,' Kao Chih said slowly. 'And no chance of intervention for Darien or Pyre?'

'The president of Earthsphere and her government couldn't care less about Darien,' Silveira said. 'And nothing, but *nothing* could push them into serious opposition to Hegemony interests.'

'You, on the other hand, came to Darien with a view to discovering how amenable to joining Vox Humana the colonists

might be. But then you heard about the surviving Pyre colonists,'
the Roug said. 'The Pyre colonists are of your species' Asiatic
subdivision and you realised that liberating them from the grip of
a monoclan, a mercantile entity, was rather different from liberating Darien. Importantly, it would foster considerable goodwill
among the Chinese Confederacy members of the Earthsphere
Overcouncil. It could even lead to the lifting of the punitive sanc-
tions imposed on Vox Humana decades ago.'

Kao Chih nodded. 'That is very similar to what he told us
before we left Darien.'

'Your corroboration strengthens our argument. So, Human
Silveira, this is what we require of you – return to your superiors
on the Vox Humana hubworld, along with all the data you have
collected; inform them of the situation on Pyre and likewise tell
them that the High Index of the Roug has been appraised of your
moves and motivations. Yet we are prepared to aid Vox Humana
in the liberation of the Human colonists of Pyre, which must take
place in a matter of days.'

'What if I refuse?'

'We will not be restrained,' the Roug said. 'We shall widely
publicise your deeds in this and previous undertakings, and
include in the documentation details of your likeness, dental and
retinal patterns, and your DNA markers. There is no corner of the
tiernet that we cannot reach.'

'You may find it hard to find similar work in the future,' Kao
Chih said.

'Of course,' Mandator Reen said, 'for your part in this arrangement you would be eligible for an intermediary's fee, to be lodged
in an account of your choice.'

Silveira looked thoughtful for a moment, then nodded.

'Very well, Mandator Reen, I will be happy to act as your
intermediary with the Vox Humana authorities. I shall communi-
cate to them all you have specified.'

'Excellent. Then you must depart without delay.'

Silveira nodded to the Roug, looked at Kao Chih and said,
'My apologies for the ruse.'

Kao Chih made no reply, just folded his arms and looked back stonily. Silveira shrugged and hurried off to the *Oculus Noctis*. As the small ship floated through to the outer lock, Kao Chih's mood seemed to swing between extremes, anger at Silveira's lies, anger at himself for being duped again, grief over the situation on Darien, and a certain weary relief, and a kind of hope. Then the upper and lower bulkhead shells met and sealed, and he turned to the Roug.

'Honoured patron, now that Silveira and his ship are gone, may I suggest using the *Retributor* to chase after the Ezgara kidnappers?'

'Apart from the time required to untether and reactivate the rock habitat's drives, it is doubtful that it possesses sufficient offensive capacity to force the Ezgara craft's surrender. But do not be concerned, Human Chih – we shall provide a vessel appropriate to that task.'

27

LEGION

Night came to the towns and cities all around the Korzybski Sea, spreading west across hills, mountains and forests. Beneath its shroud, fighting continued, invaders crushed resistance or were ambushed, the defenceless were slaughtered and the desperate fought back, the cruel refused to extend protection to refugees, and the remorseless plotted their next move.

Through the deep shining darkness of the Forest of Arawn, the Knight of the Legion of Avatars glided on its suspensors, escorted by a group of type-R combat mechs, twenty-two gleaming machines moving among the trees. In nearly five hours they would reach a steep-sided gully down on the southern ramparts of the Kentigern range, and the high, almost inaccessible entrance to the huge cavern where the droid autofactory was waiting. Once there, the Knight would undergo badly needed repairs, even though the materials were inferior, while mustering an army of droids and planning possible tactics for an assault on Giant's Shoulder.

A glow of fires was visible through the vegetation as the Knight moved along the path cleared for it. It was skirting the site of a violent clash between, in this case, Humans and the invading Spiral fanatics. A transport pod carrying a dozen or more Gomedrans had landed badly, fetching up against a couple of big mossy boulders. This had attracted the attention of a much larger band of Humans who seemed to have attacked them in unison. This was a rash decision – the heavily armed Gomedrans were carrying suicide bombs which, faced with being overrun, they detonated. The Legion Knight noted the proliferation of body parts as it passed. This was not the first such scene it had encountered, nor was it likely to be the last.

Even though it was travelling in a crepuscular gloom, where insects and growths shed bioluminescent radiance, its sensors were receiving datastreams from survey-modified mechs positioned on high peaks and other vantage points. Matched and merged, this multiplicity of viewpoints provided a grand perspective – the night sky above, with far-off stars glowing through the dust clouds of the deepzone, and the Human-settled coast below, a long crescent of bays and inlets, its inky darkness broken by the bright pinpoint-clusters of towns and villages, and by the flash of weaponry, the sudden flare of explosions, the yellow glow of burning houses.

Mid- and long-range scanners were still picking up the heat signatures of ships entering the atmosphere, stragglers from the Spiral Covenant armada. The Knight knew of the church of the Father-Sages and its Spiral Prophecy offshoot, and also knew of the specious claim laid to the old temple on Giant's Shoulder. And sure enough, by tracking comm transmissions the Knight saw that five sizeable mobs, thousands in each, were fighting their way towards the great promontory. Opposing them were bands of Humans and dislocated units of Brolturan military, who also found time to fight each other with unrestrained ferocity.

Stirring, morale-boosting communications came from Giant's Shoulder where the Hegemony ambassador, Kuros, was holed up. From the other side came stirring, morale-boosting exhortations to purge pagans and heathens from the sacred ground, the holy place where the Father-Sage was buried. Allegedly.

All precipitated by the destruction of that Brolturan warship, the *Purifier*. With it went the centralised comnet that had proved so useful, but the Knight's survey mechs had been able to pick individual channels out of the chaos, allowing it to observe the huge vessel's fiery death. It had seen the thermonuclear device explode in the ship's flank, the blast of incineration, the instant eradication of thousands of lives, and the expanding cloud of debris, most of which later entered the atmosphere, burning trails across the sky.

By a stroke of irony, the destruction of the *Purifier* saved the Human stronghold at Tusk Mountain from complete annihilation. One of the Knight's observer mechs had seen the battleship's first particle beam strike, and he'd been impressed by the way it blasted into the massif and vaporised such a large volume of rock. But the second strike never came, leaving most of the ancient Uvovo mountain complex intact. From the results produced by its age-old sensor circuits, the Knight was certain that several energy flows met there, one of which was linked to the warpwell.

But compared to the Brolturan forces gathered at Giant's Shoulder, the Humans scarcely presented a genuine threat, while the Uvovo had forgotten the useful parts of their civilisation. In addition, the Forerunners' vaunted planetary biomass sentience was confined to the forest moon, its consciousness seemingly torpid, possibly degraded. In that context, the Knight's immediate strategy was to carry out needed repairs while moving about a third of its droids to forward staging posts along the forest's eastern boundary. Meanwhile, the battle communications of all three sides would be closely monitored, skirmishes and clashes would be analysed, while the planet's vicinity would be scanned for any signs of ships jumping in from hyperspace.

And once it and its escort reached the hidden cavern, the Knight planned to set aside some time to deal with the cunning and annoying Uvovo who had been following them for nearly two days. It had a special punishment in store for that one.

28

CATRIONA

The battle for Nivyesta was going badly. In the hours since the Spiral transport crash-landed in Segrana's northern region, a squadron of Spiral fighter craft had arrived in support of their stranded fellow zealots. Most of them had homed in on the Brolturan base, which was still resisting and still knocking them out of the sky. This part of the conflict was producing a continual string of crashes, explosions and fires which Uvovo on the south-east coast were hard-pressed to deal with. Catriona was caught in the dilemma of how to use the already thinly stretched cadres of Uvovo – the depredations of the crash survivors as they bombed and shot their way across Segrana's forest floor was causing immense distress as entire communities fled their approach. As the hours ground on Catriona realised that she was no tactician and more than once wished that Theo was still with them.

Then ominous news reached her. A large craft had just left the Brolturan base and was heading north inland, and from descriptions it sounded like an armoured gunship of some kind. Meanwhile, the Spiral raiders had begun attacking townships of the upper canopy, rocketing and strafing – Highsonglade and Skygarden were now deserted. There was one piece of good news, a small Spiral vessel had been captured, complete and undamaged, along with its furry, doglike pilot. Admittedly, this triumph was due mainly to the same pilot, who flipped his craft while the cockpit was open and, crucially, while not wearing the couch restraints. This resulted in a headlong plummet into a resilient suska bush from which he was retrieved unharmed.

Apart from that, events turned increasingly grim. Down in the twilight of the forest floor, a large force of Uvovo unexpectedly encountered a smaller group of Spiral offworlders and came off worst – the zealots were armed with a wide range of heavy weapons and were enthusiastic in their use. Laser rifles, grenade launchers, even some kind of lightning-bolt gun, were unleashed against the Uvovo and the surrounding forest. The aftermath, to Catriona's senses, was a black ruin of smoke and blood.

Uvovo trackers dogging the brutal intruders' footsteps eventually deduced that they numbered no more than thirty, which accounted for roughly a third of those who fled the crash site. Therefore there were another sixty or more at large in the depths of Segrana. Suddenly anxious, she cast the net of her senses further, hunting for creatures not yet gone to ground, hoping to peer through their eyes and discover the dangerous zealots.

But it was the Brolturans who found them first.

The gunship they had dispatched was much faster than the previous vessels and after reaching the crashed transport, it followed a southward course, flying low over the treetops. According to the sparse reports that reached Catriona, the Brolturans' route closely matched that of the Spiral fanatics. Despite the dense greenery of the canopy and the mid-branch foliage, the gunship picked up the intruders' trail, stalked them through the falling night, then, when a sizeable mob was within range, it opened fire.

A few small spies on the wing had been feeding Catriona occasional glimpses of the large craft's progress. Then without warning they scattered in alarm and the next thing Cat knew, waves of distress were pulsing through the weave of being. It sharpened and took on overtones of fear and then pain. Then a few jerky images reached her, of flames ripping through dense forest, of figures ducking and running, and others pointing weapons skywards, firing chains of bright spikes.

The images chopped and shifted, a mosaic of chaos. Sheets of flame wrapped themselves around huge, ancient trees, licking and clawing higher, burning furiously despite the dampness. Then she saw a line of fiery explosions burst one after another through the forest, and realised that her worst fear had come to pass. Incendiaries, the very weapon that Catriona had dreaded from the very start.

And now the Brolturans reckon that they've got nothing to lose, she thought. *Now they're out for revenge and we're in the way.*

Yet even if the Brolt vessel rained destruction on the fleeing fanatics, this was still only a tiny portion of the vastness of Segrana, its animal population, food plants, biomass and streams self-renewing over time . . . but against the waves of terrible news flooding through the weave of being, such comparisons seemed callous, however accurate.

Fleeting glimpses of conflagration continued to filter through. So, in tandem with Segrana's far-flung influence, she caused high-level rain reservoirs to spill down into the smoke-hazed gloom. Specialised filter roots were used to pump water up from mid-branch troughs or across from unaffected areas. At the same time gangs of Uvovo scampered to and fro across the upper branch-ways, slogging through heat and ashen smoke as they bucket-chained water down onto the fires burning in the wake of the bombing. Several reports came through from a Listener crouched in a vudron dangerously close to the Spiral zealots' southerly route – his scholars were spying on them as they followed a long U-shaped valley that curved westwards. Squads of Uvovo scouts were also out there, courting peril as they tried to stay on the trail of the offworlders, who, it now seemed, had some kind of proximity detector.

Then Catriona received unsettling information. The wide valley's eastern wall comprised a line of cliffs, steep hills and ridges, all interwoven with dark, dense undergrowth, a formidable obstacle to anyone travelling on foot. Yet the zealots had turned east and were heading straight for them; on reaching that barrier they would surely be forced to turn back or continue southwards. Half an hour later came bad news – they had found a narrow, barely accessible pass between two rearing crags and were moving through it. At the other end of the pass a lush fruit vale led to the Gardentrees, five huge, specially cultivated vaskin trees. They were clustered around a scholar town called Seedspringlow; most of the youngest Uvovo children from the south-east towns and villages had been sent there soon after the Brolturans arrived on Nivyesta. Luckily Catriona had ordered them evacuated a few hours ago, dispatching them to a harvest town about a dozen miles north-east.

But then she started to get panicky messages from a Listener in Seedspringlow, which revealed that the children were still there. A group of elder scholars had decided to ignore the evac order and now the Spiral fanatics were drawing close to the Gardentrees. Meanwhile the Brolturan vessel had altered its course in the direction of Seedspringlow, still following its quarry.

The situation was desperate. The frantic evacuation of Seedspringlow was now under way but would not be completed before the zealots arrived. The town's defenders were few in number and lightly armed, and although reinforcements were being rushed from north and south they would be too late.

Children, she thought. *Hundreds of Uvovo younglings . . . this is my fault, I should have known, should have been ready . . .*

Going by past reports and observations, the Spiral zealots would slaughter all they met and after them would come the Brolturans, raining fire on the forest . . .

Segrana, help us! Her desperate plea rang out across the weave of being and there was the sense of many others, Listeners and attuned scholars, feeling that cry. *Help them! You have power, Segrana, I have seen its immensity in the depths – will you not use it to help resist the attacks on your being and your people? . . .*

But there was no reply, nothing but a tense, withdrawn silence. Catriona despaired.

Segrana, if you will not use your powers, let me . . .

'She cannot . . . and you must not . . .'

Cat felt that presence, that wise and aged intellect, and found a wavering image emerging in what passed for her visual sense, a hooded figure, hazy, as if seen through fine rain. Still in the inky darkness of the vudron, she wondered if he was real or only in her mind.

'Pathmaster,' she said. 'We must . . .'

'The powers and energies you glimpsed are very real,' the ancient Uvovo said. 'But their use demands a particular strength that neither you nor Segrana possesses.'

'She mentioned something called the Many-Eyes.'

'Yes, an old, old name for the part of her that she sacrificed during the War of the Long Night, a guiding warrior spirit that left her to dive into the underdomains and destroy the soulroots of the Dreamless.'

'I need that power,' Cat said. 'I must have it, Pathmaster. People are gonna die, Uvovo children . . . please, I cannae have that on my conscience . . .'

'The risks are terrible,' the Pathmaster said. 'You are unskilled. The consequences could be both subtle and horrible, and death is a likely outcome, although the fulsome memory of you would live on.'

'Would it let me defend Segrana and the Uvovo?'

Images flared through her mind, the Spiral fanatics, caught in flickering webs of energy, their paralysed bodies slumping to the ground, then the Brolturan transport and a dozen other craft wrapped in the same energy, losing altitude as they glide out to ditch in the shallows of the southern sea.

'Such is possible,' said the Pathmaster.

She did not hesitate. 'What must I do?'

'Recall the moment when you stretched your awareness out to the peripheries of Segrana and felt the deepness of the powers opening beneath you. You must undertake that again but you must also direct your needs downward into that power, rather than outwards. Its terrifying magnitudes will be revealed and powers will try to channel themselves through you. Then you will discover if you can master them.'

Catriona found herself assailed by doubt and she almost

changed her mind. Then thoughts of her friends and colleagues came to her and, over and over, Greg. And she wished . . . wished that she knew, just here at what might be the end, whether he felt anything for her . . .

Was there a hint of amusement in that cowled visage? Or was it compassion?

'His feelings for you,' said the Pathmaster, 'are like a flower made from the sun.'

'That's . . .' She felt overcome in the moment, by surprise and a bittersweet joy. 'Thank you.'

'Now, strengthen your inner resolve,' said the Pathmaster. 'The immensity of Segrana awaits, and you must reach out to encompass it all.'

She began.

29

THEO

The plan was simple and straightforward. Once docking protocols were complete, Theo would lead the escort guarding Captain Gideon out to the high-security buffer gate, present the access code docket and proceed on into Base Wolf and stage two of the rescue operation.

I love simple plans, Theo thought as a chime sounded in the load-out chamber and they trooped through to the main airlock. *They can go wrong in so many entertaining ways.*

According to Gideon, Base Wolf was one of four Tygran advance bases maintained around the Aranja Tesh, and the one closest to their colony world. The greater part of it was tunnelled into a craggy, four-kilometre-wide asteroid, orbiting the outer reaches of an unremarkable star system just within the boundary of Sul, an impoverished client state of the Sendrukan Hegemony. The main dock lay inside the asteroid, an immense dark space fitfully illuminated by spotlights. The scoutship *Starfire* loomed over Theo and the others as they descended a long ramp, yet it was diminutive set against the long walkway and the split-level gantries with mooring and berths clearly designed for much larger vessels.

Some of the lighting was devoted to emphasising the dramatic lines of the architecture, immense columns that angled up into the gloom, the brassy roof that sloped down over the glass-sided buffer gate, and the huge emblematic monument that hung overhead. It depicted the upper torso of an armoured warrior leaning out, shield before him, spear held chest-high and jutting forward. On the shield was a snarling wolf.

Theo, Malachi and the other six Stormlions were in full combat armour and headgear. Inside his, Theo could feel sweat running down his scalp. The sound of his own breathing was oddly claustrophobic. His armour's auxiliary arms were set to neutral, the smaller hands tucked into midriff pockets.

Gideon, on the other hand, was clad in a dun-coloured, nondescript onepiece, his hands bound, his neck hung with a muting loop. With his head bowed, he looked beaten.

Then suddenly they were standing before the buffer gate and its doors were opening to admit them. Through the transparent wall inside Theo saw three bare-headed men in partial body armour seated at holomonitors, not even acknowledging their presence. Base Wolf was garrisoned by the Shadow Watch commandery, whose captain was Nathaniel Horne. Earlier, Malachi had told Theo that Horne had a reputation for sadistic cruelty and had been known to torture his prisoners. He was also one of Marshal Becker's closest allies.

One of the gate sentries looked up.

'Good day, brothers. Let's have the prospectus.'

Theo had been coached for this and stepped forward.

'I am Field Lieutenant Brandt, Scoutship *Starfire* commanding, holding the prisoner Franklyn Gideon for conveyance to Alecto. Main drive malfunction has necessitated our stopover for repairs; also, the prisoner complains of chest pains but the shipboard automed has an intermittent fault, leading to a request for examination in your sickbay.'

The man behind the glass gave Gideon a despising look, then went back to Theo. 'Your access code docket, Lieutenant.'

Theo produced the oval laminate prepared and given to him by Gideon, and dropped it into a slot on the counter top. The Shadow Watch sentry retrieved it and swiped it over a metal pad. Meanwhile, Theo moved over to a dark, reflective panel by the inner door, unsealed his right glove, took it off and pressed his palm against cold smoothness.

Would it work or would alarms start screaming? His palm had been imprinted with a pattern virus, using a skin dye almost invisible to the eye but highly visible to the data processors running the system.

The seconds were never-ending. Theo's mouth was dry and his heart was thumping. He looked around to see the sentry frowning at his holodisplay, then shake his head and throw up his hands.

'This thing is cranked,' he said to one of his companions. 'We might have to respin the boards . . . wait, it's coming through. Okay, Lieutenant, now your retina.'

Hands trembling, Theo fingered a collar stud and his visor parted. He bent to let the panel scan his eye and when that too was verified the door opened and he walked through. One by one Malachi and the others submitted to the scan, each of them possessing an invisible tag in that same skin dye on their palms, allowing the now hijacked system to ID them as Grey Sentinels. Except for Gideon who had to be correctly identified.

Minutes later everyone was through to a seating area. Like the rest, Theo's visor was still open, exposing his face: he hoped that the improvised makeup was enough to get past any further encounters.

'Sickbay is up the corridor and to your right across the hall,' said the guard.

'Thanks, I know the way,' said Theo.

'Uh, Lieutenant, don't forget this.'

From behind an open counter, the sentry tossed the access docket through the air. Theo barely had time to react before it struck his armoured midriff and fell clattering on the floor. The Shadow Watch sentry's eyes hardened and his two companions looked up, as if aware of the sudden tension.

'Is there a problem with your aug-arms, Lieutenant?' he said.

'Only with your discourtesy.' Theo bent to pick up the docket then went over to the counter. 'Is it Shadow Watch custom to greet the brothers of other commanderies this way?'

'No, but I . . .'

'Ah, so this obnoxious, insulting behaviour was produced on your own initiative! I must relate this to Captain Horne, that a soldier of the Shadow Watch would so casually bring his commandery into disrepute . . .'

He was interrupted by a regular beeping and red and amber glows pulsing in one of the holodisplays. The aggravated guard swung away and angrily demanded to know what was happening.

'Subsystem error, Sergeant,' said one of the others. 'The cognitives are running a virus hunt.'

'Right,' said the sergeant, his hand straying to the weapon at his waist.

There was a chorus of faint clicks and red target spots appeared on the necks and faces of all three Shadow Watch guards.

'Don't,' said Theo. 'All of you, hands on heads and turn away – do it!'

As soon as they did, Theo and the other Stormlions fired trank rounds into the backs of their necks. They dropped without a sound.

'Well done, Theo,' said Gideon, snapping his tie restraints and moving to strip the tallest sentry of his body armour. 'That steel in your voice certainly had the tenor of experience.'

'Had to reprimand cadets more times than I care to remember,' Theo said. 'Most of the time a little carpeting is all it needs, but sometimes you have to wave the big stick.'

Gideon chuckled as he worked at one of the holodisplays. A moment later the beep alarm ceased and the red and amber alerts vanished. 'Okay, the virus is still in place and the comm network is down but only for five minutes, imitating a system respin. So Theo and Malachi, take Klein and Jones and get to Security – the rest of us will head for the garrison quarters and lock it down. And remember – today, nobody dies.'

This was where Malachi took the tactical lead, not least because he knew the base's layout from years of assignments and stopovers. From the waiting area, a wide corridor sloped up to a high hall decorated in a heroic fashion similar to the dockside: commandery shields and banners, austere statues in wall niches, and lamps positioned for effect. It was quiet, deserted, and the two groups went their separate ways, helm visors sealed, boots clicking on polished tiles.

Taking the security office was a textbook example of over-whelm-and-subdue. With a fibreye slipped under the door they scoped the number and disposition of the duty personnel – a man and a woman, both seated at consoles – before bursting in. Going high and low, Malachi and Klein tranked both the operators imme-diately then Jones hurried to the main command console, checking the activity logs. Then he turned to Malachi, his visor translucent.

'We've a problem – our guy here was in mid-dialogue with someone up in Holding. Whoever it was quickly cut the line then put another call through to the garrison quarters but got no reply.'

'It sounds as if Captain Gideon has succeeded, yes?' said Theo.

Malachi nodded but his frown was dark. 'Is there an updated presence log? Where is Horne and who's with him?'

Jones crouched over the holodisplay, fingering symbols, sorting and flicking data images to and fro with agile speed.

'Presence log . . . updated seventy-six minutes ago; then, Horne was up in Holding Cell Omega with five Grey Sentinel guards. Omega is where they're keeping our people . . .'

'Sergeant,' said Klein from the doorway. 'Captain's here.'

Gideon entered the now-cramped monitoring room, looked at the unconscious guards over in the corner, then nodded.

'Good. Have we control of the base's comms?'

'Seems so, sir,' Malachi said, then gave a summary report on the calls from Holding and who was up there.

'Good,' Gideon said. 'Hartmann and Boyd are heading up to level two to keep the techs out of the way. In the meantime, Jones will stay here to man the screens and comms while the rest of us head up to secure access to Holding Cell Omega. Short-range channel for now . . .'

'Sir,' said Jones from his console. 'There is a call from Holding asking for you by name.'

Gideon was silent a moment. 'Is it Captain Horne?'

'Yes, sir.'

'Put it up on the display.'

The holodisplay winked on, autoadjusted to larger dimensions and abruptly became a live feed. Theo stared as the frame pulled back to show a wall with a receding row of upright metal canisters, each containing a man, strapped and restrained, wires and tubes trailing from head and neck. The viewpoint panned to show a second row, back to back with a third, then a fourth and a fifth, while along the back wall were yet more prisoners. These had to be Gideon's men, Theo knew. The sight sent a chill down his neck.

Then the cam came to rest on a burly, bearded man clad in black body armour and, strangely, a black, calf-length cloak. Two Grey Sentinels stood behind him, both in full SLAM armour, helmed and armed with short-bodied autoweapons.

'Gideon, such an unexpected pleasure. You should have let me know – I would have had a banquet prepared.'

Gideon's features were impassive.

'Horne, no time for pleasantries. Just release my men and I'll take them and withdraw without any need for unpleasantness.'

Nathaniel Horne smiled. 'But that would lack manners, Gideon, to depart your host's residence with such indecent haste.' The cam tracked back as he stepped forward, and a metal trolley came into view, its shiny trays full of gleaming surgical instruments, some red with blood. 'But you're right, Gideon, there's no time for pleasantries so let us move on to the meat of it, shall we?'

Horne took a handgun from his waist and strode over to the nearest imprisoned Stormlion. Unsteadily, the cam followed him, clearly being carried by an operator. Horne raised his weapon and pressed the muzzle against the prisoner's forehead. The captive soldier stared at the gun, eyes unwavering, tongue wetting his lips. Theo suddenly felt for Gideon, knowing what was coming.

'Nathaniel, I'm warning you . . .'

A sudden fury tore across Horne's face.

'You don't warn me in my own base! So here is what you do – go to the quarters, rouse my men and surrender to their custody or . . . I shall execute your men, all of them, one every minute, starting with this one. In fact, just to convince you . . .'

There was a flash. The camera jerked back, simultaneous with gasps and curses in the crowded monitor room. Then there were shouts coming over as the picture stabilised to show one of the Grey Sentinels pointing his weapon at Horne, yelling at him to lay down his gun. Horne was still grinning as he held the gun to the throat of the next prisoner along. The first hung forward out of his canister, bloody and still.

'Put it down, sir, put it down! Stop this dishonouring of our commandery, stop it . . .'

'I am your captain, Villem, I am your breath, your life, you owe me your obedience, your loyalty to the brink of death and beyond! Surrender or be destroyed!'

But the rebel Grey Sentinel was shouting over the words of his captain, his voice climbing to a crescendo of rage while into the frame came another Grey Sentinel, stealthily moving in on his blind side. Three weapons aimed, fury converging, targets acquired, no going back . . .

Suddenly, everywhere, men were staggering forward out of their canister cells. The rebel Grey Sentinel glanced to the side, and Horne ducked, firing at the prisoner and missing. The holodisplay showed bolts of energy striking the rebel Grey before a freed Stormlion trooper lurched into the frame and threw a punch. The cam picture shook wildly, blurred as if dropped, then came to a rest showing a violent scramble of legs. There were shouts, agonised shrieks, and the buzz-whip sound of energy weapons.

In the monitor room all eyes were riveted to the incredible scene. Gideon continually called for anyone in the holding cell to respond and pick up the cam. Minutes went by, the sounds of struggle died away, and finally booted feet approached; the cam was lifted and the bloodied features of a soldier came into view. Theo heard Malachi and the others laugh quietly and murmur, 'Schmitt made it!' 'Well, of course!'

'Hello,' Schmitt said. 'Anyone there?'

'Yes, corporal,' said Gideon. 'We see you. What's your status?'

'Seven dead, nine wounded, and all the Sentinels are either dead or out cold.'

'How were you freed?'

'No idea, sir.'

'Right, I'm sending stretchers up for the wounded . . .' Gideon pointed at Klein and Lange, who nodded sharply and were gone. 'In the meantime, gather weapons and secure the holding area. Oh, and is Captain Horne among the survivors?'

'Just a second, sir.' The cam blurred, swayed back and forth, then was steadied to point down at a dark, gory form on the floor. It was Nathaniel Horne, half his head seared away into bloody ruin, one wide and glittering eye staring up from the other half. 'I'd say that was a negative, sir.'

After that it was a matter of getting the freed Stormlions down to the dock and aboard the *Starfire*. Theo went with Faraday up to the first floor to help stretcher out the wounded, and met Hartmann and Boyd who revealed that they'd been responsible for freeing the captives by cutting one of the power feeds to Holding Cell Omega. After that it took nearly an hour to get the 130-plus soldiers on board, berthed and quartered. Many of them were young and painfully earnest and as he spoke to them he wondered how they would react on seeing Rawlins's vid testimony. Gideon had made it plain earlier that everyone had to see it, but Theo knew that these young men were in no fit mental state to deal with the radical challenge that the testimony represented.

Finally, all hatches and seals were secured, the shipside anchors were declamped and the *Starfire*'s thrusters turned her towards the exit. Theo, now stripped of the SLAM armour, was sitting on a crate in a side corridor alongside another nine soldiers, watching exterior shots of their departure on a wall monitor, when there was a tap on his shoulder. It was Hartmann, one of Gideon's sergeants.

'Sorry to disturb your rest, Major, but Captain Gideon is requesting that you join him on the bridge.'

Theo sighed, puffing out his cheeks, then gave a weary laugh. '*Ja*, Sergeant, and who would refuse such a request, eh?' He got creakingly to his feet. 'Then let us be on our way.'

The *Starfire*'s bridge was really meant for the flight commander, helmsman and tactical officer – now it was crowded with them and Theo, Hartmann and a Tygran soldier Theo didn't know.

'Theo, my apologies for disturbing your well-deserved rest,' Gideon said, half-turning in his couch. 'But we have an odd situation – it appears that after you and Faraday finished with the stretcher parties, Captain Horne's body went missing. Do you recall seeing his body while you were there?'

'I did. No man ever looked deader.'

'Interesting,' Gideon said drily, then indicated the unknown Tygran soldier. 'This is Corporal Fleischer. About ten minutes before we cast off, I sent him back into the base to recover the captaincy datalog from Horne's body . . . Josef, tell these gentlemen what you found.'

'Yes, sir. I re-entered the base as you instructed and took the elevator to the second floor. But when I reached the holding cell, Captain Horne's body was missing. There was a trail of blood leading across to an open doorway and I saw handprints on the floor . . .'

'Surely not, sir!' said Malachi. 'The man was utterly lifeless – it must have been one of the tech staff.'

Gideon looked back at Fleischer. 'Any evidence of the body being carried or dragged away, Corporal?'

'None, sir, no footprints in the blood trail, no sign of anyone else.'

'Captain, I saw Horne's body,' Theo said. 'Half of his brains were charred meat – it would be impossible . . .'

'No,' said Gideon. 'It is possible, if Nathaniel Horne was only outwardly Human.'

'Field barrier ahead, sir,' said the helmsman, Berg. 'Transit in twenty-three seconds.'

The entrance to Base Wolf was an immense ragged oval across which a forcefield stretched, a tenuous curtain of glitter against the deep black interstellar night. Set to sensor functions only, it brushed against the hull of the *Starfire* as it manoeuvred its way through.

'Now clear of Base Wolf,' said Berg.

Gideon nodded and turned back to Theo and the others. 'I

think it would be wise to consider Captain Horne still, in some way or fashion, alive . . .'

'Contact! – vessel at 490 kiloms, following intercept vector . . .'

'Dammit! – shields to full, all weapons fire on acquisition! Why didn't you see it?'

The helmsman Berg was both appalled and angry. 'Sir, my displays showed inner and outer vicinity clear and empty, then suddenly it was there . . .'

'Intruder about to appear over the asteroid horizon, sir,' said Malachi at tactical. 'All weapon banks primed . . .'

Theo caught a momentary glimpse of something flying into view before needling rays of blinding light stabbed out from it. A burst of dazzling whiteness flooded the bridge for a second, fading to reveal blank holodisplays and screens showing only cyclic patterns. The helmsman and tactical officer tried keying in commands but could only obtain limited sensor data, while ahead of them loomed a ship several times as big as the scout. Its lines were swept back with odd edges that curved out of the smooth hull. Theo nodded to himself – this was a predator and they had just become its prey.

'It's the *Chaxothal*,' murmured Malachi. On seeing Theo's puzzled look, he added, 'Becker's flagship.'

A voice spoke suddenly from comm speakers in the bridge, and probably elsewhere in the scout.

'Pirated vessel *Starfire*,' came a voice rich with measured tones. 'This is Marshal Becker. All your main systems are now under my control and all those on board should now consider themselves in my custody. Former captain Franklyn Gideon is directed to stand down and disarm all personnel prior to boarding by a senior officer.'

Gideon was silent for a moment, staring so intently at the other ship that Theo thought he was about to let out a bellow of rage and futility. Finally, the man set his jaw and said:

'No, I will not stand down.'

Screens and displays suddenly flashed into life, showing the image of a grey-uniformed man, head and shoulders against a large dark blue command couch. The man had a long face with a powerful jaw, buzzcut dark hair and oddly mild brown eyes.

'Oh, you will, Gideon. You see, I have in my hold a large number of prisoners, Human prisoners. You have heard of the Humans indentured to the Roug, I assume.'

Some of the screens switched to overhead view of a few dozen people crammed into some kind of cargo chamber watched over by armed guards from a high gantry. Theo leaned forward to study the picture – some wore formal-looking robes and their features, he realised, were Asiatic.

'They're Pyreans . . . you've raided the *Retributor*,' Gideon said in disbelief. 'But Tygran troops are not to be combat-deployed against other Humans! – that was the core of the agreement with the Hegemony . . .

'Don't be naïve, Gideon. These Pyreans have become a threat to the Hegemony and therefore to Tygra. Now, unless you obey my instructions I shall have one of them shot every five minutes, or perhaps two every ten minutes . . .'

'This is nothing short of barbaric.'

'This is methodology, Gideon,' said Becker. 'For the sake of Tygra, what must be done shall be done. The goal glorifies the path taken to reach it . . .'

'A small craft has just flown out of the base entrance,' said Malachi. 'It looks like a personnel shuttle and it's heading our way.'

'Ah, that will be Horne and his men,' Becker said. 'He will accept your surrender and take command.'

'You do know he's not Human,' said Gideon.

'He is Human enough to serve Tygra,' said Becker. 'And strong enough, and loyal enough. So what's it to be, Gideon – surrender or bloodbath? I'd give you time to think it over but I have a busy schedule ahead . . .'

'Space–mass disruption!' said Malachi. 'Close-proximity hyperspace transit . . . very close!'

And as the bridge quivered around them, space distorted, star positions sliding outwards as a huge, incredible form emerged into solid reality directly behind Becker's ship, staring down at it with blank stone-grey eyes.

30

KAO CHIH

Two hours earlier, Kao Chih was strapped into one of the padded recesses of a two-man short-range stealthed pursuit pod locked to the hull of the *Vyrk*, the Roug ship, waiting for the launch to begin. Most of the pod's carapace was translucent, with autofilters regulating the light that passed through, the light of hyperspace. His companion, Ajegil, was calm and quiet, an experienced operative, apparently, although Kao Chih did wonder how and where a Roug would obtain this kind of experience. But his thoughts returned to brood upon the people taken prisoner by the Ezgara ship, the *Retributor*'s Duizhang as well as all the senior officers and some of the advisory elders. He did not think of himself as a traditionalist, but the abduction of these figureheads and mainstays had affected him deeply, making him wonder if he was in some way responsible. Clearly it was meant to be taken as a warning, that the Human Sept should refrain from sending anyone outside the Roug system, that they should cower in fear of stern punishment.

Punishment really only works on the defenceless, he thought. *Or at least those who think they are defenceless.*

At last the order came, a stream of whispery Roug syllables to which Ajegil responded, then glanced round at Kao Chih with his mesh-covered eyes.

'Human Kao Chih, prepare yourself.'

Suddenly the pod fell away from the *Vyrk*'s hull and spun several times before stabilising, the harsh hum of the reaction drive hurling them through the coiling void of hyperspace. All around walls and seas of impermanent matter rushed and flared into fleeting curtains of abraded light before swirling back to the former state. A flickering, flashing, heaving ocean of chaos through which they swung, their intercept vector leading them straight to that ship of kidnappers, itself powering on through hyperspace ahead of them.

As the pursuit pod stabilised in flight, Kao Chih caught sight of the Roug ship from beneath and ahead. This was only the second time he'd seen the *Vyrk*'s astonishing shape – the first had been only hours ago, not long after discovering the terrible truth about Silveira, that there was no prospect of intervention by Earthsphere with regard to Pyre or Darien. He had never experienced such angry despair before, not when Drazuma-Ha's betrayal became manifest, not even while he was captive aboard the Chaurixa terrorists' ship.

Yet the Roug Mandator Reen had promised assistance, saying that they would provide a ship appropriate to the task ahead. And when the Roug shuttle flew him and others over to the orbital Agmedra'a it was into the superior upper docks, where the sight that met his eyes gave that promise an unexpected edge. The *Vyrk*'s stern had a basic triform shape, with three clusters of reaction drive outlets jutting at the periphery. The simple lines swept forward, bulging and curving into a hull fashioned to resemble the features of an animal-like head. A blunt snout, a powerful jaw, thin lips drawn back in a snarl, and great eyes that were blank orbs staring forward. At first Kao Chih had been convinced that it had been modelled on some mythical beast from the Roug's own far distant past. Then he realised that the eyes and the brow lent it a vaguely simian cast, and was uncertain again. The name *Vyrk* was little help, being a kind of presyllable to several similar words meaning valiant, or constant, or indomitable.

Now that bizarre visage dwindled and was lost as they sped after the Ezgara ship. Kao Chih was intensely grateful at being chosen to go on the rescue mission, and excited, especially after Mandator Reen revealed exactly how they intended to effect the rescue.

'The pursuit craft in which you and Assessor Ajegil will travel contains a stasis-locked tesserae field generator. This field is a sub-quantal mirror image of one that will be generated aboard the *Vyrk*. When both are activated simultaneously, the generated fields extend through the subspace boundary, sense each other and join seamlessly together, creating a wormhole doorway.'

Kao Chih had been on the Roug shuttle when Reen had revealed this part of the plan, that the pursuit pod would latch onto the Ezgara's hull, neutralise any sensors, then cut through to the interior. Once Kao Chih and Ajegil were inside, they would remove the couches and supporting frames from the pod, revealing the stasis-locked generator. Then a signal would be sent to shut off the stasis fields of both generators, activating the field generators, creating the wormhole.

'It sound incredible, honoured patron,' Kao Chih had said. 'Is it similar to the warpwell Sentinel's translocations?'

'It was developed in an effort to emulate that function but the technology remains imperfect. Intrinsic limits restrict its usefulness over distance, while matter degradation within the generators themselves disrupts the wormhole after a brief time period. In Human terms, a little over four minutes.'

Kao Chih's eyes had widened. 'That is . . . brief.'

'Which is why you are going, Pilot Kao Chih,' the Roug had said. 'The prisoners will recognise you and follow your instructions, therefore you must be confident and organised, thereby ensuring an orderly and swift evacuation.'

Confident and organised, he thought to himself, strapped into the pod couch as the chaotic continuum of hyperspace roiled and flickered past outside. *Giving instructions . . . to the Duizhang?* He pursed his lips for a moment then shrugged. Being an adventurer meant having to face all manner of hazards, after all.

An opaque side panel displayed the parameters of their progress, one of which said that the time till intercept was less than eight minutes. Soon their field of vision was filled by the Ezgara ship, its hyperspace drive field shimmering, gently undulating as it carried the ship onwards. While Kao Chih watched, Ajegil matched velocity with the Ezgara ship then adjusted their own hyperspace field until its resonation pattern allowed the Roug pod to slip smoothly through. Dwarfed by the warship, the pod swooped in close to the underside. As it did so, Kao Chih felt four faint thuds. Ajegil was quick to explain.

'I have dispatched four scanner probes, Human Kao Chih. They will affix themselves to the hull and survey the interior in order to discover the captives' whereabouts.'

'Understood, honourable Ajegil, but what about their exterior sensors and visual pickups?'

'I have already performed relevant scans on approach,' Ajegil said. 'Counter-detection measures have been deployed.'

Moments later, a new schematic appeared in the opaque data panel, a 3D deck layout of the Ezgara ship's stern. Lifeforms were white dots, mostly scattered about the decks apart from a large stationary cluster located in a secondary hold on the aft port side, not very far from where the pod already was.

'Ah, friend Ajegil, we are practically on top of it . . .' Kao Chih said, tailing off as he realised that he might have overstepped the courtesies.

'Indeed, colleague Kao Chih,' came the Roug's whispery reply. 'However, we must assume that the captives are under close guard, necessitating that we find an entry point that is nearby and in an unoccupied space.'

They quickly found eight secluded possibles, which were whittled down to two. Examining their proximity to both the hold and the patrol routes, Ajegil discarded one in favour of the other. Moments later the pod had traversed the hull to that very spot.

'Be ready, Human Kao Chih,' said Ajegil as the pod pressed itself against the Ezgara hull, clear carapace inwards. Once a solid seal was established, they sat back while an automatic cutter sliced an oval out of the hull. Minutes later the pod's translucent carapace split open and by the light of slow, wriggling tendril lamps they clambered out. Then Kao Chih stood back as Ajegil swiftly removed the couch assemblies, revealing the portal device, a metallic oval encased in some clear substance. When he prodded it, Ajegil reminded him about the stasis field.

'The apparatus is charged and ready,' Ajegil said after checking a readout panel inside the pod shell. 'When we have the prisoners released and brought here, I shall send the signal to the *Vyrk*, which will activate both generators and create the wormhole portal. Transfer to the *Vyrk* will then be straightforward.' The Roug paused to consult a display on the back of his broad hand. 'My superiors' conjecture is that the Ezgara vessel will reach its destination in 8.6 minutes. The *Vyrk* will exit hyperspace within wormhole range 5.1 minutes after that. Therefore we must have the captives present and ready in less than 14 minutes.'

'With respect, friend Ajegil,' Kao Chih said as they went to the storeroom door, 'but I feel that may be an optimistic aspiration.'

He turned and saw the Roug's form rippling and altering into a Human one, that of an Ezgara commando in light armour. Kao Chih had already shrugged off his onepiece to reveal a formal plum-coloured suit similar to *Retributor* issue.

'Understood, friend Kao Chih,' Ajegil said in a more Humanlike voice as he completed his transformation. 'But my examination of the deck layout suggests that it is achievable – depending on the degree of guard presence in the hold.'

Ajegil turned out to be wrong, but not because of the guards. A short side passage, which the layout scan suggested led through to a maintenance access, was in fact a dead end with a drink dispenser. After a hasty study of the deck layout they ventured further along and found a companionway winding down to a corridor leading to a door and an armed guard. The door was labelled Aux Hold B.

'Returning this one,' Ajegil said as they approached. 'He's just out of interrogation so he'll give you no trouble.'

The guard gave a bored nod, punched a code into the touchpad and the door swung inwards. Ajegil prodded Kao Chih in the back, and he shuffled forward, trying to look subdued. Ajegil told the guard he was to take another out for questioning and got another nod, after which the door locked behind them.

Inside, a grille fence divided off a narrow section from the rest of the hold. Within it metal steps ascended to a walkway running round three of the walls, where four guards watched the people below, between muttering to each other. As he followed Ajegil up the steps, Kao Chih glanced at the groups of people that he knew well. Some eyes widened in recognition but nothing was said. The silence was eloquent with tension.

Aware of their regard, Kao Chih strove to shut them out as he reached the gantry ahead of Ajegil, who beckoned the guards to join him. Kao Chih's bonds were faked; in each hand he held a single-dose injector of fast-acting narco-stun, as did Ajegil, who waited till the Ezgara guards were gathered together before speaking.

'This one was found wandering the corridors. Who let him out?'

There was a chorus of denials at which Ajegil shook his all-too-Human head.

'You'd better decide. When senior officers hear about it, they'll want someone to punish . . .'

Punish was Kao Chih's cue. He fell to his knees with a groan then stabbed out at the legs of the two nearest guards. The Ezgara barely had time to react before the narco-stun hit their bloodstreams and they crumpled like disconnected puppets. Turning, he saw Ajegil standing over the prone forms of the other two while from below came a growing chatter of excitement.

'Four point seven minutes, friend Kao Chih. You must persuade them to follow us without delay.'

Kao Chih nodded and hurried downstairs, unlatched a plastic-frame door in the fence, and came face to face with Kang Lo, the Duizhang of the *Retributor*.

'Pilot Kao,' he said. 'Are you here to rescue us?'

'Indeed so, honourable Duizhang, myself and an . . . ally. Please, time is precious, so if you follow my colleague he will lead you all to safety . . .'

Kang Lo quickly and firmly mustered all his officers and the others into an orderly line. As they hurried from the hold, faces passed Kao Chih by, many exhausted and openly fearful, others more resilient, although Tan Hua looked as blank-eyed as ever. However, there was no sign of a short-legged, long-armed Voth pilot of his acquaintance. Worried, he asked Shang Ko, one of the high administrators, who pointed to a deck-level slotted wall vent.

'The Voth person was convinced that he could escape via the vent ducting and asked us to group near there and obscure his departure.'

'When was this, may I ask?'

'Just a few minutes before you arrived, Pilot Kao.'

Kang Lo was not pleased. 'You did not think this important enough for me to know, Shang Ko?'

The administrator was suddenly nervously contrite. 'Deepest apologies, Duizhang! We were firmly of the belief that the Voth would realise the futility of his actions and return.' He glanced at the vent as if willing the Voth to appear.

Yash, you fool! Kao Chih thought, then turned to Kang Lo. 'We must leave him, honourable one. If we delay we may be seen and recaptured, or we could miss the chance to leave. Quick, we must keep up with the others!'

Cursing himself and the fatefulness of the predicament, he urged the Duizhang and the last few to hurry. At the exit, Ajegil had dealt with the guard, whose unconscious form lay stretched out against the bulkhead. The line of escapees reached the companionway and climbed energetically, apart from some of the elders, whose slowness already had them bringing up the rear. They had just reached the final stretch of corridor when Kao Chih felt a wave of vertigo and a pulse of nausea, a sure sign that the ship had dropped out of hyperspace. From further ahead came groans and a faint spattering sound – someone's stomach had rebelled.

It seemed almost incredible to Kao Chih that they managed to get all twenty-four freed captives up to the storeroom without being spotted or some other mishap. Ajegil glanced at his wrist-pad as he approached the oval gap in the storeroom bulkhead.

'We took longer to retrieve the prisoners,' the Roug said. 'But the Ezgara ship was likewise late in reaching its end point. Friend Kao Chih, it is time to signal the *Vyrk*.'

The Roug reached inside the oval recess and tapped a code into the small console. The stasis field encasing the metallic portal abruptly vanished and wavery lines of radiance began to cris-scross the oval space. Kao Chih quickly turned to the Duizhang.

'A gateway will soon appear, Duizhang, and everyone must hurry through as it will close in just over four minutes. There must be no hesitation.'

'This is understood, Pilot Kao. I shall see to it . . .'

Suddenly the air within the silvery oval seemed to break up and ripple for a moment, like fragments of stained glass floating on turbulent waters, before flattening into the image of a broad spacious room with several consoles at which dark-clad, spindly Roug stood. A honey-yellow light suffused the decor, just as Kao Chih remembered . . .

Then Kang Lo was rushing his people through, watched over by Ajegil. The Roug tapped Kao Chih's shoulder and pointed to the elders hobbling along the corridor – he nodded and went to offer assistance. He was helping one of the high family elders, Uncle Hwa, when he heard a metallic tapping from back along the corridor, along with a faint rasping sound. Suddenly old Hwa stopped, frowning.

'Do you hear it, young Kao Chih?'

'Hear what, honoured father?'

'Someone is calling your name . . . back there . . .'

Kao Chih shook his head. 'I can't quite make it . . .'

'. . . *Kao Chih* . . .'

That time he heard it quite clearly, and as Hwa limped on into the storeroom Kao Chih darted back along the corridor, past an intersection, and spotted a vent high up on the bulkhead . . .

'Pilot Kao!' said Ajegil as he helped the last couple through the portal. 'Quickly, there are only seventy-six seconds left.'

He nodded but moved along to peer up at the vent and, sure enough, there was Yash, wide eyes glaring down at him.

'Help me, Human – the jelking vent cover is stuck!'

He turned to the Roug. 'I need a tool, something to get this cover off.'

Fifteen yards away, Ajegil snatched up something from the tools he had used earlier and dashed down the corridor. Elbowing Kao Chih aside, he levered the vent open then reached in and grabbed the Voth by the collar of his jacket garment.

'Just . . . *hey!* . . .' said Yash as the Roug dragged him out, slung him over one shoulder and ran back to the storeroom with Kao Chih following.

And almost predictably, the wormhole portal quivered with waves of distortion just as they charged into the small room. Kao Chih caught a glimpse of Kang Lo and the others staring back before the portal dissolved into nothing.

'What . . . what the jelk was that?'

Ajegil put the Voth down carefully then stood back and shook his head, mouth firmly closed, eyes blazing with fury.

'That was our means of escape,' Kao Chih said, panic making his heart race. 'We're trapped here . . .'

'Because of this careless creature,' said Ajegil.

'That sounded like an insult, you Human jelker.'

'I am not Human, careless Voth.'

Yash bared his yellowing teeth. 'If I have to get really careless, O ugly biped, you'll . . .'

'Quiet!' Kao Chih said in a strangled whisper.

They were suddenly silent and the sound of approaching footsteps was immediately audible.

'Just one,' said Ajegil, producing another narco-stun injector. 'And we need another Ezgara uniform.'

Understanding, Kao Chih grinned, snatched up a length of plastic tie from a shelf and wrapped it about his wrists. Ajegil nodded.

'The Voth remains here,' he said.

Yash fumed but said nothing as the door was closed.

The ambush was a copy of the action against the guards in the hold. A minute or two later they arrived back at the storeroom, carrying the snoring Ezgara guard between them. After a few adjustments, the man's light armour proved an acceptable fit, but unfortunately he had been wearing no helmet.

'So what do we do?' Kao Chih said. 'Find someone with a helmet and persuade him to lend it to me?'

'Or break into an armoury,' said Yash.

Ajegil shook his head. 'Too time-consuming. The shuttle bays are three decks down in the midsection – we must proceed to the nearest one with all speed. For all we know, the captives' absence may have already been discovered.'

'No, so far those jelkers know nothing,' said the Voth, tapping his ear in which a red audiobead was just visible. 'When I was crawling about in the walls I found a few handy bits of equipment left behind by some comms tech. Also found a monitor system piping a video feed from that hold up to the jelking bridge network. So I recorded a nice, boring segment, looped it and streamed it into the feed. So, no alarms yet, but can't last for ever.'

Ajegil regarded the Voth with faint respect. 'Exactly, which is why we must go. Now.'

'What of my face?' said Kao Chih. 'The very first Ezgara we meet will raise the alarm.'

'I can use my talents,' said the Roug. 'I can temporarily alter your features.'

Yash's eyes widened. 'Now that is some talent.'

'I told you, I am not Human,' said Ajegil.

Kao Chih almost smiled at the subterfuge. 'Will it be painful?' he said.

'To begin with you will feel only a tingling numbness. But after less than an hour your facial tissues and musculature will reassert their normal configuration and there will be some . . . discomfort.'

Kao Chih breathed in deeply. 'Very well, I'll do it. What will I look like?'

The Roug pointed at the semi-undressed, comatose prisoner. 'This one. Now, stay calm and keep your eyes open for now.'

Ajegil raised his hands and laid them against Kao Chih's face.

The sensations were minor, subtle, sometimes barely noticeable. An icy prickling came and went. Skin seemed to be tugged and muscles shifted but these were ghostly, foggy feelings, distant and painless. Several minutes later, Ajegil lowered his hands and regarded him a moment then took out a small folding mirror and held it up. In it Kao Chih saw his own eyes staring out of a stranger's face, the face of the man on the storeroom floor. The eyes were round and the chin was jutting and heroic but the mouth seemed frozen in a kind of smug half-grin. And when he tried to mention this to Ajegil he found his jaw and lips unresponsive.

'Your face muscles are locked into this expression,' the Roug said. 'Otherwise you would have no control over it and your mouth would hang open, allowing its fluid to trickle out. Therefore, try not to talk . . .'

He was interrupted by a warbling alarm from out in the corridor. 'An alert! – they must have found the empty hold.'

But Yash shook his head. 'Something else entirely. This ship had reached its destination a short while ago, a base of some kind, and it was making a stealth approach when another ship emerged from its entrance . . .' The Voth listened for a moment then smiled. 'Jelking perfect! – the captain of this ship has just told the other one to surrender or he'll start shooting the prisoners . . .'

'No more delay,' said Ajegil, tugging open the door. 'The *Vyrk* will be here very soon, after which our safety may become problematic . . .'

'Whu' 'u yu 'ean 'y 'o'le'atic?'

Kao Chih's attempt to ask the Roug what he meant unfortunately came out as a string of grunted syllables.

'Please, Kao Chih, don't talk,' Ajegil said. 'Just follow my lead and keep alert.' He handed Kao Chih one of the captured heavy beam pistols. 'Only use this as a last resort.'

Yash the Voth was grinning widely as he led the way.

'Can't speak, eh, Human? What a jelking shame – must be like not being able to use half your brain . . .'

As the Voth sniggered, Kao Chih could only glare at his hairy neck as he hurried along at Ajegil's side, silently vowing to exact a verbal riposte. Eventually.

31

THEO

Even as the bizarre alien vessel loomed ominously on the *Starfire*'s sensor displays, Gideon was conversing in low tones with Malachi who was crouched nearby. To Theo, the situation looked desperate, with the *Starfire* drifting, her controls rendered useless by some kind of coded transmission from Marshal Becker's flagship. And yet, for all that Gideon seemed to have no options left, he still appeared to be planning something.

The Tygran commander straightened.

'Open the channel,' he said. Becker's features came up on the main display.

'You're wearing out my generosity, Gideon,' said the Marshal. 'Choose your path – capitulation or death.'

'Who's the newcomer, Becker?' said Gideon. 'Has it changed the game for you?'

The Marshal shrugged. 'They refuse all comm hails but they look to be even lighter-armed than you. Now, decide.'

'Very well, sir – I would rather die with a blaster in my hand than submit to you. Clear enough?'

And with his last word, every panel and display on the bridge went dead, along with most of the lights. The starry depths of space outside the viewport suddenly took on a new prominence.

'Everyone keep calm,' said Gideon. 'I had Malachi here trigger a full shipwide shutdown. The plan is to respin the systematrix while leaving all exterior sensors and receivers disengaged.' He turned to the tactical officer, who was feverishly working away on the holofield display of a small standalone console. 'Malachi is creating an amended version of the main initialiser code with which we can restart the ship systems.'

'And all the time, Becker's got us in his sights,' Theo said.

'Yes, Becker could destroy us at the touch of a button,' Gideon said. 'We're sitting dead in space. But he would much prefer prisoners to corpses.'

An urgent thudding interrupted him. Theo tugged open the bridge entry hatch to admit Klein, who went straight to Gideon.

'Sir, we've got intruders on board. Came in through the drive assembly maintenance access, and they now hold Engineering. They were aboard the shuttle that came from the base.'

'Nathaniel Horne,' said Gideon, who then looked sharply over at Malachi. 'How?'

'When the systematrix shuts down, all hatchlocks shift to their default access codes,' Malachi said. 'Which Becker would know, of course, sir.'

'Of course,' Gideon said acidly. 'How much longer?'

'A matter of minutes, five, six maybe.'

Gideon nodded, got up from his command couch and made for the hatch.

'That thing calling itself Nathaniel Horne is on my ship, and I won't permit it. Klein, you're with me. Theo, I trust you with the bridge.'

A moment later they were gone. The helmsman, Berg, seemed at a loss for words but Theo just smiled and went to sit in Gideon's place. At the tactical station, Malachi gave him a slight smile and kept working.

I hope Gideon knows what he's doing, Theo thought. *I've not commanded anything bigger than a sailboat, and I don't think these two fellows would appreciate me ordering them about.*

He was about to share his misgivings with them, along with an offer to endorse their more experienced recommendations, when Malachi made a satisfied sound and snatched a small tab module from the side of his console. Quickly, he stood and climbed the few steps to the bridge's plain back wall, pressed something at the top of the bulkhead, crouched to do the same at the bottom, then at shoulder height pressed an indentation that Theo had taken to be nothing more than a moulding pattern. There was a faint whine and a slender full-length section slid out of the wall. Not so much shelves as layers of incomprehensible components were revealed, visually an array of grey, blue and transparent blocks.

'Bypass, bypass, bypass,' Malachi muttered as he scanned the rows from the top to about two-thirds down where he pulled out a blue block, slotted in the tab, then closed it all up. He was back at his station even before the complex array had fully retracted into the wall. He fingered a few controls and an image appeared in the hazy darkness of his holodisplay, a cluster of glowing circular symbols that intersected at different angles, shimmering as they rotated. The tactical officer turned to Theo.

'Sir, ready to respin the shipboard systems, by your command. Captain Gideon is apprised of the situation.'

'Then proceed, Malachi.'

The tac-sergeant put on a webby headpiece, bent over his console and touched a few control symbols. An instant later lights came up, consoles and displays flickered back into life and ghostly schematics flitted across the main viewport.

'Environmental initialised, helm controls back online,' said Berg at the helm.

'Weapons and tactical now online,' said Malachi. 'Internal comms are nominal. Externally we have no way of contacting or being contacted.'

'Can you adapt a receiver to filter out whatever they were using to override your systems?' Theo said.

'I could cut the bandwidth and resolution,' Malachi said. 'Chop down the colour data, leave it in monochrome. Yes, that would do it. May I ask why?'

'It would be advantageous for the captain to be able to converse with Becker, rather than presenting a blank face, don't you think?'

'I can see the sense in it, sir.'

'Will it take long?'

'A few moments, sir.'

Theo gazed at the stars as he waited, wondering if political prisoners on Tygra were allowed to go fishing.

'Done, sir.'

'Good, and can you get us a view of those other ships?'

'I can overlay one on the main viewport if you like, Major.'

'Excellent – go ahead.'

A moment later he was looking at Becker's vessel, all sleek menacing lines, like some winged predator poised to strike. While beyond, the silent and mysteriously alien, almost sculpted craft hung in the starry blackness. A magnified view of it showed that only the forward section was shaped like the head of a beast – the aft had a plain design, although the silver-grey hull colour was the same all over.

'No sign of any activity, Malachi?'

'None before the systems went down, nor since they came back online, sir.'

'Any news from the captain?'

'Just that the intruders are offering fierce resistance . . . I have an incoming comlink from Becker.'

Theo hesitated but only for a second. 'Very well, my boy. Put him on the screen, eh?'

Malachi activated the receiver with a gesture. Immediately, there was a burst of flickering light which soon switched to the man Theo had seen before, Marshal Becker.

'You're not Gideon,' said Becker, frowning as he leaned a little closer. 'And you seem a little old, even for the Stormlions. Identify yourself.'

'I am Major Theodor Karlsson of the Darien Volunteer Forces, currently on secondment to Captain Gideon's task force, and also his acting second-in-command. And you are?'

Theo ignored the barely concealed looks of incredulity coming from both bridge officers. *Well if you're going to play the rank game, boys, play it with bells, whistles and brass neck, by damn!*

Becker's piercing gaze seemed to bore through the screen at him. Then a faint smile of contempt came over the man's features.

'Darien, eh? Gideon didn't waste time finding new allies, such as they are. I am Marshal Matthias Becker, high commander of the Shield of Tygra, namely twelve commanderies of elite, battle-hardened troops. You know, I can sympathise with your colony's predicament, Major, but you have to realise that you cannot defeat the Brolturan Compact, or the Hegemony. Your people would be as well to sue for peace and request repatriation to Earth or one of the Integrated Colonies.'

Theo offered a polite smile. 'Would you give up your world so readily, Marshal?'

'I admit, I would not.'

'Exactly. The patriot is the easiest person to convince, and the hardest to defeat.'

'A well-framed conceit, Major, but my patience is running thin. I want to speak with Gideon.'

'So sorry, marshal, but he is otherwise engaged.'

Becker laughed. 'So Nathaniel and his men managed to board your ship – excellent. Then it is only a matter of time before you and whoever survives are back in my custody . . .'

'You're such an optimist, Marshal,' came another's voice. 'Especially when you place your trust in flawed servants like Nathaniel Horne, who is now scuttling away in his shuttle, having left most of his men dead on the decks of my ship.'

Captain Gideon stood in the open hatchway to the bridge, his armour marred with scorch marks. Theo grinned and got up from the command chair, which Gideon settled into.

'That's the great thing about him, Gideon – he always comes back.' Becker smiled, then shrugged. 'So we are back to the basics – my ship can outrun and outgun you and I have a hold full of prisoners whose lives hang in the balance. Surrender and they and some of your men may live. Refuse and I will kill them and all of you.'

Gideon was silent for a moment.

'I'll do what you want,' he said at last. 'But first I want to speak with one of the Pyreans before I decide anything.'

Theo regarded him, saw him exchange a look with Malachi, and knew he was playing for time.

'A defeated cur makes demands? Don't test me.'

'What do you have to lose?' said Gideon. 'Set it against what you stand to gain.'

The Marshal seemed to consider it for a moment, then nodded. 'I shall extend to you a shred of magnanimity, Gideon, just this once.' He turned and gave orders to an unseen subordinate, waited for a moment, then frowned at some unheard response. 'Then fix it – how can four personal comms cease functioning? . . .' Someone spoke to him and he stiffened. 'Get any crew members down there now! . . . Empty? Sound the alert! Find them!'

Becker then swung back to the visual link, his face contorted in fury. 'I don't know how you managed this, you anti-Tygran vermin, but this game is at an end. Surrender or I will open fire!'

'Berg, intercept course, full thrust!' said Gideon. 'Malachi, shields! Ready all weapons.'

'You're such a fool, Gideon, a fool to rely on senile dotards and a backwater majors.' Becker leaned in close. 'This will be a sweet justice . . .'

'*You will refrain from the use of your weaponry. Conflict is not permitted. We have sought you out, Marshal Matthias Becker, and we shall have from you a humble and fitting repentance!*'

A second visage appeared in Theo's holodisplay, a slender, spindly-armed creature with a conoid head narrowing to a thin neck. It seemed to be completely swathed in dark brown wrappings while odd metallic meshes covered the eyes and mouth.

'You are far from your homeworld, Roug,' said Becker. 'And you have chosen to meddle in matters that are none of your concern . . .'

'*My name is Reen of the High Index,*' said the being that Becker had called a Roug. '*Your actions are central to our purpose, specifically those relating to the abduction of twenty-five Humans from their culture-autonomous habitat while residing under the protection of the High Index of the Roug . . .*'

'Your jurisdiction is worthless in this region,' Becker said loudly, trying to break in, but the Roug was inexorable.

'*. . . and your violation of Roug system territory without announcement of your presence or intention constitutes an Act of Malfeasance in addition to the aforementioned abduction. We have already retrieved those individuals from your vessel by means of an advanced technologic. All that remains is a satisfactory demonstration of contrition on your part.*'

Theo exchanged a look with Malachi who whispered, 'He'll never apologise, never in a million years.'

Becker's features, however, had settled into a kind of intense composure. Watching him, Theo recognised the unwavering steadiness of someone who had already decided on a course of action.

'The leaders of the indentured Human Sept faction, liberated from your domination, were being held aboard my ship under protective custody,' Becker said smoothly. 'I regarded them as guests of the Black Sun commandery and thus of the Tygran Bund. If they have decided to place themselves under your authority again, then I must simply acknowledge that as their decision. All I require is proof that they are safely aboard your craft, rather than elsewhere.'

'Now you're playing for time, Becker,' said Gideon. 'Get it over with. Give the newcomer their apology.'

'*I am not obliged under the protocols of response to an Act of Malfeasance to provide such verification but in the interest of clarity I shall do so . . .*'

The frame pulled back from the Roug and panned round to show an amazingly wide and spacious ship's bridge, Theo guessed, with a few console-like installations spread out in a curve, each one attended by a dark, spindly Roug. Off to the side were a group of low chairs and padded benches where some two dozen Humans sat or stood, most engaged in conversation with a pair of the Roug. Theo stared, amazed and relieved to see visual proof of the descendants of the colonists from the *Tenebrosa*. In fact, including himself, there were representatives from all three of those old colonyships, which should count for something . . .

And in the holodisplay Becker gave a cold smile and said, 'I've seen all I need to see,' and his image vanished.

Suddenly Theo's display broke up in zigzags of static, along with several others on the bridge.

'External comms are down,' said Malachi. 'Internal comms very patchy, random dropouts. We still have environmental . . .'

'Is it the same as before?' said Gideon. 'Are they trying to shut us down?'

Malachi shook his head. 'It's different, sir – these cutouts seem more symptomatic of something else . . .'

Theo ground his teeth. 'Damn, sorry, this is my fault.'

'We don't know if that external channel is the reason, Major,' said Gideon. 'Let us wait and see . . .'

'Main thrusters have just ignited,' said Berg at the helm. 'New course laid in too – I can't get into the system, it's out of my hands.'

'Weapons coming online, targeting as well,' said Malachi.

'Let me guess,' Gideon said. 'The target is that Roug ship.'

'Very cunning, these Black Sun dogs,' Malachi said. 'It's a worm, built it up in the comm data buffer, very slowly, never noticed, a work of twisted genius . . .'

Theo was staring at the main viewscreen where Marshal Becker's ship had wheeled round to angle that beaklike prow towards the Roug vessel, that huge grey head, which was maintaining its position. Gideon's *Starfire*, however, was now moving towards it in a straight, undeviating line.

'Malachi,' said Gideon. 'If the weapons are beyond our control, what about trying to get through to the Roug, just to explain that it only looks as if we're firing on them?'

'I'll try to clear that channel, sir,' Malachi said, not lifting his gaze from his console. 'As soon as I've countered that worm with my own antiworm . . .'

'A small craft has just launched from Becker's ship,' said the helmsman, Berg. 'It's heading in the opposite direction . . . wait, now it's coming round, trajectory curving towards us, sir . . . Becker's ship is targeting it with their aft projectors . . . shuttle's evading . . . missed . . .'

The bridge lights flickered. Theo gripped the auxiliary console he stood at as he felt a wave of weightless vertigo, then a moment of heaviness that made his legs bend a little, followed by a swift return to normalcy.

'Enemy worm disrupted, sir,' said Malachi. 'There was a brief interruption in deck-grav regulation, and the worm is still operational, but we are no longer focused on the Roug ship.' Then he looked at his holodisplay. 'System is retargeting, sir, right on that small shuttle, the one that flew off from the flagship . . .'

'*Starfire* coming around on a new heading,' said Berg. 'Intercept course with the shuttle.'

'Beam battery opening fire,' said Malachi.

A volley of energy bolts sprang towards the oncoming stubby-winged shuttle. Its shields rippled, flared and were gone, its main thrusters dead and leaving a trail of grey vapour as momentum carried it tumbling along on the same course as before.

'Incoming communication,' said Malachi.

A grainy visual popped into Gideon's display, a head-and-shoulders image of, surprisingly, a Roug. Theo heard an angry voice in the background cursing – 'Jelking Humans!' – before the Roug spoke.

'I am Assessor Ajegil – please cease your attack! This vessel is unarmed and poses no threat . . .'

'My apologies, Assessor,' Gideon said. 'Unfortunately, I am not in control of my ship's weaponry, but I intend to ensure your safety.' He turned to Malachi. 'Hit the powerdown again – would a respin clear the data incursion?'

Malachi shrugged. 'It might, but not if it's lodged a backup in the initialiser code.'

'Do it anyway.'

A moment later, just as the weapon system was about to launch a missile at the coasting shuttle, the *Starfire*'s systems went dead. A hushed darkness fell on the bridge, peppered with the glowing pinpoints of standbys. Theo sighed and sat on the step next to the recess where Gideon sat in his command couch. A few emergency lamps came on as Gideon fumbled in a pull-out drawer and produced a couple of drink ration tubes, handing one to Theo.

'Any way we can see what's happening out there, Malachi?' Gideon said.

'I'll have limited viewscreen functionality shortly, sir.'

'And what options for a respin do we have?'

Berg gave a wintry smile. 'Limited. A respin on the bypassed initialiser would risk loading the incursion worm again; respinning with the original one lays us open to Becker and his access codes.'

Gideon looked thoughtful. 'If we time it right and wait until Becker's ship is fully engaged in combat, then respin on the original initialiser, we could get away, make the jump to hyperspace. Yes, that's what we'll do. Malachi, how's that viewscreen . . . ah, yes, very good.'

The stars of deep space blinked out and were replaced by an enhanced overlay of the imminent clash. Becker's flagship, the *Chaxothal*, was hurtling towards the Roug ship, that grotesque beast-head hanging motionless in the blackness. It had not moved from its original position, other than turning to face its oncoming adversary.

'Becker was right about the intruder vessel, sir,' Malachi said. 'When our systems were up, long-range scans revealed no conventional weapons or shield signatures.'

At about 800 kiloms, the Tygran ship was the first to commence hostilities, small flocks of missiles launching in waves as beam projectors opened up. Some were super-coherent lasers, and almost invisible, while others directed dense pulses of energised particles. From what the viewscreen showed, with enhanced closeups, the beams seemed to tear into the face of the Roug ship, cutting through its grey exterior which shattered and burst into an expanding haze of debris and pulverised fragments. Then the missiles arrived and Theo saw curved, shell-like pieces flying out of the pale turbid cloud.

Moments stretched by as the Tygrans pounded the Roug with not the slightest retaliation or response.

But that Roug sounded so confident, Theo thought. *Surely you don't make promises that your fists can't keep.*

Then the Roug ship began to move.

With that great, blank-eyed and now battle-cratered visage still facing its opponent, the Roug vessel sideslipped into a flightpath curving in towards the Tygran's port side. Becker's vessel continued firing as it manoeuvred to present itself prow-forward – in response, the Roug ship performed an impossible turn then hurtled forward along a course that brought it to within a hundred metres. Even as the Tygran tried to turn, the Roug ship's huge jaws gaped and a spear-straight column of dazzling energy stabbed forth.

From the Tygran ship's upper aft section, two wings curved out, up and forward, their widening tips carrying a multiplicity of beam batteries and missile launch bays. It was the starboard one that bore the brunt of the Roug's first assault, a coruscating column of power which brushed aside the force shielding. Shredding brilliance ate into the hull plating – with the viewscreen's magnification Theo and the rest could see metal pit and flake off or glow red then white before melting and sloughing away. It took mere seconds to reduce the starboard weapons wing to a charred, twisted stump.

Despite the Tygran's attempt to withdraw, the Roug vessel kept pace with it, and cut the port wing down to a deformed remnant. Next were the thruster-tubes, blasted into useless wreckage, then the hyperspace nodes, then the remaining weapon batteries. By now Becker's ship was a battered, powerless hulk adrift in space but the Roug did not stop there. With pencil-thin beams it proceeded to scar and burn the hull, even as it seized it with force grapples and towed it back towards Base Wolf.

'Well, gentlemen,' said Gideon. 'I think we can assume that it's safe to respin the *Starfire*'s systems, eh?'

In the hours that followed, Theo couldn't stop thinking about the Roug's wholesale demolition of the Tygran ship. It must have been humiliating for Becker, he thought, and thoroughly deserved. Now, he and Gideon were aboard the Roug ship – called the *Vyrk* – and actually standing on that broad, roomy bridge. They had been personally greeted by the *Vyrk*'s commander, Mandator Reen, and were now waiting to meet representatives of the 'Human Sept of V'Hrant'.

One entire wall of the *Vyrk*'s bridge was an immense viewport from which they could look out at the vicinity of the Tygran asteroid base. The *Starfire* hung off to upper port, with fixer mobiles hovering around it, while some way out to starboard the wrecked, wretched-looking Tygran vessel was being towed back to Base Wolf by automatic drones. It seemed that Mandator Reen had only permitted this retrieval after inflicting upon Becker and his crew an extensive detailed remonstrance (excerpts of which were circulating among the troops and crew of the *Starfire*).

'With Becker and his men alive,' Theo said, 'I imagine that the news of this humiliation will reach the ears of all Tygrans, yes?'

'It's inevitable,' Gideon said sombrely, his eyes fixed on the slow-moving hulk. 'I'm not sure what consequences will follow, however. Becker's scope of action is determined by Hegemony interests – he wouldn't have seized the Human Sept leaders unless it was what Hegemony planners wanted, so it is unlikely that he'll make independent retaliatory moves against the Roug.' He glanced at Theo. 'But the Hegemony might, if they felt that the Roug presented a threat to their interests and plan.'

He broke off at the sound of approaching footsteps. Three were heading their way across the bridge's shiny deck, a Human of Asiatic cast, a dark-hued, spindly Roug, and a short bow-legged being which to Theo looked uncannily like an orang-utan. Except that, unlike those he'd seen in those books of Earth natural history he had read, this one wore odd, corrugated leggings and several layers of upper garments. These were the occupants of the shuttle that had escaped Becker's ship.

The Roug spoke first.

'Our meeting is tinged with irony, although I am glad to be here . . .'

'Too jelking polite, that's your problem,' said the shortest of the three. 'Maybe you should thank them for not blowing us to pieces . . .'

The Asiatic Human smiled brightly. 'Our friend Yash's view-point only sounds scathing and cynical – really, he is the most amiable and supportive of travelling companions . . .'

'Well, jelk you, Human!'

'I am remiss with introductions,' said the Roug. 'I am Assessor Ajegil; this Human is Kao Chih, gravity-tug pilot of the formerly indentured Human Sept of V'Hrant; and this is Yash of the Voth species, whose cloud-harvester I am informed burned up in the atmosphere of Darien, seemingly an untimely demise.'

'You've been to Darien?' said Theo. 'Oh, sorry, I am Major Theodor Karlsson, Darien Volunteer Forces, retired.'

Kao Chih's eyes widened. 'You are Gregory's uncle!' He laughed and the two men shook hands.

'Indeed, that I am,' said Theo, grinning. 'So you've been on Darien, too. What's my nephew been getting up to?'

'I was there several days ago,' said Kao Chih. 'Greg is very busy, many responsibilities. He is in charge of the resistance in the mountains . . .'

'In charge?' Theo said, stunned. 'How, and when . . . you know, we should sit down and talk later, eh? Tell each other some amazing stories . . .'

'There will be no time for exchanges,' said the Roug Ajegil. 'The *Vyrk*'s commander wishes to return to V'Hrant with great dispatch. I persuaded him to allow this meeting so that we may ascertain the intentions of your three colonies as this crisis develops. First, Major Karlsson, please complete the introductions.'

'Of course. My comrade-in-arms is Franklyn Gideon, Captain of the Stormlions commandery, and of the scoutship *Starfire*.'

Gideon gave an amused nod in Theo's direction before his expression grew serious.

'I'm afraid that I am in no position to speak on behalf of my people – due to political intrigue I and many of my officers and men are now considered outlaws. I can tell you, however, that the great majority of Tygrans will stay loyal to their leaders and to the pact with the Sendrukan Hegemony.'

'A people convinced of absurdities is capable of terrible things,' said Ajegil. 'What do you and your men believe in, Captain?'

'In the principles of the founders and in the defence of our world. We may be outcast for now, but we shall uphold these principles and demonstrate our worth by going to Darien and fighting for the freedom of our brothers and sisters there. In any case, who can tell what the future has in store for the likes of Becker and his cronies?'

Ajegil nodded and looked at Theo.

'Major Karlsson, what will Dariens do?'

'Argue, I should think.' He smiled. 'Even in the face of disaster, my fellow Dariens usually find time for a good disagreement on fundamentals. Then afterwards we'll fight as one, throw stones and empty beer bottles if we have to. But we'll fight – no one strikes at us with impunity.'

'Brave words, Major,' said Ajegil.

Theo shook his head. 'When someone's trying to take away your home, my Roug friend, you don't stop to wonder what's the brave thing to do, you do the right thing and fight.'

Last, the Roug faced the Pyrean.

'I am well acquainted with the tragic situation of your people, Kao Chih, but tell our new colleagues of your purpose.'

'Free our people on Pyre, firstly and most urgently,' Kao Chih said. 'Free them from dust and death and bring them eventually to somewhere like Darien, to be reunited with their dislocated relatives, my own folk from Human Sept. Gregory approved of this, as did Mr Vashutkin . . .'

'That would be a damn fine idea,' Theo said. 'Once we've got this little local difficulty cleared up.'

'When I look at you,' said the Assessor Ajegil, 'I see three quite distinct Human variants yet there is a basic bond and a common quality that motivates and unites you. In the light of your species' widely differing cognitive and cultural heterogeneity, it is interesting to see this concord.'

'One of our devotional texts is called the *Celestial Litany*,' said Gideon. 'And there are a few lines from it that you might find interesting:

Humanity's Fire enfolds us all,
Its light can bring forth truth,
Its heat can forge great souls,
Yet that light can also blind,
And that heat can devour,
Humanity's Fire can burn us all.'

'An intriguing viewpoint,' Ajegil said. 'I would like to learn more but Mandator Reen tells me that our time together is at an end.'

Farewells were made, and even Yash, the Voth, said formal words of departure, which clearly amazed Kao Chih. The effect was slightly spoiled when he then said:

'Just wanted to prove that I've got some jelking manners!'

Parting company with them, Theo and Gideon were swiftly ushered by a pair of Roug attendants to a small-craft berth where the *Starfire*'s skiff was moored. Ten minutes later they were aboard, strapped in and heading back to the scoutship.

'So, next port of call – Darien,' said Gideon.

'That is the truth,' Theo said, considering the few details that he had learned from Kao Chih. 'I'm just hoping that there's something to come home to.'

32

ROBERT

The journey back up to normal space followed an erratic route through a succession of tiers and eye-challenging scenes. Ring orbitals braceleted together in an immense, extravagant world-girdling chain. Hourglass-shaped structures, their hexagon-patterned outer surfaces missing sections, the hollow interiors lined with curved spines. Hundreds of domed asteroids, some containing desiccated gardens, others with clusters of buildings, and all linked by a lattice of walkway conduits, which time and neglect had tangled together. Huge spheres of opaque ice hanging in orbit around a barren rocky world, all clasped by metallic grids which in places had burst or snapped. When their ship, the *Evidence of Absence*, came near enough, magnified shots revealed the foggy shapes of creatures inside them. And no sign of life anywhere – everything was deserted, the abandoned relics of dead civilisations.

The last spectacle they encountered before arriving back in normal space was a massive world lit by the dull glow of three slow-orbiting suns. In the shadow of low, rounded mountains stretched vast stony plains scarred and gouged by immense mechanical behemoths, gigantic mobile mounds of compacted technology. Rusting armour sections, cut and shaped ship hulls, hammered vehicle shells, roof sections, and a multitude of other fabricated materials formed the huge carapace from which pipes and girders poked, chains and cables trailed, and oily effluent trickled. The upper slopes bore solar panels to catch the suns' feeble rays while at the crumbling, corroded base scores of mam-

moth caterpillar track assemblies groaned and rasped as they bore
that stupendous burden across the stony plain.

According to Rosa, these were the last remnants of huge mechanised armies that had escaped the control of their creators.
Fortunately, their programming, while ingeniously self-perpetuating,
carried a fundamental flaw that prevented it from improving
themselves to true artificial sentience. The Construct, she said, was
confident that these shambling, hill-sized hulks would in a century
or so weaken and degrade and grind at last to an exhausted halt,
never to move again.

'An interestingly long-term perspective,' Robert said. 'What if
some outside agency meddled with this setup and, for example,
gave some of these ramshackle monsters a serious upgrade? How
would that affect the Construct's assessment?'

She regarded him for a moment. 'This tier and several others in
the Upper region are being continuously monitored. Any atypical
behaviour would trigger surveillance and analysis, with units of
the Aggression on standby. Does that answer your question,
Father?'

They were both sitting on blue-padded benches in the bridge
of the *Evidence of Absence*, an oblong, pale green chamber. Other
than the benches there were almost no other furnishings, consoles
or displays, apart from the big viewscreen that curved across an
entire wall. And an interaction node, a kind of floating holoconsole with a rounded base, hovering on suspensors next to Rosa.
The ship had somehow omitted to assign one to Robert.

'Yes, it answers my curiosity which, as you know, is considerable, especially about worlds I've never visited before. Like this
one . . .' He indicated the screen, currently showing images
from a probe flight. 'I mean, does it have a name? What were
the inhabitants like? What are those war-factory mountains
called . . . ?'

'I see, I understand.' Smiling, Rosa stood. 'The world was
known as Ulorthagandin, the inhabitants called themselves the
Phovada, and the mech-amalgams were the Zoanry . . .'

'And what about . . . ?'

She silenced him with a raised hand and said, 'Ship, would you please provide my father with an interaction node?'

'Certainly, Sim-Rosa.'

A niche opened in the wall next to the screen and a second holoconsole glided smoothly over to stop at arm's length from Robert. Pleased, he gave Rosa a small bow of the head.

'I appreciate it, thank you.'

'I hope you make good use of it.' Rosa headed for the door, which opened. 'We'll be arriving in the Omet deepzone in an hour, right inside the Achorga star system, and an hour after that we'll be in orbit around the hiveworld, known as Purliss Two.'

Robert nodded. 'I am sure that this will keep me occupied till then.'

After she was gone, he sat looking at the door for a few moments, smiling. *I always wondered what my daughter would be like as a grown woman, and even if the Construct's version of her is only partly right, she is still impressive.*

Then he turned to the floating console, configured the holofield for keypad and fingertipping, then started an infosearch. And paused, frowning.

'Ship, can you put this node's display up on the big screen?'

'Yes, Robert.'

At once, half the screen was occupied by Robert's workfield, embellished with the Canyon interface he'd learned to use back on the *Plausible Response*.

'Excellent. Now let's see what your databanks have under the heading "Achorga".'

There was a pause, and then canyons of data rushed by in a dizzying blur.

Two and a half hours later, Robert and Rosa were gearing up in the *Evidence of Absence*'s armoury while the Ship carried out a stealthy approach to the Achorga hiveworld. It also delivered a running commentary on the inbound vector, interspersed with odd factoids on the hives, the worlds, and the invasions of territories adjacent to the Omet.

Rosa, he realised, was actually slightly taller than he was, prompting him to wonder if she had chosen to be so. Like him, she had dressed in dark blue form-fitting body armour but Robert had insisted on a heavier, knee-high boot, keeping in mind what he'd read about the types of parasites that infested Achorga hives.

'Twenty-two minutes until orbital insertion around Purliss Two,' said the Ship. 'Atmosphere-capable pinnace seventy-two per cent partitioned.'

Moving to the weapon racks, Rosa picked out a flechette carbine plus grenade attachment, with a hand beamer for backup. Robert chose a heavy-calibre slug gun with a variety of different ammo; the weapon had a cold, solid weight that was oddly reassuring to his senses, to his recently implanted skill-instincts. He had never fired a weapon in combat or training, yet this new part of him knew this gun intimately and was looking forward to using it. And when he thought about the historical associations, the Swarm invasion 150 years ago, the siege of Earth, he knew that the rest of him was too.

'Pinnace now eighty-nine per cent partitioned. Purliss Two has seventy-eight minor Achorga nests, fifteen lesser hives, and three dominant hives that vie for supremacy. The target lies beneath the dominant hive, which controls the eastern regions of the northern-temperate landmass.'

Before they left, Robert also selected a plain-hilted sabre as his secondary weapon; its edge might not be quite as irresistible as the *kezeq* shard yet it was still well suited to close-quarters work. It came with a silver-inlaid scabbard harnessed for over-the-shoulder use, which suited him perfectly.

'We are now assuming para-stationary orbit over Purliss Two's northern hemisphere and the target hive. Pinnace is now operational – please proceed to the Forward Utility chamber for boarding.'

The pinnace was a rounded, flattened pod with stubby wings and an array of suspensors for propulsion. The cockpit had a transparent canopy that curved flush with the upper hull. As they fell away from the *Evidence of Absence*, Robert felt a queasy lurch but it passed in a moment, leaving only a calm readiness, even a certain anticipation. *I must be getting used to this* Umhang und Dolch *business – a week ago I'd have been fighting my own terrors.*

Robert surveyed the view above the planet's rim, the foggy haze of the Omet deepzone, vast swirls of interstellar dust that covered a volume of space almost three thousand light years across at its widest. It bordered on the Indroma Solidarity, Ginima-Fa, and Urdisha, all of whom suffered regular migratory swarm attacks, although on a somewhat smaller scale than the invasion of the Solar System a century and a half ago.

And a quarter global turn away, a cluster of bright points hung motionless above the planet, a fleet of fleets, a gathering of nest-ships and transports, waiting for the next swarm.

He felt a slight vibration as they entered the atmosphere under suspensor-controlled descent. Hull camo was active and stealth countermeasures ensured that the little craft gave off an objective profile no bigger than a leaf. Cloud cover was widespread and it was several minutes before they broke through to get their first view of the Achorga-modified landscape.

At one time, a civilisation had spread across this world. The patterns of habitation, vehicle highways, cultivation lattices, and the darker, more concentrated layouts of city centres were all clearly visible from high altitude, as were the scars of war. Massive craters spread across grids of built-up conurbation, their edges blurred by weathering and plant growth, while dark, barren swaths bore testament to an ingrained toxicity.

And it was on the ruins of one smashed city that an Achorga hive had been built. Tapering, asymmetrical spires climbed from the centre, a cluster of towers in purple, ochre and crimson, the highest reaching nearly a kilometre. The Swarm Hive on Mars during the Achorga invasion had topped a kilom and a half in the lower Martian gravity, and had relied on environment differentials to power its internal microclimates. Here, huge wind-gathering sails curved out from the secondary towers in

long, trailing triangles of some pale yellow substance, a few showing holes or tears. Along the top edge of each ran a thick cable;
anchored at regular intervals all the way down were the moor-
pipes of rain-funnellers held aloft by a knot of gasbags.

The phantasmagoric scene was repeated out towards the horizon and beyond, conglomerations of towers and sails resembling
a fleet of grotesque, garishly coloured vessels ploughing across a
broken landscape, interspersed with stretches of overgrown ruin.

None of the spires was their destination. From his earlier
research, Robert knew that most of an Achorga hive lay beneath
the surface and it seemed likely that the Zyradin, the lifeform
they had come to retrieve, also lay underground. According to the
Construct the Zyradin emitted a very specific and exotic particle
that caused several secondary particles – a signature that could be
detected and tracked. Just such detectors were provided for them
both, and as the pinnace swept lower they began to register.
Robert and Rosa compared readouts.

'Definitely in the vicinity of that greater hive,' she said, pointing. 'And very likely underground.'

'So, do we take our handy little boat in through one of the big
openings, guns blazing?' he said, gazing at the console display
where the sensor system was continually updating a layout of the
hive's various entrances. 'Or do we go creeping in like cautious
mice?'

A ghost of a smile touched her lips. 'Caution is good.
Remaining undiscovered for as long as possible.'

'The mice strategy it is then,' he said. 'You never know – it
might actually survive contact with the enemy.'

Landing half a mile from the greater hive, they hid the pinnace
in an ancient, disused hillside tunnel then proceeded on foot in the
dull light of an overcast afternoon. Wearing a small filter mask,
Robert followed Rosa, using what cover was available. The vicinity and approaches of any hive were watched over by several
tevorga, an Achorga variant bred for acute eyesight and obsessive
attention to detail. To that end there was around the hive a wide
zone cleared of anything that would provide concealment or cover

to fire from. As they paused behind the crumbling remains of a wall made from odd triangular bricks, Rosa produced a pair of small, silverglassy hemispherical objects and gave them to Robert. She took out a second pair and pressed them onto small square platelets on the shoulders of her body suit. Robert did the same.

'Holofield projectors,' she said. 'Set for contour cloaking, but the camo effect is time-limited to fifteen seconds after which the cells need to recharge.'

'How do I turn them on?' Robert said, studying one of them.

'Yours are slaved to mine,' said Rosa. 'So remember, Father, once they're on we have fifteen seconds to reach that cluster of small openings.' She pointed.

Robert nodded, fingering one of the little silvery domes. 'Okay, I'm ready.'

'Short-range comm functioning?'

He tapped the neck pickup and the earbead. 'I hear you loud and clear.'

'Good. We go on my mark – three . . . two . . . one . . . go!'

Rosa activated the holocloaks on two, and Robert had just a moment to smile at her disappearing act before the *go!* spurred him into a mad dash.

They made it with seconds to spare and, visible again, they climbed into one of several low tunnels that sloped in and down. Inside, the sides were ridged and unpleasantly tacky, gleaming in the light of the redlamps clipped to their chests. The moist air was laced with an acrid odour and as he moved along at a crouch he thought he could hear a scuttling sound behind them. Frowning, he glanced back towards the pale radiance from outside.

'Did you hear that?' he said.

'These hives contain tens of thousands of Achorga,' said Rosa as she peered down at the handheld detector. 'And the acoustic qualities of these tunnels probably transmit sound and vibration quite a distance. Perhaps we should keep the conversation to a minimum . . .'

They continued on down the gently sloping tunnel for several minutes until Rosa stopped, gesturing for quiet. The silence revealed nothing for a moment, then Robert heard a ticking sound which grew and multiplied. A second later, up from below came a carpet of small, finger-sized insectoids. He recognised them as a species of secondary symbiotes, just as Rosa tripped and trod on several of them, staggered back and trod on several more. She had a pained look as she regarded the splatter of bug innards underfoot, which then drove the still-oncoming insects into a feeding frenzy.

'The smell's going to spread quickly,' he told her. 'Come back up here . . .'

Too late, a section of wall came apart as a crowd of larger insectoids smashed their way in and pounced on the writhing heap of cannibalistic small bugs. Then the tunnel floor near Rosa heaved up and split, throwing her off her feet as snakelike creatures with snapping jaws lunged out, straight towards the ongoing slaughterous feast. Rosa had edged away from the gap, flechette pistol out, when the floor behind her tore open and a gleaming yellow tentacle coiled about her and dragged her out of sight.

'Rosa . . .!' he snarled as he snatched out his beam pistol and cut a swath through the ghastly mêlée to the ragged hole. Beneath was another tunnel so he jumped down and was immediately startled by a group of tentacles suddenly battering themselves against the transparent membrane that formed one side of this passage. Against an odd, pale green luminescence, the membrane was translucent with patches of opacity, and also bore a large, flapping tear next to which Robert found one of Rosa's little holoprojectors.

'Rosa,' he said. 'Can you hear me? Are you okay?'

'Yes, Father, I am . . . unwounded. Are you in the tunnel below?'

'At the moment, yes. Was it one of these ferocious tentacles that grabbed you?'

'It's a feeder arm, I think. It grabs food and drops it into an enclosure full of Achorga larvae.'

'My God, is that where you are now?'

'I managed to get out, and I'm looking for a way down to the egg chambers which are usually arranged concentrically around the Hive queen throne room. If you follow that passage it will take you to a split-level intersection near one of the main aisles into the throne room. I'll meet you there.'

'Rose, I found one of your holoprojectors.'

'I knew I was missing one, Father. If you press the little stud on either of yours, you will find that you now have independent control. Now, you had better get moving.'

'Right. See you soon.'

He spent the next ten minutes negotiating the downward, undulating tubeway, thankfully without hazardous interruption, apart from sidestepping another stream of minor symbiotes. Reaching an opening, he paused to peer down. Bioluminescence streaked rough walls as if daubed there, while a similar glow came from knobbly, milky ropes that snaked all around the intersection. Rounded ramps and walkways linked most of the openings to each other and the floor, and a couple of flimsy-looking gantries spanned the gap. Here was where Rosa said she would be, so it was just a question of whether to stay here or use the holocloak and sidle round to another minor opening with a better view . . .

Suddenly he realised that the pickup on his neck and the bead in his ear were getting warm. No, not warm but hot – hastily he backed away from the opening while tearing off the pickup and yanking the red-hot bead from his ear. Letting them fall to the ground, he leaned against the wall, wincing as he gingerly touched neck and ear. Next thing he knew, a diminutive figure rushed out of the shadows, scooped up his comm devices then dived back into the gloom.

'Hey!' he cried, stumbling after the thief.

By the feeble glow of his redlamp Robert almost tripped over the short fellow just as he raised a stone and smashed the devices into tiny glittering fragments.

'What are you doing?'

The creature scuttled off to the side, muttering to itself.

'Human . . . Human-Human . . . Human-Anglic . . . yes, Human-Anglic is . . . is!'

Then it lunged towards him and grabbed his arm.

'Come! – we go. We go now. Vilorga are awake, vilorga can smell transmittings, vilorga are hunting you and the other one! I know of place of safety – come, now . . .'

The strange creature tugged on his arm, half-crouching in the glow of his redlamp, its neat, small-featured face, short, all-over fur and slender lithe frame presenting a form too familiar for coincidence.

'Are you a Uvovo?' he said. 'How did you get here?'

'Am I . . . ?' The small face was startled, wide eyes darting side to side. 'Ah, remember, recall. My people, the Rivovo, not Uvovo. I am called Taklos. Now, we go.'

Half in curiosity, half in fear of being lost and cut off, Robert let the Rivovo Taklos lead him round the intersection's upper slope to another tunnel which wound and twisted downwards. It wore a plain, grubby shiftlike garment and although Robert was uncertain of its gender, he decided to think of the Rivovo as a he. Taklos muttered and mumbled continuously, sometimes in Anglic, other times in a profusion of languages, of which Robert recognised a few. Thus he learned the names of some of the insectoid symbiotes and heard Taklos talk of several dangerous Achorga variants like the Lysorga which could wrap its quarry in narcotising webs, or the Jikorga which could disable or kill with acid spit, or the Marorga which could deliver a lethal shock through long spines.

Robert recognised a couple of these from historical accounts of the Swarm War, and from vee and Glow dramas. He just hoped and prayed never to encounter any of them.

Sure enough, they had just reached a low-roofed, poorly lit chamber when Robert heard a rapid thudding coming from a wider tunnel leading off. A moment later a full-grown, bull-sized Achorga rushed into the chamber, slowed and approached them. At once the Rivovo bent over and began to make a strange wavering moaning sound, cupping his hands around his mouth to focus it on the restless, oddly indecisive creature. Robert felt weirdly calm, despite being possibly the first Human to get this close to one of these things in a century and a half.

I wonder where Rosa is, he thought. *She would have some good advice for this situation, I'm sure.*

Then the Achorga seemed to lose interest as it turned away and hurried off up another exit. Robert almost sagged with relief.

'Safety is this way,' said Taklos, indicating an oval passage that sloped up, a yellowish glow some way along. 'Getting close to halls of Empress – keep feet and mouth quiet.'

The yellow glow brightened as they drew near. Surreptitiously Robert checked his beam pistol, not sure if he should be trusting the Rivovo so completely. Then they came out in a sweet-smelling grove of small trees with shiny dark green leaves and low-hanging reddish-orange pods. This was a medium-sized chamber with a high ceiling, a kind of grass underfoot and the sound of water trickling in the undergrowth somewhere.

'This is a surprising place to find underground, Taklos,' he said, reaching for the detector to see how near he was to the Zyradin. 'I wonder if you can help me find . . .'

Glancing round, his voice trailed off. The Rivovo's face was slack and twitching as the tapered end of something membranous, something grey and slick, wriggled away into a now-visible slit in Taklos's neck. Abruptly, the Rivovo stood straighter and his eyes stared levelly at Robert.

'Humaniform subject,' he said. 'Earthsphere, Earth, the Grand Exodus, the many Battles Glorious, ah, we remember . . .'

'Taklos, what are you saying . . . ?'

'This one only an intermediary, although sometimes we steer him, enjoy bipedal intrinsicality when we tire of the Achorga modes . . .'

'Who is "we"?'

'Guides, pilots, advisers, mentors,' said the thing inside Taklos. 'Choose.'

This is some kind of mind parasite, Robert thought, curious despite the menacing situation. 'So why did he bring me here?'

'Poor Taklos thought to barter you for his release, his freedom to leave.' A shake of the head. 'Unfortunately, his biology was altered long ago, longevity, cellular resistance, blood acclimatisation – if he left the confines of the hive he would be dead in a single sky-cycle.'

'How long ago was he altered?'

'Hundreds of Earth years, at least a thousand.'

Robert frowned at this, then noticed that some of the pods near the possessed Rivovo were extruding thin, pale grey tongues which wavered as they lengthened. Glancing round he saw others protruding from pods close by. He shifted his position slightly.

'We need you to stay,' the Rivovo said.

Calmly, Robert took out the beamer pistol. 'Your offer is most kind but sadly I have other more pressing matters to attend to.'

The possessed creature gave a grotesque, gaping smile as it saw the weapon.

'What exceptional Construct handiwork,' it said. 'You . . .'

There was a cluster of sharp hisses and three dark marks appeared on the Rivovo's neck. It jerked in surprise, tried to speak then slumped to the floor. All around the sinister grey tongues retracted back into their pods. Robert looked round to see Rosa appear from a previously unseen doorway, flechette carbine in hand.

'This way,' she said.

Keeping his distance from the pods, he followed her out to a narrow tunnel which led steeply upwards.

'Is he dead?' Robert said. 'What were those things?'

'Those things are Sarsheni, Father, and if I'd killed that host creature while one was inside it, every other Sarsheni in the hive would have felt its psi-death, which is why I used knockout flechettes.'

Robert was astonished and horrified. The Sarsheni were a psi-parasitic species that had ruled the vast Indroma domains for nearly ten millennia. It had been thought that the Sarsheni were wiped out in the Bargalil revolution, so their presence here was a profoundly disturbing discovery. When he voiced such worries Rosa agreed.

'It makes the success of our mission still more imperative,' she said. 'The Construct must be informed.'

As she consulted the detector, Robert went over some of what the Sarsheni said – *Earth, the Grand Exodus, the many Battles Glorious, ah, we remember* . . . Which almost implied that those creatures were around at the time of the Swarm War, or were even involved . . .

Rosa snapped shut the detector's cover and looked up. 'When we were separated, I found some disused passages behind a wall built over the underground remnants of the original city. They lead down and straight towards the Zyradin trace. I've made sure of the route we need to take – we should reach our destination quite soon.'

Trusting to this, Robert followed only to discover that Rosa had omitted to mention that said route led along a wall gallery overlooking the Empress's birthing hall. Several times they had to pause and activate their holocloaks as smaller, paler Achorga hurried past with clusters of glistening eggs fastened to their backs with sticky strands. Once, Robert paused to steal a glance out at the hall and saw scores of red Achorga crawling all over a huge, lopsided spiral dais. Only when he saw a line of apertures along one spiral level suddenly squeeze out small white eggs, one after another, did he realise it was no dais.

With that grotesque image fixed in his mind, he hurried after Rosa.

Some fifteen minutes later, in a secluded corner of the hive's lowest levels, they clambered through a hole Rosa had mentioned making. A musty-smelling passage with walls of irregular stone curved round to a low, square room with another three doorways. Two were blocked by age-old cave-ins, but the third led to a downward slope of shallow steps. Up till now they had been lighting the way with their redlamps but as they descended the stepped ramp they saw a pale, wan glow coming from below. Some minutes later the ramp emerged into shadowy open space, and Robert's eyes widened at the sight.

The ramp had been cut from the rough wall of an immense cavern whose heights and far end were lost in shadows and haze. The dark mirrored surface of a placid underground lake almost filled it, covering all except a thin strip of dry higher ground that ran around the edge. The craggy ceiling dipped in many places, forming here and there complete columns of knobbly pale rock that reached to the floor. Pendulous rock formations served as anchor points for webs and masses of foliage whose stalks, tubers and tendril meshes gave off a pearly radiance. That, however, was outshone by the forest that they paused to survey.

Dense thickets of slender pale trees formed a tangled forest on a broad island at the centre of the lake. From their higher elevation, Robert could see that many other plant-forms were intertwined with the trees: bushes and creepers, long grasses, crooked stalks holding odd translucent cones aloft, clusters of glassy orbs and outbreaks of bulbous fungi. It was these rather than the trees whose radiant luminosity reached into all but the most shadowy of corners.

Rosa had her detector out – she smiled and pointed at the forest. 'The secondary particle source is at the centre.'

They continued down to the foot of the slope then along to a narrow neck of ground, one of several that connected the outer shore to the island forest. The air was warm and humid and numerous clouds of insects hung over the still waters. The closer they came, the more Robert noticed the faint colours of the vegetation, delicate blues, limpid yellows, gauzy pinks. This all combined to give the underground lake and forest a mysterious and pleasing lustre, a kind of immaculate tranquillity. Once at the island they pushed on through the pale, luminescent foliage, and Robert smiled to himself, remembering some of the stories his mother told him when he was very young, tales of brave knights venturing across wastelands and into forests on the trail of treasure or a princess or the Holy Grail.

And here we are, he thought. *Strange knights in search of a stranger grail.*

Finally they reached the heart of the pale forest, a clearing with a pool, dark and undisturbed. Detector in hand, Rosa walked over and stopped at the edge.

'There are secondary particle readings all around,' she said. 'But they are concentrated here.'

'So now you set up the container and it draws the Zyradin to it, yes?'

Rosa nodded, took a flat object from inside a midriff pocket and tugged a plastic strip away from its edge. Immediately it expanded and filled out into a dark grey cylinder as long as his lower arm. The lid was a disc peeled from the cylinder's base. It grew rigid in seconds.

'The cylinder is designed to emit a specific pattern of subsonic frequencies,' Rosa said. 'The Zyradin responds by converging on the subsonic source and compressing itself into the container . . .'

** OR NOT **

The voice was quiet, speaking in near-accentless Anglic, and sounded as if it was coming from nearby, yet all around, like a chorus of many voices. Robert exchanged a look with Rosa, who seemed both puzzled and amused.

'Who are we speaking with?' she asked.

** WHO DO YOU SEEK ** YOU SEEK AN IT BUT I AM AN I ** THE GREAT DESIGNERS CREATED AN IT FOR THE WORK OF WAR ** AFTERWARDS, THE IT CHANGED OVER THE LONG AND MANY YEARS AS IF TIME ITSELF WAS THE SOIL FOR IT TO GROW IN ** AND IT BECAME I ** I AM HAPPY HERE ** WHY SHOULD I LEAVE **

'Because the work of war is not done,' said Robert. 'Because powerful forces are trying to set free your ancient enemy, the Legion of Avatars. Because if we fail worlds will burn and count-less billions will die. Because the Construct sent us to find a Zyradin, a counterpart for the world-forest known as Segrana, in the hope that the worst can be avoided.'

Rosa gave him an approving look.

** AH, THE CONSTRUCT ** THAT EXPLAINS A GREAT DEAL ** THE CRISIS MUST BE ABOUT TO BLOOM ** VERY WELL, I SHALL ACCOMPANY YOU **

Taken aback, Robert glanced at Rosa, who seemed equally surprised.

'You change your mind quickly,' said Robert.

** I MIGHT HAVE TAKEN MORE TIME TO CONSIDER YOUR

REQUEST ** EXCEPT THAT THE ACHORGA HUNTERS THAT YOU FOOLISHLY LED HERE WILL SOON ARRIVE ** MAKE READY YOUR CONTAINER ** PUT IT IN THE POOL **

Quickly, Rosa placed the lidless cylinder in the water at the edge of the pool. A moment later tiny bright motes began rising from its depths, like glowing beads with a trailing, electric-blue aura, or the stylised image of a comet. Or eyes . . .

'The orchestra of eyes,' he muttered.

** THE FANCIFUL NAME BESTOWED ON THE ZYRADIN BY EBRINALDR ESISK, THE HIGH SCIENTIST LORD WHO DESIGNED US **

'Is there another way out of here?' said Rosa.

** THERE IS ** IT MAY NOT LEAD YOU BACK TO WHERE YOU STARTED FROM HOWEVER **

Now the pool was actually glowing from the hundreds of motes that were converging on the container, pouring into it. As Robert watched, more began appearing at the edge of the pool, as if entering from the surrounding ground. Still they kept appearing or ascending from the depths, funnelling together into the open cylinder, thousands of them.

How is this possible? he wondered. *Unless the actual physical component is a lot smaller than it appears . . .*

Suddenly the myriads thinned out to a stream and dwindled to nothing.

** YOU MAY NOW AFFIX A SEAL **

In one smooth movement Rosa retrieved the dripping cylinder and attached the lid with an audible click. At the same time Robert heard a thrumming rushing coming through the pale forest.

'Time we were leaving,' he said.

** GO AROUND THE POOL AND THROUGH TO THE OTHER SIDE OF THE FOREST ** CROSS THE WATER AND GO TO THE NARROW END OF THE GREAT CAVE ** AT THE HEAD OF THE DESCENDING STAIRS THERE, CLIMB ON THE STONE LEDGE ** BEHIND THE PILLAR ON THE LEFT IS A DOORWAY ** GO THROUGH AND FOLLOW THE PASSAGE DOWN **

They followed the Zyradin's instructions to the letter and, sure enough, the hidden doorway was where it said it was. Cradling the Zyradin's cylinder, Rosa hefted her flechette carbine in her other hand and stepped through. Robert paused to peer back at the lake and its forest island. The dense, pale tangles seemed to have lost some of their spectral lustre. The luminescence was dimmed and the shadows were taller and darker. As he watched, a few Achorga emerged from the vegetation. Quickly he withdrew behind the pillar and went after Rosa.

Stone stairs descended the sides of a square shaft, the steps deep yet worn and rounded. Every footfall raised a puff of dust and every cold breath was tainted by the smell of ancient decay. Had the original civilisation of this world built all these subsurface areas, and if so why? Occasionally he slowed to peer over the brink but there was only an impenetrable darkness that gave no sense of depth. What, he wondered, would drive a society to burrow down so far?

Red lamplight revealed no patterns or lettering, no marks or decoration of any kind, which was somewhat atypical. After nearly twenty minutes he was starting to question inwardly how this escape route could possibly lead back to the surface. He was about to voice his doubts when Rosa stopped and turned, eyes wide.

'Quiet,' she said.

For a moment, nothing. Then a sharp ticking and clicking far above, swiftly growing louder. Then a rushing sound and a dark shadowy form that fell past them. In the red gloom few details were apparent but a glimpse of thrashing insectoid limbs told them all they needed to know. A few seconds later they heard an echoing thud.

'They've found the concealed door,' Robert said.

** NOW YOU MUST HURRY ** THERE ARE NINE MORE FLIGHTS TO GO **

Rosa leaped ahead, taking the steps two, sometimes three at a time. Robert tried to keep up and was gasping for breath by the time he reached the bottom. Dark ichor splattered the floor around the smashed Achorga corpse – he spared it the briefest of glances before dashing after Rosa, who had ducked through a wide exit. Beyond it he almost stumbled when he saw what awaited there.

There was some light, faint glows coming from strange narrow panels that looked vaguely like stained glass. There were columns of similar panels all around the walls, which went up at least two hundred metres. This huge hall had straight sides and semicircular ends and was perhaps three hundred metres in length. But what caught his attention from the moment he entered were the big circular platforms, one at either end. He recalled the chamber under Giant's Shoulder, back on Darien.

'Forerunners,' he said. 'Are these . . . warpwells?'

** THESE ARE TRANSFER PLATFORMS ** WARPWELLS UNDERTAKE TRANSFER FUNCTIONS IN ADDITION TO THEIR OWN VERY SPECIAL NATURE **

'I suspected as much,' Rosa said. 'Which one?'

** TO THE RIGHT **

'And naturally I'm the last one to know,' Robert said, running after her. 'I think I can guess how we're getting out.'

Drawing near he could see the same swirling, interlocking patterns he had noticed at Giant's Shoulder, except that this platform was at least twice as big. Also, it had a tenuous yet perceptible aura about it, as if energies slumbered within, waiting to be awakened. By contrast, the other looked grey, dusty and lifeless.

** PLACE ME UPON THE CONTROL PEDESTAL **

Steps led up and at the edge of the platform was a waist-high plinth of pale, featureless stone. Rosa carefully set the cylinder on its flat top then stood back. A shifting blue radiance appeared around the container and suddenly glowing symbols flickered up and down the plinth. At that moment, Achorga began streaming in through the entrance.

** SENTINEL PRESENCE IS ONLY RESIDUAL ** OUR DESTINATION IS SET ** RETRIEVE ME THEN STAND ON THE BRIGHT EMBLEM **

Rosa grabbed the container while Robert darted over to where a large symbol like an embellished filigree letter O glowed brightly. All the time horribly aware of the clicking, clattering sound of Achorga limbs as they scrambled towards the warp-well. Then Rosa was standing next to him and dazzling curtains of light sprang up around them, completely obscuring the huge Forerunner hall . . .

For a long, drawn-out moment he felt as if the light was pouring through him, its brightness invigorating his mind and senses, an exhilarating cataract of cold fire filling his head . . .

Then abruptly it was gone and he staggered, eyes blinking at a sudden dimness.

'Father, are you okay?'

'Yes, I'm . . . I am fine. That was quite an astonishing experience,' he said. 'I don't recall the transfer from Giant's Shoulder being quite as visceral as that . . .'

He paused, eyes adapting to normal light levels as he became aware of his surroundings, then amazed.

The Forerunner chamber beneath the Achorga hive had been imposing, but this edifice was built on an altogether more stupendous scale. They were now standing on another big circular platform, like the others made of stone but this was a pale material and the grooves of the intricate convoluted patterns were sharp and clean, as if freshly cut. Dark, glassy walls rose straight up to a dome with a silvery octagonal pattern. Curved ramps led down to a side avenue which ran straight for perhaps half a kilometre to a similar dome and platform. On one side was a steep-sloped wall from which immense empty plinths protruded at regular intervals, interspersed with huge square frames filled with blank silvery surfaces that offered no reflection. Along the top of the wall, itself about two hundred metres high, were more of the silvery frames and behind them pillars supported a long balcony provided with numerous small buildings and structures. Nowhere was there any sign of life.

The other side of the huge avenue consisted of a single unbroken and transparent wall which rose up to curve over the high balcony and meet a dark, shiny wall that formed a backdrop. But there, beyond the transparent wall, was a sight fit to render insignificant anything devised by mortal or transient sentience. Above them, vast and beautiful, was the galaxy.

** THIS IS THE SEAT OF REGARD **

'All references I have ever seen discount it as a myth,' said Rosa, cradling the Zyradin container in her arms.

Robert stared up at the stellar lens. They were seeing it from the side and perhaps ten degrees off the ecliptic, so he was able to make out the spiral arms, the clumped densities of stars and hot gas, the darker swirls and patches, and the brightness at the hub.

'It's breathtaking and magnificent,' he said. 'But I thought we were going to Darien.'

** THE SEAT OF REGARD IS NOT A MERE OBSERVATION POINT ** IT ALSO SERVES AS A TRAP ** THE SILVER APERTURES DEPLOY COUNTERMEASURES AGAINST ANY AGGRESSORS WHO ENTER ** I BROUGHT US HERE AS A PRECAUTION ** TO CONTINUE OUR JOURNEY WE MUST TRAVEL TO THE PLATFORM AT THE FAR END **

'Let's go,' said Rosa. 'We can afford no more delays.'

At ground level they found a couple of passenger floaters parked in a booth set into the stairway. The controls were simple and intuitive and moments later they were gliding leisurely along the avenue. As they did so, colossal holoprojections appeared on the jutting plinths, opaque, full-colour representations of many different species which shifted their stances and looked down as the newcomers passed by. Robert recognised a Kiskashin, a Vusark, and a Makhori, but the others were a mystery to him.

One hundred millennia separates us from the peoples of the Forerunner alliance, he thought. *But compared to the thirteen billion-plus years of the galaxy's existence, that's almost recent history. Who knows what primordial eras and conflicts the Forerunners looked back at and drew inspiration or caution from?*

Halfway along the broad avenue, Robert spotted something sitting off to the side not far ahead. As they drew closer he saw that it was another floater vehicle, abandoned and deactivated. Further on was another, and a third.

Rosa looked grim. 'Zyradin, are you seeing this?'

** THE SITUATION APPEARS ANOMALOUS ** MY ATTEMPTS AT ESTABLISHING EXCHANGE PROTOCOLS WITH THE SEAT OF REGARD'S WARDENS ARE BEING IGNORED ** PERHAPS THE PASSAGE OF TIME HAS ALLOWED DYSFUNCTIONS TO OCCUR AND PERSIST **

Without warning, the floater started to slow, losing height.

'Father,' said Rosa. 'Arm yourself and be ready to run when we come to a halt.'

The moment the floater finally scraped to a stop, she leaped to the floor and took off in a full-pelt headlong dash. Taken by surprise, Robert charged after her, straining to catch up. At the same time, the lighting dimmed and a harsh voice boomed throughout the interior, uttering incomprehensible words.

'What's . . . it saying . . . ?' he shouted as he ran.

'That we are a violation . . . and we must be erased.'

'At least they're . . . taking us . . . seriously . . . *What's that?*'

The silver frames spaced along the avenue were starting to distort. Their silver faces warped, pointed shapes pushing forward against metallic yet elastic membranes.

'Trouble,' Rosa yelled, slowing to push the Zyradin cylinder into his grasp. 'Take it and go on ahead – quick. I'm right behind you.'

Even as she gave him the container, a shape broke free from one of the frames. On five limber legs it fell to the floor, a fist-sized, chrome spiderlike thing, creature or mechanism, he couldn't tell. But it was like a signal because now every silver frame began spilling them into the avenue. With the cylinder tucked firmly under one arm, he aimed the beam pistol and fired as he ran.

** THERE HAS BEEN A SERIOUS BREACH OF THE SEAT OF REGARD'S DEFENCES ** THESE THINGS ARE THE LESSER XEZRI, AND THEY COULD NOT HAVE INFILTRATED THE OVERSYSTEM BY THEMSELVES ** ANOTHER AGENCY IS AT WORK HERE **

Robert felt too gripped by fearful determination to answer, too focused on burning aside any of the spiders that scuttled too near, as well as ducking and dodging the ones that sprang into the air. Behind him he heard the whining hiss of Rosa's flechette carbine. Ahead the steps to another platform were less than a hundred metres away.

Then a grabbing silvery shape flew at him from the side. He cried out as it scrabbled at his neck and he flailed with his pistol, trying to knock it loose and succeeding. But another group of them were rushing to intercept, the front runners suddenly launching themselves towards him. Somehow he managed to cut them into burning, melting fragments with a single sweep of the beam pistol. Then he executed a tight turn, sprang past the remainder and found himself with a clear run at the steps. But when he glanced back he saw Rosa surrounded by a surging, glittering horde that reached her legs and began to climb.

'Rosa! No!'

** YOU CANNOT SAVE HER ** CLIMB TO THE PLATFORM **

'Run, Father!' she cried out as she fought, kicked and lashed out. 'Save the Zyradin and get away . . .'

Robert cursed in helpless fury, wavered, then turned back towards the platform. But a line of the spider things had flanked him and were advancing across the steps. He fired, shrieked, stamped and jumped over them, lunging up towards the top. He was nearly there when several of them landed on his back, knocking him forward. Panicking, he pushed himself back up but then something needle-sharp lanced into his back, between the shoulder blades, into his spine. Cold and hot at the same time, it made him think that he was almost reliving the fight aboard the *Plausible Response*, in that pocket universe.

His sight split, seeing double, and he staggered up onto the platform. Then another spike drove into his neck. He gasped and fell to his knees, hands numb and releasing their burdens. He didn't remember falling over . . .

. . . but his next conscious thought found him lying on his side on the carved, heavily patterned surface of the Forerunner platform. His outflung hand was empty and as it came into focus so did the horde of silver spider things waiting in a surrounding mass just metres away.

In reflex he quickly retracted his arm then levered himself into a sitting position.

** MOVE WARILY ROBERT HORST ** MY CONTAINMENT VESSEL IS AT YOUR BACK **

Carefully he retrieved it, regarding the enclosing circle of silver enemies. His breathing was shallow and there was a wheeze in his chest, and his muscles seemed weak and quivering.

'What did you say these things are?' he said.

** THE LESSER XEZRI ** A DEADLY PARASITE LONG THOUGHT EXTINCT ** A BILLION YEARS AGO THE GREATER XEZRI RULED HALF THE GALAXY AND MADE THE OTHER HALF TREMBLE IN FEAR ** LISTEN ROBERT HORST ** YOU ARE DYING ** THE XEZRI INJECTED YOU WITH A NEURAL DISAS-SEMBLER ** IT IS SLOWLY EATING AWAY YOUR BRAIN AND REPLACING IT WITH THEIR OWN STRUCTURES ** YOU MUST GET UP AND CARRY ME ACROSS TO THE CONTROL PEDESTAL ** I AM EXERTING MY OWN ENERGIES TO KEEP THE XEZRI AT BAY ** THEY DARE NOT COME ANY NEARER ** SO ROBERT HORST ** TIME TO COMPLETE YOUR MISSION **

But no time for any more living, he thought, a certain despair tingeing his woozy thoughts.

Tucking the cylinder inside a chest pocket, he got to his feet, somehow. Then he faced the control pedestal and strode forward, got a few paces, yawned, blinked a slow blink which on opening showed a sideways view of the platform, from where his head lay upon it. So heavy, his head, but he managed to lift it, imagining that he was carrying it under one arm with the Zyradin under the other. He laughed, a weak, throaty sound.

No walking this time. On all fours he crawled for an eternity across the cold stone patterns, which drew his eyes to them, their fabulous complexity, grace of line and intertwining enigmas. At one point he thought he was talking with Rosa, with the older, more mature version, discussing her mother and the previous younger Rosa-sim, almost as if she were a younger sister. And with every shuffle and drag of the way, the waiting myriad xezri paced him, the eerie, restless swaying of a forest of deadly silver blades over which he towered like a dying giant . . .

** SLEEP NOW ROBERT HORST ** DIE NOW WITH HONOUR **

And he was lying slumped against the control pedestal, now alive with glowing symbols. He'd made it somehow, and as for dying, well, he wasn't ready for that but to sleep, to lay down his head and rest after all of that terrible effort, ah yes, what a rest that would be . . .

Beautiful veils of light burst up out of the stone platform, out of the patterns, wrapped him in radiance, and he knew no more.

33

CHEL

After days of stealth and nights of guile in the shadows, he came
to a rocky hillside overlooking a deep, densely forested valley
some distance north of the Kentigerns, and roughly two days'
walk from the coast. He knew that the enemy machine was down
there, now, and with all that he had gleaned it was imperative to
find out what it was planning. His new eyes, Segrana's gift, had
shown him visions, glimpses of what had been, of oddly different
events with different outcomes or involving different people. He
also saw fragmentary scenes of the now, Greg on a devastated
mountainside, directing construction and helping with refugees
while sunset approached; Kao Chih aboard a small spaceship
with two others, his face appearing oddly distorted; Catriona
looking ill and distressed as she sat on a high branch with heavy
rain falling through the gloom.

Then his eyes had shown him chains of strangely grey images –
Greg dead and buried at the heart of a mountain, Catriona dead and
buried at the foot of a tree, and himself, face-down in a river flowing
down to the sea while indistinct, enslaving machines marched across
the hills towards Giant's Shoulder. Was he being warned about actual
futures, or were these symbols of some other kind of conflict?

He stared calmly at the darkening forest. His task was clear –
find out all he could about the bizarre tentacled machine-creature,
track its course, determine its destination, then lead Greg and
others there to destroy it. The consequences of failure looked to
be full of dread.

By now the sun had set so he stood and started down to the valley below.

Tonight, Umara's sky unfolded a plentiful display of purple and orange swirls while the points and glows of the forest seemed especially lustrous. Chel smiled, half-imagining a conspiracy between ground and sky to illuminate matters as he stole through the trees. Yet he had his own ploys and stratagems by which he intended to avoid detection and slip past the eyes and ears of the enemy's machine servants.

Which had taken up sentry posts, proof of a kind that the enemy itself had come to a halt. One of the advantages conferred by his new eyes was the ability to vary certain aspects of his body's inner workings, like heartbeat and skin temperature. Adjusting his external presence to merge with the susurrus of the forest, he crept past the gleaming lenses and pickups of war machines standing guard. He could have used the altered-air shell to be sure of complete concealment but it would have left him exhausted and vulnerable in the middle of the enemy camp.

With steady, deliberate movements he crept past the inner and outer circles of sentries, using every scrap of bush and foliage as cover. An after-dusk misty haze drifted over the undergrowth, haloing the soft glows of ineka beetles and clusters of ulby roots. Finally he reached the enemy's lair, a sharp dip sheltered beneath a stand of larger, mature trees. Hidden by a dense, prickly syldu bush, he peered down at a great dark shadow, then gazed upon it with the eyes of Segrana . . .

Within the long blocky form of the factory machine rested the enemy – its shape was like a creature with a flattened carapace and a number of tentacles protruding from one end. But Chel had seen their like before, during the visions of his husking at Tapiola daughter-forest, visions of the deep past, of the great war against the Legion of Avatars. Twisted minds bound lifelong within armoured shells, beings who embraced what they called convergence, a union with machines, a cold pain and a mechanised anger that faced outwards, directed at all and any who would dare defy them . . .

And now he changed the intensity and focus of those eyes, shifting from the images of now to the images of after. This was a Knight of the Legion of Avatars, whose only conceivable purpose had to be the release of the Legion survivors, imprisoned in the deepest levels of hyperspace, then unrestrained retribution. But he had to know the very darkest of the consequences gathering beyond the limits of the now, he had to see . . .

Night's gloom lay upon the forest, speckled with creature-glows and overlaid with an ominous hush. All six of his eyes gazed at its shadows, which trembled like a membrane, like a skin. Which dissolved into cold, black devastation, the land and the hills and ridges to the north merging into the mountains to the south, except that it was all burnt. All the forests, the meadows, the wildlife, all around for as far as he could see was incinerated to ash, black and grey wastes congealing in a steady, heavy downpour, cold, black and dead . . .

The vision melted back into the now, into Chel crouching behind a leafy bush, drawing a deep, shaky breath. The horror of it, even just as a potential envisaging, was almost overpowering. A part of him wanted to run far and fast and find a deep cave to hide in. But that was only the youngling in him, whereas resolve led him to start climbing down the foliage-curtained slope towards the enemy's machine lair.

He was near the bottom when he paused, sure for a moment that he'd heard voices. Keeping motionless he listened, got nothing, then heard it, one voice, a man's. Chel finished the descent cautiously and slowly while the voice came nearer through the trees. The man was alternately yelling for help, virulently cursing his captors, and trying to cajole them into releasing him. Worst of all, Chel knew who it was – it was Gregory's friend Rory.

'. . . aye, ye better let me go 'cos if I get ma hands on one o' they plasma cannon I'm gonnae stick it where the sun don't shine and let rip! . . . aaaagh! – right, I'll no' need a gun, just a hammer'll dae!'

Chel could see metallic forms emerging from shadowy curtains of creeper. Rory had been bound hand and foot then strapped to the back of one of the big combat droids. The sight was disturbing – for all the days of this long, taxing pursuit, not once had Chel seen any evidence of the Knight or its servants taking prisoners. Rory, still shouting and swearing, was being carried towards the rear of the huge factory machine where a hatch had folded open. It was easily wide enough to admit a Human lying prone, and as he watched a thick shelf with a Human-shaped recess slid out lengthways.

Chel shook his head, a Human gesture for a Human predicament. But there was no conflict in his intentions – he would have to try and save the man. With his eyes, his Seer's eyes, he looked at the air, at the infinitesimal motes of which it was consisted, then looked for the shell of air, knowing that his perception of it would bring it into being. The strain of observation-alteration was already noticeable but he held steady as the air around him grew opaque with faint glowing swirls. At once he rose and walked straight towards the machine that bore Rory along.

He was yards away when he suddenly realised that the machines were all closing in on him from all sides. There was a flash of light, a dazzling burst, and the concealing air-shell vanished. From the back of the now-motionless droid, Rory stared in disbelief.

'Chel! – Greg sent me to find you . . .'

'I am sorry, Rory, so sorry,' was all he could say before cold metal talons seized him and a needle slid into his neck, blackening all sight.

LEGION

Resting within the autofactory's rebuilt storage bay, the Knight of the Legion of Avatars considered his two prisoners: one was a male of the Human species, the other the Uvovo whose steady, untraceable pursuit had been a constant irritation for days. But at that very moment when it had employed its special talent, a form of psi-cloaking, the Knight's sensors, attuned to Forerunner methods, spotted the intrusion immediately. Then it was merely a matter of neutralising the creature before it could deploy any other trickery.

Up till now, the Knight had been rigorous in the extermination of any primitive sentients who strayed too near, whether Human or Uvovo or Sendrukan, or any of the score of other species who were part of the infantile invasion of fanatics. Now, however, as the rhythm of events picked up and his chosen strategy carried him still closer to inevitable triumph, his new prisoners presented an opportunity for an experiment in convergence. Once the appropriate controls were established both subjects would undergo a series of implants and augmentations, thereby discovering which race would be best suited to true evolution.

Initial preparations would begin now, ensuring biophysical compatibility with the embedded technology. In the meantime he would continue to direct the buildup of his mech army while analysing the reports from his monitor droids. The situation across the Human colony of Darien had deteriorated in the last forty-eight hours. The majority of the population of the central coastal plain had fled, either to settlements near Trond in the north, where Brolturan remnants maintained a significant presence, or south-east to the towns of the deepwater inlets where Humans were in complete control. The main city, Hammergard, was now in the hands of the Spiral Prophecy zealots, who, having put Human places of worship to the torch, were now attempting to convert the remaining Humans by coercion. Elsewhere in the south, a large force of Humans had either been wiped out by the fanatics or chased off in a rout, leaving the road to Giant's Shoulder open. Another army of fanatics was already there and meeting heavy resistance from Brolturan troops who were holding the northern gullies, ravines and gorges leading up to the great ridge that led straight to Giant's Shoulder. The ravines and hilly slopes had been extensively mined, while up on the promontory itself, the Hegemony ambassador, Utavess Kuros, resided with over a thousand crack troops dug in, fortified and protected by weapon batteries.

Against the poorly armed host of the Spiral Prophecy, such a garrison could probably hold out indefinitely. But when his army of modified war mechs went into attack mode, the Knight did not expect the Sendrukans to last much longer than ten to fifteen minutes.

He broke off from strategic considerations to study the operations being undertaken by the autofactory, reprogrammed with schemators from his own contingency store. The Uvovo's body had started rejecting the embeds almost immediately, requiring genemorph treatments. The Human, however, was accepting the basal systems without a qualm.

That was when a sensor alert went off, an urgent-priority one. And when he saw what it was announcing, he checked the sensor webs for any flaws, checked the datastream for anomalies, but the processed outcome remained doggedly the same. A Zyradin, a powerful artificial psi-symbiote, the key element of the Forerunners' citadel worlds, the being that unified each of those worlds with its accursed biomass, the sentience that directed the ferocious energies of the warpwell against the Legion's countless warriors . . . the very thought, the remembrance, and now this terrible, stark fact of its existence. That it should appear on the field of battle at this crucial moment . . .

He paused to regain composure, to recall his duties, loyalties and warrior purpose. He also looked more closely at the locational data and felt a spike of irritation – it had appeared in that mountaintop stronghold, the insurgent hideout he had dismissed as irrelevant to his campaign. A mistake that he would take great pleasure in rectifying.

He began issuing orders to more than half his mech forces, sending them south towards the Kentigern Mountains.

<This fear will be a source of strength. I feel it cutting to my

core, but it is the memory of fear, not fear itself. Perhaps this enemy is weak and unprotected but I shall face it and fight. Such a battle would be glorious and such a triumph would be incomparable. I am of the Legion and we fight to the end>

34

GREG

'. . . on our way to one of the Uvovo hideouts when a pack of them machines, those big, hefty buggers, jumped us. It was really dark in the gorge and things went mad all of a sudden. Didn't know where Rory and the others were, and I got clouted by one o' them which threw me on the ground. I was scared out my wits, and wounded and dizzy, I . . . I crawled into a hollow under a fallen tree . . . Guess I was lucky . . .'

Murcheson's voice trailed off, shame writ openly in his face as he gazed down at a piece of strapping his fingers fiddled endlessly with. Greg felt a certain sympathy for him, but it was personal anxiety that gripped him.

'And you're absolutely sure that Rory's body wasn't with the others?' he said.

'After the machines were gone, I looked and looked, Mr Cameron,' Murcheson said miserably. 'I couldna find him – he must have been taken prisoner.'

There were four of them in the small hut, Greg, Murcheson, a Uvovo healer who was attending to his wounds, and Alexei Firmanov.

'Are you willing to lead another search party to that same spot?' Greg said. 'If we can pick up the trail . . .'

'Greg, the forest's far too dangerous now,' said Alexei. 'We cannot afford to lose any more men . . .'

'Rory's my friend, Alexei – I can't just abandon him.'

'He is also *my* friend, but we must face reality! – we have to hold on here, rebuild what we can . . .'

'Aye, in time for when the next Hegemony ship comes along to finish the job . . .'

He stopped the bitterness in midflow, leaned on the rickety wall and hung his head in despair. Was this grinding conflict going to take away every last one of his friends? Catriona, Uncle Theo, Nikolai, and now Chel and Rory . . . and he found himself recalling the aftermath of his father's death and how his mother had soldiered on through it, dealing with the paperwork, the relatives, the cremation, the never-to-be-fulfilled obligations, and the outstanding debts. And the only answer she had given to his need to understand her fortitude were the words 'Do the work now, mourn later.'

She was right, he thought, thankful that she and his brothers were finally safe in Camp Sanctum away to the west. *I can't afford to be distracted by my own worries – I don't have time for that luxury.*

He looked up at Alexei with a smile.

'We won't be able to send out a search party, I guess, although perhaps the Uvovo can help, perhaps one of the Listeners.' Greg patted Murcheson's shoulder. 'Ye did well to stay alive and get back here in one piece, mostly. D'ye feel up to regular activities? I can have ye assigned to light sentry duty if you want.'

'I think I'm okay, Mr Cameron. Could do with a few nights' sleep, though.'

'Couldn't we all?' said Greg. 'Right, take tomorrow morning off. Have some of that sleep for me, okay?'

'Thanks, sir.'

Greg nodded and left the hut, followed by Alexei.

Outside, a cold evening breeze struck him and he shivered. The healer's hut was one of about a dozen hastily erected on the few level areas around the big blast crater in the mountainside. Most were for storing lumber cut from the wooded hills below, the rest was for stone, building materials for constructing stairs and walkways to allow access to the ancient Uvovo stronghold. The entrance, battered and half-melted, was still serviceable, and, importantly, the stronghold itself remained unbreached by enemy forces. There were still a few figures loitering around the scaffolding and even down in the bowl of the crater, some smoking pipes. Everyone else had trooped back indoors to eat and gossip and rest.

God knows there's enough to gossip about, he thought, after the last forty-eight hours.

A young Rus called Pavel, one of Vashutkin's men, came up and handed him a folded piece of paper.

'And this is?'

'Report on the fortress main figures, sir,' said Pavel as Alexei took out his squeeze-torch to light up the sheet.

Greg looked it over quickly, took mental note of the figures on population change, food and water supplies, and armoury reserves, then nodded, folded it and slipped it away.

'Any word on the hunt for a radio?' he said.

'There was a rumour this afternoon that there's a trapper town in Nazarova Valley south of Gangradur that has a working short-range.' Pavel shrugged. 'Mr V sent a couple of scouts but we won't know for two or three days.'

'What about Varstrand? – he said he might be able to get the *Har*'s radio working again.'

'He's still working on it, he says.'

Greg gave a resigned grimace. A radiation burst from the orbital strike had fried most of the comms equipment, leaving them unable to contact their agents and observers still present over on the coastal plain. With a few pocket receivers, however, they were picking up broadcasts from both the Spiralists and the Brolturans claiming that the 'terrorist nest' in Tusk Mountain had been obliterated. This propaganda clearly spread quickly as the previous night they had to chase off two separate groups of looters, fortunately without any casualties.

'Where is Mr Vashutkin now?' Greg said.

'He is with foremen, giving assignments for tomorrow.'

'Could you give him my thanks for the reports and say that I need to speak with him soon? Thank you, Pavel.'

As the youth hurried off, Greg looked at Alexei with an amused, sardonic expression. Alexei rolled his eyes.

'You see?' Greg said. 'He's moving in and taking over, just as I said he would . . .'

'My friend, you have to admit that he's a better organiser than you—'

'Better organiser? Based on what, exactly?'

Alexei grinned. 'Greg, I love you like a brother but Mr V knows how to motivate people. He gets them enthusiastic, makes them think that they're vital to the resistance . . .'

'Ah, that's just the usual smarmy politician's guff . . .'

'*Nyet*, it's more than that. It's charisma . . .'

'Right, I see. Didn't realise I was such a nonentity, Mr Forgettable, or Mr F as I'm known around these parts . . .'

Alexei gave him an exasperated look. 'Are you really so angry about this?'

'Nah, not really . . . well, I am, a bit. I just wish Uncle Theo was here – he'd cut him down to size . . .'

He broke off when he heard someone shouting his name, then saw a diminutive robed figure clambering up one of the three access ladders leading out of the crater. Hurrying round, Greg and Alexei were in time to help a breathless Listener Weynl up over the temporary steps.

'Friend Gregory . . . once more I come to you . . . gasping for my breath,' Weynl said. 'In the Hall of Discourse . . . Robert Horst has returned . . .'

'Horst?' Greg was suddenly fully alert. 'My God, he made it . . .'

'He is . . . fatally wounded and unconscious. The Sentinel said to bring you as quickly as possible . . .'

'Did he manage to bring back this Zyradin thing?'

'Yes. Please, Gregory, go.'

Less than ten minutes later he and Alexei were hurrying into the high-walled Hall of Discourse. Glowing veils shone up from the solitary working Forerunner platform. On its intricately patterned surface a figure lay motionless, watched over by a couple of robed Uvovo. One of them, Listener Churiv, looked up as they approached, met Greg's gaze and shook his head.

'He has gone to join with the eternal.'

Sombrely, Greg mounted the steps and went to crouch beside the body – and stared in puzzlement.

'This isn't Robert Horst,' he said. 'The ambassador was in his late sixties and grey-haired. This guy is a lot younger . . .'

A patch of the platform's glowing radiance brightened, thickened and coalesced into the image of a slender young woman.

'Hello, Gregory Cameron,' she said. 'I am the Sentinel – as you can see I have adopted a Human appearance as an aid to communication.' She indicated the still form. 'I can assure you that this is the body of Robert Horst – soon after I translocated him to the Garden of the Machines, the Construct carried out rejuvenation procedures to enable him to undertake certain demanding tasks.'

Greg gazed at her, then at the corpse. Looking closer he saw familiar lines in the face, the long jaw, that strong nose, the defined cheekbones. The younger Horst must have been quite formidable, he thought, but clearly not formidable enough.

'How did he die?'

'He and another Construct agent were attacked by hostile creatures while retrieving the Zyradin. That he managed to reach the transfer platform to get here is a great tribute to his willpower.'

A few feet away sat a sealed grey canister. Regarding it, he frowned.

'Is it in there?' he said. 'This Zyradin thing – is that it?'

** THAT IS A CONTAINER ** I AM WITHIN IT **

Eyes widening, Greg got to his feet but before he could say anything, the Sentinel spoke.

'To refresh your memory, Gregory, the Zyradin is a psi-sentient symbiote, an artificial lifeform designed by the High Ancients to focus and direct all the energies of planetary eco-entities like Segrana. That voice is the voice of the Zyradin – with its help, Segrana can take an active role and move decisively against unfriendly forces.'

'A clever old bunch, those Forerunners,' Greg said. 'Creating a planetary defence system that won't work without the cooperation of an exotic symbiotic creature. Add to which – Segrana is up on the moon! If we have to steal a shuttle like Uncle Theo did, we'll have to fight our way through a war zone first, not exactly my strategy of choice.'

'There are no ground-to-orbit craft available at Port Gagarin,' said the Sentinel. She gestured and a small block of vidage frames appeared, showing glittering clouds drifting in orbit above Darien. 'Even if a suitable one could be found, the incidence of debris, mines and hostile monitor probes of both Spiralist and Brolturan provenance makes a crossing extremely hazardous. The only other way to ensure delivery of the Zyradin to Segrana is via the transfer platforms.'

'And you've not done this already because . . .?'

The opaque young woman spread her hands. 'Unfortunately, the transfer link between this stronghold and the platform chamber on the moon was irreparably corrupted a long time ago. However, the link between Giant's Shoulder and the moon is now operable.'

For a moment Greg said nothing as he absorbed the implications, then slowly he said, 'You cannot be serious.'

'There are no other options left to us, Gregory.'

'Look, Kuros is dug in behind heavy fortifications with hundreds of veteran troops and a battery of those tasty beam cannons. He might even have some air support for all I know. In short, it's a suicide mission. There has to be another way.'

'I was being accurate, Gregory. There are no other options. I would advise that you assemble a team and be ready to leave with the Zyradin as soon as possible. The zeplin would be ideal – with its speed you would be able to draw the droids away from attacking the stronghold.'

'Whoa, what droids? There's been no sign of any for days.'

'This is because they have been gathering at a staging area over a hundred miles to the north,' said the Sentinel, pulling up a satellite image of the Forest of Arawn. 'The Brolturans no longer control the mech factory, the Namul-Ashaph. It was taken over by a Knight of the Legion of Avatars several days ago. It detected the Zyradin the moment it appeared here; he knows how important it is, which is why an army of mechs is heading for this mountain.'

Greg glared at the Sentinel. 'One of those things is here on Darien? And you didn't think to tell me?'

** NO ONE KNEW **

'I had vague suspicions that maybe another of those Instruments was meddling in affairs on Darien, but was unable to scan for it.'

** I KNOW THE ODOUR OF THEIR SPOOR WELL AND I DETECTED THE KNIGHT'S PRESENCE ON YOUR WORLD SOON AFTER MY ARRIVAL ** I DONATED SOME ENERGY TO THE SENTINEL SO THAT IT COULD SEE FOR ITSELF **

Looking around him at the sombre faces, Uvovo and Human, Greg noticed Vashutkin standing over by one of the entrances, leaning against the stone, arms crossed.

'So if we keep the Zyradin here,' Greg said, 'we get massacred by a mob of war droids. If we fly off to Giant's Shoulder with it, we get shot to pieces by Kuros and his Brolt troops . . . or massacred by a mob of war droids along the way. Did I miss anything out?'

'I will take on this task,' said Vashutkin, his voice booming across the chamber. 'If no one else will.'

Greg laughed and shook his head. 'Concerned for our welfare, Alexandr? Och, I'm touched . . .'

'Gregory, dearest of all my friends, you are too valuable to be lost to such a risky adventure.'

'Aye, I know, but I'm sure ye could struggle along without me, somehow.'

'Gregory Cameron, on reaching Segrana, the Zyradin must be given to the Keeper of Segrana, to Catriona Macreadie. There will be changes, alterations.'

Taken aback, Greg gave the Sentinel a narrow look. 'What kind of alterations?' he said, thinking of Chel's Seer eyes.

'Unknown. She is Human.'

'C'mon, you've got to give me more than that!'

** SHE IS THE KEEPER OF SEGRANA ** SHE IS THE TRUE
VOICE AND EYES OF SEGRANA ** THROUGH HER I CAN REACH
EVERY PART OF SEGRANA **

'Which still doesn't explain how I'm supposed to get through
the Brolt defences,' he said.

** I CAN PROTECT YOU ** I CAN PROVIDE YOU WITH AN
ENCLOSING ARMOUR **

'Is this feasible?' Greg said to the Sentinel.

**'The Zyradin are powerful entities with a wide range of abili-
ties.'** She turned to the sealed container. **'Would you care to give
a demonstration?'**

** WITH PLEASURE **

The cylinder's lid lifted slightly and slid off. A pale blue radiance bloomed at the opening, then a few glowing motes drifted up
into view, then some more, then many more. Greg stared in the
excitement of recognition – the bright points surrounded by a
corona that had a tail when in motion, just as he'd seen repeatedly
on walls all over the Uvovo temple site for years.

'Well,' he said. 'Fancy meeting you here. Must admit, your pictures and carvings don't do you justice.'

** I HAVE SEEN SIMILAR DEPICTIONS IN THIS PLACE ALSO **
MAKE YOURSELF READY **

'Ready for . . .'

Before he could speak further, the cloud of glowing blue motes
swooped to surround him. Startled, he staggered back, seeing
everything through a veil of glowing points. Then some of them
settled onto his bare hands and began to sink into his skin.

'Now, wait a second, what is it doing?' he said, panic rising.

** THIS MERGING IS ONLY TEMPORARY BUT SERVES TWO
FUNCTIONS ** IT PROVIDES THE PROTECTION YOU NEED ** IT
ALSO ALLOWS ME TO DERIVE ENERGY FROM YOUR OWN
RESOURCES **

'And there's no permanent side effects, then?'

** OTHER THAN CONTINUING TO LIVE THERE ARE NONE **

Greg gazed at his hands and down at his body. The bright
motes seemed to cling to his form, passing in and out of his

clothing as if it wasn't there, meandering around like a restless nimbus. He glanced at the Sentinel. 'So, all I have to do is get to the warpwell chamber and you'll do the rest.'

'**I shall be there when you arrive.**'

'Okay,' Greg said. 'Let's go gatecrash Kuros's party.'

It took twenty minutes to organise the team he wanted, and get Varstrand over to the blustery eastern slope in the *Har*. In the company of Alexei, Maclean and Bessonov, they waited in the windy downwash while a rope ladder came snaking down from the dirigible. While there was fascination over Greg's blue glow, there was also a disconsolate feeling; Rory's absence was being sorely felt. Maclean and Bessonov pointed torches upwards for Varstrand's benefit and soon mooring lines were coming down as well, caught by accompanying helpers.

'Hey, Mr Cameron,' yelled the Finnish pilot. 'If we are going on the night trip, it is usually a secret reason or a crazy reason. Which one, do you say?'

'Both,' Greg shouted back as he clambered into the gondola.

At the Zyradin's insistence, he was carrying the cylinder in a webbed harness strapped to his back, over his padded combat jacket. Weapon bundles were heaved in next, followed by the others. Last was Bessonov but before he could close the hatch another figure appeared and hauled his brawny frame inside. Vashutkin grinned and nodded at everyone then reached outside and dragged in a long object, a Brolturan beam rifle.

'Alexandr,' Greg said. 'My great and dear friend, have you lost your mind? This could well be a one-way trip – nae votes in it.'

Vashutkin dogged the hatch and gave the thumbs-up to Varstrand, then came and sat across the aisle from Greg.

'Very true, Gregory, very true, but the greater truth is that if you fail because I was not there, how do you think that will make me feel, eh? Apart from probably being dead when this Legion of Avatars overruns the planet. So I decided to throw all my dice along with yours. After all, you've been pretty lucky so far.'

Greg uttered a low whistle. 'Would ye credit it! So that's what I've been feeling since I got up this morning – lucky!'

The others chuckled, then grasped their seats as the dirigible surged forward and up. Minutes later the dirij levelled off, course set for Giant's Shoulder.

'What's with the extra artillery?' Greg said, indicating the Brolt weapon Vashutkin had carried aboard.

The Rus shrugged. 'Insurance. No such thing as too many guns on an operation like this. What about you, Gregory, what's your weapon of choice?'

It was Gregory's turn to shrug. 'Usually a Gustav handgun . . .'

** YOU WILL NOT REQUIRE ANY OF THESE WEAPONS ** MY ABILITIES WILL PROTECT YOU **

He laughed, ignoring Vashutkin's puzzled look, and leaned on a crooked arm, wishing for a good stiff shot of whisky. Outside a nearby grimy oval window, he could see a vast expanse of the Forest of Arawn's eastern marches, a sea of treetop foliage, details rendered ashen in the meagre light from the night sky's starmist, yet brightened here and there by ulby roots. His thoughts turned inward, thoughts dwelling on those he loved and those who might be lost in one way or another. Chel, Rory, Catriona, Uncle Theo, and what of Kao Chih and his mission to save his people? He sighed, held up one blue-veiled hand, turned it, studied it. He had never imagined that this conflict could widen so radically and become so complex and at times bizarre.

Our enemies seem to multiply and get stronger, he thought. *While our abilities seem to shrink . . .*

** ACCIDENTS ARE INEVITABLE ** THE COSMOS DEPENDS ON THEM **

You're hearing my thoughts . . . aren't you? No chance of privacy in my own head, then!

** YOUR ANXIETY OVER THE MACROCONFLICT WAS CLEARLY STATED **

And you said that accidents are inevitable – what's that supposed to mean?

** SIMPLY THAT THE GREATER THE POWERS EXERCISED BY THOSE OPPOSED TO LIFE, THE GREATER THE UNFORESEEN CONSEQUENCES ** IN GATHERING POWER TO THEMSELVES

THEY MAKE THEMSELVES THE FOCUS OF ACCIDENTAL OUT-
COMES ** USUALLY THESE OUTCOMES ARE NOT WHAT THEY
WANT **

Well, that's all very pretty and mystical, he thought. *Don't see
how it helps, though.*

** I SEEK TO PROVIDE PERSPECTIVE ** ACCIDENTS ARE
ANTICIPATED **

Greg gave a mental shrug and tried to settle into a comfortable
position while keeping the canister strapped to his back. Twenty
minutes later, and about three-quarters of an hour from the vicinity of Giant's Shoulder, he heard Varstrand calling to him from the
cockpit.

'For you,' said the pilot, holding out his headset. 'Someone
urgently asking for Mr Cameron . . .'

Puzzled, Greg lurched up to the cockpit, accepted the frail-
looking headset and put it on.

'Greg Cameron here – who's this?'

'Finally! – I was getting a wee bit worried there, chief!'

'Rory?!' he cried out in relief. There was a commotion back
along the gondola as the others heard him.

'Naw, it's William Wallace calling up for a blini home delivery –
aye, it's me! Look, I'm here wi' Chel but he's not doing too good.
Are you in that dirij that's heading west?'

'Aye, where are you?'

'About three mile north of ye, on a hilltop, ye canna miss it . . .'

Vashutkin crouched down next to Greg, his face serious.

'How did he escape the droids? – ask him . . .'

'That Vashutkin?' said Rory.

'Aye,' Greg said, turning the headphone outward for all to
hear. 'So how did you get away?'

'Pure chance. Two of they big combat machines were carrying
us away from some robot camp when they both started shaking
and fell over. I got free then dealt wi' Chel's bonds, and that was
us. We got tae this hill then found there's droid patrols to the
south and west – we could head north but Chel's not looking so
great. So, are yiz coming to get us, then?'

'Yeah, Rory, just hold on.' Greg looked at Varstrand. 'Head north and watch out for a hill.'

'I know the one, I think,' the Finn said, changing direction.

But Vashutkin shook his head and Greg covered the headset stalk-mic.

'I don't believe they could escape,' Vashutkin said. 'In fact, I don't even believe it's him. Sorry.'

** I CONCUR **

Greg agonised over these similar judgements, all too aware of the doubt in the eyes of the others.

'And what if you're wrong?' he said.

Vashutkin got up and leaned on the backs of the seats on either side of the aisle. 'You will lose two good friends,' he said. 'If you are wrong, perhaps we die or they capture us and kill us, or turn us into slaves. And all of this is for nothing.'

'I've got to know,' Greg said. 'If there's a chance . . .'

'We are getting near the hill,' said Varstrand.

'Can you hover over the top, about a hundred feet up?' he said.

'Maybe could go higher. It is breezy tonight.'

'Okay, do that.' He uncovered the microphone. 'Rory, we're nearly there . . .'

'We can hear ye! – and so can them droids. Ye'll have to come in low . . .'

'Can't do that, Rory. We'll send down ropes with body slings,' he said, making encouraging gestures to the others.

'No, listen, Greg, ye gotta come down . . .'

The gondola cabin was a whirl of activity as Alexei and Maclean, going with Varstrand's directions, dug lengths of rope out of a locker along with a body sling. At the same time, Bessonov and Vashutkin were opening the hatch, securing it as Alexei lashed one end of the rescue rope to a hull stanchion, then gave the okay. A turbulent gusting added to the noise of the dirigible's engines and Greg had to yell into the headset mic.

'Okay, that's the rope going down now. Ye see it?'

'See something – it's too high, come lower . . .'

'Is it long enough to reach the ground?' Greg yelled to Alexei.

'It should be, but difficult to see,' Alexei came back. 'It's shadowy and bushy down there . . .'

** SOMETHING IS BENEATH US **

'Come lower, Greg, come lower,' said Rory's voice.

Varstrand shook his head. 'Too dangerous.'

'Rory, we can't . . .'

Suddenly the gondola jolted and the rope hanging out of the hatch snapped taut.

'Rory, was that you?' Greg yelled. 'Have you got the body sling?'

'Lower, Greg, come lower . . .'

** WE MUST LEAVE ** THINGS ARE GATHERING BENEATH US **

They did get him after all, Greg thought brokenly, just as the entire dirigible lurched downwards.

Everyone cried out while Varstrand, wrestling with the control column, shrieked, 'Cut the rope! Cut it!'

Bessonov snatched a hatchet from clips over the hatch but before he could chop the hawser, a thing like a segmented silver snake lunged up from outside and fastened its jaws on his shoulder. Next to him, Vashutkin grabbed his Brolt rifle, swung it round to press the muzzle against the thing's head, and fired off a short burst. Instead of the expected explosion of deadly shrapnel, the machine slackened its jaws and fell limply to the floor where it was kicked out of the hatch by Maclean. As he did so he looked down.

'My God, the place is alive with them!'

But Greg had tossed aside the headset and dived for the hatchet, with which he attacked the rope. There was a loud bang as it gave way, the severed end whiplashing against the side of the hatch. At once, the dirigible surged upwards. Varstrand gave a triumphant bellow as he gunned the engines, and for a second it seemed that they were in the clear. Then something struck the rear of the gondola and it swung drunkenly, tilting up. Knocked off his feet, Greg slid towards the rear, halting himself by grabbing at a seat rest.

There was the slam of an impact against the stern, and another. The wood-and-composite hull cracked and split and a taloned metal hand punched through then ripped a ragged gap across.

Then some major seams just parted like cardboard and most of the stern was torn aside, exposing the interior and everyone to the horrifying machine that was weighing down the aft.

In the meagre cabin light, framed against the night-shadowed forest, it resembled some grotesque machine-hybrid of tiger and gorilla, serrated talons, armoured limbs and chest, back and shoulders sprouting clusters of black vanes. Greg could feel the heat on his face. And there was a faint, strange aura, a flickering layer of hexagonal patterning.

** FASCINATING **

As the beastlike droid tossed away the wrecked chunk of hull, the others were yelling at Greg to hit the deck and give them a clear shot. Instead Greg's glowing hands came up, seemingly of their own accord, stretched out towards the brutal machine as it dragged itself further inside and in his direction.

'What . . . what are you doing?' he gasped.

** YOU SHOULD THROW YOURSELF TO THE FLOOR IN ABOUT THREE SECONDS **

Tiny glittering points burst from his outflung hands and splashed across the front of the oncoming monster.

** NOW **

Greg spun away, diving towards the deck, arms wrapped about his head.

A deafening chorus of weaponsfire filled the cabin. He craned his neck to glance back and saw the beast machine holed and battered by an onslaught of volleys, one of which reduced its outstretched, bulky arm to a punctured, torn wreck shorn of its taloned grab. Another ferocious volley hit, and lights went out in its squat head, in the chest and arms, and it toppled backwards out of the gaping stern.

As Vashutkin and Maclean hauled Greg to his feet he stared at his hands, at the blue glowing motes just visibly moving beneath the skin.

'What was that?' said Vashutkin.

'The Zyradin . . . did something, I don't know what,' he said, slightly dazed. 'How about you – what did you shoot that snake thing with?'

Vashutkin grinned and patted the big Brolturan beam weapon, which was resting across two seat backs.

'This is a variant on the usual design,' he said. 'This one fires some kind of emp bolt, blows out their nasty, evil circuits . . .'

'My ship!' wailed Varstrand from his cockpit. 'You see? This is the crazy trip!'

'We need more height,' Vashutkin told the pilot, then glanced at Greg. 'And back on course to Giant's Shoulder.'

They exchanged a slight but definite nod. Greg then sidled towards the stern, trying to ignore the icy, whistling gusts whipping through the opening. Holding on to an overhead stanchion he peered out at the receding hill, thinking about Rory and contemplating another addition to his burden of grief and loss. And then, for a moment, he saw a number of gleaming shapes appear in a gap in the hillside foliage, fast-moving and in pursuit.

'What can you see?' said someone.

'Hellhounds on our trail, boys,' he said. 'Looks like it's gonna get ugly.'

35

KUROS

Uvovo Ambassador Utavess Kuros had intended to fly north to Trond to inspect the remnants of the surviving units. He wanted to study their officers' summaries, set their tactical and strategic objectives, and get an accurate sense of the readiness of the remaining airworthy craft before returning to Giant's Shoulder. But recent reports confirmed that yet another horde of Spiralist fanatics had closed in from the south and were attempting to fight their way up to the ridge, part of the pincer movement that now had the promontory as its focus. And they were armed to the teeth, including a variety of portable missile launchers more than capable of bringing down Brolturan vehicles, as they had already discovered to their cost. In addition, the chaotic valleys to the west were swarming with renegades and insurgents of every kind, all eager to take pot-shots at anything in the air, thus making flights in or out too hazardous.

He thought morosely on these matters while seated in what passed for personal chambers in the science facility. Now fully built and functioning, it sat over the huge access trench he had ordered cut into the promontory soon after his forces had taken possession just a few weeks ago. Below lay the chamber with the Forerunner warpwell, now being exhaustively probed, measured and fussed over by a frequently incomprehensible coterie of scientists whose babble often threatened the underpinnings of his sanity. Yet even their jargon and occasional lapses in manners were preferable to the cold and deadly presence of the Clarified Teshak.

Ever since the destruction of the *Purifier*, the Clarified One had devoted himself wholly to the defences of Giant's Shoulder, the newly installed tactical barriers, the squat towers providing crossfire on the approach from the ridge, the fortified emplacements guarding the gullies and ravines to north and south, and the beam cannon battery. This left matters relating to the warpwell in Kuros's hands, as well as coordination of the Brolturan remnant units. Without the *Purifier*, the communications network had fallen apart and calls for tactical support never got through. The first twenty-four hours after the death of the *Purifier* were a chaotic whirlwind of violence and retribution, and by the time partially secure stopgap comms were operational the Spiral fanatics were landing in their thousands.

Now, nearly three days later, the outlook was much improved, despite the Spiralists' successes. A couple of mobile builder drones were retrieved from the Lochiel depot before it was overrun, lifted to Giant's Shoulder and put to work. Almost all Brolturan troops had rejoined their own units, or formed into patchwork ones. The Trond encampment was well dug in and equipped with power and supplies, and would soon be in a position to move against Spiralist elements who had occupied several towns south of Trond. And his comms technicians were working to re-establish contact with their sensor satellites, which would provide the kind of strategic overview that had been sorely missed.

Only two things marred this progress: the loss of all contact with the Namul-Ashaph, the mech factory, and the complete lack of response to his priority signal from either Hegemony or Brolturan listening posts. For the former, it was possible that the comms crash critically damaged the autofactory's systems, while for the latter he was for the time being assuming that, somehow, the Spiralists were jamming extraplanetary communications.

And while all of this was going on, the investigation into the warpwell had proceeded in leaps and bounds. According to the Chief Scientist, almost the entirety of the warpwell's upper layer had been successfully analysed, with more than half the energy pattern pathways now subverted and working for the Hegemony technicians. With these pathways, they had prepared an elaborate trap for the guardian entity, an array of sensor clusters preset to pinpoint the entity's originating substrate then flood it with disrupting energy, effectively erasing the guardian from the warpwell and thereby unlocking its secrets. All they were waiting for was a visit from the entity, the Sentinel.

Kuros leaned back, smiling in the certainty that he could hold out at Giant's Shoulder almost indefinitely. When Hegemony forces finally arrived and took possession of the orbits and skies of Darien, assault brigades would be sent down to scour away the Spiral zealot filth. And when the Overcommander and his accompanying Tri-Advocate stepped down onto Giant's Shoulder, he, Utavess Kuros, would be able to unveil the fruit of tireless labours carried out beneath his aegis. In the light of such self-evidently illustrious expertise, not to mention his aura of modest dignity, the bestowal of honours and promotion would practically be a necessity . . .

He was suddenly aware of Gratach's presence off to the side, standing with his back to the blank, as yet unpowered holowall. His AI mind-brother's opaque figure stood spear-straight, garbed in segmented gold and red armour, his arms crossed, his head bare, his fierce face regarding Kuros.

'*You have a visitor, one of those prating technologists, the chief one. He is agitated.*'

'He is always agitated over some minor detail or other.'

Gratach gave a grin that was half a snarl.

'*This does not concern a mere detail.*'

Kuros shrugged. 'Admit him.'

The doors to his chamber slid open and Chief Scientist Tabri hurried in. At the edge of Kuros's field of vision the still-grinning Gratach faded away.

Tabri was attired in a high-collared, dark blue and crimson robe whose high-status shoulder insignia were somewhat negated by the virulent yellow chemical splashes adorning its lower folds.

'Chief Scientist, what brings you—'

'Most High Monitor,' Tabri cut in. 'Esteemed Ambassador, pray tell me why we are being punished.'

Startled, Kuros straightened in his chair. 'Punished? What do you mean?'

'Please! – do not play with me! I refer to the order for all my personnel to cease their activities and prepare to depart from the facility immediately, an order received from you not fifteen minutes ago!'

'I have issued no such order,' Kuros said. 'Clearly, there has been a gross administrative error . . .'

The Chief Scientist's expression was sour. 'Ah, of course, Ambassador – errors, minor faults, misunderstandings, the usual regalia of courtly intrigue! Let me be blunt – if you wish some favour or gift from me, say what it is so that I may return to my work . . .'

'I gave no such order,' Kuros repeated angrily, rising from his chair. 'And I require no favours from you or any . . .'

Then the door opened and the slender, black-garbed figure of the Clarified Teshak entered.

'Is there a problem with your orders, Chief Scientist?' Teshak said pleasantly.

Tabri looked round in surprise. 'You are aware of them, high one?'

'Indeed – the ambassador discussed them with me earlier. You're not thinking of questioning them, are you?'

'No, ah. . .' Tabri met Teshak's icy gaze for a moment and seemed to shrink visibly. 'If these are the orders, I must . . . carry them out. I shall see to my staff, without delay.' Looking miserable, he then left.

Kuros had tried to interject but found that his voice was dead, his throat soundless. The moment the door closed behind Tabri his voice returned. And his mind-brother General Gratach appeared right beside him. For a moment Kuros's gaze flicked between Gratach and Teshak.

'Was it you who issued that order to my scientists, your Clarity?'

'I issued that order to all personnel on Giant's Shoulder,' said the Clarified Teshak. 'Several transports will be landing on the pad shortly.'

Stunned, Kuros sank back into his chair. 'What could possibly justify abandoning this place, just whèn we are making such excellent progress with the warpwell?'

'The reasoning is quite straightforward,' said Teshak. 'The failure of this mission and the subsequent disastrous military clash with an Imisil Mergence fleet – they've been assembling it under conditions of extreme secrecy but every secret can find an ear – will lead to the downfall of the Hegemony's governing faction and a crisis of policy and authority. The Clarified will then step forward, in league with certain traditionalist groups, to propose a new direction for the Hegemony, one less hampered by consideration for the feelings of half-hearted allies.'

Gratach grunted in agreement, smiling.

'What will happen to this facility?' Kuros said.

'Several groups want to gain control of it,' said Teshak. 'Some want to wreck the warpwell, others to unleash its powers against enemies. Hostilities will ensue, turmoil and killing that will only serve our cause by blackening the governing policy, whose representative is, of course, you.'

'But you would sacrifice something that might give the Hegemony a crucial advantage . . .'

'Many such possibilities have been explored by Hegemony officials in recent centuries, and usually they turn out to be a waste of effort and a drain on financial resources. We Clarified are confident that our vision of the future will bring tangible and long-lasting benefit to the Hegemony, as well as widening our dominance of the greater region.'

Kuros felt fear quivering in his chest and his limbs.

'If you're telling me this, you must be planning to have me executed.'

'Oh, Kuros, how dramatic! That would be a waste, in more ways than one.' The Clarified Teshak strolled across the room, hands locked behind his back. 'We need you to carry out the tasks allotted to you. This is how it will be explained – surrounded by enemies and under pressure from your own feelings of inadequacy, your nerve broke and you ordered a full evacuation of Giant's Shoulder. Later, after relocating to the northern camp, your sense of shame was so great that you decided to atone for your craven cowardice by choosing the path of clarification. By giving your spirit into the hands of Voloasti you allowed your mind-brother, Gratach, to ascend to full sentience, thereby furthering the aims and glory of the Sendrukan Hegemony.'

Kuros glanced uneasily at the opaque image of his mind-brother, Gratach, scarcely able to believe that it would turn against him. And when he made to speak once again his vocal cords were silent. When he tried to turn his head, to move his hands, even to stand, he found he was locked in position, every muscle unresponsive, his body an impervious block.

'Clarification is an intricate process,' said Teshak. 'Therefore, we'll need to ensure that your role is played without flaws or risky notions of sabotage.'

Off to the side, Gratach's image faded, melted away. When it was wholly gone, Kuros's hands drew back to the edge of his desk, pushing as he stood up. The Clarified Teshak came into view, smiling as he indicated the door.

And not one movement, not a single muscle, was controlled by Kuros. His body had become a cage.

36

GREG

** NO SIGN OF OCCUPANCY AND NO ENERGY SIGNATURES **
NO POWER IS BEING GENERATED AND NO DATASTREAMS ARE
BEING RELAYED FROM THE TELEMETRY POINTS ** I ADVISE
CAUTION **

'Aye, that sounds sensible,' said Greg, peering through the
gloom towards Giant's Shoulder.

'What did it say?' said Alexei.

Greg repeated the Zyradin's comments and Alexei chuckled.

'A trap,' he said. Maclean and Bessonov nodded but Vashutkin
was puzzled.

'No signs of anyone at all? Why would they abandon such a
place – it makes not any sense.'

'The fortifications are not patrolled,' said Varstrand, handing
his binoculars to the big Rus. 'See it for yourself.'

They were in the ice-cold gondola of the *Har*, Varstrand's dirigible, hovering low over dark ridges and wooded gullies a mile to
the west of Giant's Shoulder. The hill where they'd been
ambushed was half an hour behind them but a force of about
forty enemy machines was in hot pursuit and would be arriving in
less than twenty minutes, by the Zyradin's reckoning.

'Looks deserted,' said a frowning Vashutkin, who then prodded
Greg with his forefinger. 'But time is running out – decide what to
do. I say we go in fast and low, tie up at one of those sentry
towers, then you and I make the dash for the big building – the
way to this chamber must go through there.'

'How come *we* have to wait behind?' said Maclean.

'Because I have my special gun and Gregory has his special friend. You guys will be our eyes and ears, watching for when those crazy-mad machines come into view, then you sound alarm and get away with Varstrand.'

'And no heroics,' Greg added. 'Don't hang about – just get in the air.'

Vashutkin regarded Greg. 'So, you like my plan?'

Greg gave a half-shrug. 'It's good enough.'

'What does your silent partner say?'

** A RASH AND RISKY PROPOSAL ** IT CORRESPONDS CLOSELY WITH MY OWN THOUGHTS ON THE MATTER **

'He likes it.'

The next ten minutes went unnervingly according to plan. The Har glided smoothly in over a squat, square sentry tower where everyone disembarked. Before Greg and Vashutkin left, Bessonov gave everyone a small two-way with a stubby antenna. They nodded and stowed the transceivers away.

Large, Sendrukan-scale steps led down from the tower roof to ground level. This far from the foliage of the forest, the shadows were dark and impenetrable, especially with no artificial light from the tower-mounted lamps. But the Zyradin's aura gave him an enhanced view of his surroundings as they hurried through the concrete barriers towards the large, slope-sided building. Vashutkin seemed to have no problem adjusting to the darkness.

As they approached the main building, Greg saw that none of the ancient Uvovo temple ruins remained – the Brolturans had cleared them all away. He was appalled and furious. This was a wanton, criminal demolition of irreplaceable artefacts. Every stone and carving and potsherd was like a syllable in the language by which the past could speak to the present. And now the past had been struck dumb by heedless destruction.

A large landing pad lay between them and the building's darkened main entrance. The doors, predictably, were locked. They were also heavily armoured.

'I might be able to burn off the hinges,' said Vashutkin.

'Take too long,' said Greg.

** I CAN SEE THE LOCKING MECHANISM ** PLACE YOUR
HANDS AGAINST THE SURFACE **

But before he could do so, panicky voices came from the two-
way, wedged into a chest pocket.

'Hostiles! – they're here, now! – we need backup . . .'

A volley of shots came from the two-way, overlaid by the
actual sound from a hundred or so yards away, then a crunching
impact, and an awful, throat-tearing scream. Greg and Vashutkin
took one look at each other and turned to dash back to the sentry
tower . . . and saw heading their way two heavy biped-type droids
similar to the one Greg and his team had confronted in the shadows beneath the hill-covered tree.

'I'll take the one on the left,' Vashutkin said, bringing up the
Brolturan rifle. 'The hard one . . .'

'Aye, keep telling yerself that,' Greg said, unsure of what to do
next.

** MOVE QUICKLY TO YOUR RIGHT ** IGNORE ANY
WEAPONSFIRE **

He followed the Zyradin's directions but when one of the droid
pair veered off towards him and began firing he instinctively
quailed and turned his back. There was a cluster of curious thuds
and he felt a wave of heat across his side.

** YOU MUST TURN AND RAISE YOUR ARMS AS IF TO GRASP
ITS ARMS ** YOU WILL COME TO NO HARM **

Greg obeyed, keeping his eyes open as the armoured machine
rushed towards him, taloned limbs extended for a simultaneous
heart strike and decapitation. Suddenly it was upon him . . . and
he was savagely thrown backwards by a cushioned impact, which
he hardly felt. The Zyradin's blue aura had expanded to enfold
the droid's upper limbs. Greg almost laughed as the droid tried to
shake him off, then began battering him against the ground. Yet
Greg felt no motion sickness or sensations of collision, although
his heart was racing and sweat made his neck and chest slick.

Then the mech began to fire its weapons, all of them, and that
was absolutely the worst thing it could have done. Instead of a

hail of energy bolts and explosive shells pouring into the Zyradin's nimbus, it was all confined by the mech's own force shield, with which the Zyradin had meddled. Destructive incandescence wreathed the droid's upper torso; Greg saw armour twist and crack, cables flare into ash, and processor substrate melt and run. In seconds the unleashed fury reached the main power matrix and the force shield abruptly vanished, spilling forth mangled, smoking wreckage onto the landing pad.

Breathing heavily, Greg stepped back, amazed and exhilarated.

That was . . . incredible! he thought. *So this is what Catriona's got to look forward to!*

** ATTEND TO THE BATTLE **

He looked around in time to see a weaponless Vashutkin execute a balletic duck and roll to avoid the raking sweep of metal talons. As he did so, one hand stabbed out to slap a small charge on the mech's midsection. Coming out of the roll he lunged at the big Brolt rifle, lying off to the side, and came up with it in one hand as the other thumbed a small, boxy trigger unit. The charge went off with a bright flash that made the mech stagger but not fall. At the same time, the machine's force field scrambled and pulsed for a couple of seconds, which was all Vashutkin needed. Without even aiming he brought up the rifle and directed a string of emp rounds into the unprotected carapace. Electromagnetic disruption tore into the mech's vitals. Deranged datastreams burnt out control nodes and overloads raced through the gyro-motile systems. Wrecked from within, the droid fell to the ground, a shuddering, jerking ruin from which threads of smoke rose.

Backing away, Vashutkin glanced over at Greg, who nodded and jabbed a thumb over his shoulder in the direction of the sentry tower. The Rus grinned.

** YOU SHOULD TAKE THIS OPPORTUNITY TO ENTER THE BUILDING AND LOCATE THE WARPWELL CHAMBER **

I can't abandon my friends, he thought as he ran towards the tower, just ahead of Vashutkin. *I hope you can deal with more than one of these things at a time.*

** THEIR SHIELD PATTERNS ARE TRANSPARENT TO ME **

HOWEVER, THE NEEDS OF BATTLE WILL PUT A STRAIN ON YOUR PHYSICAL RESOURCES ** BE AWARE OF THIS **

I'll do what has to be done.

There were another seven mechs at the sentry tower, three trying to break open the ground-floor entrance, three firing rounds in through upper-floor weapon slots, while another was going after Varstrand who had fled up onto the Har's gasbags. In the gloom, sparks flew from the clash of metal claws on stone. In the Zyradin's enhanced vision, Greg saw them all clearly.

Then they saw him. Torso- and shoulder-mounted weapons opened fire. Trusting to the Zyradin, Greg had his hands raised and outstretched as a storm of energy bolts, explosive slugs and minirockets converged on him . . . and time seemed to slow as the missiles entered the blue radiant nimbus of the Zyradin.

** THE ENERGY FROM THE BEAM WEAPONS CAN BE ABSORBED AND REUSED ** THE SOLID-MATTER MISSILES CAN BE OVERLAID WITH A TRANSIENT FIELD MATCHING THEIR SHIELD PATTERNS THEN RETURNED TO THEIR POINTS OF ORIGIN ** OBSERVE **

In an eyeblink, explosions flared on the three mechs' upper torsos. The chest and right arm of one burst into flame while the left arm and claw swept up and tore its own head off before swivelling to attack one of its companions. As the second one fended off the flailing blows, the third launched another wave of ordnance as it leaped forward.

It was barely able to take two strides before its own reflected volley punched through its armour and wrought destructive havoc within the chest cavity. As it keeled over, the headless droid was being hammered and bludgeoned to the ground when something inside gave way. A dazzling explosion engulfed the decapitated mech and the machine attacking it, a white-hot eruption that left several twisted, blackened lumps of metal scattered across the concrete.

That got the attention of the other four, who, recognising a genuine threat, lost interest in those trapped in the tower and descended to the ground. The droid hunting Varstrand likewise dropped onto the tower roof and quickly reached ground level. Greg began backing away in the direction of the promontory's southern edge, drawing them away from the tower.

'Guys, time you were leaving,' he said into the two-way. 'How are ye doing up there, anyway?'

'Bessonov's dead,' came Alexei's voice.

'Dammit,' he muttered. 'Right, don't hang about, move yer-selves!'

'Yes, yes, it is what we are doing! Why aren't you with us?'

'Because I have a special friend,' Greg said. 'And someone has to keep their attention while you get yer arses in gear ... Vashutkin, get aboard with them ...'

'Ah, so you've been elected president as well, eh? Sorry, my good and dear friend, but I think you may need a little help, here. How is it with you now?'

'*Kharasho*,' he lied. 'I'm doing okay, maybe a wee bit *oostalli*.'

** THIS IS FALSEHOOD ** YOU ARE FEELING THE STRAIN OF MY ENERGY DRAIN ** THE NEXT CLASH WILL REQUIRE A COUNTERATTACK THAT MAY RENDER YOU INSENSIBLE **

Do it.

Almost as if his thoughts were a signal, the four combat mechs, all moving in quadruped mode, shifted formation to herd him towards the edge. In the background, the *Har* swayed away from the tower and began to gain height.

'Alexei, why didn't you see them coming?' he said into the two-way.

'They didn't arrive from the north-east,' said Alexei, voice raised against the sound of the dirigible's engines. 'They must have stealthed their way in, or they were here already.'

'Vashutkin up there with ye?'

'What do you think?'

He was about to come back with a good bit of banter when, suddenly, the mechs went from amble to breakneck charge in roughly a second.

** FACE THEM ** BRACE YOUR STANCE ** ARMS RAISED AND SPREAD **

The Zyradin's aura brightened. The glowing motes emerged from his skin, swarming, looking exactly like strange, wandering eyes. The tide of metal closed on him, and even though the fear was choking him he knew what the Zyradin was capable of and a demented, exhilarated part of him was actually enjoying it.

The mechs had learned from the demise of the others so no ranged weapons were being deployed. Then the full-tilt charge reached its launch point and in unison they leaped, trajectory arcs finely calculated to converge on the place where he stood. Greg could feel his body temperature rising, heartbeat speeding up, a rushing in his ears accompanied by a deep bass drone that seemed to resonate down to the cellular level . . .

As before, time slowed. To his eyes the machines blurred at the edges, and the strange blue light smeared faintly. The four mechs were past the high points of their leaps, glinting metal claws out-stretched, spined lower limbs also coming up, They were close, less than a couple of metres away and still in motion, slow, imper-ceptible. Sharp, icy light bloomed from his outflung arms, a web of glittering radiance, like a froth of star-glints, that extended to caress the inward-flying killing edges and spikes.

For Greg it was like having the strength physically wrenched from his body. His senses swam, his extremities tingled and trem-bled, and bitter cold started climbing his spine. At the same time his mind was flooded with images of mechanisms, interlocking, turning, sliding elements, bearings, power systems, subassemblies, sensor webs, data networks, self-repair nodes, processor hubs, weapon batteries, ammo magazines . . . he saw their construc-tion, saw the improvements and upgrades to earlier designs (some he recognised from those early mech attacks on Tusk Mountain) . . . He saw the production chamber where they were put together, saw something after, a long alien shape, a flattened carapace, segmented metallic tentacles . . .

Like an avalanche's first moments, the first stone dislodging a few more, the disassembly began at the heart of the Zyradin's zone of slow time. Greg could see pins, linkages and bolts undo themselves from the claws that were aimed at him, saw this unlimbering move back along the armoured limbs, past the shoulder joints and into the chests, into compressed assemblies of processors and power generators.

One part of Greg's mind saw the immaculate disassembly, revelling in the attention to detail, and in the sheer torrent of detail . . .

While the rest of him gasped as the four merciless, inexorable machines sprang apart in midair, a spreading cloud of components still flying forward, cascades of metal pouring straight at him. Only to rebound from a hazy blue barrier which leaped up at the last moment. A deafening roar of clashing and crashing filled the air as the disconnected debris formed a rough U-shape surrounding him. Then everything turned grey and tilted over. Lying on his side he could feel exhausted muscles twitch in his face, neck, back, almost everywhere. The air wheezed in his chest with every breath, and there was just no strength in his arms and legs. He pressed one shaking hand against the hard ground but there was nothing to push with.

Footsteps approached, the only sound in the silence. A familiar figure crouched down next to him.

'Impressive,' said Vashutkin. 'Micro-distortion of subspace combined with causal state inversion, with various effects. The Forerunners certainly were master craftsmen.'

A cold dread crept over Greg. It was Vashutkin's voice but without so much as a hint of Russian accent. Feeling a trickle of returning strength he levered himself up onto one elbow.

'Who are you?' he said hoarsely.

** AN AUTOMATION **

Vashutkin's smile was almost hidden by the darkness. 'Your passenger is correct, Gregory. Remember when you were handed over to the custody of the High Monitor Kuros? And how you became the recipient of that special dust? After your Uvovo friends removed it from your bloodstream, Kuros had to find another useful figure among the rebels – and here we are.'

'What are you after?'

'My orders were to bring you here for interrogation, but as we've seen, the facility is deserted.'

'Renounce Kuros, join us, work with us . . .' Greg said, breaking off to cough drily.

'Not an option, and time is short since the main force of
combat droids will soon be here.' The big Brolturan rifle swung
round, rounded muzzle pointed directly at Greg's head. 'Actually
my orders in full said capture or kill so it would seem that the
latter is now my imperative.'

Purely on impulse, Greg reached out and stuck his forefinger in
the rifle's muzzle.

'That won't save you,' said the possessed Rus.

'Maybe not,' Greg said. 'But *they* might.'

Off to the west, waves of gleaming metal forms were cresting
the main ridge.

** SOMETHING ELSE IS COMING **

As Vashutkin turned to glance at the oncoming droids, Greg
found himself looking through a rising haze of grainy, blurring
greyness which brightened and began rushing upwards, brightened and smoothed into a flowing, glowing whiteness that
snatched him away . . .

He had glanced sideways for only the briefest of glimpses but
when he looked back the Human was gone. A quick scan of
the area revealed no footprints or clues of any kind. Reasoning
suggested that some form of matter transfer had taken place.

The entity occupying Alexandr Vashutkin's body was really a
coalescent persona comprising various groups of the self-organising
nanoparticles with which Vashutkin had been impregnated during
the escape from the cliff caves. The entity had no especial instinct
for self-preservation but when it looked and surveyed the dozens
of armoured mechs pouring onto the promontory it could feel an
emotional-physical response from the host, whose sentient awareness was still linked to the perceptions. Urgency, causing increased
heart rate and alterations in hormonal balance in preparation for
fight or flight.

The droids were gathering around him, cutting off avenues of
escape. His orders were clearly no longer adequate to the wider

situation, therefore he had to have them either clarified or replaced with new ones. In both cases, Utavess Kuros had to be located.

The immediate task, however, was survival. The droids were only moments away from rushing him or opening fire. Dropping the Brolturan weapon, he spun and dashed towards the edge. The droids were a rippling mass of metal converging but following him past the brink. And when probes were aimed over the side, sensors revealed the hundreds of lifeforms gathered far below and the heat signatures of explosions and weaponsfire. But of the solitary fugitive there was no sign.

Satisfied that no threat could come from that point, the mechs spread out across Giant's Shoulder, preparing for their master's arrival.

Amid a swirl of fading, shredding whiteness, Greg found himself stretched out on cold, hard stone. His fingers brushed over it and discovered incised grooves with rounded edges and pitted surfaces. He was lying on the warpwell, with the shape of the Zyradin canister pressing into his back.

'Gregory Cameron, listen closely to me.' The Sentinel was standing over him, its young-woman features displaying something like weariness. 'I have less than a minute of existence left – the Hegemony scientists decoded the deeper patterns and set a trap. My foundation pattern has been destroyed and the auxiliary will soon be overwhelmed. I am going to send you and the Zyradin to Segrana but this will leave me with insufficient resources to hold off the Knight of the Legion of Avatars. His servants are gathering above.

'Nor can I harm the warpwell. But I shall send a message to the Construct – it may be able to provide help. Farewell, Human Gregory Cameron.'

The storm of whiteness descended again. For what felt like an interminable period he hung suspended in the white, body numb, thoughts circling in despair. All the planning and struggle and fighting had led to this, the warpwell in the hands of a servant of the Legion of Avatars, the myriad-strong bogeymen who had brought the Forerunners and half the galaxy to the brink of disaster so many millennia ago. According to what the Sentinel told him after the defeat of the machine Drazuma-Ha, the Legion had originally numbered in the billions. The warpwells had sent them plunging through destruction to the deepest, most inescapable tiers of hyperspace, a place called the Abyss. Solid proof was hard to come by but the Sentinel said that any survivors might number only a few million . . .

Then the braided whiteness whirled and swirled away, melting into darkness. New odours came to him as his sight adjusted to gloomy surroundings, smells of wood, soil and decay and overlaying them an acrid whiff of smoke.

He was sprawled on an expanse of damp stone. The Zyradin's container was still safely strapped to his back, which he made sure of first. Then his fingers felt the intricate grooves and indentations in the stone surface almost before his eyes picked out the curved edge of a Forerunner platform. It sat at the bottom of a four-sided pit with stepped sides. What little light there was came from one end of this low, shadowy temple-like building so he carefully climbed the slippery tiers of what looked like seating.

Where are we?

** THE HEART OF SEGRANA ** IT HAS BEEN NINETY THOUSAND YEARS SINCE I LAST SHARED THE GREAT UNITY WITH ONE OF THE WORLD-MINDS **

So now all we have to do is find Catriona, he thought. *Then what?*

** THE KEEPER IS THE GATEWAY TO A GREAT WEAVE OF BEING ** THE KEEPER CHANNELS THE ZYRADIN TO EVERY ROOT AND BRANCH AND EXTREMITY **

As Greg climbed out of the strange pit the air grew noticeably smokier and he coughed as it caught the back of his throat. It was woodsmoke. Somewhere, trees were burning.

You're avoiding the question. What happens to her? Suddenly he was angrily speaking out loud. 'Is she still human afterwards? Tell me – I've a right to know!'

** I CAN ALREADY SENSE THAT SHE HAS MOVED BEYOND HER OWN LIMITS ** WHAT YOU THINK OF AS HUMANITY CANNOT SURVIVE INTIMATE CONTACT WITH THE MULTIFAC-ETED PRESENCE OF SEGRANA **

Greg shook his head but made no reply as he half-staggered through the shadows, along a low passage, and round to where a wide door led out to the smoke-hazed green gloom of the forest. Ominously, from far off came the sound of gunfire. The temple was situated on a bushy rise, looking down at the huge bulging, twisted roots of the massive trees that towered over the forest floor. And even as he emerged from the doorway, a figure stepped into view from behind a mass of foliage, and Greg's heart suddenly began to pound as he recognised it as a Brolturan trooper. It saw him at the same time, bringing its heavy rifle to bear even as he reacted, half-turning to throw himself back inside . . .

A darkened form suddenly flew down from above, landing on the Brolturan's shoulders, joined by another half-dozen diminutive Uvovo wielding clubs with vicious rapidity. In seconds the invader was subdued, and an older Uvovo clad in pale brown folds appeared from round the side of the temple and hurried towards him.

'I am Scholar Rinavi. Forgiveness is begged, visitor,' he said. 'Are you the Benevolent scholar Gregory, leader of the freedom-seekers on Umara?'

'That's me.'

'I am to take you to the Keeper immediately. Please follow – we must be swift, as this area was overrun just hours ago and we had to fight hard to push both the Brolturans and the Spirals back.'

'I can appreciate your problems,' he said, pacing the scholar as he set off. A moment later, his legs suddenly felt weak and a wave of dizziness assailed him.

'Do you require assistance?' said Rinavi.

** I CAN NOW PROVIDE YOU WITH SOME ENERGY **

A clean warmth flooded into his chest, arms and legs. His head felt clearer, his eyesight sharper.

'I can manage, thank you, Rinavi. Please, lead the way.'

After twenty minutes of hasty tramping across boggy ground and through sometimes heavy undergrowth, they reached the crest of a low hill, rounded and free of any foliage. A small three-sided stone temple sat there, its lines and design reminding him of the structure on Giant's Shoulder. Other Uvovo were gathered there, silently watching as he approached the wide, curved entrance directly ahead. Greg gazed up – smoke drifted in high layers, lit weirdly by the tessellated fragments of sunlight that filtered down from above. A light shower had begun to fall, tiny glittering droplets coming down in gauzy curtains. He felt them in his hair, on his face, his lips, and tasted a sooty grit in them. Sombre in the rain, he entered the temple.

The building had no other entrances and a triangular opening in the centre of the roof. The ground was an uneven expanse of grass and tilted, mossy flagstones, and there, seated on a long stone bench was a familiar figure. As he approached she rose and hurried towards him. Without hesitation they put their arms around each other and kissed. It was an unselfconscious act, tenderly, gently done.

When they broke apart, he saw that she had been crying, her eyes reddened, face streaked with tears.

'What's wrong?' he said. 'What's the matter?'

She shook her head, wiped away the wetness. 'I . . . harmed Segrana, Greg. I was trying to defend against the invaders and the bombings and I forced her ancient energies to surface, so that I could give the invaders a clout, make them leave! But I couldn't control it . . .' Catriona sighed and took hold of his jerkin. 'I canna tell you what it means to see you again.'

Greg leaned forward and kissed her once more. She smiled, a little sadly.

'Well now, Mr Cameron, am I right in thinking that you have intentions towards me? These lips of yours seem to be trying to tell me something.'

'My lips, Miss Macreadie, are the very bletherers of candour.'

'So tell me – do you love me?'

Taking her hand, he nodded. 'Aye, I'm afraid that I do.'

'Then tell me what'll happen when you give me the Zyradin.'

'I don't know but I can tell you what it did to me.'

And he related his experiences as the Zyradin's host, and tried to summarise events on Darien, all that struggle and intrigue and insane, daredevil heroics. He also told her a little about Kao Chih, the Roug, and the colony of Pyre. She in turn told him about Theo and how he helped in the initial defence of Segrana, and how he and the Ezgara-Tygran Malachi were abducted by unseen attackers. That a deadly enemy was now in control of the warp-well cast a dread pall over their mutual embrace.

'I know that the Zyradin will alter me,' Catriona said. 'And I don't want to do it! I don't want to lose what I am and what I know and I especially don't want to lose what we ... what we might have together.' She closed her eyes, as if in pain, and gave a small shake of the head. 'But there are things that have to be done, and errors that must be put right.' Tears were trickling down her cheeks. 'All the damage that I did ... aye, and now there's huge areas where Segrana cannae even see or feel, while the fanatics and the Brolturans fight it out and Segrana burns ...'

** THE INTRUDERS CAN BE DEALT WITH ** THE INJURIES AND THE BLIGHT CAN BE REPAIRED ** THE GREAT WEAVE OF BEING CAN REGROW AND RENEW ** THIS IS MY PURPOSE **

Catriona straightened, eyes wide. 'Was that him, it ... the Zyradin? Can I see it?'

For a moment, Greg half-expected a cloud of blue motes to emerge from his skin but there was nothing as he unfastened a chest strap, swung the harness off his back and took out the canister. He removed the flexible lid and looked in at the restless mass of glowing blue specks, filling the container to the top.

'I can't even tell if all of you is in there,' he murmured.

** I AM THAT WHICH YOU SEE **

Greg looked up at her. 'Ye ready?'

Catriona met his gaze and something requiring no words passed between them. Then slowly, reluctantly, he handed the canister to her.

She held it in both hands as if judging its weight. 'Hmm – all that advanced Forerunner tech surviving for millennia. Thought it would be heavier, somehow . . .'

Then with a calm, resolute gaze she looked inside, studying it, eyes widening before she drew back, a rapt expression on her face. The blue motes of the Zyradin began pouring out, filling the air around her and becoming a dense cloud. The canister fell from her clasp, empty, turning end over end, while she raised her hands and swept them slowly through the hovering, drifting myriad blue points. Then the radiant cloud drew inward, condensing around her, brightening. The collective luminescence lit up the stone floor and walls, a pure blue glow that showed up every groove and chip, every maker's mark, as well as every spreading patch of lichen and sprigs sprouting in notches.

Now the Zyradin's blue points were sinking into her skin, watched over by Catriona who marvelled at the sight, occasionally giggling. Eventually every last one had been absorbed, and she looked up.

'Is that how it went for you?' she said.

Greg nodded. 'Pretty much. Doesna look too bad from where I'm standing. With the Zyradin in your corner, there's not much that can touch ye, as long as ye eat properly, keep up yer strength . . .' He paused. 'So, is that it? Can we nip off for a bite somewhere? Dunno what the restaurants are like on Nivyesta, but I'm telling ye, I could eat a large domesticated farm animal, hooves an' all . . .'

Catriona's upraised hand halted his desperate chatter. 'It says there's more,' she said. 'Much more.'

Abruptly, her skin started to brighten and there was a quick intake of breath. She was starting to glow, not blue but a faint roseate hue as she drifted up off the ground. The simple robe she wore slipped off her shoulders, and the seams of her other garments unstitched themselves. Soon she was utterly naked, her slender form radiating that rose-coloured flush, almost as if she had been exposed to the sun too long, yet without any kind of angry redness. Greg's eyes prickled with tears at the beauty of her.

She smiled at him and held out one small hand.

'Goodbye, Greg,' he heard her say, though her lips never moved.

He lifted his hand towards hers but was too late. One moment she was standing there before him, the next her form disintegrated into a slow-swirling mass of radiant roseate specks, undulating and stretching like a vast flock of birds surging this way and that. Then the expansion accelerated and the motes in their millions flew outwards in every direction, a wave of enigma racing out to every corner of Segrana.

The Brolturan gunship, still soaring over the treetops of Segrana, hunting the Spiral zealots through the dense forests, was on the trail of a heavily armed group moving east along the banks of a broad river. Its captain never noticed the roseate radiance that was rising from the canopy beneath in a wave, until it engulfed the craft fully, from prow to stern. The fleeing zealots below, who had for hours been desperately dodging missiles and explosive rounds, suddenly found themselves ducking and hiding from a deluge of parts and components, armoured hull sections, uncased ammunition, interior fittings, couches and deckplates, all the elements of the former gunship which were scattered over a wide area.

Similar treatment was meted out to the Spiral interceptors and fighters. Their swooping trajectories turned into a terrifying ride for their pilots as the craft disassembled and came apart around them. Any Brolturan ship that ventured out across Segrana's green ocean received the same treatment.

Those on the forest floor holding flechette rifles, pistols, beam carbines, flamers, shoulder launchers and grenades one by one saw their weapons fall apart into useless piles of junk. Faced with the abrupt loss of the means of attack and defence, both the Brolturans and the Spirals armed themselves with cudgels improvised from branches and gathered together in larger numbers for mutual protection. Some headed for higher ground or the coastal regions, while others set up camps to wait out the night.

Later, the new unity of Zyradin and Segrana used specialised midlevel plants to produce a gaseous soporific that drifted down through the foliage onto the unsuspecting intruders. After that teams of Uvovo transported the narcotised antagonists to places where they could not cause harm to Segrana, the Brolturans to their battered base off Pilipoint, and the Spiral zealots to an isolated island several miles off Segrana's west coast.

In the Uvovo temple, after Catriona's transformation and transcendent disintegration, Greg had stood there under the circular roof opening, staring up at the smoke-veiled, branch-interwoven heights, watching the bright shafts and gleams of sunshine shift and fade, studying the night's progress through the layers of foliage. The faint radiance of ineka beetles and ulby roots began to appear, and before the last shreds of daylight faded some Uvovo scholars entered and quietly lit several lamps. The realisation that she was not coming back finally became bleakly real in his thoughts, and slowly Greg sat down. After a time, he began to weep.

37

LEGION

Flanked by two bodyguards, the Henkayan general Hurnegur followed the Spiral Prophet up the hillside track leading to the immense promontory. Sunup was less than an hour away but the feathery greyness of pre-dawn was lightening the horizon. The darkness atop Giant's Shoulder remained unbroken. As they approached it from the ridge, the only light came from the torches and lamps carried by their guards and attendants. This place was, according to the Prophet, the sacred repository of the tomb of Agiserri, one of the founding Father-Sages, but the Brolturan fortifications that came into view lessened the impact somehow.

Behind him, Jeshkra, the Gomedran general, cleared his throat.

'Still reading no lifeforms, Exalted One.'

'Good,' said the Prophet as he limped along. 'You see, Hurnegur? Our enemies disperse, by virtue of our divine purpose and the guarding presence of Arigessi, praise the light of his words.'

'Praise their everlasting light,' Hurnegur and Jeshkra said in unison, but Hurnegur couldn't shake off an imperceptible thread-like sensation of menace. The Brolturan units guarding the passes had been broken by his fervent battalions and, as the Prophet had promised, the Hegemonic enemy had abandoned their citadel. Such desirable outcomes caused the believer in him to give hearts-praise to the spirits of the Father-Sages, but the tactician in him could not stop being cautious and wary.

By torchlight they came out onto a wide expanse of rocky

ground which became an area of rough concrete. It was flat and empty, overseen by squat towers and broken up by sections of low wall angled to force a ground attack into a bottleneck, a gap opening onto the next crossfire arena. Probing cones of light revealed signs of battles, charred lumps of metal which, on closer examination, proved to be the remains of battle mechs. This only served to provoke stronger feelings of unease in Hurnegur as they proceeded onwards to a large, multi-levelled bastion. When he voiced these fears, the Spiral Prophet was dismissive.

'Trust to the Father-Sages, General. Gaze upon these impregnable yet vacated fortifications and see how that vaunted power has been rendered impotent by unseen hands and invisible intent. Ahead lies an abomination, built over that sacred resting place – picture it torn aside to allow that divine presence to rise to the celestial spaces, to its rightful and illustrious station. Come, walk with me, you too, Jeshkra.'

With Hurnegur in the middle, the three of them continued with their guards following.

Now they were crossing a well-surfaced plascrete landing pad. Two more wrecked droids came into view, some distance apart, and Hurnegur began to wonder if some horrific ambush or booby trap awaited them within the darkened structure. The Prophet indicated the main entrance, a pair of doors made from some opaque material and adorned with a stylised interlocking-gears symbol. They were just a few paces away when a deep synthetic voice boomed out across the promontory.

'Wily and dauntless Hereditants, be welcome in this place of my triumph!'

Suddenly combat-alert, and angry at not having paid more attention to his instincts, Hurnegur drew his hand projector and scanned the surroundings. Then he realised that the Prophet and Jeshkra showed no sign of alarm or agitation. Instead, they had stopped to smile at each other.

'He is here,' said the Prophet.

'He is indeed formidable,' replied Jeshkra.

Hurnegur stared at them in fearful incomprehension. 'Revered

One,' he said to the Prophet. 'Who is it that is here? Is it . . . Arigessi? . . . Jeshkra, old friend, what is this all about?'

But neither responded. The Gomedran and the crippled Henkayan turned to gaze up at some point in the dark and shadowy upper air.

'We greet you, Illustrious Progenitor, and stand humbled in the light of your mastery. How may we serve you?'

'Cast off your disguising shells, my Scions. The final phase awaits us.'

With a trembling hand, Hurnegur brought up the projector and aimed it at the Gomedran.

'Jeshkra, my friend, if you do not tell me what is happening, I will shoot you dead, I promise.'

Jeshkra and the Prophet glanced sideways at him but said nothing, just smiled. Hurnegur uttered a prayer for forgiveness, and blew Jeshkra's leg off at the knee.

The Gomedran went down, making no sound even as blood gouted from the ragged stump. Then Hurnegur swore as Jeshkra forced himself up onto his knees, smile fixed, unvarying. This time he aimed at the head, but before he could fire Jeshkra jerked as if struck in the back and his head lolled forward. There was a grinding sound, then a wet tearing. The Prophet too had fallen to his knees but his head was leaning further and further to one side until there was a terrible crack, a ripping noise, something spattering on the ground. And the Prophet flopped forward like a boneless husk, revealing the thing that had been inside him, a metallic object like a tapered cylinder less than a metre long. Streaked with blood, it rose to hover in midair while Jeshkra's tormented body split apart in a dark spray to expose a similar monstrous passenger.

In all his years of combat, Hurnegur had encountered many examples of vileness and base depravity but this superseded them all. Awash with incredulity and seized by an unanswerable terror, he flung out his beam projector and emptied its charge. Bloodstains were crisped and charred to ash but otherwise the two metal things were unaffected. He threw away the weapon, turned and ran.

He heard other weapons firing behind him, and only got as far as the edge of the landing pad when he felt something needle-sharp stab into his neck. He staggered a couple of paces before a spreading numbness reached his legs and he slumped to his knees. The next thing he knew he was being lifted into the air.

His senses swam. He tried to bellow his fear but even his throat had rebelled. Then whatever it was that had him in its grip turned him to face it, and a grotesque shape swung into view. With a flattened hull, it seemed to be a craft fashioned to resemble certain sea creatures he knew of – it even had several tentacular limbs protruding from the forward section. The hull was adorned with a hooked pattern, dark reds and greens with silver details. There were no obvious weapon ports but it was hovering, which meant that it had to have suspensors on board . . .

His vision blurred a little, followed by a wave of dizziness which he fought against. Then he realised through the fear that a few of the tentacles were no more than stumps but before he could complete the thought everything blurred and just fell away from him.

The Knight regarded the unconscious Henkayan, held aloft in one of its lesser tentacles.

<Why do you wish this one kept alive?>

>The Henkayan is greatly respected by the followers of the Spiral Prophecy sect. Through him the movement can be manipulated to your advantage<

<To the advantage of convergence, my Scions>

>Only and for all time and beyond, honoured Progenitor<

The Knight considered the captive and recalled the other two experimental subjects, the Human and the Uvovo.

<I shall investigate its uses. Now, your duty awaits, O fearless Hereditants>

The Scions moved away from the organic guises that had been sloughed off, a symbolism that the Knight chose to ponder with approval. The Brolturan building was entered with ease and the Knight began to receive datafeeds from his Scions as they descended to the warpwell chamber, the very heart of their ancient enemy. Before long he was receiving images of the chamber and the broad circle of the warpwell, which was strewn with odd stone blocks, many of them fitted together.

And as far as could be made out, the Sentinel was not present.

>Illustrious One, it appears that the Sentinel of the well has been destroyed<

A stream of data came through, directly from the crude devices employed by the Hegemony scientists. Crude or no, they had successfully provided Ambassador Kuros and his advisers with detailed information about certain warpwell functions. The Knight could see where their investigations were leading before their inexplicable halt. Together with his own knowledge, gleaned from the ruins of other Forerunner warpwells down the millennia, the data offered the key to warpwell operation. And, of course, it was knowledge that his Scions also possessed.

>Illustrious Progenitor, once the well is activated we propose that one of us enters it and makes the descent with the aim of contacting the Legion's survivors and guiding them to the well if necessary. Soon after the first has gone, the second shall follow with the logic bomb, intending to detonate it within the warpwell pattern access field. There is an 8.3 per cent chance that the first of us will survive the journey into the abyss. The second of us has an 11.1 per cent chance of surviving the warpwell's inversion, although the chance of a successful detonation is 92.6 per cent<

<92.6 per cent?>

>Unforeseen factors, Illustrious One. In the event that the inversion attempt fails, it is our recommendation that you dispatch another Scion to carry out the task>

<Understood. This meets with my approval. Proceed>

The Knight watched as his Scions used the well's patterns to bring it up to full activation. The various stone blocks and pieces of equipment abruptly vanished into the dazzling, churning maw. Even here, floating on his suspensors above ground, he could feel that dragging force, that insensate hunger. Yet even as fearful as it was now, when controlled by the full bioentity of a Forerunner citadel world it could reach out into space almost a light year away and drag any enemy down its throat.

Then one of the Scions floated out over the burning bright portal and plunged in. The Knight was receiving a video feed which lasted less than two seconds before cutting out. A minute and thirty seconds later the second Scion followed. The Knight's attention was split between the stream of data coming from the warpwell chamber, and the view from Giant's Shoulder as the sun edged up over the horizon. Then the datastream suddenly spiked with state-change information . . . and the Knight *felt* it, felt the warpwell's alteration ripple outwards from Giant's Shoulder. He was sure that even if he had been miles away just then, he would still have felt the alteration. As for how long the inversion wave would take to reach the bottom of the Abyss, that was indeterminate, three or four days, perhaps, then the same for any survivors to make the ascent.

But one thing was utterly certain – a hundred millennia after that ignominious defeat, the Legion was returning from the Abyss.

EPILOGUE

CHEL

Cold and tireless, the pulse of machinery regulated all functions within the autofactory. The extraction of base material from the forest floor, the preparation, the conversion, the schedule of power allocations, the finely coordinated production process, the internal repair and monitoring systems, the external service racks. And the special project section, a chamber provided with environment control and arrays of surgical equipment that hung over a scoured metal plinth flanked by recesses. In two of them, still forms lay, lifesigns readouts blinking nearby. One was Human, his open yet blank eyes darting to and fro after invisible things while his lips moved but made no sound. The other, a Uvovo, lay still with his eyes, all six of them, closed, his face calm and expressionless while his chest rose and fell unhurriedly. Both bore evidence of surgery and at their necks, shoulders and upper limbs the skin had been replaced by panels of some grey, flexible material.

Behind those closed eyes, Chel hung in a kind of delirium, his semi-aware self swaying between despair, pain and the temptation to surrender to the malign machine fragments now invading his body. He could feel how they were meant to merge with his flesh, with the feeling-paths and the thought-paths, and he had so far resisted. This had resulted in a persistent fever and a steady weakening of his forces. Chel had nothing left except the willpower to resist, and even that might not shield him from any use of drugs. He just regretted not being able to help Rory escape.

Thinking to take one more look at the Human, he forced his

awareness to focus on the physical so that he could at least open an eye or two. Pain flooded in from the nine separate implant wounds but he endured it as he opened his ordinary eyes.

The compartment was essentially a large metal box harshly lit from a single source. Except that just now it was blinking erratically, more than enough to reveal the opaque, fold-draped and cowled form of the Pathmaster floating next to the surgical table.

'Great Elder, I . . . am I imagining this?'

'Your birth eyes are open, Cheluvahar, and your senses are seeing and hearing me.'

'Am I dying, Great Elder?'

'There is no death, but it may be that the universe will offer you a new path. Many dark and terrible possibilities are emerging from the seething no-time of the future into the dim periphery of becoming-time. The turn of events has benefited our adversaries and laid a still-greater burden of necessity on your shoulders.'

'But Great Elder, I am their captive and . . .'

'Hear this! – a Knight of the Legion of Avatars, the same one that you were tracking, has taken possession of the Waonwir and activated the warpwell, reversing its flow. It will take at least three days for the change to reach that dark, deep prison in the Abyss and as long for any Legion survivors to travel up its full length. It may be that only you and this Human will be able to prevent it.'

Chel was stunned, and irritated that somehow stopping this terrifying event was his responsibility while his mind and body were being eaten away piece by piece.

'Please, Great One, can you help us escape? If I can just get free of the mechanisms and the implants . . .'

'But Cheluvahar, you must not fight but accept. You must embrace the machine in order to defeat it!'

This time he felt a wave of anger.

'How can this be? I am to become one of that monster's mechanical slaves in order to . . .'

'I see that you are yet to be convinced. Seer – attend!'

Chel's sight flared suddenly, then cleared to reveal a dark, overcast scene, an expanse of skeletal trees set in a blackened landscape, a charred Darien. But as his vantage point began to drift across this gloomy forest he saw that they were trees of metal, and that tunnels sloped down into the roots. Human and Uvovo came and went from below but their faces were blank and their bodies were patchworks of sickly skin and artificial grey. Chel saw immediately that the metal forest was a depraved parody of Segrana, a cruel copy stripped of natural life. Meanwhile, the vision still glided onwards until he reached the hills and ridges east of the Kentigerns. Further on was the coastal plain, a scarred and poisoned desolation, and when he turned to look at Giant's Shoulder there was nothing there. The upper section of the promontory was gone, leaving the chamber of the warpwell open to the skies. Clouds darkened, rain fell, thunder rumbled . . .

Abruptly he was back in the recess, in the metal compartment, a prisoner and experimental subject, yet not alone.

'Hard as it is to believe,' said the Pathmaster, 'there are other far grimmer futures gathering, ones where implacable tyrannies wage pitiless wars that consume the stars.'

'What do you want me to do?' Chel said brokenly.

'Use the talents Segrana gave you,' the Pathmaster said. 'And use them with cunning and guile. Accept the machine implants but use the eyes of the Seer to see and change. Observation alters what is observed.'

Pain gnawed at Chel's neck, arms and chest, as he looked across at poor Rory, his darting eyes and restless head.

For Rory I will do this, he thought.

'Many, many others will be spared lives-like-death if you succeed.'

'But new potential is then created,' Chel suddenly realised. 'Potential for good and evil.'

'Which those yet to be shall have to face, Cheluvahar. You can only face today's challenges.'

And like mist melting away, the Pathmaster was gone. Chel regarded Rory, locked into machine-made delusions, then opened his Seer's eyes and directed their unveiling gaze inwards.

JULIA

Cool, blank emptiness stretching out, silent and indivisible, was all she could see.

She remembered being carried to the virtuality chamber, limp from the sedation patches, almost laughing as they put her in the tank and hooked her up to the bioreg web. Then they'd activated the cortical interface field, and the laughing and the tank and Talavera's face and sensation all went away.

And then there was this, only now that she thought about it, the cool blank emptiness wasn't quite blank and not entirely empty. An indistinct dividing line passed across it, gradually taking on definition and contrast, as well as perspective. It was a horizon, with dark grey above and something textured below, a sea, she realised, at the same time as she felt a sense of presence.

So this is their virtuality, she thought. *Is it responsive or adaptive? I wonder if I can consciously modify the context.*

She dug through her memories for childhood moments, like the summer holiday to an Enhanced residence by the sea, along the coast from Hammergard. The place had its own fenced-off stretch of beach, complete with sand and rock pools. She remembered warm sand between her toes, the cold and slippery feel of pebbles underfoot while paddling in the shallows, the acrid smell of washed-up tube-kelp. And when she opened her eyes (which suddenly she had) there it was, the shallows of a wide, placid sea and yes, she was paddling along, barefoot but otherwise wearing a blue checked shirt and yellow slacks rolled up to the knees.

A figure was strolling along the beach towards her. The beach was a sloping expanse of even, pale sand scattered with small stones and fragments of driftwood. As the newcomer drew near, she saw that it was Corazon Talavera, attired in red and carrying a parasol.

'Very pretty,' she said. 'Although I kinda imagined that your metacosm would be, hmm, a bit more practical, like Konstantin's laboratory.' She uttered a low whistle. 'Thing is like a city, it's huge.'

By now the sky had brightened to an even summer blue. There was no actual sun but there was a soothing ambient glow that Julia quickly found irritating. That aside, she said nothing, just splashed her toes gently in the shallows (now dressed with rocks and pebbles), stirring up little billows of sand particles.

'I liked your last escape attempt, by the way.' Talavera chuckled. 'Reassigning your room as storage and a storage closet as your confinement. I suppose the next stage involved the movement of large cargo cases from here to there and ending in one of the shuttles.'

Julia gave a cold smile. 'I expect you found my polymote.'

'Uh huh, and the one on timed deactivation. See? – I know how you wily Enhanced types think.' She shrugged. 'But all that is behind us now. Despite all your plots and sabotage, you are here in my virtuality to work for me.'

There were a number of clouds near the horizon. Talavera made a gentle beckoning gesture and the clouds rushed towards the shore, growing huge and dark. They all merged into one immense, sprawling bruised continent of cloud, looming and ominous. Then the ground fell away as Julia and Talavera rose into the air, passing through veils of intricate vapour to a point overseeing the great cloudscape. Only now, up close, she could see that the cloud was composed of numbers and symbols and fragments of symbols and hanks of fine tendrils linking them all together, with myriad glittery flecks strewn all through it. Out of curiosity Julia reached out to touch a nearby shining speck . . . and a burst of condensed data sprang into her mind, the gravity gradation effects of one planet on another in a five-planet system, full statistics laid out in tabular and graphic depictions . . .

Then it was gone.

'Five hundred worlds,' Talavera said with a theatrical sweep of the arm that encompassed the vast cloud. 'Fully detailed information on their astrogational coordinates on a specific future date, complete with true-path trajectories and velocities, in-system gravity matrix, and plenty of etcetera!' She glanced at Julia with one of her twinkly, malicious smiles. 'That's only a hundred worlds each, and all you have to do is use that admirable brain to produce course data similar to your recent success.'

Julia stared at her. 'Course data for more missiles?'

'I've got five hundred of them and they ain't gonna get to their target by themselves.'

Struck by the enormity of Talavera's suggestion, she fell silent.

'Look, it's not what you think,' Talavera went on. 'This isn't meant to be some high-profile mass slaughter – it's all precision attacks on specific pro-Hegemony actors, monoclan nobles, military industrialists, cultural influencers, pro-war politicians, interrogators, and plenty of other unsavoury types. And you may be interested to know that most of your associates are already hard at work, without any need for a dose of the magic nanodust. Apart from Thorold – he needed a little persuading.'

At some unseen signal, Julia descended through the dark data cloud, returning to the shore, to the shallows of an electric sea.

'You do have a choice, I suppose,' said Talavera. 'But there's not much to it since you'll end up doing the work anyway.'

Now Talavera was dressed in black while a couple of strange snakelike things wound and writhed about her feet. They seemed to have no faces or sense organs and the closer Julia looked the more it seemed as if they were made of dense, dark smoke.

'Think it over,' Talavera said. 'You've got an hour – well, subjectively anyway!'

And with a laugh, she and her black snakes were gone.

Some choice, Julia thought. *Which is no choice at all.*

And all that stuff about targeting pro-Hegemony types just sounded like a calculated lie that, coupled with the remark about Thorold, was supposed to weaken her resolve. Yet she felt like smiling, or even skipping along the shore and kicking up the water.

Because it now looked very certain that they hadn't found the very last polymote, which she had hidden in her hair before they came for her.

Soon it will reactivate, she thought. Then we'll see who really has a choice!

THEO

He was on the bridge of the Starfire when it entered Darien orbit. Sensors were completing their sweeps of the planet's extra-orbital sphere, but many shocking details had been apparent from the moment they'd dropped out of hyperspace at the edge of the system. The huge Brolturan battleship, the Purifier, had been destroyed by a thermonuclear weapon – some of the twisted wreckage was still circling the planet, hurled along widely differing orbits by the force of the explosion. There were also signs of a second similar attack, but the attributable debris did not indicate a similar obliteration.

Theo knew that this debris had to be from the Earthsphere ship, the *Heracles*. Any strategy to move against Darien would logically involve neutralising such warships, but it did raise the question of the *Heracles*' whereabouts. Had it retreated to somewhere else in the system, or did it somehow escape into hyperspace? Or had a failing orbit sent it plunging down into the atmosphere, burning up as it did so? He shuddered at the thought.

Then information on planetside comms traffic began arriving at the tactical station. The tactical officer, Berg, tidied it a little before sending it to Captain Gideon's station and to the auxiliary set up for Theo's use.

There were transmission frequencies, ground coordinates, encryption levels, and expandable transcript summaries. Many were in Anglic, or Anglic variants, others were in Brolturan–Sendruklan (and had been translated), but there was a swath of others in several other languages, mainly Henkayan, Gomedran, and Kiskashinan, according to the onscreen commentary. As he read through some of the transcripts, the appalling outlines of recent events emerged, leaving him feeling angry and impatient.

'I've known nothing like this in my time,' Gideon said. 'A few generations ago the Dol-Das-ruled Yamanon suffered a wave of divine sieges, mostly taking place within this or that solar system. Interstellar divine sieges are rare, successful ones rarer still. But these zealots call themselves Followers of the Spiral Prophecy, a very new splinter-faith of the Father-Sage religion.'

Theo stared at the screen and shook his head.

'The Winter Coup was nothing like this,' he said. 'Not even the New Town Successions caused this kind of havoc. If only I knew what's happened to my nephew . . .'

'Excuse me, Major,' said Berg. 'Is his surname Cameron?'

'Yes, why?'

The tactical officer gazed at his holodisplay. 'Right, I'll slot that name into the filters. I'm sure I saw a few entries with that name . . . yes, here's one: ". . . Varstrand's *Har* flew Greg Cameron and some others to Giant's Shoulder for God knows why, and no one's heard anything from them since," and the reply is "The place is crawling with machines now – I'm not surprised," and it then goes on about refugee camps south of Lake Morwen . . .'

Theo sighed, trying to grasp the storm of conflict and confusion that had descended upon his world, toppling all certainties.

'Captain,' he said. 'Can you tell when these fanatics began their invasion?'

'Radiation and ionisation analysis puts it at nearly two days ago,' said Gideon.

'The Brolturans would not be pleased to lose such a vessel, I'm thinking, yet no sign of reinforcements.'

'Retaliation will come,' said Gideon. 'The Brolturans and the Hegemony are very likely assembling a large task force with the aim of enforcing a major interdiction.'

'Sounds serious,' Theo said.

'It is very serious – all inhabitants are documented down to the gene map, then tagged, usually with ankle clasps, but sometimes with neck ones . . .'

'Sorry to break in, sir,' said Berg. 'But the filter has just flagged up a mention of Greg Cameron . . . okay, it says, ". . . picked up my passengers, *ja*, and a risky one, the big man. He said that Cameron got through with the cargo, which I say makes me feel better about having my boat ripped up, hah!", and the reply is, "How soon will you be back?", and he says, "Maybe five hours, if I must be the safety pilot, eh?"'

Suddenly Theo felt energised. 'That man is a zeplin pilot – can you raise him, contact him?'

'Shouldn't be a problem,' said Berg, fingers working at his holodisplay control interface. A moment later he said:

'Calling unidentified vessel, this is scoutcraft *Starfire* – please respond.'

'*Starfire*, eh? Never heard of you, which makes you unidentified, eh? Well, this is the sturdily built and expertly flown zeplin *Har*. How are you doing there?'

Theo laughed out loud. 'Hey, Varstrand, you old spanner shaker – still flying that leaky gasbag, eh?'

'Well, well, so either my ears have gone mad or I'm hearing the wheezy voice of Theo Karlsson. I hear you flew up to Nivyesta, but now you're back to help us all, maybe, eh?'

'That's more true than you know, but first I need to know about my nephew, Greg – is he safe, do you know?'

'Hmmph, not so sure. You should talk to the man who knows . . .' There were scratching, clicking noises, then a different voice spoke, with a Rus accent. 'Hello, Major Karlsson?'

'Yes – who is this, please?'

'I am Alexandr Vashutkin – I was the last one to see Greg alive.'

Theo swallowed, suddenly sombre. 'What happened, exactly?'

'I cannot go into details – this connection is not so secure. All I know is that he gained entrance to the Brolturan building while I did what I could to draw off the attention of a pack of combat droids. But eventually I had to escape, and I was lucky enough to find a hiding place and then to get picked up by these guys . . .'

'I see,' said Theo, then recalled something. 'Mr Vashutkin, are you the same Vashutkin who was in Sundstrom's cabinet?'

'Yes, sir, I am. Can you come to Tusk Mountain? – we have a

base there. Perhaps I can persuade you to join us. I know that your experience would be invaluable.'

Theo glanced at Gideon, who smiled and nodded.

'Yes, Mr Vashutkin, I should be able to find it. I'll be bringing some more bodies to help, so I look forward to meeting you.'

'Already you are making the difference, Major! Be seeing you soon.'

The line went dead.

'So it appears that there is some kind of organised resistance,' said Gideon. 'This Vashutkin must be resourceful to evade a pack of combat mechs.'

Theo nodded but his thoughts were going over what the Rus said about Greg. He must have been on a mission involving that damned warpwell, and if he managed to reach it safely, who knows where he could be? The disappearance of Ambassador Horst was for ever seared into his memory.

Ah, Greg lad, he thought. *What have you got yourself mixed up in?*

THE CONSTRUCT

The body lay on a white C-table, which sat out on a balcony over-looking the stepped terraces of the Garden of the Machines.

'He looks so peaceful,' said Rosa, one of the taller military variants. 'Which is fitting after what he went through.'

The Construct made no reply as it continued the autopsy scan. Real-sample blood and tissue biopsies would soon be complete but they were not expected to reveal any divergence from the earlier resonant field scans.

'Multiple puncture wounds by lesser xezri barbs,' it then said. 'Each barb delivers 0.5 milligrams of synaptic inhibitor designed to pass through membranes, spread and shut down all control and distributed functions. The inhibitor has been isolated and analysis shows no evidence of modification.'

'Someone must have uncovered a pre-Forerunner biocache,' Rosa said. 'Perhaps something left over from the Zarl Empire. I was reading about them earlier.'

'Documents concerning the Zarl are inherently suspect,' the Construct said. 'As is any file claiming to date back longer than a million years or more. Mischievous minds have lain behind many a believable hoax . . .'

Rosa straightened. 'You have an important visitor approaching. I shall leave.'

'It is not necessary that you depart.'

'I think that my presence would be unproductive.'

Rosa moved away, leaving by a small side door. Moments later, the main balcony access sighed open and someone else entered and came over to stand on the other side of the C-table.

'He succeeded in his task,' said the Construct. 'He was brave, resourceful and determined. You should be proud of him.'

Robert Horst looked down at the body that was like his body, with a face that was his own.

'I'm not sure what to think,' he said. 'Although there's the feeling of having lost a brother, almost.' He closed his eyes, shook his head. 'Which is foolish.'

'Imprinting your mind on one of my semiorganics was the simplest, quickest way of retaining your skills and knowledge for the Zyradin mission, a crucial and pressing matter now successfully concluded.'

'I agree that I was in no condition after you rescued me from that pocket universe,' Robert said. 'But I still feel guilty.'

'From my observations, it seems that guilt is an overbearing emotion, especially since it was I, not you, who employed this lifeform this way.'

'Guilt is powerful,' Robert said sombrely. 'It can have strange effects.'

'Ah, so we come to your own mission to the region of the Godhead,' said the Construct. 'I have read the concise, even compact, report that you so kindly wrote out for me. Now I am wondering if you are ready to give me a verbal account, subject to my own interjections and requests for clarity.'

Robert regarded the lifeless form's peaceful face, and took a deep breath.

'Yes,' he said. 'I'm ready.'

ACKNOWLEDGEMENTS

This being the first time I've written a proper middle book of a trilogy (well, *Shadowgod* didn't really count since *Shadowmasque* took up the story 300 years later), I feel kinda apprehensive. But hopefully it does what it's supposed to do, and if it does it's mainly due to the skilled perception of the editorial team at Orbit, specifically their point-woman Bella, whose graceful persistence and illuminating insight got me thinking and rethinking about how the story's balance should play out. Thanks also go forth to Dave W. whose rock-steady, eagle-eyed scrutiny always keeps me attentive to the Detail (in which is the devil, I'm told).

A joyful brandishing of the sombrero goes out to John Parker and John Berlyn, my agents at Zeno, to Joshua Bilmes, to the team at Thomas Schluck, to my German publishers Heyne and my French publishers, Bragelonne. A big Dia Duit to Gary Gibson over in Taiwan, to Stewart Robinson in Musselburgh, to Ian McDonald in Belfast, to Eric Brown, Ian Sales, Jack Deighton, Neil Williamson, Keith Brooke, Debbie Miller, the whole GSFWCers, the Edinburgh Writers Group, to Ian Whates, to Pete Crowther, to Trevor Denyer, to the indefatigable Charlie Stross, to Cuddles and Scottish conrunners everywhere. And a salute to Graeme Fleming, progmetalmeister of the Southern Domains (AKA Paisley), and a tip o' the hat to Ronnie and Katie, to Spencer and Adrian, and absolutely every metal fan in Glasgow and beyond.

Limitless thanks go, of course, to Susan, who was very patient with my woolgathering and absentmindedness while the book gestated and emerged onto the page.

The soundtrack for this particular literary journey was provided by Rammstein, Megadeth (new CD is a stormer, I kid you not), the mighty Pallas, Gazpacho, Wobbler, Black Water Rising, the brilliant Red Flag, Gandhi's Gunn, Heaven & Hell, IQ, the long-lost Mudshark, Sensational Alex Harvey Band, Porcupine Tree, Eternal Elysium, Younger Brother, and Glass Hammer. From here on out, the music just keeps getting better and better. Venceremos!